Praise for Lora Leigh:

"A MUST-READ."
—*Affaire de Coeur*

"TITILLATING."
—*Publishers Weekly*

"SIZZLING HOT."
—*Fresh Fiction*

"WONDERFULLY DELICIOUS . . . TRULY DECADENT."
—*Romance Junkies*

TITLES BY LORA LEIGH

Rugged Texas Cowboy

MOVING VIOLATIONS SERIES
One Tough Cowboy
Strong, Silent Cowboy

THE BRUTE FORCE SERIES
Collision Point
Dagger's Edge
Lethal Nights

THE MEN OF SUMMER
Hot Shot
Dirty Little Lies
Wicked Lies

THE CALLAHANS
Midnight Sins
Deadly Sins
Secret Sins
Ultimate Sins

THE ELITE OPS
Live Wire
Renegade
Black Jack
Heat Seeker
Maverick
Wild Card

THE NAVY SEALs
Killer Secrets
Hidden Agendas
Dangerous Games

THE BOUND HEARTS
Intense Pleasure
Secret Pleasure
Dangerous Pleasure
Guilty Pleasure
Only Pleasure
Wicked Pleasure
Forbidden Pleasure

ANTHOLOGIES
Real Men Last All Night
Real Men Do It Better
Honk If You Love Real Men
Legally Hot
Men of Danger
Hot Alphas

LORA LEIGH

Her Renegade Cowboy

St. Martin's Paperbacks

This is a work of fiction. All of the characters, organizations, and events portrayed in this novel are either products of the author's imagination or are used fictitiously.

First published in the United States by St. Martin's Paperbacks, an imprint of St. Martin's Publishing Group

HER RENEGADE COWBOY

For information, address St. Martin's Publishing Group, 120 Broadway, New York, NY 10271.

www.stmartins.com

ISBN: 978-1-250-25201-2

Our books may be purchased in bulk for promotional, educational, or business use. Please contact your local bookseller or the Macmillan Corporate and Premium Sales Department at 1-800-221-7945, ext. 5442, or by email at MacmillanSpecialMarkets@macmillan.com.

Printed in the United States of America

St. Martin's Press hardcover edition / June 2020
St. Martin's Paperbacks edition 2021

10 9 8 7 6 5 4 3 2 1

Chapter One

The song "Save a Horse (Ride a Cowboy)" popped into Lily Donovan's head as she leaned over the rail fence, her gaze fastened on a perfect male ass, hugged by a pair of Wranglers. From there she couldn't help but lift her gaze higher, from the narrow waist to a wide, strong back and equally powerful shoulders that flexed against a tight T-shirt. The wide brim of his hat cast a shadow on his neck, hiding any glimpse of his hair. He'd yet to turn around, but did that really matter? The view was perfect from where she stood.

"Yee-haw. Am I right?" Her companion snickered from beside her. "Who's the new talent?"

Lily cast a sidelong glance at her sister, Shay, who happened to be admiring the same view.

Lily stifled a grin. "I don't know, but he sure knows how to wear a pair of jeans."

And she'd noticed over the years that most men hadn't acquired that talent. Or the backside to carry it off.

"I'm more interested in what he looks like without them," Shay remarked, more teasingly than serious.

"Of course you are." Lily resisted the urge to roll her eyes. Cowboys, no matter how good looking, were not usually her sister's thing.

"You saw him first, though, so I'm giving you dibs." Shay waved graciously, her perfectly manicured ruby-red nails glinting in the sunlight.

Lily gave in to the urge to roll her eyes. "Gee, thanks. That's awfully generous of you,"

"Oh, I know." Shay was always so magnanimous. "You can owe me later."

"And I'm sure you'll remind me of it regularly." Lily couldn't help but laugh at the thought.

"You know I will," Shay remarked. "But you need a man more than I do. You have to get back in the saddle, girlie."

Shay's intentions were good, but Lily had her reasons for staying single for so long. She admired. Flirted every once in a while. Ogled on occasion. But for the past year Lily had been a strictly "look but not touch" sort of a woman.

Hypotheticals were comfortable. She could talk a good game, and it was safe to banter about a guy's ass with Shay when his back was turned to her and she wasn't required to engage in conversation. This was better. Safer. And safe distances like this were likely to be the norm for a while longer.

As if he'd heard them, the cowboy in question turned in their direction. Though the hat shaded his face, the sparkle of honey-gold eyes stood out from the shadows. His gaze locked with Lily's and held it for the briefest moment.

"Wow!" Shay exclaimed a little too loud. "The front side is just as damn good as the backside!"

"Shay!" Lily hissed. "Shhh. He's looking right at us."

"He's looking right at *you*," Shay corrected her. "You might want to offer him a tissue so he can wipe the drool from his mouth."

Lily scoffed, but she didn't look away. Strong jawline, high cheekbones, a nose that was just imperfect enough to ground his good looks, and those eyes. They practically glowed. He continued to stare, his gaze unwavering. Lily tried to look away, but his eyes captivated her.

"No one stands around here, girls. You know that." Lily's cousin Jacob's voice boomed from the group of men setting up the cattle chute, breaking the spell. "Fence leaners get put to work, so you'd better get moving or get down here and get dirty."

He was teasing, but Lily wanted to kick Jacob in the shin for drawing attention to them. It was his ranch, after all, and it wasn't the first time she and Shay had been given a hard time. They weren't there to hang around and get dirty, though. They were picking up Jacob's wife, Sallie, for a shopping trip in Sacramento.

"Sorry, Jacob!" Shay called back. "We're supervising. But we probably should stay. There's not a single woman out there to make sure you're doing it right!"

Jacob grinned and shook his head. He was a good sport. They really did harass him on a regular basis. But they'd been doing it since they were kids, and neither she nor Shay could find a good reason to stop doing it now.

"Aren't you going to Target or the mall or something?" Jacob swept his hands at them as though to shoo them away. "Maybe you should go make a shopping list."

"You don't make a shopping list for Target," Lily quipped. "Target tells you what you need when you get there."

She reached a fist up and Shay bumped her knuckles against Lily's. From the corner of her eye, she kept her attention on the mysterious cowboy and found him watching her again. For the past year, that sort of attention had made her a little anxious. This time, however, it gave her a bit of a thrill.

"Lily, will you please control your sister?" Jacob said with mock exasperation.

"You know she's uncontrollable," Lily reminded him with a laugh.

"Boy, you've got that right."

He gave them a wave in parting and headed back to the chute. Lily stepped down from the fence.

"Are you sure you want to go shopping today? Looks like everything you need is right here. Might not be a bad idea to get down and dirty if you know what I mean," Shay suggested as she followed.

"You're hilarious." Lily jabbed at Shay with her elbow.

"Oh, I know." Shay could always be counted on to be modest.

As they headed toward the house, Shay continued to talk, but the words faded to the back of Lily's mind. She fought the urge to turn around and look one last time, to try to get a glimpse of the gorgeous cowboy with the light honey eyes. But Shay would never let her live it down if she did, and so Lily kept her gaze straight ahead, nodding here and there, going along with whatever it was that Shay said.

"So, you agree with me? I bet we could get Jacob to introduce you."

"Wait. What?" Lily snapped out of her reverie.

"Lily, I'm hurt." Shay feigned a pout. "You're the one person I can count on not to tune me out when I ramble, and you let me down."

"What did you say?" Lily demanded as she stared at her sister suspiciously.

Shay released a long-suffering sigh. "I said that I think it would be good for you to go out on a date. I could totally go too. I mean, not on the date. That would be weird. But I could be, like, undercover. Sit at the next table and wear a wig and sunglasses. Keep an eye on you in case someone needs his ass kicked."

Lily pictured her sister sitting in a booth at Merrill's Café, full trench coat, dark curly wig, and overstated sunglasses. She stifled a laugh, and though she wanted to get on Shay's bandwagon, she knew she just wasn't ready.

"No dates for me."

Shay's shoulders slumped like a four-year-old who was just denied a sucker.

"It's been almost a year," her sister reminded her, her voice quiet.

The conversation had turned damned serious and they hadn't even made it to the house yet. Lily had hoped they'd at least make it out of the county before the conversation circled around to her love life, or lack thereof.

Lily's cell vibrated in her back pocket, and for once she was thankful for the interruption. She pulled it out and a rush of adrenaline coursed through her veins. She didn't recognize the number, but she knew the area code.

"Go ahead and grab Sallie," Lily said as she swiped her finger across the screen. "I'll meet you guys at the car."

Shay's brow furrowed with concern, but she did as Lily asked and hustled up the front steps and into the house.

"Hello?"

"Lily Donovan?"

The formal tone of the man on the other end of the line only added to her worry. She took a steadying breath.

"Yes."

"This is Chief Deputy U.S. Marshal Seth Miller calling from the U.S. Marshals Service. Do you have a moment to talk?"

Lily's throat went dry. She turned and walked toward her car as she tried to stay calm. "Um, sure. I don't have much time, though."

"I'm sorry to be calling, but I need to inform you that Graham Brisbee escaped from the California Correctional

Center in Susanville two days ago. The media hasn't been alerted yet. I wanted to make sure you were one of the first to know. We'd like to put you in protective custody until he's apprehended. I can have a deputy marshal pick you up immediately and transport you to Sacramento."

"No." The word left Lily's mouth before she could think better of it. Her hands trembled and she worried she might not be able to keep her grip on the phone. It took a conscious effort to draw air into her lungs, but she forced herself to keep her shit together. "He escaped? How?"

"I'm sorry, but I can't share that information with you right now. Excuse me, but did you just say no?" He sounded almost incredulous.

She wasn't surprised by his incredulous tone. But Lily had made her mind up a long time ago. No one was ever going to be in charge of her life but her. She'd managed to keep this part of her life a secret, and she wasn't about to change that.

"I said no. And I don't want any deputy marshals following me around either. Your job is to catch him. I'll look out for myself. Have a good day, Chief Deputy."

She ended the call and released a shuddering breath. Sallie and Shay walked toward the car and Lily stuffed the sudden fear and anxiety that had overtaken her to the soles of her feet. In a single moment, one of her worst nightmares had been awakened. She just prayed that the marshals would do their job and not make her regret her decision to look after herself.

Levi Roberts stepped away from the group of ranch hands. The persistent, rhythmic buzz of his cell let him know it was a message that couldn't be ignored. He retrieved it from his pocket and quickly read the text message. Disappointment puckered his brow as he fired off a quick response and tucked the phone away. He turned toward the driveway, his attention drawn to the three women climbing into a Toyota 4Runner. He pulled the brim of his hat down lower over his forehead, shielding his gaze from the sun as he watched the car drive off, sending a plume of dust into the air behind it.

"Levi, what do you think?"

Now that was a loaded question. He turned toward Jacob Donovan and jerked his head toward the acres of sprawling pastures beyond the ranch. "This is a bigger operation than the one I worked near Waco. But I can handle it."

"Good," Jacob replied. "Because I can always use another set of hands around here, even if it is only temporary. We have a bunkhouse on the property that you can stay in. If it works for you, I'd like for you to start tomorrow."

"I'm here now. I'd rather start today if that's not a problem." Levi fought the urge to look back at the road and the car that sped down the lane. Before he'd even been made aware of who she was, Levi had been drawn to the woman with auburn hair. The sunlight played off the red-gold strands setting them afire. Her voice and spunk had piqued his curiosity. Only after he'd heard her name had Levi made the connection. *Lily Donovan.* He hoped to see her again, soon. "Might as well hit the ground running, you know?"

"Sounds good to me. You've already pretty much met everyone here. John Grange, who you met earlier, is in charge of the day-to-day stuff. He'll line you up. If you have any questions, go to him." Jacob reached out his hand and Levi took it in his, returning the firm shake.

Levi nodded. "Thanks. I appreciate it."

"Not as much as I do," Jacob said. "The spring calving season is the busiest around here. I'm glad to have you join the crew."

Jacob left Levi to get straight to work. He was anxious to get to know the crew and the operation. Learn more about

Deer Haven and the people who lived here. The best way to do that was to talk his co-workers.

The Rocking D Ranch was a decent-sized operation. Large enough to employ a crew of about a dozen or more. From what he'd heard, Jacob hired mostly ex-military, which was what made Levi a perfect fit.

"Jacob says you were an Army Ranger?"

Levi hoisted up a section of metal fencing, waiting for the other guy to secure it to the section they'd just set up. "Yup. Eight years. Joined straight out of high school."

"I'm Chris, by the way. Navy. Twelve years. Nothing fancy, just an enlisted guy."

"Levi," he introduced himself. "And no one is 'just' anything. Every job serves a purpose."

"Ain't that the truth," Chris agreed. "I thought about being a lifer, but I missed home."

"You're local?" Levi asked.

"Born and raised here," Chris said proudly. "Once a California boy, always one, right?"

"So you know the family?" Casual conversation was always the best way to find anything out. Especially in a small town. In order to get to know the area and the people who lived here, all he had to do was be friendly and initiate conversation.

"Oh sure. I'm five years older than Jacob, but everyone sort of knows everyone in a small town."

"His cousins hang out here a lot?" He tried to pose the question casually.

Chris grinned as he reached for another section of fencing that would make up the temporary corral. "You mean Lily and Shay? They're here every once in a while. Tara too sometimes."

"Another cousin?" *Exactly how many cousins ran around loose on this ranch anyway?*

"Yeah." Chris nodded.

Levi hoisted the fencing up and waited for Chris to put the pins in place, securing it to the section before it. "Be careful, though. Jacob's super-protective of the girls and he'll kick anyone's ass who does them wrong, if you know what I mean."

"Noted," Levi said with a laugh. "Though they seem like they can take care of themselves without any help from Jacob."

"You've got that right," Chris said. "Don't let those innocent good looks fool you. The Donovan girls won't stand for any bullshit."

Feisty. Levi liked that.

"Shay's a firecracker for sure, but it's Lily that you have to watch out for."

Levi grabbed another section of fence. "How so?"

"She's like a stealth bomber. Seems harmless enough and then, *bam!* She lays you out before you know what hit you."

Levi laughed. "Sounds like a handful."

"Last year, Jacob's wife, Sallie, was in a bit of trouble. Jacob did what he always does and made sure that everyone in his family was safe. Told Justice Culpepper to keep an eye on Lily. Lily and Justice have sort of an antagonistic history, and she wasn't super-happy about Jacob dumping Justice on her. Guess she let Justice know by chucking a cast-iron skillet at his head."

"Handful" was an understatement. He didn't even know who this Justice Culpepper was, but he almost felt sorry for the guy.

Levi didn't have any information about the situation with Jacob's wife last year, but in the couple of days he'd been in town he'd heard enough gossip to have found out the basics. Sallie had gotten mixed up in something that had to do with her stepfather, a diplomat. Some dangerous men had come to

Deer Haven looking for her and learned the hard way that you don't fuck with people Jacob Donovan loves. Levi admired Jacob. He had a reputation for being a good man and force to be reckoned with when crossed. He was definitely the guy you wanted on your side when shit went south.

"It definitely sounds like Lily is the one to watch out for," Levi remarked. "Unless you're looking to get a concussion."

"She's got a temper on her," Chris said. "But she's a catch."

"Single?" Levi tried not to sound too curious.

"Yeah. For a while now."

"No one's willing to risk a skillet to the head, huh?"

"I doubt that's it." Chris laughed. "She's a prize and any man with eyes in his head has tried to snag her. She's a cold one when she wants to be."

Lily had a wall up. Levi could see it in her eyes when she'd looked at him. He knew all too well what that felt like. She wanted to push people away, but it only served to draw him in. His curiosity grew to a point that Levi knew it wouldn't be squashed until he got to know her better.

He was determined to melt that cold exterior of hers, even if it meant feeling the icy burn in the process.

Chapter Two

Levi sat at the bar at the Broken Horn Brewery, the local sports pub, finishing up his burger and fries. A lot about a town and its people could be gleaned from watching, listening, and even just chatting up the bartender.

Deer Haven, California, was a small enough town that everyone knew everyone and no one's business stayed private for long. Gossip flowed like whatever beer was on tap, and the locals seemed to drink it up just as eagerly. Curious eyes watched him as well, regulars curious about strangers and newcomers. Levi made a point to introduce himself to the bartender and let her know that he'd been hired at Jacob Donovan's ranch. No need to draw attention to himself when he could squash curiosity by putting the word out easily enough through the grapevine.

"You want another beer?"

Levi looked over at his nearly empty glass. "I'm good. Thanks, though."

The bartender—Amelia—grinned. "Okay, sugar." She slid his check along the bar and secured it under the glass. "Let me know if you need anything else."

He gave her a nod and went back to surreptitiously scanning the bar. The front door swung wide and a group of four women crowded the entrance. He perked up at the sight of light auburn hair and watched as Lily, her sister, Shay, and two other women walked through the bar and took seats at a booth.

Levi got Amelia's attention and jerked his chin in the direction of the booth. "I'd like to buy those ladies their first round."

She gave him a knowing smile. "You've got it. Which one do you have your eye on?"

Levi replied with a wry grin, "What makes you think there's just one?"

Amelia laughed. "Good answer. Keeping your options open."

Hardly. He waited as a waitress took their order and came back to the bar. Amelia mixed four drinks, set them on the tray, and leaned over the bar with instructions. Again, he watched as she wound through the maze of tables back to the booth and set down the drinks. She propped the empty tray against her hip as she talked to the group for a few moments and pointed over to where he sat. Four heads turned in unison and Levi tipped his hat. The darker-haired of the women, Shay, if he remembered correctly, smiled wide and waved. Lily, on the other hand, gave him a suspicious, narrow-eyed gaze, her lips pursed petulantly. So much for making a good impression.

Rather than approach the table and invite himself to join them, Levi let it be. He turned his attention back to his burger and watched the preseason baseball game on the big-screen television above the bar. Amelia passed by and he said, "You know, I think I will take another beer."

She reached for the taps and produced an already full glass. "I knew you would," she said, and set the glass in front of him.

Levi popped a fry into his mouth. From the corner of

his eye, he caught movement from the table Lily sat at. He dipped his head, angling it to the right, and watched as she slid from the booth and crossed the bar in his direction.

She wasn't carrying her drink. At least she didn't mean to throw it in his face.

She stepped up to the bar beside him, one hand moving to rest casually at her hip as he turned to face her. His gaze swept the length of her frame, from the shapely calves and thighs hugged tight in a pair of skinny jeans to the supple curve of her hips that gave way to her torso. A vanilla and spice scent surrounded her, and the soft waves of her auburn hair shone like strands of silk. Levi's fingers twitched at his sides, eager to reach out and touch. To see if it was truly as satiny soft as it looked. She was a good head shorter than him, affording Levi a glance at the generous swell of her breasts that disappeared in the V neck of her blouse.

"Thanks for the drinks." She was all but glaring at him.

"Any time." He tipped the beer in reply but watched the frustration and confusion that edged at her expression.

This woman wouldn't be an easy sell where a man was concerned. He'd have to work for this one, he knew.

"Did you even know who you were sending the drinks to?" Her eyes narrowed in suspicion.

If he'd ever seen a woman itching for a fight, then it was this one. Pent-up anger all but burned like flames in her gaze.

"Boss's cousins and his wife." He sipped at the beer again, his gaze never leaving hers. "I saw you and your sister at the ranch and met Mrs. Donovan later. I'm Levi Roberts. I just hired on with your cousin's spread."

"Jacob will kick your ass for flirting with his wife." The prediction was made with no small amount of glee as she ignored his introduction.

Levi couldn't help but chuckle. "Can't say as I'd blame him, but I wasn't trying to flirt with her. Or your family."

Her lips parted as though to speak, then pressed into a firm line.

Yeah, it was Miss Lily he was after.

He sipped at his beer again, wondering what she'd accuse him of next. She was like a little cat, all wary and ready to scratch.

A second later, her chin lifted defiantly. "We thank you for the drink." She seemed to force the words past her lips. "Good evening, Mr. Roberts."

Lily swung her arms in time with her stride as she walked with purpose back to the booth. Up close, Levi Roberts was even more strikingly handsome, so much so, it was difficult to take a deep breath in his presence. At least six feet five, with an impressive frame that complemented his height. His muscular build was created by hard work and nothing else and stretched the light cotton fabric of his T-shirt perfectly. His hair was short, mostly hidden by the hat, but tawny with a few errant curls that poked out around the edge near his ears. The cocky smile he seemed eager to show off must have caused more than a few women to breathe a little harder. He knew he was good looking and was confident enough to use it to his advantage. Guys like that were dangerous. Lily knew from experience.

"Did somebody make a new friend?" Shay sipped innocently from her straw before reaching for a mozzarella stick.

"Not damned hardly," she muttered, casting the cowboy's back another glare.

Shay tilted her head to one side and gave Lily a disapproving look. "Too bad, he's cute. But you know I don't do cowboys. Maybe Tara will take him on,"

Tara rolled her eyes as she sipped at her drink.

"Since when have you sworn off cowboys?" Sallie asked, the amusement in her voice thick.

Shay pursed her lips and turned to Sallie. "Since I've decided to broaden my horizons."

Lily grabbed a mozzarella stick and dipped it in a cup of marinara sauce. Shay continued to watch her and she pretended not to notice. Meanwhile, Sallie and Tara seemed to enjoy observing the quiet standoff, neither one willing to step in and break the silence.

"He smelled your hair," Shay said at last.

"He did not!" Lily exclaimed.

Shay looked to Tara, who shrugged apologetically. "Sorry, Lily. He totally leaned in."

"Doesn't matter." Lily helped herself to another mozzarella stick. "I'm not interested."

"Because you're blind?" Shay wasn't going to let it go.

"Because I'm not interested. I don't want to date anyone in this town. You know how the mentality can be. 'You don't lose your girlfriend; you just lose your turn.'"

"Okay, so it's true that the dating pool is more like a puddle here, but that's the beauty of new blood," Shay argued.

"Yeah," Lily said. "Until the breakup. Then you have to watch your ex move on with someone you went to high school with. No thanks."

"Who says you'd break up? Don't be such a pessimist, Lily," Shay objected with a roll of her eyes.

"I'm not being a pessimist. I'm being a realist." That was her story and she was sticking to it.

Shay opened her mouth to speak, but Sallie cut her off. "She's not ready, Shay. Leave her alone."

Lily looked at Sallie and smiled a silent thank-you. Recently, she'd thought that she might be ready to try to date again. But that was until two days ago, when she'd gotten a call from the U.S. Marshals Service. She had bigger things to worry about right now than whether or not Levi Roberts had smelled her hair. Though she had to admit, knowing he'd leaned in made her heart beat a little faster.

Sallie graciously changed the subject, showing Tara a pic from an interior design account on Instagram that was the inspiration for her living room makeover, proving again to Lily that she was definitely a ride-or-die friend.

Though she tried to ignore him, Lily was painfully aware of Levi sitting not fifty feet away at the bar. As far as she could tell, he hadn't turned to look at her table, and for some reason that annoyed her more than if he had walked over and invited himself to sit down. A pleasant shiver rippled over her skin as she thought again about him leaning in to smell her hair. What could it hurt to take a chance?

Lily had learned the hard way that taking a chance could cost almost everything.

The front entrance door swung open, bringing with it a chilly gust of spring wind and Justice, Rancor, and Pride Culpepper, a trio of trouble if Lily ever saw one. Motorcycle-riding, leather-wearing playboys with more arrogance than good common sense. Lily ordered another drink. Damn it, after the past few days she'd had she deserved it.

As the night wore on, more familiar faces passed through the door. The double-edged sword of living in a small town was that everyone knew everyone. Lots of people stopped by the table to chat before moving on, and of course word had already gotten out among the women in town that Jacob had hired a hot new ranch stud. But as annoying as it could be, the comfort of being somewhere that felt safe was far worth the other drawbacks.

"You guys want to stay a little later?" Tara thumbed through the dessert menu on the table. "There's live music tonight."

"I need to get home early," Sallie said. "I promised Jacob we'd watch a movie together."

“I’m out too,” Shay chimed in.

“Lily?”

“I’ll stay for a while longer.” Even in a small town, it was safer to be out with a wing-woman. She’d never leave Tara—or anyone else—alone at a bar. Besides, it was Friday night and the thought of going home alone tied Lily’s stomach into an unyielding knot. She had too much on her mind, and if she spent the rest of the evening at home she’d just overthink things that were out of her control. Better to hang out here with Tara and let the music and crowd distract her.

“Yes!” Tara held up her hand and Lily gave her a high five.

The music started up not long after Shay and Sallie left. Lily and Tara moved from their booth to one of the tables near the dance floor. The band wasn’t bad. Some country group making the rounds of the local bar circuits. A few couples had begun swing dancing and Lily watched while she nursed a glass of wine. She’d had enough to drink tonight, just enough to be relaxed without being too buzzed. She never overdid it. Never put herself in a position where she was out of control.

“Wanna dance, Tara?” Pride Culpepper bent over the table, his head between them. Tara held out her hand and he pulled her from the chair, leading her out to the dance floor.

Dressed in a black T-shirt, snug jeans, and motorcycle-riding chaps, like his brothers, Justice and Rancor, he resembled a *Sons of Anarchy* reject.

Her gaze strayed to the bar again, only to be caught, and held, by Levi’s.

What was it about him? There was an undefined something that caught her attention from the first moment she’d seen him at the ranch. She knew plenty of men with confidence, arrogance, and sheer bravado. That wasn’t what made him stand out, though she was certain he possessed all three qualities in spades.

Lowering her gaze to her nearly empty drink, she forced herself to remain seated, not to go over to the bar for whatever reason she could conjure up. But she did need a fresh drink, after all. Maybe an order of hot wings.

Gripping her glass in her hand, she made to stand up, looking toward the bar again. But Levi was gone.

Her gaze swung to the dance floor, but she didn't glimpse his tall, distinct figure. Moving around the bar, she just did catch a glimpse of him leaving. The need for the drink or the hot wings was gone just as quickly.

Dammit.

Chapter Three

Nothing rounded off a long day of educating Deer Haven's finest better than a hot pizza and cold beer. Lily had always wanted to be a teacher, but now that she had a classroom of her own to manage, she'd come to realize why all of her teachers growing up had always looked so damned exhausted. Kids were great, but they could sure drain some energy.

The long week of state standardized testing was over, and she couldn't be happier to get back to her normal classroom routine. But she needed the weekend to recoup, spend some time with her girlfriends, and try to have a little fun.

Jacob had promised to stop by the next morning to check out the brakes on her car—they'd been acting a little iffy lately—then he and Sallie, Tara, and Shay were supposed to meet her at her favorite bar.

But that was tomorrow, and this evening wasn't, which left her with too much time on her hands alone and way too much time to think.

A week had passed since her unsettling phone call from the U.S. Marshals' office. So far, there hadn't been anything on the news about the prison break, which piqued her curiosity. The marshals must have had some impressive pull to keep it a secret for this long. She couldn't even begin to wonder why that was. Wouldn't it be better to have the public looking out for a few escaped convicts? Then again, maybe the marshals didn't want to cause a panic by letting people know there was a murderer and serial rapist on the loose.

Despite the stress and worry from her past that had compounded on her professional one, Lily was determined to try to live a normal life. She might have been a teacher and, lately, an obsessive worrier, but she wasn't an old schoolmarm or a shut-in. Yet. She wanted to at least try to enjoy what was left of her twenties. That is, as much as she could in a small town where everyone knew your business and your family kept an even closer eye on you than the local gossips.

Lily was good at keeping secrets, though. Very few people knew everything about her.

Even if she hadn't been exhausted from a week of cranky kids tired of taking tests, Lily would have spent tonight at home. Sallie and Jacob were having a date night and Shay wasn't feeling well. They'd promised her a night out tomorrow, but without a wing-woman to have her back, Lily wasn't going out alone. Not even in her own hometown.

Pizza, beer, and a *Below Deck* marathon on Bravo. It might not be an exciting Friday night, but sometimes boring could be good.

"You gonna eat that large pizza all by yourself?"

Lily nearly dropped the pizza on the hood of her car as her heart jumped into her throat. She recognized the cocky drawl and knew before she spun around to face him that there'd be an arrogant smirk on his achingly handsome face.

She swore if given the chance, Levi could coax the panties off a nun.

Sure enough, when she whipped around he met her with a closed-lipped smirk that spread into a wicked, panty-melting grin. Curls of tawny hair peeked out from the wide brim of his hat—*did he ever take that damn thing off?*—to frame his face, and his bright gold eyes twinkled beneath the shadow of it.

Lily clutched the pizza box in front of her, as though it would provide some sort of barrier. "I sure as hell am," she quipped. "And I'm not going to regret a single bite."

In the past week, Lily had seen Levi at the grocery store, the gas station, and of course the ranch. She didn't know much about him aside from the fact that he was insufferably full of himself and not in the least bit shy. In the past week, he hadn't wasted a single opportunity to give her a hard time and Lily had no doubt he enjoyed getting her wound up. She gave as good as she got, though. She refused to let his charm or his otherworldly good looks get under her skin.

For one insane second, she entertained the thought that she could invite him to share the pizza with her. She could text Sallie to check in on her, though she didn't believe anyone who knew her cousin would dare to try to hurt her. Even as she rejected the thought, her cheeks warmed. Levi was hotter than a Southern California summer, and every woman in the county seemed interested in him. She'd be a fool to invite him. As tempting as he might've looked, Lily had built tall walls to keep men out. Especially gorgeous slick talkers like Levi.

But the walls of the house seemed to be closing in on her this week and this man had occupied far too much time in her thoughts.

He tipped his hat to her and shot her another of his devil-may-care smiles.

"Enjoy every bite of it then," he drawled, and the way he said it made her wonder if he'd enjoy tasting her.

She barely kept a flush from rushing up her cheeks again.

Turning, she opened her car door and tossed the pizza box to the passenger seat before sliding in. Closing the door, she gave him a half-hearted wave, started the engine, and pulled away from him.

Damn him, he made her feel like a teenager. A very awkward teenager at that.

She knew he was still standing near the sidewalk, his gaze trained on her car as she drove away. Her skin tingled with the weight of it. Lily's hands gripped the steering wheel too tight and she forced herself to relax as the color returned to her knuckles. She blew out a breath and focused on the air entering and leaving her lungs as she had countless times to keep the anxiety at bay. Lily had seen her fair share of excitement in the past year, and some of that in Deer Haven. Because of it, Jacob protected his family almost obsessively. She couldn't blame him after someone had tried to kill Sallie almost a year ago. Lily had been present for one of the occasions Sallie had been attacked and they'd both barely escaped with their lives. Funny, it had scared the shit out of her, and it hadn't even been the most terrifying experience of her life.

Her brain switched to autopilot as she drove home. Overthinking just dredged up memories she didn't want to revisit and stirred the worry and anxiety she didn't want to deal with. All she wanted was to watch some fun, mindless television, stuff her face with pizza, and drink enough to put her to sleep. God, that sounded bad.

She was simply too tired to deal with anything right now. It had been a long week and a half and she needed some downtime. But damn if seeing Levi didn't just wind her up even more. So insufferably sure of himself and aware of every single one of his assets. Lily wished she could be so confident. Maybe she had been at one time. Now all she had was a smart mouth and a shit ton of bravado. And it was going to have to be enough to get her by on for now.

* * *

Levi watched as Lily's 4Runner pulled out of the parking lot and onto Main Street. She sped down the road as though running from something. Or someone. He let out a measured breath as he adjusted the Stetson on his head and headed into the pizza place. Lily was a tough nut to crack. He'd been trying for a little over a week now, to no avail. As cold as an Idaho winter and bullheaded to boot. He wondered what a man would have to do to melt that icy exterior. Whatever it took, Levi knew it would be worth the effort. As he had come from Sacramento, it had taken Levi a second to get re-acquainted with a small-town vibe. Everyone knew every-one here, and where it had worried him at first he'd grown to find it comforting. Not to mention safe. Outsiders were noticed regularly and regarded with a fair amount of curi-osity and sometimes equal suspicion. Lucky for Levi, his employment with Jacob Donovan allowed him the benefit of an almost instant trust with people in town. Jacob ran a tight ship. If he trusted Levi, then they did too.

Too bad Lily didn't share in the rest of the town's opinion of him.

Lily was notorious for her sharp tongue and fiery spirit. She had no problem standing up for herself. She didn't need anyone, not even her cousin apparently, to have her back. Levi blew out a breath. Jacob was fiercely protective of the women in his life, and if he found out Levi was trying to get close to Lily, Levi worried he'd find himself flat on his ass. Levi could be stubborn too, though. And when he set his sights on something, he didn't quit until he got it. Lily was dead center in his bull's-eye; he'd be damned if he didn't win her trust.

It damn well might kill him to earn it too.

As he neared the door to the pizzeria his phone buzzed im-peratively from his pocket. Pausing just outside the entrance, he pulled it free of his jeans and flipped it open as he brought it to his ear with a quick "Hello."

"Hey, Levi, Grange said you were headed to town earlier," Jacob's voice came over the line. "You still there?"

"Yeah, what's up?" He stepped farther back from the door as a couple left the pizza house.

"If you're not too busy I wanted to see if you'd run by Lily's place for me. I promised I'd stop by and check her brakes for her. She said they were acting, 'iffy' was her word." There was a wealth of amusement and no small amount of concern in his voice. "I'd head out and do it myself, but that new bull just took down the fence to the main yard and now I have cows trampling the lawn and Gran threatening to pull out Gramps's rifle on them."

Levi could hear Sallie laughing at the rancher in the background. That bull had taken out that same fence the week before.

"I'll head there now." Levi chuckled. "Have you thought about hiding your grandfather's rifle?" He turned and headed back to his truck.

Jacob snorted at the thought. "Considered it until I remembered how vengeful she can get. She'd just shoot me with it once she found it."

The problem was that Levi could see her doing just that.

"Can't have that," Levi agreed, grinning. "Have fun with those cows."

He was pretty sure he didn't want to know what Jacob muttered as he disconnected the phone. But it didn't matter. His boss had just given him the perfect reason to stop by Lily's and further his own goals. And if he was lucky, she just might offer to share that pizza with him.

Lily had no more than pulled a beer from the fridge and returned to the living room to sit down in front of the television with dinner when a decisive knock sounded at her door. Clenching her teeth at the interruption, she set the bottle next to the pizza box and stomped to the door. Dammit, her cousin just had lousy timing; that was all she could say for him.

"You would show up just in time to eat," she announced as she swung open the door, then stared up at the man on the other side in surprise. "What the hell are you doing here?"

She knew better than to open the door without checking to see who was on the other side, she berated herself. Dammit to hell, if she'd just checked the little peephole she'd had installed in the door maybe she could have ignored the knock.

"Orders." He grinned as he tipped his Stetson back on his head with such cocky confidence it made a woman want to knock it off just for the hell of it. "Boss called. The cows got out in the yard again and he asked me to check your brakes for him. Since I was in town anyway."

Since he was in town anyway. Just great.

"But since I didn't get to order my own dinner, you could share a slice or two of that pizza in exchange. Maybe a beer," he suggested with a lift of his brow and far too much charm.

Men like him should be outlawed. Locked up. Kept away from women craving a little sanity in their lives.

Now, to keep from being a pure bitch, she was going to have to do just that. Share her pizza and her beer.

"When you're done with the brakes, fine," she agreed. "I don't pay for work that hasn't been done, though."

Amusement flared in those golden eyes and tugged at his well-molded lips.

"Understandable." He nodded, stepping back from the door. "You eat all that pizza before I get done, though, and I'll be mighty disappointed. I'm a hungry man."

The way his gaze drifted over her face and the sensual

smile that tipped his lips, Lily had a feeling it wasn't the pizza he was talking about. And that should piss her off. It should terrify her. Instead, it sent a spike of excitement racing through her that had very little to do with fear.

"Don't worry, I'll be sure to save you some." She'd wrap it up nice and neat and hand it to him when he was finished.

He scratched at his cheek thoughtfully for a second. "You wouldn't make me eat alone now, would you, Miss Donovan? That would just be downright mean of you."

"No, refusing to share my pizza would be mean." She shrugged. "Count yourself lucky I'm nice enough to save you a slice. Let me know when you're done."

She closed the door, then lifted her lip in a little snarl as she heard his laughter from the other side.

She wasn't bored any longer, though. Peeking from the curtains at the side of her window, she watched him as he returned to his truck and pulled out a toolbox before moving to her vehicle.

God bless America, that man filled out a pair of Wranglers like it was nobody's business. Then that army green T-shirt he wore molded some fine muscles too before tucking into said jeans. If she wasn't mistaken, there wasn't an ounce of fat beneath the material. Just hard, powerful male.

There was a time when she would have done some sketchy shit to catch his attention and probably ended up with her heart broken. He was the type of man women prayed for while lying in their lonely beds playing with their vibrators. An unapologetic bad boy with a knowing grin and a body to die for.

As he moved to check the brakes, Lily left the window. Nibbling at her thumbnail, she tried to tell herself all the reasons why it was insane to allow him into her house to share her pizza, but those arguments were as weak as the ones she'd come up with for the past week. For some reason, thoughts of Levi Roberts did nothing to inspire the fear other men had in the past two years. Nor could she convince herself that she really didn't need a broken heart to add to her nightmares.

Hell, she had enough problems. What was she doing allowing herself to add to them?

She was lonely, yes, but no news there. She'd been lonely since she'd moved out of her parents' home years ago. It was the reason she'd gone to college away from home, the reason she'd found herself living a nightmare. And now here she was, more fascinated with a man than she had ever been.

A man she didn't know and had no idea how to read. All she had was the fact that her cousin didn't hire men he wouldn't allow around his female cousins or his wife. And Jacob knew how to run a background like nobody's business.

She was still pacing the living room when another firm, decisive knock came at her door nearly an hour later.

Levi's knock. It was distinctive, like the man himself.

Damn him. She'd been pacing the living room for nearly an hour. So much for a nice evening relaxing with a pizza and a movie.

Swinging the door open, she met his gaze with an arched brow and distinctive mocking look.

"Figure it out?" Of course he had. She had no doubt of it.

Chapter Four

Damn, she was fucking beautiful.

Levi kept his expression amused, careful to keep the lust crawling through his balls under control. He'd been hard since he's first laid eyes on this woman, and he was damned tired of aching for her.

"Brake line was loose. I tightened it up and checked everything out. You shouldn't have any more problems." He couldn't help but be concerned by that brake line, though. According to Jacob, he and one of his cowboys had changed those brakes themselves.

"Come on in." She huffed out a heavy breath as she stepped back from the door to let him in. "I'll get you a beer and a plate."

This was going to hell in a handbasket, Levi thought, He'd never begged a woman for the time of day and he was damned if he was going to start now.

"So gracious." He chuckled with a shake of his head. "Tell you what, I'll stop at a drive-thru somewhere. Enjoy your pizza."

"We had a deal." A frown furrowed her brow and her hands propped on slender jean-clad hips.

At that Levi paused. Glancing down at her bare feet and

the soft pink polish adorning the nails, he found himself having to force himself not to touch her. This wasn't going to work. As much as he wanted it to, it wasn't happening.

"Yeah, we had a deal." Lifting his head, he caught her gaze again. "You're a scared little girl, Lily. You watch me like I'm going to attack you any second. Shit's hell on my ego, so I think I'll just roll out. I'll let Jacob know about the brakes."

Her eyes widened, incredulity and anger filling her expression as he leaned against the doorframe and watched her struggle to hold on to her temper. From what he'd heard since coming to Deer Haven, Lily rarely tried to contain the fireworks. It was obvious she was working at it now.

"A scared little girl?" She all but snarled the accusation back at him. "Where the hell do you get off saying that?"

He tilted his head, watching her curiously, wondering how far he could push that temper of hers. If she fucked like she fought, then she'd burn down the night.

"Observation," he replied with a shrug. "You hung around that bar last week, but wouldn't dance. Word is, you used to close the place down on that dance floor with your sister. You stopped dating, stopped dancing, stopped doing all the fun things a woman likes to do." He frowned back at her. "What surprises me is that Jacob hasn't figured out yet that someone hurt you."

She flinched and paled. He saw the fear that flashed in her gaze as well as the instant rejection that he could know anything.

"You're crazy!" she snapped back at him. Taking a step forward, she suddenly stopped herself before stepping back once again.

His lips tilted knowingly at the action.

"What happened, Lily?" he asked her then. "What made the fun-loving, dance-till-dawn hellion too scared to do what she loved doing? Or should I say who?"

"Well, since you're so fond of gossip, why don't you tell me?" Anger suffused her voice and her expression. But at least she wasn't throwing him out.

"Don't worry, Lily, your secrets are safe," he assured her, his tone lowering as he watched her eyes darken and saw the fear flash in her expression. "No one knows why, but it's been noticed. And commented on."

Levi had to force himself not to reach out and pull her into his arms, to promise her that everything was going to be fine. To allow her to keep her secrets. She was destroying herself, locking herself in her home or maintaining a frozen distance between herself and the activities she enjoyed.

"I have no secrets," she assured him, that anger still vibrating her voice. "Now do you want the goddamned pizza and beer or not?"

"No, that's not what I want when I step into your house. But I have a feeling what I do want would scare the hell out of you." He didn't move from his position against the doorframe, nor did he let his hands drop from where he'd hooked his thumbs in his pockets.

He watched her. Her eyes, her body language, the flush on her cheeks, the anger that bloomed in her gaze. She was scared, but not of him. At least not yet. The problem was, he didn't want her scared of him, but he wanted her. Her touch, her kiss, all that wildfire he sensed burning inside her. And he wanted to give her the same in turn.

"I'm not scared of you either, cowboy," she sneered.

What she did then he hadn't expected. Should have, but it wasn't something he'd ever thought she'd do to counter his unspoken dare.

She stepped forward; one hand was behind his neck as she lifted herself and her lips were on his. Sharp little teeth nipped at his lower lip, and an inquisitive, silken tongue licked over the bite.

Self-control was never so hard to maintain as it was when Lily's lips moved over his. He wanted to throw her against the wall, lift her to ride the hard ridge of his cock, pull her hair and take her kiss and show her all the ways he wanted to taste her, pleasure her. Instead, his head lowered, his hands went to her hips, and he let her have her way instead.

And she was destroying him.

Her lips rubbed, her tongue licked against his, her nails scraped along his neck, and she explored every second of pleasure she found in it. Her breathing roughened along with his, and she pushed him to the very edge of control. That place where he knew he'd never make it another second. And yet he did.

Lily needed someone to trust. She was a woman who needed touch, ached for it. And she could deny it till hell froze over, but she wanted his touch above all others'.

He could work with that. He'd make himself work with that.

Just as his fingers tightened, as the need to grip her hips and jerk her to him was overriding every other impulse, she drew back slowly, hesitant, as though uncertain she wanted to break the contact. She stepped back, releasing him just as slowly as he slid his hands back from her hips.

Her lips parted as though to speak, closed, and parted again.

"I think I'm ready for that pizza now," he told her, aware his voice was rougher, deeper. "I could definitely use that beer."

As she turned and led the way from the living room, he blew out a silent breath.

Hot enough to singe. She'd end up burning him alive and he knew it.

Knew it, and he sure as hell looked forward to it.

Chapter Five

Lily fought for air. The force that held her down was immovable. The hands that squeezed her throat constricted tighter. He was stronger than her. Weighing her down. But she wasn't about to give up. She refused to go down without a fight. For a moment, she was free, and she took a large gulp of air into her lungs. Before she could release her breath in a violent scream, a palm pushed over her mouth to stifle the sound and a powerful forearm crushed down across her chest.

She tried to draw in air through her nostrils that were partially blocked by the hand covering her mouth. Her heart thundered in her ears as fear-infused adrenaline dumped into her bloodstream. The darkness of the room permeated her vision and cast the body looming above her in a sinister shadow. Her fingernails dug at the hand blocking her airway. She kicked her legs to try to wiggle free. If she could just fill her lungs with enough air to call for help, surely someone would hear her. . . .

Lily clawed at her throat as she sat upright in bed. The covers had wound around her legs and she gave a frantic kick as she tried to free herself from the tangle. Stars twinkled in her vision and her mind swam as she drew desperate gulps of air into her lungs. Her heart beat a wild rhythm in her chest. She struggled to stay calm as she fought the dregs of sleep and nightmare that still clung to her. God, she was going to pass out.

The sheet and blankets released their grip and Lily flung herself from the bed. She made her way to the bathroom on wobbly legs and fumbled on the wall to flip the light switch. She squeezed her eyes shut against the intrusion of sudden bright light. She braced herself on the counter and took a deep breath before slowly opening her eyes and turning on the faucet.

She hadn't had a nightmare for a couple of months, but this one had been bad. Vivid. Bad enough to steal her breath and leave her shaking. Bending over the sink, she splashed cold water on her face and cringed as the icy droplets ran down her neck to the scratches she'd inadvertently given herself. Lily reached for the hand towel and dried her face. Forced her gaze to the mirror. Three red slashes marred the right side of her neck from where her dream had invaded reality. Not the worst injury she'd ever given herself during a nightmare, but it would be tough to hide the marks for at least a day or two. She snatched a tissue from the box on the sink and dabbed at the tiny droplets of blood that formed where she'd broken the skin.

What she wouldn't give for a solid night of peaceful sleep.

Lily tossed the tissue in the trash and folded the towel to hang back on the rack. She left the bathroom light on and headed back to the bedroom. The sun hadn't crested the horizon yet, but the first gray signs of dawn were starting to show. She reached for her cell and selected "Sallie" from her favorites list. She was taking her friend up on her "call anytime" offer. Thank God she had friends and family she could count on.

"Lily, you okay?" Sallie didn't even bother with a hello.

"Nightmare." She still found it tough to fill her lungs with enough air to even form a word.

"It was a bad one, wasn't it?"

Tears welled in Lily's eyes and she fought to keep her voice steady. "Yeah. I'm sorry I woke you up. I just—"

"Just nothing," Sallie interrupted. "Don't you dare apologize to me. You call me whenever you need me. Day or night or first thing in the morning. Do you want me to come over? We can make some coffee and find a mindless movie to watch."

No, she wanted out of the house, as far away from being alone as possible.

"Can I spend the weekend at the house, instead?" She wouldn't be alone, and Levi would be there.

The need to see him was so overwhelming she nearly used the number he'd left with her, to his cell phone. If she called him, though, she was afraid he'd expect far more than she could give. If she went to the ranch instead, she could see him, talk to him, with no pressure.

"Do you have to ask?" Sallie asked gently. "We don't care how long you stay, sweetie. I'll put the coffee on. Get your ass over here."

"Give me time to shower." She was sweaty from the nightmare and still far too shaky. "I'll leave as soon as I get ready."

Ending the call, she drew in a deep breath and let it out slowly.

She was going to get through this, she promised herself. The marshals would do their job, she'd be safe, and no one need ever know that Lily Donovan hadn't been able to pull herself out of trouble. No one would know she'd been weak or that she hadn't been in control.

Swallowing against the bile that threatened to build in

her stomach, she grabbed clean clothes and headed for the shower.

Levi knew she'd been weak, though, she reminded herself as she stepped into the shower. He knew someone had hurt her. He hadn't pressed for information, and there hadn't been pity in his expression. Just acknowledgment and regret. He hadn't known her all her life, hadn't known how she always maintained control, how she could set any cowboy she met back on his heels. He didn't see her as Jacob Donovan's hell-raising cousin. He just saw a woman.

A woman he wanted.

And that should terrify her. The knowledge of the lust she'd seen in his face, burning in his eyes, should have scared her to death. Instead, it fascinated her, drew her.

He wasn't a man who would want a quick little tumble in bed and then go his separate way. He'd be thorough, rough, dominant. She could sense it in him, see it in every shift of his powerful body. If he wanted to, he could force a woman to do whatever he wanted her to do.

But she had a feeling Levi would never be satisfied with force. He'd want every kiss, every touch, every acceptance of who he was and what he wanted from her, to be given willingly. Not being in control would mean something totally different with him than it meant in any other situation or with any other man.

The sun sank beneath the western horizon, painting the evening sky in brilliant shades of deep orange, pink, and purple. A light breeze stirred the air, bringing with it the sweet scent of field grass and the wildflowers that dotted the far pasture. They'd be gone in a few days, as soon as the cattle were turned out to graze, but right now the brilliant late-spring landscape looked as though it had been painted by a master. A moment, a season, caught in time.

Levi wondered if he'd ever seen anything so beautiful in his life.

Yes, he had. And she was sitting on the porch swing, gently swaying back and forth as she watched the very same sunset he admired.

The same deep lines marked her brow, and she worried her bottom lip between her teeth. The breeze stirred wisps of her hair in front of her face and she reached up to brush them away and tuck the strands behind her ear. Levi watched her for a quiet moment, wondering what she could be thinking about. Or remembering.

"Stop staring at me if you don't mind." The demand was nothing less than imperious as she turned her gaze on him.

Damn, he was really starting to like her. She was damned spunky and determined. She might be running scared right now, but she was doing it on her own terms. Or what she thought were her own terms anyway.

Levi wasn't a bit chagrined at being caught. He wasn't trying to hide it in the least.

He followed her gaze for a brief moment before pushing himself away from the fence post he'd been leaning on and crossing the driveway toward the front porch. Lily's feet paused, slowing the sway of the swing, and her expression turned wary. Almost panicked. Like a small animal that had been cornered by a much larger predator. Her hand moved to her throat for a moment and she tucked her sweater tight around her before she forced her arm down and grasped it in her opposite hand. Levi frowned as he picked up on her subtle body language. Years of training had made him aware of even the most minute tells, and Lily's practically screamed her discomfort.

"You okay?" Something was wrong. He may not have known Lily most of her life, but there were a few things that weren't hard to discern about her.

Lily's shoulders relaxed and she resumed the easy rocking of the swing. "I'm fine. Just getting some air."

It wasn't unusual to see Lily or any of Jacob's other cousins at the ranch.

But something about her being here warned him that everything wasn't so good at the moment.

"Do you think I'd hurt you, Lily?" Leaning against the porch in front of her, he watched her curiously. "Did I hurt you yesterday?"

She glared back at him. "I am not scared of you, Levi Roberts. But I also don't want you thinking that kiss yesterday meant anything." Her lips clamped together for a second before they parted, and her tongue ran nervously over her lips. "Because it didn't."

His brow arched.

The lying little hellion. She was sitting there lying to his face without a hint of remorse.

He couldn't help but chuckle.

Lily intrigued him. The shadows of secrets lingered behind her eyes. Levi knew more about those secrets than Lily realized. But he'd never be able to gain her trust if she refused to open up to him. She was a tough nut to crack and he was hell-bent on getting through to her.

"Keep telling yourself that, cupcake," he drawled, his gaze raking over her and taking in her flushed cheeks, the need in her gaze and in the hardened little points of her nipples beneath the thin material of her tank top. "You might actually convince yourself of it. Eventually."

She might convince herself of it eventually? Lily glared up at the arrogance and sheer male confidence in Levi's expression and wanted to kick him for it. Damn him, he shouldn't draw her the way he did.

"You're an ass, Levi," she informed him rather than arguing

a point that she knew was a lie. If that kiss hadn't meant anything to her, then the nightmares might not have been so bad.

That low, amused chuckle came from him again and it sounded way too sexy. A sound that made a woman want to challenge him, dare him, just because of the arrogance inherent in it.

"So I've been accused a time or two," he surprised her by agreeing. "But would you be as attracted to me if you could walk over me? Admit it, Lily, all those doormats you went out with before were boring. Maybe it's time to try a real man on for a change."

Good God, he hadn't just said that.

Lily's eyes widened as she found herself torn between incredulity and anger.

"And of course, you're the man I should 'try on,'" she snorted. "I wouldn't try that line too often if I were you; it could end up getting you kicked where it hurts the most."

His lips curled as a grin flirted with them. "Now that wouldn't be in your best interests, sweetheart," he chided her gently. "Just think of all the fun we'd miss out on for a minute or two. Or the spanking I'd be certain to deliver to that pretty ass of yours for trying. Of course, that could end up being fun as hell too."

Her ass clenched at the thought and that was dangerous. Intriguing.

"Time for me to go inside. The bullshit out here is getting deep." She rose to her feet. "Good night, Mr. Roberts."

She moved to shift past him when she suddenly found herself pulled to him. Hooking one arm behind her back before she could stop him, Levi pulled her flush against his body, against that broad, powerful chest, strong thighs. Right where she couldn't help but feel the length of his erection beneath his jeans.

"Lie to me, Lily," he told her. "Go ahead; tell me you don't want this."

Not that he gave her a chance to say much of anything. His head tilted and his lips slanted over hers in a kiss that she was certain fried important brain cells. Because she couldn't make herself push away from him, couldn't deny herself the pleasure just one more time.

He kissed like a man who knew exactly what he wanted and had made his mind up to have her. A man who knew pleasure, how to give it and no doubt how to receive it. And she couldn't even hate him for it. As bad she wanted to, he drew her instead, made her think about him when she shouldn't, ache for it when she knew it was no doubt a dead end. He'd end up breaking her heart or worse, and she could do nothing to stop it.

When he broke the kiss, his breathing was not less fast than hers and the gleam of male hunger in his gold eyes was fascinating to see.

Had any man ever stared at her with such unabashed desire in his eyes? Not just lust, but a hint of the same confusion perhaps that she felt. The question was, why was it so much better, so much hotter, than any kiss she'd had in the past?

Now wasn't the time or the place for this, Levi knew. At any second, her cousin, his boss, could walk out the door and catch Levi with his hands filled with Lily. More than one cowboy had felt the blunt end of Jacob's fist, not to mention found himself in the unemployment line, for being caught in such a position.

"Do you want to go for a ride tomorrow?" he asked her then, wondering just how brave she was going to allow herself to get. "I need to ride the south end of the fence line tomorrow and see what needs to be mended before we turn the cows out. I can always use a little company."

Lily swallowed, her breathing fast, her expression still drowsy with passion. "Jacob's making you working Sundays now?"

Levi shrugged, releasing her when she moved to step back. "I don't have anything else to do. Might as well get a head start on the week's work."

Lily studied him as though trying to look right through him to find something hidden. An agenda, maybe? He wanted to spend time with her and get to know her better. He had no reason to hide it.

"Maybe I'd be up for a ride." Lily looked down at her feet, seemingly afraid to meet his eyes. "I'll let you know in the morning."

It wasn't the answer he wanted, but it was obviously the only one he was going to get. He'd have to take what he could get and "maybe" was a hell of a lot better than "no."

Like attempting to tame a feral animal, Levi thought his best bet for the night was to quit while he was ahead. He'd given the invitation; there was little else he could do.

"I think I'll take my tired ass and jump in the shower." Levi tucked his gloves in his back pocket and tilted his hat up farther on his head. He took in one last look, his eyes moving over every inch of her, committing detail to memory. "Enjoy the sunset, Lily, and have a good rest of your night. I'll see you in the morning."

She frowned and he couldn't tell if it was disappointment or frustration in her expression. Was it wrong to hope it was a little of both?

"You do sort of smell like a barn." Her lips curled into a saucy smirk. Finally, a little of that fire that drove him crazy. "Enjoy your shower, Levi."

Levi turned, his feet reluctant to take him away from her. But he had to play this right or he would ruin his chances of getting close to her. Besides, there was no point in trying to seduce a woman when you smelled like dirt, sweat, and stock animals. Real sexy.

Tomorrow. Another chance to win her over. And goddamn, Levi loved a challenge.

Lily watched Levi climb into his pickup and drive away. He'd traded in his usual cocky attitude for something a little more subdued. Maybe all it took to take him down from his high horse was a day of hard work. The chain squeaked as she swung, and Lily lifted her feet and tucked her legs against her body on the cushion, allowing the swing to slowly come to a stop. The sun sank lower beneath the horizon, leaving nothing but a neutral gray dusk in its absence.

The breeze picked up in intensity, rustling the trees and bushes that surrounded the house. Lily wrapped her arms around her middle. A chill raced up her back and over her shoulders, though the air was warm enough. The sight of Levi standing at the gate to the walkway with the brilliant sunset as a backdrop had painted quite the breathtaking picture. He was 100 percent cowboy, and hell if that wasn't the sexiest thing she'd seen in a long time.

Still . . . Icy fingers of nervous energy danced over Lily's skin. She wasn't ready to get close to anyone. Not with the current turmoil in her life. And especially not with a gorgeous cowboy who was sure to break her heart. Of course, that would mean she'd have to give him her heart to break. She was already so unsure. So afraid of her own damn shadow that she didn't think she had the strength to give herself to anyone in that way. Her ability to trust, to love, to be carefree and reckless had been stolen from her. Lily didn't think she would ever be the same, and no one, not even Levi, could turn back the clock and make her into the person she used to be.

"Hey." Sallie opened the screen door and leaned out. "Dinner's about ready. I'm just waiting on Jacob to finish up some paperwork in his office."

"Okay." Lily smiled. "I'll be in in just a second."

Sallie's gaze wandered to the driveway. "Was that Levi who just left?"

"Um, yeah." Lily's cheeks heated. Why did she feel like she'd been caught after curfew with a boy? "He was on his way home to take a shower."

Sallie's lips spread in a wide grin. "A shower, huh? Did he invite you to join him?"

Lily rolled her eyes. She was wishing she hadn't said anything about that damned kiss to her friend. "No. But he did invite me to ride the property with him tomorrow."

"Oh yeah?" If Sallie smiled any wider, her face would crack. "Are you going to go with him?"

Lily shrugged. "I told him maybe, but I don't think I will."

Sallie's expression fell. "Why not? I think it would be good for you."

"I don't know." Lily looked down at her hands as if the solutions to all of her problems lay in her palms. "I don't think I'm ready."

"It's just a ride. Don't put so much pressure on yourself. It doesn't have to be anything if you don't want it to be. And I'm not about to encourage you to do something you're not ready to do. A little fun might be good for you, though. Just don't think of it as a date. Simply two people hanging out together. You've got to be getting tired of me, Shay, and Tara," Sallie added with a laugh. "Besides, if Levi steps a toe out of line, it won't be Jacob he'll have to worry about, because I'll kick his ass myself."

Lily smiled. “I don’t doubt that for a second.” In the few years since she’d met Sallie, they’d become best friends. The only other person she trusted implicitly was Shay. Outside of that, Lily was a closed book.

“You have to admit, though,” Sallie said with a mischievous grin, “there are worse ways to spend a Sunday.”

Lily laughed at Sallie’s persistence. “I’m not going to argue with you on that one.” She thought again about Levi’s strong silhouette against the backdrop of the sunset and the way his gaze had raked over her body, sending a shock of tingling heat over her skin. “He’s definitely nice to look at.”

“He’s a good guy, Lil. I’m not saying that to sway you in any way. I just want you to know.”

“Do you think Jacob is finally done wasting time in his office?” She was done talking about Levi for the night.

“I’ll go check.” Sallie took the cue and ducked back into the house and the screen door shut softly behind her. “Meet you inside.”

Lily nodded as she drew in a slow breath and released it. She tried to take her friend’s words to heart, though. She knew not all guys were bad. Jacob was a good man and he only surrounded himself with other good men. Levi wouldn’t be here working at the ranch if he couldn’t be held up to Jacob’s standards. God, how she wished she was the same girl she’d been a year ago. Carefree. Unhindered. Delightfully naïve. Never suspicious. Never anxious. Always looking for the best in people instead of worrying about what nefarious personality traits might hide beneath the surface.

What upset her most was the thought that she might remain this jaded—this damaged—for the rest of her life. Would she ever be able to open up to anyone again?

Lily pushed herself up from the swing and headed toward the house. Obsessing over things she couldn’t change would only throw her into another anxiety attack. She was here to relax, clear her head, and find the calm she so desperately needed.

The screen door closed behind her and she listened to Sallie and Jacob exchange casual conversation as she made her way through the mudroom to the kitchen. She wanted that with someone. Just a quiet night at home, nothing special, but at the same time extraordinary. Was Levi the man to give her that? She'd never know if she never took a chance.

Chapter Six

Sleep would not find Lily that night no matter how hard she tried. A cool spring breeze blew in from the open window, stirring the curtains. She'd slept in this bed hundreds of times; the pillow fit her head perfectly. The down comforter wrapped her in weighted warmth and frogs sang from the pond down the road. She should have been deep in blissful sleep, but instead, she was wide awake. Her stomach churned like an angry sea and her mind raced a mile a minute.

She didn't think she'd fallen asleep until well after two in the morning. Anxiety-infused adrenaline overstimulated her body and brain, making it impossible to settle down.

Lily had never felt so pathetic in her life.

She'd never been one for sympathy. Their family was very matriarchal, and Lily's mother was every bit her mother's daughter. Gran often remarked that the apple hadn't fallen far from the tree with the same sort of pride any father would have for his own son. Lily was just as strong willed. Just as independent. With the same fire and determination. So why was it so hard to overcome what had happened to her and why did it still cripple her over a year later?

She'd tried therapy. But at the time she hadn't been ready to open up. Her wounds had still been too fresh. The trauma still too real to revisit it or talk about it. Despite her anonymity, she'd been too afraid and too ashamed to return to campus, opting instead to finish her classes online. Instead of facing what had happened to her, she'd run home to hide.

Lily's heart began to pound, resonating in her ears. The ranch was supposed to be a safe place where she could escape from the memories that haunted her, but instead, her own mind became her greatest enemy. Taunting her with the things she couldn't forget.

God, she was so sick of turning to Sallie for help when she fought against the anxiety that wouldn't release its grip on her. Sick of needing Shay as backup everywhere she went, to run interference when Lily was too much in her own head to remember that she was in control of her life. She was tired of feeling weak. Sick of the sleepless nights and loneliness.

Maybe Sallie was right and it was time to go back to therapy.

She rolled over and checked the time on her phone. Half past seven.

"Crap!"

Lily shot upright in bed.

She was supposed to go riding with Levi.

Grogginess stuck like cobwebs in her mind. She'd forgotten all about him. Though she hadn't given him a straight answer last night, she still didn't think she had the backbone to go out riding with him today. Hell, she barely had the energy to get her ass out of bed and dressed.

Her decision made, Lily sprang up and neatly pulled the blankets up and over the mattress. She set the pillows back in place and grabbed her bag from the closet. With little thought to her appearance, she grabbed a pair of joggers and a T-shirt and threw them on before slipping on her socks and tennis shoes. It was totally a quick-getaway outfit, but she didn't care. With any luck, she'd slip out of the house before

Sallie and Jacob knew she was awake and get out of there before anyone could try to coax her to stay.

She'd work on self-improvement and healing tomorrow. Today, she just wanted to hide.

Lily grabbed her bag and snuck from the guest bedroom. The house was quiet, not even any sign of Gran, who was usually up with the sun. Lily made her way through the kitchen and out the back door, easing it open, careful not to even make a squeak to betray her presence. Something akin to elation soared in her chest at the prospect of making a clean getaway. No one to answer to. No excuses to make. She was home free. Just a few more feet to her car and she could get the hell out of there and hole herself up in her house for the rest of the day.

"Standing me up?" Levi's rich sardonic tone called out to her from the direction of the barn.

"Shit," Lily muttered under her breath. So much for a stealthy escape. Her cheeks heated, caught in the act of doing exactly what he accused her of. "I don't have any jeans." The excuse was as lame out loud as it had sounded in her head. "I'm not really dressed for a ride."

"Really?" Levi scoffed.

He crossed the driveway to her car and leaned a casual arm on the roof. She hadn't really noticed until now how tall Levi was. Good lord, he was a tree of a man. Broad shoulders, strong arms that tapered to a narrowed waist, and powerful thighs wrapped in a pair of Wranglers. There was definitely something about a man in jeans and boots that made Lily's mouth water. On a scale of one to ten, Levi was about a twenty on the thirst meter. She wouldn't be surprised if every single woman in town was trying to snag him.

"What you're wearing is fine," he replied. "No one said you had to wear jeans and boots. We're riding the fence line. All you have to do is stay in your saddle and look gorgeous."

The spark of heat in Levi's honey-gold eyes as he looked her over warmed Lily from the inside out, settling low in her belly. Her heart beat faster, but not from nerves. Excitement coursed through her veins, such an unfamiliar sensation that for a moment she doubted it was truly real.

"I don't know about that." Lily averted her gaze. "I look like I just rolled out of bed." And lord, wasn't that the truth?

"I like it." Levi's voice went low, reaching out to her like a caress.

Lily cleared her throat. He wasn't kidding. How could he possibly think she looked good with her ratty clothes and hair piled on top of her head in a haphazard bun?

"You probably need your eyes checked," she said with a nervous laugh.

"Twenty-twenty," Levi replied with a wink. He reached out and gently took the overnight bag from Lily's hand. "Mind if I put this in the car for you? I don't think you need to bring it with us."

Lily's plans were being hijacked right before her eyes and she found herself helpless to stop it. "Um, yes. I mean, no. I don't mind." Did she mind? Hell, her brain was so scrambled right now, she had no idea. "Go ahead."

Levi smiled and she swore her knees might buckle. A grin like that could be a very dangerous weapon. He reached for the back door and his arms brushed against hers. Sparks of electricity ignited at the contact point, spreading outward. Lily took a nervous step back, looking down at her feet as though inspecting the knots of her shoelaces.

"Look, I'll make you a deal." Levi spoke as he reached inside the car to deposit her bag. "If you just give it a chance, you can leave the second you get sick of me. You can ditch me and leave my ass out in the field all by myself. At any time. I'm talking thirty seconds. I won't even take it personally. Promise."

Lily chewed her bottom lip. She must be giving off some serious piss-off vibes if he realized how much she didn't want to go for a ride with him. But that wasn't exactly true. Levi was gorgeous, and aside from acting like a typical cocky cowboy, he'd been nothing but nice to her. It was her own past trauma and insecurity that made her unsure. That coaxed her to build a wall between her and anyone who tried to get close to her.

"Thirty seconds, huh?" Lily remarked. "We'll barely make it out of the barn at that rate."

Levi chuckled. The sound sent pleasant chills over her skin. "If my personality turns you off in thirty seconds, I won't deserve anything less."

Lily forced her lips to stay put and not give in to the smile that threatened.

"But . . . ," Levi added. "I'm pretty damn sure I can keep you around for longer than that."

Her lips tried again to spread into a wide smile, but Lily kept the expression in check. She didn't want to reinforce his overconfidence by letting him know he might be doing something right.

"Okay." Was she really doing this? *Oh, hell.* Like he said, she could leave at any time. "Deal."

"Perfect." Levi closed the car door and gave her a wide grin. "I've already got Montana saddled up and ready for you."

Had Levi been spying on her? Or, more to the point, asking questions about her? Monty was her favorite horse on the ranch. She rode the four-year-old gelding every chance she got. It wasn't like it was a big secret or anything. It was actually a little flattering to think that he cared enough to pay attention to details like which horse she might like to ride.

"Thanks." Maybe today wouldn't be as bad as she'd imagined it to be. "I love Monty." Besides, Sallie and Jacob were close if she needed them. "He's such a sweetheart."

"He's a good boy," Levi agreed. "And he's sweet on Darby so he'll be on his best behavior."

None of the guys who worked the ranch ever wanted to ride Darby. She was a stubborn pain in the ass and more likely to do what she wanted than obey her rider. Lily could only imagine how the day would go with Levi fighting the spirited mare all day. No matter what the day brought, she was bound to be entertained.

"Are you ready to go?" Levi canted his head toward the barn.

Lily looked down at her ridiculous outfit, regretting the decision not to get dressed this morning. "If you want to wait a few minutes, I could grab my bag and see if I have something more appropriate to wear."

"Are you kidding?" Levi shook his head. "You look great. Come on." He held out his hand, inviting Lily to walk ahead. "Let's go."

Oh boy. Lily had a horrible feeling she was about to get in over her head.

Levi couldn't believe his luck. If he'd been two minutes later, Lily would have jumped in her car and sped away. He knew a runner when he saw one and she was spooked. But she was here with him now and he'd only managed to convince her to stay by the skin of his teeth. Now all he had to do was convince her to stick around and get to know him. It was high time that Lily Donovan let someone in and he was determined to break down her defenses.

Lily seemed nervous to walk in front of him, so he walked beside her. He liked it better this way. He could study her profile, gauge her reactions, and learn the little tells of her personality that he'd been dying to learn more about.

"So, Monty's got a girlfriend, huh?"

Small talk was the best way to break the ice and Levi

was happy to indulge her. "Oh, you bet." She smiled and it tugged at something in his chest. "I think he likes a challenge. Darby is a stubborn girl. She pretends like she doesn't want anything to do with him, but I think she's playing hard to get."

Lily's smile transformed, curling up at one corner and showing off a dimple in her cheek. Damn, she was adorable. He hadn't noticed until now, but her button nose was dusted with freckles that spread outward onto her face.

"She's stubborn, all right," Lily said. "I'm surprised you're riding her. No one on the ranch wants to deal with her attitude."

Levi chuckled. "I have a soft spot for obstinate females." And he'd never been one to back down from a challenge. "Besides, we have an understanding," Levi replied.

"What sort of understanding?"

Levi turned to her and winked. "That's between Darby and me, I'm afraid."

Lily's mouth formed a petulant pucker. Did she have any idea how damned sexy that was?

"Of course, we'll see how she behaves once we get out of the barn. She might be extra feisty with her beau chasing after her today."

"Monty's a handsome boy," Lily said. They walked through the barn doors and into the stable. "And there he is!" she exclaimed. Levi loved the obvious delight in her tone. "Hey there, cutie. How are you doing?"

Monty threw his head up at the sound of Lily's voice. He danced in the stall, as excited to see her as she was to see him. Levi was glad he'd done a little recon to find out which horse was her favorite. It would buy him at least a few more minutes with her, and he'd take every little bit he could get.

Lily walked ahead and opened the door to the stall. She crooned in low tones, rubbing her palm against the gelding's muzzle as she put her forehead to his. "You wanna go out and run for a bit?" she asked him. "I heard you've got a crush on Darby, though. You'd better be on your best behavior if you want to make a good impression."

Levi's curiosity piqued at Lily's words of advice and he couldn't help but wonder if she'd inadvertently meant them more for him than for Monty. He took the words to heart, because he damn well wanted to make a good impression.

Monty tossed his head and whinnied. Two stalls down, Darby replied with an anxious stomp.

"Looks like someone's ready to get out and stretch her legs," Levi said. "She'll be disappointed that it'll be slow going today."

Lily looked over her shoulder and grinned. "She can run on the way back. That is, if you think you can handle her."

The way her voice went low with the words was sexy as hell. Levi's cock stirred and he willed the bastard to settle the hell down. He'd vowed to make a good impression. Walking through the barn with a raging hard-on wasn't going to get that accomplished.

"Come on, boy. Let's go for a walk." Lily opened the door and grabbed the lead rope to guide Monty out of the stall. He brought his legs up high. Prancing as he came between Lily and Levi, he tried to head straight for Darby's stall.

"You weren't kidding, were you?" Lily remarked as she abandoned the lead rope for the bridle. "Settle down, you little rascal. She isn't going anywhere."

Lily used the bit to keep Monty under control so he wouldn't get the upper hand. Levi was damned impressed. He knew Lily could handle the horse. According to Jacob, she'd been riding since she could walk. He wouldn't have to worry about her out on the property today and he admired a woman who could hold her own.

"We'd better get these two out of here so they can work

off all of that pent-up energy," Levi joked. "Otherwise, Monty is liable to take your arm off to get that bridle out of your hand."

"I think you're right." Lily once again guided Monty with a firm hand as she wheeled him around and faced him toward the barn door. "I'll meet you outside."

Levi didn't bother to look over his shoulder to check on Lily as he headed toward Darby's stall. He knew she had the situation under control and the quicker he could get the mare out of the gate, the sooner he and Lily could spend a little quality time together.

By the time he got Darby out of the barn, Lily was already in the saddle, guiding Monty in a graceful canter at the edge of the pasture. It only took a second for him to catch the mare's scent, however, and his carefully practiced maneuvers came to an abrupt halt.

"Hey." Lily seemed more at ease, bringing a smile to Levi's face. "Ready to go?"

"Absolutely." Levi guided Darby in Lily's direction. "I thought we'd ride this fence line." He pointed toward the southern end of the property. "And then head west. I just need to get a sense of what needs to be repaired before we turn the herd out next week."

"Sounds good."

Monty fell into step beside the mare with little guidance from Lily. Like the night before, they let the sounds that surrounded them, the horses' footsteps, the rustle of the grass, and the buzzing of insects fill the silence between them.

Levi had always hated silence.

Until now.

Chapter Seven

You can leave at any time.

Having an escape clause for today's outing might have been exactly what Lily needed to put her at ease. Though she didn't know Levi well, her impression of him was that he was the sort of man who kept his word. Jacob wouldn't have hired him otherwise. She found herself wondering about Levi as they rode side by side, watching as he stopped to inspect a broken fence post. She wanted to know more about him. Where was he from? What had brought him to Deer Haven? Had he always worked in the cattle industry? She had a sneaking suspicion that wasn't the case at all. Her cousin surrounded himself with a lot of ex-military guys. And Levi definitely fit the bill. Tall. Muscular. With a shrewd look in his light bourbon eyes that hinted at a cunning and intelligence he tried to keep mostly under wraps.

It was dangerous to let her thoughts drift like this. She couldn't afford to let her guard down.

"Do you think there's much to be fixed?"

Levi propelled himself back into the saddle and took the reins. "Not really. A few posts here and there and maybe tighten the wire up a bit, but it's actually in good shape. Funny how a tight string of wire can keep a fourteen-hundred-pound Angus in."

"Right?" Lily laughed. "I always thought it was sort of ironic. Their hides are so thick, they don't care much about the barbs. If one wanted, it could barrel through a fence, no problem. But somehow, that thin string of wire subdues that thought."

"Thankfully, they only take down a fence when they're spooked," Levi said. "Otherwise, I'd never get a good night's sleep ever again."

"How did you meet Jacob?" Lily couldn't help herself.

"Through a friend of a friend." Lily expected nothing less than a vague response. Jacob talked the same way. Definitely military. "I needed a job and Jacob needed a ranch hand."

"Why Deer Haven, though? It's such a small town."

"What's wrong with small towns?" Levi asked.

"Nothing." Lily had always liked her tight-knit little community. It was comfortable. Familiar. And safe. "But I grew up here."

"What makes you think I'm not small town?"

"I don't know. I just figured—" she said with a shrug.

Levi laughed. "Last week, Justice Culpepper said to me that only wannabe cowboy assholes wear hats like mine. Did it give me away?"

"Justice is a dick." Lily appreciated a man who could laugh at himself, though. "And I would never willingly agree with him on anything, but . . ."

Levi plucked the hat from his head and tossed it out into the field. "That's all the answer I needed. It's gotta go."

"Don't throw it away!" Lily wrapped the reins around the pommel of the saddle and hopped down from Monty's back. She jogged to the spot where Levi had tossed his hat and scooped it up in her hand. "There's nothing wrong with it." Lily walked toward Darby, hand outstretched. "I like the hat. It suits you."

Levi reached down and slowly took the hat from Lily's hand. Their eyes met and the intensity of his gaze smoldered, igniting a warmth low in her belly that rushed outward through her limbs.

"Well, in that case," he said, low, "I'll never take it off."

His fingers brushed hers and Lily pulled back as though she'd been burned. That pleasant heat turned to cold fright in an instant and a familiar tightness settled in Lily's chest. The primal fight-or-flight reflexes reared up inside her as she took several tentative steps backward. Levi's brow furrowed as he studied her. The concern etched onto his handsome face made Lily sick to her stomach.

"Hey." His voice went low. Gentle. "You okay?"

Lily reminded herself that she could leave at any time. She didn't have to stay here if she wasn't comfortable. But neither could she keep running from all human interaction. "I'm fine," she lied. "I just have a super-big personal space bubble."

His soft smile showed no trace of pity. Instead, it conveyed so much understanding and compassion that it made Lily's heart constrict in her chest. He was one of the good ones. No doubt about it.

"I totally get it," he replied. "You keep that bubble as big as you need it, darlin'. And if I get too close, you tell me to back off. Okay?"

The tightness in Lily's chest eased with Levi's words of reassurance. Her first impression of him had been a little off. Not quite the cocky, full-of-himself, self-centered playboy she'd thought him to be. By slow degrees, she was peeling back his layers, and she was beginning to like what was underneath.

"Okay," Lily said. "I will. Thanks."

She headed back to where Monty waited for her and slipped her foot in the saddle. She wrapped a hand around the pommel and with a hop put herself back in the saddle. Levi wheeled Darby around and took off down the fence line at a slow trot. Lily pressed her heels against Monty's flanks, and he fell into step beside Darby, matching the mare's pace.

"So, what made you want to become a teacher?" Apparently, Lily wasn't the only one who was curious.

"Everyone always thinks anyone who chooses education as a profession does it for summers and holidays off," she said with a laugh. "But to be honest, it's not much of a perk. I've worked a lot of late nights, weekends, and holidays. I just really loved the thought of making an impact in someone's life. You never forget your favorite teachers."

Levi nodded. "Mrs. Sanchez. Sixth grade. Everybody loved her."

"See?" Lily rested her hands on the pommel, letting Monty adjust the pace on his own as Levi urged Darby to slow. "The good ones always stay with you. What did you like about her?"

"She looked like J Lo," Levi said with a wide, boyish grin. "Her butt was like . . . wow."

"Seriously?" Lily rolled her eyes.

"I'm kidding." Levi laughed. "But I had you there for a minute."

A smile tugged at her lips. "'Her butt was like . . . wow'?"

Lily couldn't contain her sputtering laughter. Levi's smile grew and he joined in, laughing alongside her.

"I can't believe you said that," Lily said through her laughter.

Levi's laughter grew subdued. "I couldn't resist."

"Really, though, was she hot?"

Levi reached down and caressed Darby's neck. Lily's

eyes followed the motion, focused on the gentle attention he paid to the mare. She was almost jealous of the horse. It had been so long since anyone had touched her in that way. Had touched her at all, really. She'd been so closed off for so long. A pang of regret tugged at her chest. She missed that sort of affection. The gentle touch of a lover. A kiss. At this point, she'd settle for a good hug.

"She wasn't hot," Levi said. "At least not that I remember. But she was enthusiastic and fun. She made learning exciting. She was happy to be at school every day and I think that made us happy to be at school every day."

"I hope that's how I make my students feel," Lily replied.

She reached forward to scratch between Monty's ears as Levi hopped down from his saddle to inspect another section of fence. She watched quietly as he pulled at the wire, checked the connections to the post, and moved on to the next.

The joy that bubbled in Lily's chest settled to a soft pulse. Her heartbeat kept pace with Monty's gait. She liked Levi. For as much as she'd tried to push him away, to make assumptions about the sort of man he was, he'd managed to turn her opinion upside down and slowly prove her wrong.

Levi tried to focus his attention on the loose wire and rotten posts that needed to be replaced. But he'd be damned if he could keep his mind on work. Lily distracted him like no woman ever had, and that was a bad thing. He needed to keep his head straight, but it was next to impossible with her soft voice in his ears, the sight of her—sweats, messy bun, and all—as she scratched Montana's head, and her sweet scent that carried to him on the breeze.

He wanted her.

God knew he shouldn't, but he couldn't help himself. Jacob would have his ass if he found out Levi was having less than pure thoughts about the other man's cousin. Hell, he'd be in deep shit even if Jacob never found out. If Levi didn't cool his lusts, he'd find himself in the sort of trouble he might not be able to get himself out of.

"What grade do you teach?" Levi asked over his shoulder. At least if he kept himself engaged in conversation, he'd be too occupied to imagine Lily naked. Which he had no doubt would be a glorious sight.

"Second," Lily said. "Seven- and eight-year-olds are my favorite age group. They're such little cuties. Carefree, affectionate, playful. They don't have much of an attitude yet and," she added with a smile, "they're old enough to take care of their own clothes when they go to the bathroom."

"That's a plus," Levi said. "I can't say I have any experience with kids that age, but I'll take your word for it."

Lily canted her head to one side as she studied him. "I'm assuming you don't have any nieces or nephews?"

"Nope." Levi grabbed Darby's reins, and he led the horse along the fence line. "No kids, no nieces or nephews. My family is pretty small."

For as much as he wanted to get to know her, he found it tough to turn the microscope on himself and open up to her. Family wasn't something he liked to discuss.

"I don't consider my family small, but it's not exactly huge either. Shay's my only sibling, but I've got aunts and uncles, Gran, and my grandpa on my mom's side of the family. I've got several cousins besides Jacob and Tara. Some of them have kids."

"You don't consider that huge, huh?" Levi said with a laugh.

"I don't know. I guess not. Why?" she asked. "How small is your family?"

Levi hiked a shoulder. "Me, my sister, Mom, and Dad."

"Okay," Lily said. "I take back what I said. My family isn't that small."

She didn't press him for any more information and Levi was thankful. Talking about his parents as though they were still alive threatened to rip open wounds that had taken years to heal. It absolutely made him a hypocrite that he expected from Lily truths that he wasn't yet ready or willing to give, but he forced any thoughts of guilt from his mind as he focused on his objective. Everyone had something they didn't want to talk about, Levi included. It was ironic that getting people to talk was one of his talents.

"No." He chuckled. "Your family is anything but small."

"Do you like kids?"

He welcomed the change of topic, though this felt more like jumping out of the frying pan and into the fire. "Sure. I mean, I don't have a lot of experience with kids, but I like them okay."

Lily flashed him a sweetly sinful grin that made his cock stir in his jeans. Damn it, she needed to quit looking at him like that or they'd have something a lot more humiliating for him to talk about when she noticed him riding around with a hard dick.

"You're the guy who holds a baby like it's a live bomb, aren't you?"

Levi paused and Lily pulled back on the reins to bring Montana to a stop. "You know . . ." Hell, it was almost embarrassing to admit. "I've never actually held a baby before."

"So basically, what you're saying is that you won't be babysitting as a side hustle anytime soon."

"No." Levi enjoyed how the conversation ebbed and flowed between them. As if she instinctively knew when he needed it to lighten up. "I definitely won't be doing that."

"You're right, though." Lily's gaze wandered with the conversation as she stared out over the expanse of grassy pasture. “The fence is actually in good shape. You won’t have much to do to get it ready.”

Her demeanor changed. She wasn’t with him in the moment anymore. Her mind had taken her somewhere else entirely. Afraid he might lose the ground he’d gained, Levi tried to keep the banter going and her mind away from whatever distracted her.

“You love kids, obviously,” he remarked. “What about pets?”

“No pets. But Sallie keeps telling me that I need to adopt a dog.”

“Funny.” Levi had hoped that Lily would have gotten down from her horse. Instead, she stayed in the saddle, keeping a respectable amount of distance between them. “So everyone keeps telling me.”

“Well, every respectable cowboy has a cow dog,” Lily said.

“I’m more of a ranch boy,” Levi joked. “At least that’s what some of the guys around town say.”

“What guys? The Culpeppers?”

Levi scoffed. “How’d you guess?”

“Because they’re a bunch of smart-asses who think they’re better than everyone else.”

Lily nailed that one on the head. Levi had dealt with men like the Culpeppers his entire career. Arrogant and hard, but also entitled to a little arrogance because they were reliable and competent. They were the type of guy you never wanted to be on assignment with but were glad they had your back when shit hit the fan.

“They’re all right,” he said. “I can handle the ribbing.”

“Ribbing,” Lily said with a smirk. “Justice could use a fist to his ribs.”

“From what I’ve heard, you’d be the one to give it to him.”

“What’s that supposed to mean?” Lily’s tone hardened, sending up a big red flag.

Shit. Levi wondered what he'd said to elicit such a sharp response. Maybe she didn't realize that she was infamous for throwing a skillet at Justice Culpepper's head.

Levi halted his horse to check another fence post.

"Just that you can hold your own. That's all," he stated before marking the post with a length of red tape before going to the next.

He was aware of Lily sliding from her horse as well and following behind him.

"I know what they say about me," she said with an edge of hurt in her voice. "Jacob's bitchy, stuck-up cousin."

He gave a bark of laughter at that as well as a quick, incredulous glance as he moved to the next post. "You're kidding, right? I've never heard a single man talk disparagingly of you, but hell, I'm new; maybe I missed something somewhere."

One thing was damned certain: Any man who spoke that way about her would regret it fast. Levi would ensure it.

Finding the next two posts to be secure, he turned back to her and watched her closely. She'd grabbed the reins to both horses, and they trailed behind her easily as she followed him. She watched him closely, uncertainly.

"Maybe you did," she muttered with a sigh.

Straightening, he turned to face her as he leaned against the fence post, noting the little flush in her cheeks, the tension that filled her body.

"You look like you're scared I'm going to attack you," he told her quietly. "Whatever happened in the past has nothing to do with me, Lily. Stop watching me like I'm going to sprout horns and ravage you."

She narrowed her eyes on him as he removed his leather gloves and tucked them into the belt cinching his hips. It wasn't fear, at least not the fear he was talking about, Lily knew, that had her so nervous. Fear of herself, of what he made her feel, made her want, was a whole other story, though.

"I'm not scared you'll attack me." She lifted her shoulder in a brief shrug as she caressed the reins she carried in her hands nervously. "I'm intelligent enough to know that all men aren't the same."

Besides, Jacob would have run a hell of a background report on him. If there was even a shadow of violence toward women in that background, then he wouldn't be working on her cousin's ranch. It was that simple.

Straightening from the post, he moved closer to her, the gold in his eyes more apparent as desire, lust, tightened his face. The sight of that male hunger had her body sensitizing, her heart racing. She wanted his kiss again. Wanted his touch. And in many ways, that was more frightening than anything else. Because she wanted him.

She'd been hurt, nearly killed, by one man, but she sensed that this man could break her inside, and that terrified her. Terrified her and drew her.

"Time we head back. Sallie and Gran will have breakfast on the table by time we get there and your gran will skin me alive if you miss it," he stated, stepping close and staring down at her, the hunger in his gaze at odds with his words. "And if I touch you right now, I may not stop before I'm balls deep in you, baby. Then we'll be evening getting you back."

"Stop babying me, Levi." She hated that feeling that he was handling her with kid gloves, refusing to touch her, to give her a chance to get over any trepidation she may feel in being with him.

She wanted him. She didn't want him to give her a watered-down version of who or what he was, though.

"Then stop babying yourself." He shocked her with the

demand, his voice low and resonating with that dark hunger she sensed inside him. "Go after what you want, Lily, and stop letting fear rule you. Because once I get you in my bed, I won't allow it."

Her eyes widened, anger and embarrassment twisting inside her and tearing at her emotions.

How dare he.

He had no idea of her nightmares. No idea what had caused them.

Damn him for being such a bastard.

And damn her for caring.

Turning, she lifted herself furiously back into the saddle and gripped the horse's reins in desperate hands.

"You don't know me at all, Levi," she bit out. "And you damn sure don't know what you're talking about."

But he did, that little voice inside her whispered. He knew far too much.

Montana stomped his feet, sensing Lily's annoyance. She pulled back on the reins and wound them in her fist to keep him still, only further serving to agitate the horse.

"Lily—"

"Don't." Montana jerked his head and Lily spun him around.

"Stop, Lily." Levi reached out his hand, a protective instinct coming over him as the horse skittered to one side. "Just settle down. He's getting worked up."

"He's not the only one!" Lily snapped. "I'm going home."

She shook out the reins and put her heels into the horse's flanks. He took a surging leap forward and took off at a full run, leaving Levi to gape after them.

"Son of a bitch!" he grumbled on a breath.

Levi hopped up into Darby's saddle and clicked his tongue at her as he let loose on the reins to urge her to run.

His heart leapt into his throat, his heart pounded with worry, as he watched Lily speed recklessly through the field toward the house. Son of a bitch, that woman was going to make him insane. If she lived long enough.

Chapter Eight

Lily didn't look back. Instead, she urged Monty faster, her attention focused on getting back to the ranch so she could get herself home. She'd never been so damned humiliated. Her flippant attitude had always been something she'd taken pride in. Her take-no-shit stubbornness had always been a trait that men had seemed to admire. It was sort of her love language. Some girls batted their lashes and giggled. Lily stepped up to the plate and gave as good as she got. She'd never considered it a personality flaw.

Until now.

The wind rushed past her and the sound of Monte's hooves as they tore up the turf thundered in her ears. She let the sound drown out the angry thoughts that spun in her mind and the spring air dry the tears that stung at her eyes.

She wasn't the same woman she used to be. The old Lily would have taken pride in her reputation and used it to her advantage. Likewise, she'd always been good about taking it in stride when someone teased her or gave her a hard time. She could always laugh at herself. In a single night almost a year and a half ago that woman had been shattered, and in her place was someone with so little self-confidence and gumption that she was afraid of her own goddamned shadow.

She was damned sick of it.

"Lily!"

Levi's voice called out from behind her and she urged Monty faster.

"Damn it, Lily! Stop!"

No freaking way. She wasn't stopping until she was back at the stable. Jacob would be pissed, because she'd have to ask him to walk Monty and put him away, but there was no way she was sharing the same space as Levi Roberts for another second.

Riding with him today had been a *huge* mistake. Not one she planned to make again.

The sound of Darby gaining ground sent a surge of anxious energy through Lily's bloodstream. The sensation of being chased triggered emotions she'd tried so hard to bury. Fight or flight. *Him or me.* Her anger clouded her common sense. Allowed for her to be reckless when she knew better. Lily was an experienced rider and she and Monty had always worked well together. She knew better than to push him in the open field where he might step in a gopher hole and throw her from the saddle, or worse.

"Lily! Slow the hell down!"

She bowed her head close to Monte's neck. Like she was about to do anything Levi *told* her to do.

She crested the top of a shallow knoll and the ranch house came into sight. Monty pushed himself as hard as he could go, instinct carrying him as he headed toward his home base. She shot a quick look over her shoulder to find that Levi was closer to catching up to her than she thought.

"Piss off and leave me alone!" *Childish? Maybe.* But at this point, she didn't care if she ever saw that sardonic grin on his gorgeous face or heard the sly turn of his words ever again. She never should have given him a chance. She never should have given herself one. It wasn't going to happen again.

Nothing mattered more than protecting herself. And if that meant being alone forever, so be it.

She brought Monty to a skidding stop at the barn door and jumped down from the saddle. Without looking back, she led him to his stall and opened the door, urging the reluctant horse inside.

"I'm sorry, boy," she said as she shut the door behind him. "I know you need to be walked and brushed and watered. Jacob will do it soon. I'll make it up to you, buddy. I promise."

She turned and marched out of the barn, her attention focused on her car. Darby slowed as Levi tightened up on the reins and they trotted toward Lily's car before coming to a stop. Lord, and he thought she was stubborn?

"What in the hell is the matter with you?" Levi barked as he got down from Darby's back. "You could have killed yourself, racing back like that!"

The last thing Lily wanted or needed was to be chastised by the man who'd just humiliated her. "How about you mind your own business?" she seethed with venom in her voice. "*Do not* tell me how to ride."

"I'll tell you whatever the hell I think is right when you're doing something foolish! Especially when your temper is high. What if Montana had tripped or gotten spooked? You could have broken your fool neck!"

"Oh, so I'm a fool now?" Levi was racking up all sorts of points with her today. "Anything else you want to insult me about while you're at it? Take your best shot, Levi! I'm all ears."

The sun played off his gold eyes, setting fire to his expression. His brows drew down sharply over his eyes and the line of his mouth hardened with agitation. It wasn't fair that he could look so mouthwateringly gorgeous, even in anger. She wanted to slap the expression right off of his arrogant face.

"You're not foolish," Levi replied. "But you might be the

most stubborn woman I've ever met. Damn it, Lily, you could have gotten hurt!"

"Which is *none* of your business," she shot back. "I've been taking care of myself for a while now. I don't need you looking out for me."

"Oh no?" Levi challenged.

Lily leveled her gaze as she met him look for look. "No. Don't you have a fence line to check?"

His jaw squared and he let out a slow sigh. "You know what? I do."

"Then you'd best get to it and leave me alone."

Levi snatched the hat from his head and slapped it against his thigh as he turned his back to Lily. He muttered under his breath, words too low for her to make out, but she didn't miss the anger inherent in his tone. A momentary twinge of guilt plucked at her chest, but she forced the sensation away, determined to hold on to her own anger for as long as possible. She let it be fuel for her fire, the motivation she needed not to allow herself to grow soft.

"I hope you drive slower than you ride," Levi said, just loud enough for her to hear as he propelled himself back into the saddle and guided Darby back in the direction from where they'd come. "At least wear your damn seat belt."

Lily pretended as though she didn't hear him as she headed for the house. She couldn't leave Monte in his stall after a run like that without asking someone to cool him down. For that, she allowed herself guilt. She owed him a bag of apples the next time she came out, which might not be for a while if Levi was going to be working here for the time being.

"Lily? Everything okay?" Jacob called out to her from around the back corner of the house. "I thought you were out riding."

"I'm back early," she said as she forced her voice to calm. She didn't want Jacob to know that she'd fought with Levi.

It wasn't really any of his business and he'd just get all protective-big-brother-type on her if she said anything. Lily had trained herself over the past couple of years to keep everything to herself, and that's the way it was going to stay. "I forgot something that I need to get done before school tomorrow. Is there any way you could walk Monty and brush him for me? He had a good run this morning but I don't have time to cool him down."

"I can do that," Jacob said. "I'm just finishing up with Sallie's garden beds." He pulled his gloves from his hands and stuffed them in his back pocket. "Are you sure you're okay, though?" He tilted his head slightly as he studied her.

"I'm fine." Lily hated that she was ditching like this, but she didn't think she could bring herself to stay and risk the prospect of running into Levi when he came back. "Just a little out of sorts. I hate forgetting things that need to get done. I owe you one for Monty, though. Tell Sallie I'll call her."

Jacob's skeptical expression let her know that he wasn't buying her story at all. But he didn't question her further, just let her walk away.

"I'll let her know. Call us if you need anything, though. Okay?"

Lily threw her arm up and waved. "I will. See you later!"

"See you later."

Now she owed both Jacob and Monty. Lily cringed as she opened the door and slid into the front seat of her car. Her show of temper might have been childish, but it was too late to do anything about it now. What did it matter? She didn't owe anything to anyone and just because Levi had invited—and then practically pressured—her to go on a ride with him didn't mean she was obligated to keep him company. They were on her family's property, for crying out loud. And she was the one who was tucking tail and leaving.

Pathetic.

* * *

Levi unbuckled Darby's saddle and laid it back on the stand along with her blanket. It had taken him a good half hour to calm down after his argument with Lily and twice that long to focus on what he was supposed to be doing and not head back to the ranch, jump in his truck, and take off after her yet again.

What had started as the perfect day had gone off the rails, fast. He had no one to blame but himself and his big damn mouth. What he'd thought of as a flattering compliment Lily had seen as an insult. *Yeah, way to play that one nice and smooth, dickhead.*

"I take it today was a little rough?"

Levi turned to find Sallie standing in the doorway. She crossed the barn to Darby's stall and laid a hand on the mare's muzzle.

"Did she say anything?" No point in pretending. Sallie had to have known what happened; otherwise, she wouldn't have been there.

"No. But I heard her talking to Jacob about putting Monty up and I could tell she was upset."

"It's my fault." If he could go back and change his words, he would.

Sallie offered him a kind smile. "No, it's not."

"It is," Levi insisted. "Nothing can be done about it. Not then or now. But still, it's on my shoulders."

"Lily has had a rough past couple of years," Sallie said, her expression turning serious. "If you're truly interested in getting to know her, you're going to have to give her some slack."

He shot her a scathing look. "Seems to me that's all she's had, Sallie. Everyone's ignored the changes and just rolled with it." And they didn't want his opinion of that. "They're too scared of her ire to demand explanations or try to help her."

Sallie laughed. "Oh, she's stubborn as hell."

"She's damned scared and she knows it. Pointing it out was my mistake." Hell, his head was getting messed up where Lily was concerned and he knew it.

"Ice cream. And maybe a little less pointing out things might help." Regret and worry filled Sallie's eyes. "Chocolate peanut butter is her favorite."

"That woman's going to be the death of me and your solution is ice cream and keeping my mouth shut?" Levi put a scoop of grain in Darby's feed bag and hung her bridle on the hook next to her stall. "Seems to me like I'm going to need a miracle instead."

"Oh, for sure," Sallie replied. "You're going to need it. But she's worth it, Levi. I promise you that."

Levi sat in his truck in Lily's driveway, a knot formed tight in the pit of his gut. He hadn't felt this way since high school, riled up over a girl. But here he was, second-guessing his own nature and trying to figure out how to control it just a little longer as he tried to talk himself into preparing to eat crow and grovel at Lily's feet with a half-gallon of premium chocolate peanut butter ice cream as a peace offering.

If she wasn't willing to forgive him, he might be wearing this ice cream home on his head tonight. In which case she'd be in danger of that spanking he was tempted to deliver to that cute little ass of hers.

He let out a quick gust of breath and steeled himself for the coming confrontation. He'd gone up against hardened criminals a hell of a lot more deadly than Lily and they didn't scare him half as much as she did.

"Well," he said on a breath, "here goes nothing."

He hopped out of the truck, ice cream in hand, and climbed the front porch stairs. The sun had yet to sink below the horizon and it cast the little Craftsman-style cottage in a golden light that played off of the flower baskets that hung from the porch, giving them a stained-glass glow. The yard was small and meticulously kept, with a newer detached garage on the east side of the property. The place suited her. All she was missing was a porch swing.

Levi reached out and rang the doorbell. He waited and after several moments rang it again. The garage door was open and her car parked inside, so he assumed she was home. Ignoring him? Letting him stand outside on the porch until he got the hint and took his sorry ass home.

Hell, maybe this had all just been a huge waste of time.

As he turned to leave, the creak of door hinges stopped him in his tracks. He stayed still as he waited for some kind of reaction from the woman he knew stood directly behind him.

"Chocolate peanut butter? You've been talking to Sallie, haven't you?"

Levi turned back and stared down at her, wondering how the hell he was going to do what needed to be done. What had to be done. And not hurt her.

There was no hostility in her tone now. Something more akin to resignation and maybe a little chagrin.

"I was told it's your favorite."

"Sort of cheating, don't you think?"

Levi nodded at that. "Absolutely. And I'll take any advantage I can get."

"You might as well come in before it melts." Lily went back in the house and held open the screen door. "Want to share?"

Levi was surprised by the offer, but he wasn't about to refuse it.

"You're awfully quiet for a guy who couldn't wait to put me in my place a few hours ago," Lily stated as she took the ice cream from Levi's hands and went into the kitchen.

He followed behind her, careful not to put his foot in his mouth yet again. "I wasn't trying to put you in your place. I don't want to scare you, and I damned sure don't want to make things harder on you. But I want in your bed, and I'm not ashamed to admit it. Unfortunately, I'm afraid it might be something you're not ready for yet. The way you raced back proves my point."

"About that . . ." Lily set the carton on the counter and grabbed a couple of bowls. She kept her back turned toward Levi as he took a seat at the kitchen table. "You were right. I'd been angry and it made me reckless. I had no business riding Monty that way, no matter how I felt."

"You'd been angry?" Past tense was a good sign. "How do you feel now?"

"Maybe a little annoyed," she said with a laugh. "And a little more embarrassed."

"Neither of which you need to feel," he told her, keeping his voice low, gentle. "Whatever happened was obviously traumatic. I understand that. But that doesn't mean I'll ignore it like everyone else has. I'm not that man."

"Can we talk about that later?" He watched as she swallowed with a tight movement. "Let's just enjoy the ice cream for now."

Yeah, he could do that. He didn't like it, didn't like what this was doing to her, but he could do that.

"If that's what you want." He nodded in a short, sharp movement.

"Hey, it works for second graders, right?" Lily scooped the softened ice cream into the two bowls and set one in front of Levi along with a spoon. "So it should be good enough for two stubborn adults too."

Levi dug into the ice cream with his spoon and Lily followed.

"I love ice cream when it's sort of melty," she said. "And

honestly, I'd do some pretty sketchy stuff for peanut butter chocolate."

"Oh yeah?" The husky undertone of her voice rippled through him and settled deep in his balls. He'd never met a woman who could turn him on with nothing more than the soft purr of her voice. He suspected he'd get a hard-on listening to her read the phone book. "What kind of sketchy stuff?"

Lily laughed from behind her spoon. "I have no idea," she admitted. "I guess it would depend on the brand, the actual deed, and how long I'd gone without ice cream."

Levi didn't know about sketchy stuff, but he was imagining some pretty damned sexy stuff they could do with ice cream. He imagined sucking the sweet melting chocolate from the peaks of her stiff nipples and grew harder still. She licked her lips as she scooped the spoon into the bowl and Levi's attention was glued to the simple action. He wondered if her mouth would taste sweet. If her lips would be chilled. Would she let him deepen the kiss so he could taste her more fully with his tongue?

"What are you thinking about?" Lily studied him, a half smile playing on the same lips he fantasized about.

"Honestly?" Levi never had been one to mince words. "I'm thinking about kissing you right now."

Lily's jaw slackened a moment before her lips formed a gentle pucker. "Oh."

Levi had known better than to say it, but he couldn't help himself. For her, he'd throw all of his convictions aside. Lily wasn't the only one behaving a little recklessly today.

Chapter Nine

Lily's heart dove into her stomach and did a backflip before skyrocketing back into her chest. She'd been so angry at Levi this morning. So infuriated by what his words insinuated. She'd let her temper get the better of her and hadn't once stopped to consider that she might be blowing things out of proportion. She was ashamed for the willful fit she'd thrown and for the way she'd treated Monty, running him relentlessly back to the barn without regard for either of their safety. Embarrassment and fear had driven her away, and once again she'd put her more destructive emotions into the driver's seat.

Having Levi point this out didn't do much for her pride, but at least he wasn't chastising her for it. No, he was doing his damned best to turn her on instead. She licked her lips and Levi's eyes dipped to her mouth. A wild rush of sensation flooded Lily, settling low in her abdomen. It had been so long since she'd allowed herself feelings of any kind for a man. And as much as it scared her, it also exhilarated her. Made her feel alive again.

And, oh God, how she wanted to kiss him too.

Levi set the spoon in his bowl and pushed himself up from his chair. He leaned across the table to close the distance between them.

"I want to kiss you bad, Lily."

Her chest swelled. How could he have known that was exactly what she'd needed to hear? Lily's mouth went dry. Her heart thundered in her chest and butterflies swirled in her stomach. She pushed herself up as well, to meet him halfway across the table.

"Yes . . ."

His mouth claimed hers in an explosion of sensation that left Lily shaken. His firm, full lips moved over hers, hot and demanding of more. His tongue slid against the seam of her mouth, coaxing, teasing, testing the waters of her consent. A soft sigh escaped her as she tilted her head farther to the side and parted her lips in welcome.

Levi deepened the kiss in an instant. Now hungry and urgent. He left one hand braced on the table and the other he brought up to cup the back of her neck firmly. A momentary twinge of panic tugged at the back of Lily's mind, but she focused instead on the feeling of protection that encircled her and the strength in Levi's hand as he held her neck securely.

He put his forehead to hers as his lips pulled away. His breath came heavy and he kept his eyes closed. "Goddamn, Lily." The warmth of his breath brushed her face. "You test my self-control, honey."

It felt so good to be wanted after so many lonely months. Her pussy clenched and flushed with warmth as she tried to catch her breath as well. She wanted him too. Needed to feel his naked skin against hers so badly that it made her shiver with want. She let her eyes drift shut as well, and when she opened them he studied her intently.

"Tell me, baby, can I have you?"

Her lips parted, her breathing coming rougher as his hand slid from the back of her neck to cover her throat, his thumb exerting enough pressure to tilt her head back. "Or do you need more time?"

Did she need more time? She stared into his eyes as his hand remained in place, just the lightest pressure against her neck, not restricting her breathing but firm enough that she felt the edge of danger. Rather than scaring her, causing her to panic, it was causing her juices to dampen her panties and her clit to throb in demand

Her lips moved before she had a chance to reconsider. “Yes.”

She didn’t know if she was ready for this, but she was going to find out. Levi kissed her once and then again before pulling away to meet her gaze.

“If you want me to stop,” Levi said against her mouth, “just say the word.”

Again, he gave her the reassurance she needed without even having to ask.

“Okay.” She was too breathless for more than the single word.

Levi took Lily’s hand in his and rounded the table. He brought her fingertips to his lips before moving to her palm, her wrist, her forearm, and then her elbow. Lily’s head swam with Levi’s intoxicating male scent. His rough, callused hands rasped deliciously over her bare skin as he traced over every inch of skin his lips had just touched.

Their bodies barely made contact, but sparks ignited in the space between them. Lily felt her hunger mount with each kiss, each caress. She craved the contact. Was starved for it. Too much still stood between them and she was desperate to close the distance.

“Levi, please. I need more.”

Her words sparked a gleam of lust deep in his honeyed eyes and he snatched her to him, holding her against his hardened body, dominating, forceful. Sensation shot through her womb to her sex, causing the muscles to clench desperately with overwhelming pleasure.

His kiss was hard and demanding. Urgent. Lily's head swam and her limbs went weak in his embrace. She wanted to drown her senses in Levi until nothing else remained.

"There you go, baby," he murmured against her lips. "So sweet and hot . . . Be sure now."

"I'm sure." She didn't want to talk anymore. Didn't want to analyze anything or give herself time to feel anything but the passion that stole over her.

It seemed her permission was all he needed.

Levi's fingers threaded through the length of Lily's hair, pulling her head back firmly as he kissed her. Their tongues moved in a sensual dance, their lips meeting and parting as though starved for each other. He drew her bottom lip between his teeth and gently sucked before abandoning her mouth for her throat. She'd never been kissed this way. With such wicked intent.

His teeth grazed her chin, her jawline, beneath her ear. He nibbled the lobe, sucked it into his mouth. His heated breath caressed her ear as he moved his lips over the shell. Lily's stomach clenched as a rush of wet warmth spread between her thighs. Her clit pulsed with every beat of her heart. She waited for the panic to set in. The claustrophobic feeling that came with having someone too close. Every touch should have sent her closer to fear but instead pulled her away from that precipice and steered her toward passion and contentment.

Joyful tears stung at Lily's eyes. He handled her with such deliberate care yet with such dominant hunger.

Her hands moved from his wide shoulders to the strong hills of his pecs. The muscles flexed beneath her palms, and she moved downward over the ridges of his stomach to his narrow hips. The fingers of her left hand curled inside the waistband of his jeans, brushing against the heat of his bare skin. Her right hand ventured lower, pressing against the hard length of him. Levi sucked in a breath and released it in a low moan that vibrated through Lily's body.

"Darlin', you have no idea how good that feels."

His words emboldened her. She reached for his belt buckle, but he stayed her hand.

"No need to rush. We've got all night."

Levi wanted to take it slow, but Lily's desires demanded a much faster pace. "Sorry," she said, embarrassed. "I'm a little overzealous."

"Nothing to be sorry about," Levi said as he put his lips to her collarbone. "It's all good, baby. But we're going to savor this just a little bit."

Lily's head lolled back on her shoulders. Levi continued to kiss her, devouring every inch of her skin until the neckline of her shirt hindered his progress. He reached for the hem and dragged it up her body. His knuckles grazed the skin of her torso and she shivered before lifting her arms as he removed the shirt the rest of the way from her body.

"Goddamn, you're beautiful."

He continued his exploration of her body with his lips, mouth, and tongue. Lily backed against the table and Levi wrapped his large hands around her ass to lift her and set her on top of it. He kissed over the swell of one breast, down into the valley, and over the crest of the other. Lily's breath caught in her chest. She reached under his shirt, greedy for naked flesh, letting her hands roam as her palms brushed his nipples and moved around to the powerful muscles of his back.

Levi looked up, and as their eyes met his gaze devoured her. He kissed her, his tongue thrusting past hers as he reached behind to unfasten her bra. Lily's nipples tightened and tingled as the fabric fell away. Her arms dropped as he raked the silky fabric down her arms and reached up to cup the heavy weight of her breasts in his hands.

"Beautiful," he murmured again as he dipped his head to take one aching peak into his mouth.

Lily gasped and her pussy clenched at the shock of sensation. He teased her with gentle suction, the heat of his tongue lashing against her sensitive flesh. Teeth nibbled and tugged at the tight bead of her nipple before he paid the same lavish attention to the other side. Lily's breaths transformed to quick little gasps and she swore if he kept going she'd come.

Levi held on to his restraint by the barest of threads. Lily drove him wild with lust and it was all he could do to keep from laying her out on the table and fucking her until they collapsed with exhaustion.

She trembled against him, her full breasts a delicious appetizer. He swirled his tongue over the hard pearl of her nipple and she gasped. "Oh my God, Levi. Oh God."

Damn, he could feel her climbing to her orgasm. Knowing he could get her there with nothing more than his mouth on her nipples made him rock hard. But he wasn't even close to being ready for her to reach that point. He wanted to guide her to the edge and bring her back. Build her pleasure to the point she could no longer stand to wait. Then, and only then, would he take her.

His mouth left her breast and she whimpered with disappointment. Her breath came heavy and her chest heaved, her brows furrowed with near frustration.

"Shh, baby." He put his mouth close to her ear as the pad of his thumb brushed against her nipple. Her body twitched as though a tiny electrical current passed through him, only serving to boost his ego. "You feel so good, darlin'. Are you wet? Tell me."

"Yes." Lily's desperate reply was nothing more than a breathless whisper. "I want you to touch me. Please don't stop."

She braced her hands on the tabletop, pressing down as she lifted herself up to allow him to pull her joggers over her hips and past her thighs. It only took a moment for her to kick the fabric from her ankles. A slow sigh escaped her lips as her legs parted. Levi found himself incapable of breath as he took in the sight of her glistening pussy. He couldn't decide if he wanted to touch or taste first.

Slow. Levi reached out and brushed the backs of his fingers against the hot, slick flesh. Her thighs quivered. Her responsiveness drove him crazy as she reacted to his slightest touch.

"Do you like that, Lily?"

"Yes. It feels so good."

He was about to make her feel better still. He loved the sound of her voice, thick with passion. His balls tightened and his cock throbbed behind his fly. He couldn't wait to be buried deep inside her, sheathed in her heat. He continued to touch her. Featherlight caresses as he acquainted himself with her body. The tip of his index finger swirled around her opening and Lily's body went rigid. He went deeper, leaning over her as his mouth found her nipple once again.

Her desperate gasp spurred him on, and he laved at her breasts, sucked her nipple deep into his mouth as he withdrew his finger and plunged deeper once again. The desperate whimpers resumed and he switched his attention to the swollen bud of her clit, circling it with his fingers, dancing over the tight bundle of nerves as he suckled her until her whimpers became desperate sobs.

"Don't stop." Her words became a desperate mantra. "Don't stop, don't stop, don't stop."

Levi paused and she gripped his shoulders tightly, her nails digging in. "Hold on for me." He was so wound up, he'd be lucky if he didn't go off the second he pushed inside her. "Let me take you to bed."

Lily hopped from the table, grabbed his hand, and pulled him toward the bedroom. Once through the door, he didn't waste any time kicking off his boots and going to work on the rest. Lily's hands joined his, tugging at his belt as he pulled his shirt over his head and deposited it on the floor beside him. He patted his back pocket. *Shit.* Did he have a condom? He hadn't come here tonight expecting this.

Hands fumbling, Levi managed to pull his wallet from his pocket as he continued to kiss Lily. He all but dumped the contents on the floor until he found the smooth silver packet and discarded his wallet next to his driver's license and boots.

As hastily as he'd undressed her, Lily pushed his jeans over his ass and her hand found the length of his cock. Levi sucked in a breath as she stroked from the swollen head to the base before she cupped his sac in her hand.

"Now, Levi," she said. "I want you right now."

Despite his plan to make her wait, he couldn't deny her for another second.

They fell to the bed in a wild tangle of limbs. With his teeth, he ripped open the packet and quickly rolled the condom over his erection. His mouth slanted over hers in one last ravenous kiss as he grabbed the hard length in his fist and guided it home.

Bliss. Levi stilled as he allowed Lily a moment of adjustment. The walls of her pussy squeezed him tight, and he moved slowly, pulling out to the throbbing head before driving deep once again. Lily arched against him; the points of her nipples grazed his bare chest. As her knees drew up close to her body, he cradled one leg in his arm, and the other he braced beside her to keep the bulk of his weight from her body.

He fucked her slowly. Every thrust of his hips deliberate. Her heels dug into his ass, urging him deeper, and he obliged. Their breaths mingled, their mouths nearly touching. He pulled out and caressed the length of his shaft along her swollen lips, back and forth, teasing her clit with the head of his cock. Once again her breaths quickened and Lily's moans became louder and longer with each slow stroke.

"That feels so good, Levi." Her voice rasped in his ear. "It's perfect."

She was perfect. This moment was perfect. Levi wanted it to last forever.

Drenched in her slick heat, he plunged inside her once again. His balls tightened, aching with the need for release, but he wasn't ready for this to end yet.

Lily's arms stretched outward and she gathered the comforter in her fists. The muscles of her arms went taut, her body such a display of strength, beauty, and raw passion that it nearly laid Levi low. Her hips came up to meet his, their bodies moving in synchronicity. The pressure built and Levi didn't know how much longer he'd last. But he'd be damned if he came before Lily had her pleasure.

Harder, faster, deeper. Her moans grew louder, sweet cries that echoed in his ears and urged him on. Lily's heady scent invaded Levi's senses, the softness of her skin drove him wild. Her pussy, so wet and tight, held on to him, squeezing tight as he thrust. Several sharp breaths preceded her low moan as Lily's head came up from the mattress. The sting of her nails against his back gave him a thrill.

"Levi!"

His name burst from her lips as the orgasm hit her. With each wracking sob, her body released a small degree of tension. Levi focused on the sensation, the sound of her, the wild light in her eyes as she came. Tight contractions of wet heat held him, stroked him, and his own tension built until he could no longer withstand the onslaught and Lily brought Levi to his own release.

He let out a low moan as the contractions milked him. Strong pulses of sensation rocked him as he continued to trust, hard at first, and then slower until he stilled, buried deep inside her.

For long moments, the only sound to fill the room was that of their racing breaths. Hands wandered; lips met. Sweet caresses were accompanied with sweeter sighs.

"Thank you." The words were spoken so quietly, at first Levi had thought he'd heard her wrong.

Now wasn't the time for playful jokes. Her tone conveyed so much sincerity. His chest ached from the emotion that settled there.

"Lily . . ." Words refused to come. At least nothing to adequately match the sincerity in those two simple words.

"Shh."

Lily brought her fingers to Levi's lips. She reached up and tugged down the covers. He joined her beneath the downy warmth as she tucked her body against his.

"Can we just sleep for a while?"

He wrapped his arms around her and held her tight against him.

"For a little while, baby. Just a little while. Then I have no doubt I'm going to need you again."

And damn it, he meant it.

Chapter Ten

Lily listened to the soft sounds of Levi's steady breathing. Not quite a snore, it was more of a quiet bear snuffle. Cute, but at the same time indicative of a dangerous animal in slumber. The warmth of his body permeated hers; his hand rested on her hip, holding on to her in sleep. The gently possessive gesture caused her breath to catch in her chest.

She still couldn't believe Levi was lying beside her. The previous night seemed like a dream.

After leaving the ranch, Lily had spent most of the afternoon fuming. Trying any excuse to perpetuate and justify her anger. But the more she'd thought about it, the more she'd realized that she'd blown everything way out of proportion. She'd been looking for a reason for everything to go wrong, giving her the easy out he'd offered her. Lily had set herself up for failure and it didn't matter why. She'd been afraid to let herself like Levi. Too nervous to take a chance. Too stubborn to try to allow herself to heal and move on. Living her life had seemed too impossible a task.

And then Levi had shown up on her front porch and offered her a second chance at everything she'd pushed away.

The anxiety and doubt were still there, though. Not even a man as talented in bed as Levi could make that magically disappear. But it was a step forward, and that's what mattered. She didn't know if she was ready for where things might go with him, but maybe that's exactly what she needed right now.

Levi stirred beside her. His fingers gripped her hip as he nuzzled her neck. She'd have to get up soon and jump in the shower. Monday mornings had never been a source of dread until now. She wished she could turn back the clock and stay like this for another eight hours. But they both had to work, no matter how much she'd rather stay in bed all day.

The eastern sky let go of its darkness and gave way to muted shades of gray dawn. Birds chirped their morning songs in the trees outside, providing her with a beautiful morning serenade. Lily never missed living in the city. She hated waking up to the sounds of traffic, sirens, and garbage trucks. She loved the sounds of spring: rain, wind, the rustle of grass, birds singing, frogs croaking. She even loved the buzzing sound of insects. Who needed an alarm clock when nature provided its own waking symphony?

"Mmm." Levi's lips found her ear as he woke. He kissed her lobe and moved up to her temple. "Did you sleep good, darlin'?"

She loved the way "darlin'" rolled off his tongue. It felt good to have someone speak to her with affection. She liked the endearment and the way it gave her chills when he said it.

"I did," she said sleepily. "How about you?"

"Best night's sleep of my entire life," he said before placing another kiss to her temple.

Lily laughed. "Whatever."

"Sleeping next to you?" Levi asked. "I can't think of anything better."

A warm glow settled low in Lily's belly. All she could think of was picking up where they'd left off last night, and unfortunately, she didn't have time for that.

"I need to jump in the shower and start getting ready for school." She did nothing to hide the disappointment in her tone as she snuggled deeper into the blankets.

"I should probably get back out to the ranch too." Levi smothered a yawn, stretching his arms out wide before wrapping them around Lily and gathering her close to his chest. "But damn, all I want to do is spend the day in bed with you."

It shouldn't have bothered her to hear Levi echo the very thing she'd just been thinking. They hadn't even been on a proper date for shit's sake! And now here they were, waking up together. She'd been alone for a long time. Lily wasn't sure if she was ready to open up her life to anyone. Tension stretched her muscles taut as she tried to keep her worries at bay. She fought to stay relaxed as the walls seemed to close in on her. She needed a little breathing room, just for a second.

"I'm going to go start some coffee."

She wriggled free of Levi's grip and scooted from the bed. His appreciative gaze followed her from the bed and Lily was suddenly very aware of her nakedness. And his. Levi's erection stood up and said hello from beneath the sheet like a sexy little ghost.

In three quick strides, Lily was across the room to where her robe hung beside the door. She slipped it on and cut Levi a quick look to find him grinning widely, before she ducked out of the room.

"I'll wait for you to shower!" Levi's voice, full of smug amusement, drifted out to the kitchen.

"Um. . . . no, go ahead!"

Lily didn't know why in the hell she was suddenly so shy since she'd been practically begging for it last night. Or why the house felt too small for them both to be in it at the same time. Everything was happening so quickly. Levi seemed so comfortable, so insufferably at ease. Her heart had been racing since he'd woken up. She'd only been out of bed for a couple of minutes and already she felt as though she'd run a mile. Who needed coffee when you had a sexy, naked cowboy in your bed to give you a little rise and shine?

"I'd rather wait for you if it's okay."

Levi appeared at the edge of the hallway and crossed the living room toward the kitchen. He didn't bother to cover himself. Just stood there in all his naked glory, wearing nothing but that cocky smile and impressive erection.

Oh God. Her cheeks heated at the thought of what they'd done last night.

"Coffee?"

Lily snatched the half-full pot from the coffeemaker and thrust it toward him. The hot liquid sloshed from side to side, nearly spilling over the spout. Levi's smile grew as he sauntered toward the counter, so damned confident.

"Sure." He took the pot from her hand. "Maybe after the shower?"

Did they have time for what a shower might lead to? "I have to be at school by seven-thirty—"

"Lily, relax." Levi's dark gold eyes twinkled with amusement. "It's just a shower. You won't be late; I promise."

Her shoulders had managed to creep to her ears in the time it had taken him to cross the dining room to the kitchen. Lily let out a breath and forced herself to relax. Why in the hell was she so damned tense? "Let's shower," she said with a nervous laugh. "And then coffee?"

Levi grinned. "Perfect. I'll meet you there." He turned, giving her a view of his perfect backside as he headed back toward the bedroom.

Lily rounded the counter and paused, leaning her hip against the edge. Levi had seemed to make himself at home, and modesty obviously wasn't an issue. Lily had spent most of the morning overthinking everything while Levi didn't seem to have a care in the world. The sound of the shower turning on coaxed Lily to push herself away from the counter. She wouldn't put it past Levi to throw her over his shoulder and carry her to the bathroom if she didn't show up.

She truly didn't understand her own reluctance. A drop-dead gorgeous man was waiting for her—naked and possibly soapy—in her shower. She should be running down the hallway, leaving her robe on the floor behind her.

Lily swallowed her doubts. She let the robe fall to the floor and padded to the bathroom. Steam filled the small space, and from behind the shower curtain Levi began to sing the chorus of "Place Out on the Ocean." She pulled the curtain aside and he flashed her a sheepish grin as he continued to sing.

"Sounds good," Lily said as she climbed into the shower. Levi moved back to allow her access to the warm spray and she let her head fall back to wet her hair. "You'll be ready to cut your own solo album soon."

"Nah, the spotlight isn't for me. But I did teach Jamey everything he knows."

"Sure, you did."

He reached for the shampoo and squirted some in his hand. Lily's brow furrowed.

"Turn around, stubborn woman." Levi laughed.

"Not stubborn," Lily said as she turned, letting the water rush down her chest. "Suspicious."

"Trust me," Levi replied. His hands met her scalp as he began to massage the shampoo into her hair. "You're in good hands."

Her scalp tingled as pleasant rivulets of sensation danced down the back of her neck and spine from Levi's artful scalp massage. She was indeed in good hands. And that was exactly what she was afraid of.

* * *

Levi had seen abused animals that behaved much like Lily. Wary. Spooked. Wanting to trust while their instinct told them not to. Ready to run at the first sign of danger or fight to the death if cornered.

Someone had hurt Lily. He already knew that, though she hadn't spoken a word about it.

He drew a deep breath of steamy air into his lungs and held it. His gut churned with anger not only at the thought of anyone hurting her but of Lily trying so hard to erase it from her life. And after last night, Levi vowed that no one would ever hurt her again.

He gathered the length of her hair on top of her head and lathered it with another dollop of shampoo. Scrubbed his fingertips gently against her scalp all the way to the nape of her neck and back up again.

"Mmmm."

Lily's contented sigh was better than the warm air and water that surrounded them. The way her body began to relax filled Levi with pride. He wanted to be the man to make her feel safe and content. Whatever it took.

"You know, women pay good money to get their hair washed this well," Lily said dreamily. "If things don't work out with Jacob, I bet I could get you a job at the salon."

"Good to know." Levi chuckled. "Turn around."

Lily turned to face him, her eyes closed. Levi urged her head back to allow the spray to wash the suds from her hair. He studied her as he rinsed out the shampoo, her delicate features, button nose, and the way her lips parted slightly as she tilted her head back. He couldn't resist himself and seized the opportunity to place a gentle kiss on that delicious mouth. Her eyes opened as he pulled away and she smiled.

"I definitely don't get that kind of service at the salon."

"That's good for me," Levi said. "Gotta do something to keep you interested."

Lily's brow furrowed. He still didn't know her well enough to read her expressions, but he could tell something worried her. He did his best to keep things light. No pressure. But with every moment he spent with her, Levi found himself wanting more.

"I'd offer to do the rest, but . . ." He handed her a sponge and the bodywash. "I'm afraid that if I put my hands on your soapy naked body, I'll break my promise that you won't be late for work."

The worried crease smoothed from her brow. Levi's heart sank at the expression, the look of utter relief that he wasn't planning to touch her.

"It's a good thing." She quickly hid the relief with a too-bright smile. "Because there would be a classroom full of second graders running around like wild animals without me to rein them in."

Levi forced his own concerns to the back of his mind. It was too early to make assumptions. He had time, and he was patient. He couldn't expect Lily to trust him in one night and this wasn't about a one-night stand. If it had been, he'd have been out the door before she'd fallen asleep last night.

"Well, we can't have a bunch of little banshees overthrowing the school, can we?" He leaned down and kissed her forehead. "Finish your shower, darlin'. I'm gonna dry off."

"I owe you a shampoo," Lily said.

"Already done," Levi replied as he moved the curtain aside. "But I'm taking a rain check on that for sure."

Lily's gaze followed him as he climbed out of the shower. "There are towels on the rack beside you," she said as he put the curtain back in place.

He grabbed a fluffy brown towel from the rack and dried

off. The sound of the shower drowned out his thoughts as he went into the bedroom to get dressed. Levi had always had great instincts. He could read people. It had made him good at his job and helped him move up the ranks quickly. But Lily was an enigma.

As he pulled on his jeans, his gaze wandered to the bed and his lust stirred. The sounds of Lily's sweet moans echoed in his mind. As did the memory of the soft skin of her thighs, the slick, wet heat of her pussy, and the way she'd gripped his shaft so tightly.

They'd only had one night together and already Levi knew that one night would never be enough.

He made the bed and put the decorative pillows back in what he hoped was the order in which they'd found them last night. He folded his towel and hung it back on the rack. The water continued to run and he decided to give Lily a little space. The last thing a woman needed when she was getting ready for work was an audience.

The aroma of coffee filled Levi's nostrils and he walked into the kitchen to hunt down a cup. For a small space, it wasn't cluttered in the slightest. Lily's cupboards were meticulously organized. The plates, bowls, and mugs all belonged to a matching set and were stacked neatly side by side. Rather than grab one of the stoneware mugs, he closed the door and continued his exploration.

Each cupboard revealed a little more about Lily. She liked Frosted Mini-Wheats, granola, and Cool Ranch Doritos. Typical farm girl, she kept the pantry stocked with canned goods and other nonperishables. Rather than clutter the counters, she stored most of her appliances. The dishwasher was empty and so was the trash can.

"Cups are in the cupboard to your left," Lily remarked as she walked into the kitchen. "Above the coffeemaker."

Levi shot her an abashed look. "Busted." He cupped the

back of his neck in his palm as he offered Lily a sheepish grin. "Sorry."

"It's okay." Lily's hazel eyes sparkled with humor. "Nothing stands between me and coffee either."

She'd dressed in a pair of slim gray slacks that hugged her shapely thighs and a white blouse, cut just low enough to remain professional. Her hair was gathered up in a high ponytail. Levi's breath caught. Did she have any idea how damned beautiful she was?

Levi grabbed another cup and filled it for her. She smiled her gratitude and she joined him in the kitchen. "I can't do black," she said as she grabbed sugar from a cupboard and a carton of cream from the refrigerator.

"My mom liked cream in her coffee." The heavy stuff, just like Lily. She would scoff at milk or half-and-half.

"It's the only way," Lily said as she took a sip and let her eyes drift shut dramatically. "It's like having dessert for breakfast."

Levi leaned against the counter as he studied her. Since the day they'd met, she'd proven to be a force of nature and then some. Her emotions blew like spring winds: fierce and blustery cold, warm and sultry, soft and easy as breath.

"Levi." Her tentative tone demanded his attention. She leaned a hip against the counter and she looked into her cup as though gathering her thoughts. "Please don't take this the wrong way, but I'd appreciate it if you didn't tell anyone you stayed here last night." Was she regretting last night? His expression must have given his emotions away, because she quickly added, "It's just because people in town like to gossip, and I hate to say it, but my gran is one of the worst. If anyone out at the ranch finds out, her entire social group will know about it by noon and they'll have our wedding planned by dinner."

"Gotcha." Though Lily seemed mortified at the idea, Levi found it amusing. "I was planning on posting it on a billboard outside of town, but if you want me to be a little more discreet, I understand."

Lily's lips formed the petulant pucker that drove him wild. He loved teasing her just for the reaction.

"I'm kidding. You don't have anything to worry about, Lily. I don't kiss and tell. And honestly, I'm not interested in having my wedding planned behind my back either."

Her cheeks flushed and she quickly averted her gaze. "Thanks. I'm just a really private person."

He knew that better than she realized. "You have nothing to worry about, darlin'. What's between you and me stays between you and me."

Lily studied him for a quiet moment as though trying to gauge the truth in his words. Levi had every reason to keep what had happened between him and Lily a secret, the least of them being town gossips and her cousins.

"I should probably get to work." Lily set her empty cup in the sink and poured a second cup into a to-go mug. "I have extras if you want to borrow one," she said, indicating the steel mug. "Help yourself."

"Thanks," Levi said. "But I've got to get going too."

An amazing morning had slowly devolved into something stilted and awkward. This was why Levi tended to choose hookups and one-nighters over something that might be lasting. When you left before the sun came up, there was little time for small talk and the unavoidable, uncomfortable parting of ways.

"Okay." Lily seemed reluctant to leave. "Well, have a good day."

Levi took the cue, but not before he pointed to her cell. "Do you mind?"

She swiped her finger over the screen and handed him the phone. He smiled and quickly tapped his phone number into her contacts.

"My number. Just in case." He leaned over and placed a quick kiss on her cheek. As he headed for the door and opened it, he shot over his shoulder, "Don't forget, you owe me a shampoo." And closed it quickly behind him.

Levi had been sent to Deer Haven to watch over Lily Donovan. And if his superiors found out just how closely he'd been watching her, he could lose everything he'd worked so hard for.

But as he thought again of Lily, soft and willing in his arms, Levi realized that there were far worse things to lose than a job.

Chapter Eleven

The busy Monday had been a welcome distraction for Lily's racing mind. She'd worked through lunch and used her prep periods to line up field trips for next week's fire awareness and prevention week with the fire department. She hadn't had a free second to think about Levi or their wild night together, or how her body ached for more of his commanding touch. But now that the day was over and she was alone in her classroom, her thoughts began to wander.

To him.

The way he looked at her.

The way he made her feel.

Lily opened her desk drawer and pulled out her cell. Levi was nothing if not persistent and thank God he'd insisted on entering his number into her phone before he left the house this morning. She swiped her finger up the screen. Though she hadn't made him any promises, dinner was beginning to sound like a good idea.

A news alert popped up on the screen, drawing Lily's attention. Her blood turned to ice in her veins as she read the headline and her limbs began to quake.

"*Surveillance Footage Leaked in Susanville Prison Escape:* Convicted university professor and two other inmates escaped from the California Correctional Center in Susanville more than a week ago. The FBI and the U.S. Marshals Service are conducting a nationwide manhunt, focusing their attention on the U.S./Mexico border."

She stared at the images of a grainy security camera picture beside photos of two other men and the faculty photo of Graham Brisbee that accompanied the news story.

That face haunted Lily's nightmares. The man she'd thought she'd trusted as a mentor and teacher had stolen her peace of mind, destroyed her confidence, and nearly killed her. He'd been her psychology professor for two years. Brilliant. Charismatic. Charming. And the vilest predator Lily had ever encountered.

She'd been foolish to separate herself so entirely from what had happened, shunning support groups and the solidarity that might have helped her to heal. She'd managed to keep her name out of the headlines during the trial. No one in Deer Haven besides Shay and Sallie knew. She'd sworn both women to secrecy and forbidden either of them from telling Jacob or Gran. Instead, she'd made up a lame excuse about being homesick and opting to finish her last year of college remotely and through the local community college. No one had questioned it. But now Lily was beginning to regret her secrecy.

If the headline was correct, Graham could be several hundred miles away or more. And honestly, he couldn't possibly know where she lived. She couldn't remember ever mentioning her hometown, and she could have moved anywhere after the trial. The marshals service wanted to put her in protective custody. Did they believe Graham wanted revenge on the woman who'd testified against him? He'd managed to intimidate his other victims. Used his psychological games to control them. Lily had refused to cower. Before his arrest, Graham had graduated from serial rapist to murderer.

Lily would have been the second life taken, but she'd gotten lucky and managed to escape before he could choke the life out of her. She wanted to trust the headline and believe he and the other two inmates were heading for the U.S./Mexico border. If he had any sense at all, that's what he should be doing. Every law enforcement agency in the country would be looking for them now. It was only a matter of time before they'd be caught.

Too bad Lily found it hard to believe her own reassurances.

She stared down at her cell phone and swiped away the image of Graham Brisbee. Anxiety tightened her shoulders and stretched taut across her chest. She hadn't heard from Chief Deputy Seth Miller since she'd blown off his offer of protection over a week ago. She guessed he'd taken her rebuff to heart. But if she felt abandoned, she had no one to blame but herself.

Lily stared at the message she'd been about to send Levi. She no longer felt like having dinner. What was the point in trying to start fresh and live her life when her past so actively haunted her? Why drag him into her messy life? It was best to leave last night as it was. A one-night stand.

A deep sense of regret settled like a stone in Lily's stomach as she gathered her things and turned off the lights before leaving her classroom. Her phone rang as she walked down the hallway and she checked the caller ID, releasing a sigh of relief as she answered the phone.

"You seriously have the best timing," she said.

"Are you okay?" Shay questioned her, worry and fear lacing her voice. "I just saw the news. Sallie called too. Did you know about this? Did anyone call you or anything? Victims have to be notified when something like this happens! And oh my God, how could they just let him walk off the property like that? Is no one at that prison doing their goddamn job? I mean seriously, are they going to catch this asshole or what?"

If Lily had a reputation for being feisty, then her sister was downright hostile. There was no one Lily would rather have to watch her back, however. Even if they hadn't been related, they'd still be best friends.

Lily took a deep breath and held it in her lungs. "The marshals service told me over a week ago. They said they were trying to keep it on the down low and wanted to put me in protective custody."

"What?" Lily pulled the phone away from her ear as Shay's incredulous shout boomed from the receiver. "Then why aren't you hiding out in a hotel somewhere, surrounded by armed cops?"

"I told them no." Lily could picture the infuriated expression on Shay's face right now.

"Are you crazy?"

"I'm not going to let him take my life away, Shay."

"Lily—"

"I'm not going to argue with you about it." They'd been through this after Graham's arrest. Prosecutors had wanted Lily to go into witness protection, but she'd refused, instead making a deal that she'd testify as Jane Doe and retain some sort of anonymity. If she had to give up her life, her identity, and her freedom, Lily might as well have been dead. Thankfully, Graham had confessed instead. His arrogance so high he'd been certain he could talk his way out of it. He was too insane to accept the fact that he could lose. She refused to let that happen. "I'm hoping he's running scared and headed for the border." Lily fought to keep the quaver from her voice. She wanted to at least give the illusion she was standing strong. "But yeah, I hope they arrest the son of a bitch and put him away forever this time."

"Amen," Shay said solemnly. Lily was grateful that Shay

didn't press the issue of protective custody. "For what it's worth, I hope you're right. I can't imagine him wanting to hang around now that he's one of America's most wanted. If he's smart, he'll head straight for the border."

Shea played the confidence game as well as Lily did. They were both full of shit.

"You want me to come over? I'm off at five, but I can get out of here a little early if you need me to."

It was sweet of her to offer, but Lily was sick and tired of having to be babysat. She was so over being scared all the time, looking over her shoulder and feeling unsure. She couldn't keep letting the people she loved put their own lives on hold for her.

"I'm okay." The words didn't even sound convincing in her own ears.

"No, you're not," Shay said as a matter of fact. "And it's okay not to be okay."

Lily knew that. But damn it, she had to start standing up to her fears. "I know. I'm just going to take it easy tonight."

"Okay. But call me if you need me," Shay said. "I'm serious, Lily."

Lily smiled. She meant business. "I will. Promise."

"Okay, good. I've gotta get back to work; I swear this place would fall to pieces without me. I'll call you later."

"Go save the world," Lily said with a laugh before she ended the call.

She crossed the nearly empty parking lot to her car. Might be a good idea to start parking closer to the building or at least asking one of the custodians to walk her to her car in the afternoons from now on. Just because she was trying to master her fear didn't mean she was about to take her own safety lightly. She unlocked the door with the fob and climbed into the driver's seat, taking a quiet moment to breathe before starting the engine.

Would there ever be a day when she could finally put all of this behind her? Or would something that was never her fault follow her for the rest of her life and stand in the way of her happiness?

So much for dinner with a sexy cowboy. Lily just hoped that Levi wouldn't hate her for blowing him off.

Levi checked his phone for what felt like the hundredth time that day. He'd never been the type to wait for a call. None of Levi's past relationships were what he would consider serious. Flings, one-night stands, a couple of short-term hookups that lasted a week or two here and there. Nothing serious. He'd never met a woman who occupied his thoughts for long. When it was over, it was over, and he never lost any sleep over it.

But Lily was different.

All day he'd been preoccupied, his concentration for shit. He'd nearly been kicked in the thigh by an agitated calf this morning, and in the afternoon he'd almost taken Chris's head off with a shovel. That certainly hadn't earned him any points, and he'd been catching a lot of dirty looks for most of the day.

He couldn't blame them. He was the guy dropping the ball.

Five o'clock had come and gone. He'd hoped Lily would call and agree to go to dinner with him. Instead, she'd effectively ignored him. But then again, maybe he'd misread the situation. Maybe she was waiting for him to call.

He scrolled through his recent calls and selected Lily's number. He waited as the phone rang once, twice . . . five times before going to voice mail. He cursed under his breath as he disconnected the call. Ghosted? Sure as hell felt like it.

The phone vibrated in his palm and his excitement crested before taking a sharp nose dive. "Damn it," he growled as he read the name on the caller ID. This couldn't be good.

He pressed his thumb to the screen and answered. "Roberts."

"Have you seen the news?"

"No."

"So much for keeping things quiet," Seth Miller, the chief deputy director of the Sacramento Bureau of the U.S. Marshals Service, replied with disgust. "We knew we wouldn't be able to shut the media down for long, though."

"Fill me in," Levi replied. *Shit.* This was going to be a long phone call.

Levi paced the confines of his room in the bunkhouse, agitated as fuck. The news he'd gotten hadn't been good and the fact that he still couldn't get hold of Lily made his bad mood even worse. He'd called three times in the past hour only to be sent to voice mail. He didn't bother texting. If she'd wanted to talk to him, she would have answered.

Unless she wasn't able to answer.

Stomach acid churned like an angry sea in Levi's stomach. His heart thundered in his chest as a wave of anger stole over him. He'd always prided himself on his ability to stay calm and levelheaded no matter the situation. But this was different. She was different. And he'd be damned if he sat around and did nothing, no matter what he'd been ordered to do.

He grabbed his keys and his holstered Glock from the bedside table and stormed out the door, letting it slam behind him. He took off at a jog toward his truck and jumped in, jamming the key in the ignition. The engine roared to life and the tires kicked up gravel as he pulled out of the driveway. The time it took to get to town from the ranch felt like an eternity as Levi slowed to enter the city limits. He turned down Main Street and took a left on Colorado Street as he left the town proper behind and headed for Lily's house on the outskirts.

In a matter of minutes, he turned onto her lane. He slowed the truck to a crawl, taking in every detail around him as he pulled up to the house. Lily's car was parked in the garage. There were no other vehicles in sight. Everything seemed absolutely normal, and instead of calming him down, it sent his blood to boiling.

Levi practically kicked the truck door open and hopped out, slamming it behind him. He tucked the holster into his waistband at his back and marched up the stairs, doing nothing to mask his presence. He pulled open the screen door and laid his fist to the wooden planks, not bothering with the civility of the doorbell. A few quiet moments passed, and he pounded on the door once more. His gut tightened with anxious energy and he reached for the holster at his back, ready to bust down the door and storm inside.

Before he could lay the bottom of his boot to the heavy door, it flew open. He released his grip on the holster and relaxed as he came face-to-face with the angriest female he'd ever laid eyes on.

"What in the hell is wrong with you?" Lily practically shouted as she stepped out onto the front porch. The screen door slammed behind her, echoing her rancor. "You scared the shit out of me pounding on the door like that. Do you have a problem with using the doorbell?"

Levi let out a slow breath. He wasn't exactly calm either and her indignant attitude wasn't doing anything for his annoyance.

"You're not answering your phone," Levi said through gritted teeth.

Lily's eyes went wide with disbelief. "Last time I checked, I don't have to."

Anger burned in her expression and colored her cheeks. Levi should have seen the warning signs and backed down, but he was too damned angry and too damned worried about her to exercise any amount of caution.

"Yes, you do."

Lily let out a chuff of laughter. "Are you for real?" She took a menacing step forward, but Levi refused to budge. "I don't have to do *anything* I don't want to do and that includes answering phone calls from arrogant pains in the ass who think I owe them something after spending a night together!" Lily poked her index finger into Levi's chest. "You have seriously got some set of balls on you to come over here and demand that I answer my phone."

Levi's anger melted away in an instant. Sweet mercy, she was the sexiest thing he'd ever laid eyes on. Even more desirable in her anger. He wanted to strip her naked, bend her over the porch railing, and fuck her right then and there.

"Has anyone ever told you how sexy you are when you're angry?"

Lily's jaw went slack. "Excuse me? Do you really think that works?"

"I'm hoping." He grinned before sobering an instant later. "It's your fault I went overboard. I know you're running from something, baby. When you didn't answer the phone my imagination went crazy. Until you get more forthcoming, you're just going to have to deal with it."

He didn't give her any slack there. The fact that he was lying to her by omission wasn't going to be allowed to factor in.

Lily cocked her head to one side as she studied him, her brow furrowed. "You were . . . worried about me?"

It seemed impossible to her that anyone would worry and it made him want to grab her and crush her against his chest in a tight embrace. At the same time, he wanted to shake her for forgetting the fact that people did worry about her.

"Why?" The word hung in the air between them as her gaze held his.

"I . . ." Levi laughed. Good lord, was there any way to salvage this without looking like a complete chump? "Because I care about you," he said simply. "I thought something might be wrong." He hiked a shoulder. "Blame it on my ego if you want."

Lily smiled. "Oh, you've got an ego," she agreed. "And then some. But I'll give you a pass this time. We're kind of bad about miscommunicating, aren't we?"

"Yeah," Levi said. "We are."

"You drove all the way out here," Lily said on a sigh. "You might as well come in."

Ouch. That ego he'd bragged about took a stabbing hit with the resignation in her tone. She'd clearly not wanted to have dinner or anything else with him tonight.

Levi was in uncharted territory. He'd never put effort into a relationship before and it showed. Put him in a combat situation or send him after a fugitive and he owned every word, every action, with unwavering confidence. Lily scared him more than a storm of enemy fire. He hated feeling out of his depth here and she had an uncanny ability to strip him bare and reveal the chinks in his armor that he worked so hard to hide.

"Since you asked so graciously," he growled.

Lily huffed a heavy sigh. "It's been a hell of a day, Levi. I'm sorry it sounded bad."

Levi fluffed the back of his shirt to cover the holster as he followed Lily into the house. A pot boiled on the stove, sending a cloud of steam toward the ceiling, and Lily sped around the counter to turn down the heat.

"Shit." She grabbed a slotted spoon and stirred the pot. "There's nothing worse than overcooked pasta."

Levi grabbed the colander from the counter and put it in

the sink. He was never one to stand around and he wasn't going to pass up an opportunity to be closer to Lily. He breathed in her sweet vanilla scent as she gripped the pot handle and tipped the contents into the colander. Her arm brushed his, sending an electric zing through Levi's body.

"What's for dinner?" Levi turned on the faucet, drenching the pasta in cold water.

"Baked ziti with sausage," Lily said. She stood silently beside him watching the water pour over the pasta. "I blew you off today."

Yeah, he'd figured that one out.

"Yes," Levi said. "You did. Remind me to spank you for that later."

She tensed just a little. Just enough to assure Levi that the thought of that spanking just might be more intriguing to her than she wanted to let on.

"Why are you so persistent?" Lily turned to look at him. "Why even bother when I've been such a pain in the ass?"

"Because I want to get to know you." Levi turned off the sink and shook out the pasta. He smiled. "And who says you've got the monopoly on being a pain in the ass?"

Levi had been sent to Deer Haven. Not only to keep an eye on Lily Donovan. He was hunting a dangerous predator who might have his sights set on her. Getting close to her had been a part of that assignment. But now everything had changed.

He leaned in close to her, almost close enough to brush his lips to the top of her forehead. Dying to touch her and yet afraid to take the chance and scare her off.

"Guess we've both got that whole pain in the ass thing going for us," she whispered.

"You're not a pain in the ass, Lily," Levi said, low. "What you are is the most beautiful thing I've ever laid eyes on."

She turned to face him, her expression guileless, her lips

parted invitingly. A powerful surge of lust overtook him as he seized her to him. His mouth hovered near hers as he stared into the depths of her hazel eyes. He'd risked everything to have Lily and he'd risk it all again. There was no turning back, no coming to his senses. He was lost to her. And damn it, he was going to have her.

Chapter Twelve

Lily's head swam. Her senses were full of Levi. His leather and spice scent, the soft strands of his hair as they slipped through her fingers. His muscles that flexed and bunched as he moved against her. It was the most sensual thing Lily had ever experienced with her clothes on. His proximity drove her wild. Her breasts tingled in anticipation of his touch, her stomach knotted and her pussy clenched, as though already wrapped around the hard, wide length of him. Their mouths hadn't even touched, but her lips felt hot and swollen. Her body was hyperaware of his every movement, drawn to him like a magnet to metal.

"Lily, I need to fuck you. Right now."

"Yes." She pushed the word past her lips on a desperate breath.

Levi's powerful arms caged her against the countertop. She reached for the hem of his shirt and he took a step back. "Hang on, baby. Let me taste you first."

A thrill rushed through Lily's center as she contemplated just what part of her it was that he wanted to taste. Her eyes drifted shut and her bones seemed to melt as her lips parted in anticipation of a kiss.

"Ahhhhhh!"

Lily's front door crashed in with a battle shout. Her eyes flew open as her heart leapt into her throat. Levi spun around, putting himself between Lily and the potential threat rushing at them. He reached behind his back and in a motion too fast for Lily to comprehend pulled a gun from a holster and pointed it at the tiny—and enraged—form rushing toward them.

"Get away from her, asshole!" Shay stood at the other side of the counter, a baseball bat held tight in her grip. Her eyes burned with fire and her jaw was set in a stubborn sneer. "I swear to God, you'd better shoot me right now, because if you don't, I'm going to beat your head in with this bat!"

"Levi, stop!" Lily came to her senses as her brain caught up with what was happening. Levi stood poised to shoot, a gun pointed straight at her sister. "Why in the hell do you have a gun? Put it down! And Shay! I'm okay! Can everyone please just calm the hell down?"

Tension thickened the air as neither one made a move to back down. Shay looked Levi up and down with suspicion.

"Oh, good lord!" Lily threw her arms up. Shay's arms loosened, though she didn't lower the bat entirely. "Shay! He's okay. I'm fine. I swear."

Levi lowered the gun and tucked it back in its holster. Rather than tuck it back into his pants—and who in the hell carries a gun in his pants?—he took a step forward and carefully placed the gun on the counter. Shay lowered the bat but didn't let go. Lily fought the urge to laugh. Only Shay would bring a bat to a gunfight and be confident enough to think that she'd come out on top.

"Has everyone lost their damn minds?" Lily stepped out from behind Levi so she could look the both of them in the eyes. "Seriously? What's wrong with you guys?"

"You didn't answer your phone," Shay said.

The absurdity of it all made Lily let out a snort of humor. It bubbled up from her chest, unbidden, and refused to stop. Giggles turned to rolling laughter that brought tears to her eyes. She sucked in a tight breath and laughed even harder, drawing looks from both Shay and Levi.

"Girl, are you okay?" Shay asked.

"No," Lily replied through her laughter. She wiped at the tears that spilled over her eyes. So much for her "tough-girl" reputation. She was so damned helpless that she had everyone rushing to her front door when she didn't answer her phone. "I'm definitely not okay."

"Lily." Levi reached out to take her hand, but she waved him away.

"Just give me a second." Her sides ached from the humorless laughter that shook her. Her emotions were too raw. Too much had happened in the past twenty-four hours and she was trying to catch up.

"So." Shay grinned as she propped her free hand on her hip and sized Levi up. "What brings you out here tonight? You have some sort of rejection fetish that gets you off?"

Lord have mercy. Leave it to Shay to lead off with a smart-ass remark to put Levi in his place. Another round of spluttering laughter threatened, and Lily pushed it to the soles of her feet. Shay was the saltiest person Lily knew and she had not one shit to give.

Levi's smirk grew into a wide smile. "Damn, I love blunt women."

Shay grinned wider and plopped down on one of the barstools at the counter. She set the bat in front of her, next to Levi's gun. She mostly ignored him and focused her attention on Lily. "What's for dinner?"

"Baked ziti with sausage." Looked like she and Levi weren't going to be getting cozy anytime soon. Shay wasn't going anywhere. Good thing she had enough pasta to feed an army. "But no one's getting anything to eat as long as there are weapons on the table."

Levi took the gun in his hand and reached for his back.

"No weapons anywhere on your persons as well," Lily said.

Levi cocked a questioning brow.

"You heard her," Shay said, resigned as she plucked the bat from the countertop and set it on the floor by her feet. "When she uses her teacher voice, she means business."

"Teacher voice?" Levi laughed. "All right, guess I'd better leave this by the front door if I want dinner."

He rounded the counter and headed for the living room. Shay's eyes went wide as she shared a moment of silent communication with Lily and mouthed the words, *You hooked up?* Lily grinned sheepishly. To which Shay replied with an appreciative thumbs-up. Shay's expression turned serious, though, as she jerked her head toward the living room and popped up her thumb and stuck out her forefinger.

The gun had thrown her for a loop as well. "I'm okay." She shrugged as she gave her sister reassurance in a low murmur. "It's just been a hell of a day."

"You can say that again," Shay agreed.

"Say what again?" Levi came back to the kitchen, ready to join the conversation.

"That," Shay said, deadpan. "You can say *that* again."

Her response invited no other comment. Lily hid her amusement behind a cough as she went to the cupboard for plates.

"You always carry around a baseball bat?" Levi tried to sound congenial, but Lily sensed an edge to his tone that piqued her curiosity.

"What can I say?" Shay hiked a shoulder. "I'm a regular Boy Scout."

Levi replied with a tight-lipped smile that was anything but friendly.

Lily wondered at his sudden hostility. He couldn't possibly be that put out at being interrupted. And why in the hell did he have a gun with him? This wasn't Texas, after all. Though Deer Haven was mostly a ranching community, it was unusual for anyone to be packing. She could understand why Shay would come rushing over here looking for a fight, considering news of the prison escape making headlines. Levi, on the other hand, had no reason whatsoever to be concerned. His excuse for coming over—being worried that she hadn't answered her phone—seemed a little too sudden a response for someone she barely knew.

Barely knowing him didn't seem to matter when you slept with him last night.

She forced the self-deprecating thought from her head before she let her guilt get the better of her. She was a grown-ass woman and could sleep with a man if she wanted to. No need for justification, explanation, or apology. Of course, that didn't mean she couldn't be concerned when said man showed up with a gun and wanting to know why she wasn't answering her phone. She knew what Shay would say to that.

Stalk-er!

Deep down, Lily didn't believe that. Levi wasn't a stalker. In fact, she felt safer with him than she had in a long damn time. Something was up, though. And she planned to find out what.

"Puhleaze tell me you made garlic bread." Shay had effectively ignored Levi and turned her attention to what truly mattered to her: food.

"I made garlic bread," Lily said.

"Wine?"

"Red and white."

"Dessert?"

"Okay." Lily laughed as she tossed the ziti, cooked sausage, and sauce into a baking dish and popped it into the oven. "Now you're pushing it."

"Bullshit," Shay replied. "I know you have ice cream."

Levi remained silent, but Lily felt his attention as he observed her and Shay's interaction. She tried to brush it off, focusing instead on setting out the wine and silverware. Shay turned her attention to Levi, her lips quirked in a wry smile.

"How's life on the ranch, Levi?" Her tone dripped with honey and Lily cringed.

It was going to be a long night.

Levi scowled. The night had taken a sharp turn from the direction he'd hoped it was going and Lily's party-crasher sister was beginning to get on his last nerve. Though he had to give her credit, Shay was fiercely protective of Lily, and he was thankful that someone was watching her back. He'd met seasoned interrogators who could learn a thing or two from Shay about intimidation tactics. She certainly knew how to throw down the questions.

"We just finished branding and tagging." Levi could play her game, and he'd play it better. He left Lily in the kitchen and rounded the counter to join Shay. He slid onto the barstool next to her and reached for the bottle of merlot and poured himself a glass. "Lily and I rode the fence line on Sunday and the crew replaced some poles and wire today. Turned the herd out this afternoon."

"Oh *really*?" Shay cocked a brow and looked at Lily.

Lily shot her sister a warning look and Levi hid a satisfied smile behind his wineglass.

"Shay, eat something." Lily dug into a foil-wrapped loaf and produced a slice of steamy bread that she put on a plate and slid across the bar. "You're obviously hangry."

"You're right about that," Shay agreed. "Since *someone* blew me off for dinner tonight."

Lily handed Levi a plate with a slice of bread as well. Better to keep their mouths full so they couldn't talk. He took a big bite of bread as he set the plate in front of him. "Funny," he said through a mouthful. "I got blown off for dinner too."

His eyes met Lily's. She looked from him to Shay and her cheeks flushed.

"I feel so sorry for the both of you." Her expression was pure sympathy while her tone was 100 percent sarcasm. "It's a shame neither one of you wound up with anything to eat—oh wait! Yes, you did."

Shay chuckled. "Lucky for us you always cook for an army."

"Super-lucky," Lily agreed.

"Ranch girls." Shay took another bite of bread. "It's in our DNA."

"That's the truth," Levi agreed.

"Oh yeah?" Shay turned her attention to Levi. "You have a lot of experience with ranch girls?"

She was fishing for information. Exes, family, whatever she could get. Levi didn't like to open up. He kept his personal life personal. But to smooth things over with Shay and put Lily more at ease, he'd bite the bullet and play along.

"My mom grew up on a peanut farm just outside of Willow, Oklahoma. I swear she cooked enough in a day to last a week. And she was always canning and freezing something." Levi smiled at the fond memory. Damn, he hadn't thought about that in a long time. "She was always putting food in front of us."

"Remember Gran?" Lily said to Shay. "I swear, she was cooking all day long when we were kids. Breakfast, lunch, and dinner. She fed the ranch hands back then too, and she always had a pie or cake or cobbler for Grandpa. That man had such a sweet tooth."

Shay giggled. "He had a candy bar stash in the truck! Do you remember that?"

"Oh yeah." Lily grabbed a couple of pot holders and took the ziti out of the oven. "In the glove box." She brought the baking dish to the bar and scooped out servings for both Shay and Levi before making a plate for herself and joining them at the bar. "He didn't think Gran knew about it, but she totally did."

Levi sat quietly and listened to Lily and Shay reminisce. It took the pressure off him to join in the conversation and allowed him to learn a little more about Lily. Plus, anything that kept him out of Shay's sights was a good thing. Lily had been fond of her grandpa. She'd spent the majority of her childhood on the ranch with Shay and Jacob. The two women laughed as they recalled the antics of their youth as well as some wild times as teenagers. Levi ate quietly, enjoyed his wine, and drank in Lily's brilliant smile and bright eyes. He could spend all day just sitting next to her, watching the expressions on her face, and listening to the lilting tones of her voice.

"Anybody home, cowboy?" Shay's joking tone tore him from his thoughts.

He raised his brows in question.

"We're just rambling," Lily remarked. "We're probably boring you with all of our childhood memories."

"Not at all." Levi reached for the bottle of chardonnay and refilled Lily's glass. "I love the sound of your voice."

Lily's eyes sparkled as she graced him with a dazzling smile.

Shay snorted, but there was no malice in it. "You're quite the sweet talker, aren't you?"

Levi was ready to fire back at Shay, but Lily cut him off. “What’s wrong with a little sweet talk, Shay? I like it.”

Though his back was turned to her, he imagined that Shay rolled her eyes.

Levi’s chest swelled with emotion. He liked that Lily would stick up for him. Especially with a member of her family. He was used to watching his own back. He’d never really had anyone in his life he could count on. His professional life had always been a different story, but when the workday was over Levi had been mostly alone. Lily made him realize that he’d been missing out on something important. A partner. Someone to share the day with and to create memories with. Someone to protect and be protected by. Maybe Lily could be that person.

And maybe he was kidding himself.

“Do you have any Parmesan?” Without waiting for a response, Shay went into the kitchen to dig through the fridge.

Lily leaned in close and murmured next to Levi’s ear, “I’m sorry about Shay. She’s actually really awesome.”

“Anyone who has your back is awesome,” Levi replied. “Not gonna lie, though, her timing sort of sucks.”

Lily flashed a sensual smile that hardened Levi’s cock in an instant. “I’ll make it up to you later.”

“Promise?”

She reached for his lap and brushed her palm against his erection. “I promise.”

“Hope you weren’t planning on leftovers, Lil, ’cuz I’ma smash what’s was left of the pasta.” Shay didn’t bother to sit back down. She stood at the counter opposite them as she took her plate in one hand and sprinkled the grated cheese over the ziti with the other.

“Why would I be planning on that?” Lily said with a

laugh. She rested her hand on Levi's thigh and gave a gentle squeeze. "Just be gentle on the silverware, would you?"

"You're lucky I don't bite right through the fork," Shay teased, playing into Lily's joke. "I haven't eaten all day."

"She's lying," Lily said in a conspiratorial tone. "Eating is Shay's favorite hobby."

"I consider it more of a pastime," she said with pride. "I'm world champ material."

Levi found that hard to believe since Shay couldn't be more than a buck-ten soaking wet. Then again, he'd just watched her consume a heaping plate of pasta without flinching.

Lily continued to massage his thigh. Gentle passes of her palm that started on the outside of his leg by his knee before rounding to his inner thigh and brushing against his cock. It was a delicious torture that wound him tighter with each round she made. He stabbed his fork absently in his pasta, no longer hungry. He wanted his hands on Lily's body and their present company made that impossible. Lily pretended to be interested in her dinner as well, picking at her plate and sipping her chardonnay. She reached for his cock and gave it a gentle squeeze, bringing their play to a damn near inappropriate level. If she didn't watch out, he'd have her laid out on the counter, legs spread. No matter who was there to watch.

In the meantime, Shay managed to finish off a second serving of pasta and took her plate to the sink. She gathered up the rest of the dirty dishes and began to load the dishwasher, turning her back on Lily and Levi. He leaned close to her ear, brushing his lips against the outer shell.

"You're driving me crazy," he murmured low. "You have no idea how badly I need to fuck you."

"Give me ten minutes," Lily whispered, "and I'll have Shay out of here."

"Perfect."

Chapter Thirteen

"You're ditching me for a boy? Lame."

Shay acted put out, but Lily knew that secretly her sister was thrilled. "I am, in fact, ditching you for one of the most gorgeous men I have ever laid my eyes on."

"I gotta say, you know how to pick them." Shay gave Lily a nudge. "I'm a little jealous. When is Jacob going to a hire a guy for me?"

"You don't do cowboys, remember?"

"For one that looks like Levi?" Shay replied. "I'd revisit that self-imposed guideline."

Lily laughed, though she knew better. "I'm sure that's what Jacob's concerned about. Finding eligible men for his cousins."

"He should be," Shay quipped. "Can you imagine how much easier his life would be with the both of us out of his hair?"

"Easier?" Lily asked. "If we snag all the good help, he'll never let us live it down!"

"True that," Shay agreed solemnly. She reached out a closed fist and Lily met it with her own knuckles in a bump. "Honestly, though, I'm glad Levi is here. I'll sleep better knowing you won't be alone tonight."

"I love you," Lily said. "You know that, right?"

"You have to love me," Shay scoffed. "We're family."

"I love you in spite of being family," Lily teased.

"Call me tomorrow." Shay stepped out onto the back porch to leave. "And I want details. I'm talking de-tails."

"Gross," Lily said with a laugh.

She strode across the lawn toward her car. "You think I'm kidding," she said as she opened the car door. "I will hound you to the ends of the earth. Who else can I live vicariously through? Talk to you tomorrow!"

Shay got in the car and started the engine. She pulled out of the driveway without giving Lily a chance to reply; she simply stuck her hand out the window, giving one last wave as she drove off.

De-tails. Lily shook her head and laughed. Shay would absolutely hold her to it.

A thrill of excitement chased through Lily's bloodstream as she walked back into the house. There was no more buffer, no one to come between her and Levi and force them to behave. Her body warmed at the prospect of being naked with him once again. Feeling his body move against hers, enjoying the sensation of his lips on her skin.

Why stand out on the porch and fantasize about it when the real thing was right on the other side of the door? Lily strode back into the house and shut and locked the door behind her. She'd be damned if anyone else barged in to interrupt them tonight.

"Levi?"

He was no longer in the kitchen. Lily poked her head around the corner to check the living room and found it empty. Maybe he was in the bathroom? Lily finished tidying the kitchen and took a carton of ice cream out of the freezer. They had all night together and there was no need to rush.

As much as she enjoyed Levi with his clothes off, Shay had inadvertently pointed something out to her tonight.

Lily knew virtually nothing about Levi. Aside from the fact that he worked for Jacob, his story about his mother's cooking was the only personal detail he'd shared with her since they'd met. And whereas so far she and Levi had had only last night together, she was beginning to think that she wanted to spend a lot more time with him. Worry scratched at the back of Lily's mind. Was she in the position to let someone into her life? Especially with everything that was going on. She didn't know if she was ready to open up about what had happened to her. And was it even fair to drag Levi into all of this drama?

She had no idea how he'd react if and when she chose to tell him everything. If he decided that it was all too much, Lily wouldn't blame him. It was way too much for her to deal with and she was the one living it.

Lily grabbed a couple of shallow dishes from the cupboard and two spoons. She gathered a large scoop of chocolate brownie batter ice cream and dropped it into one of the dishes. A second scoop went into her own dish before she put the carton away and took their desserts into the living room.

She waited for the sound of the toilet flushing or the sink running, but the house stayed eerily still. "Levi?" she called out once again only to be answered with silence.

Nervous energy gathered in her stomach as Lily set the dishes on the coffee table. Had he left? Just walked out the door and ditched her while she'd said goodbye to Shay? The wild assumption began to grow in Lily's mind until her worry turned to annoyance. He'd been the one butt hurt over the fact that she hadn't answered her phone. And now he was just going to leave without saying goodbye?

The front door opened and closed, and Lily nearly jumped

out of her skin. Levi locked the door behind him and once again set the holstered gun on the entryway table. What was up with him? You'd think he was the one potentially being stalked by an escaped prison inmate. Lily shook her head. And she thought *she* was paranoid.

"Hey," Lily said. "Everything okay?"

His eyes met hers, and he relaxed the stern set of his jaw. "Just looking around," he said. "You should be careful living out here, Lily. You're pretty far from town."

"I'm not that far. And I can take care of myself." Good lord, even she had a hard time buying that line of bullshit.

Levi gave her a look that let her know he was about to disagree. She sensed an argument over her capabilities coming, and the last thing she wanted to do was spend the rest of the night agonizing over words that were better left unsaid.

"We can agree to disagree later," she said, holding up her hands to stay any further argument. "Get over here and have some ice cream."

Levi cocked a sardonic brow. "I've been thinking about that ice cream ever since Shay mentioned that you had some in your freezer." He crossed the space between them and settled down next to her on the couch, taking one of the bowls in his palm.

"Oh yeah?" Lily asked. "What were you thinking?"

"That I wanted to smear it on your nipples and suck it off."

Lily's jaw hung slack and she paused with the spoon held halfway to her mouth. The nipples he'd just mentioned tingled as though already cold and waiting for the heat of his mouth to soothe them.

He scooped a large spoonful of ice cream into his mouth. Lily followed the action, but the rich chocolate and chunks of brownie batter barely registered as she continued to imagine the icy chill on her breasts and the ensuing heat that would follow.

Levi dipped his spoon into the ice cream again and this time held the spoon to Lily's mouth. She parted her lips and closed her mouth over the spoon, imagining the hard length of Levi's erection sliding against her tongue as her eyes drifted shut for the barest of moments.

"What are you thinking about, Lily?"

Her lids came open and she held his gaze. "You," she replied. "In my mouth."

Levi's nostrils flared and he sucked in a sharp breath. "Damn, darlin'. You sure know how to make a man rock hard."

Lily's chest swelled with a smug rush of power at being able to affect Levi in that way. She reciprocated, offering him a spoonful from her bowl, and watched with satisfaction as he sucked the spoon into his mouth.

"I doubt it tastes half as good as you do."

Holy hell. Lily's heart pounded in her chest as heat swamped her. Her pussy clenched, already anticipating the sensation of Levi's mouth sealing over her clit. Every nerve ending in her body fired with hyperawareness. His words and the low timbre of his voice were as good as a touch. He caressed her with wicked promises that she hoped he would follow through on.

Levi plucked the spoon from Lily's grip and set it along with his in the discarded bowl. He brought his hand to her face and cupped her cheek while the pad of his thumb traced her chin and jawline before passing over her bottom lip and dipping inside her mouth.

Her teeth grazed his flesh as she sucked gently, hopefully giving him a taste of what was to come. His heated gaze burned into her, searing her with the intensity of passion in their depths. His breath came heavy as he pulled his thumb free and put his mouth against hers in a ravenous kiss.

If she didn't control her lust and pace herself, Lily feared she'd succumb to her pleasure from a single kiss. She knew one thing for certain: one more night in Levi Roberts's arms was likely to ruin her for other men for the rest of her life.

Levi crushed his mouth to Lily's, desperate for her. He took her bottom lip between his teeth and sucked before letting it go to thrust his tongue against hers. He'd never been so starved for a woman before. So desperate and eager to claim every inch of her and make her his. Levi wanted her in a baseless, primal way. He wanted his mark on every inch of her. He wanted to nip at her skin, suck her nipples until they became swollen, dark pink beads on her perfect breasts.

Lily's passion matched his. She didn't shy from his advances. Didn't bother to pretend to be shy or demure. No, she met him as an equal. Unafraid to express her wants and desires.

She was brave, wanton, and full of life. Levi couldn't get enough of her.

As much as he wanted her mouth wrapped around his cock, he couldn't wait to taste her. Her scent permeated the air around them, tempted him to bury his face between her thighs and lap at her until she screamed her pleasure.

He gripped her hips and scooted her toward him, urging her to lie back on the couch. Her gaze drank him in, expectant, as he unfastened her slacks and pulled them, along with her underwear, off her. Levi guided one of her legs over the back of the couch, opening her up to him. He sucked in a breath, captivated by the sight of her glistening pussy, already swollen and ready for him.

Lily's back arched as he dragged the pad of his index finger from her mons, over the bud of her clit, and downward. She let out a quiet moan that caused his balls to draw up tight. He'd be lucky if he didn't come the second his mouth met that sweet flesh. No longer able to wait, he gripped her ass in his palms and angled her hips upward, lowering his mouth between her supple thighs. Lily let out a shaky breath that hitched the moment he sealed his mouth over her.

Damn, she was heaven.

The honey sweetness of her covered his tongue as he dipped it briefly in her tight opening. Her thighs twitched against his cheeks and she drew in tight little breaths as he ventured upward, sweeping the flat of his tongue gently over the pearl of nerves at her center. He pulled it into his mouth and sucked gently, eliciting a gasp from Lily. He swirled his tongue over her clit. Lapped at it and teased it until she shuddered in his embrace and her breaths ended on desperate whimpers.

Lost to the moment, the taste and smell of her, Levi kissed her swollen labia, up along her pubic bone, nipped at her inner thigh, avoiding the area she wanted him to touch the most. She thrust her hips, twisted to maneuver her body where she wanted it. But Levi was in control and she needed to understand that before he gave her what demanded.

"Please, Levi. Oh God."

He didn't respond. Didn't relent. Simply kissed and teased her, blew gently over the flesh she begged him to touch. She gripped the couch cushions, let her knees fall wide to open herself fully. By small degrees she began to settle, to allow him to hold her and kiss her, and as her frenzy calmed he rewarded her with exactly what she wanted.

Levi thrust his index finger into her opening as his mouth sucked gently on her clit. A second finger joined the first, moving possessively, firmly, as his tongue flicked out in a steady rhythm. Lily's body went rigid. Her back arched and her legs trembled. She released a low moan that built in intensity, ending on a keening cry of pleasure that turned Levi's cock to steel.

He brought her down slowly. Controlling her pleasure, her climb to release. Laving at her swollen flesh with alternating firm and whisper-soft caresses that elicited tiny gasps and moans. He kissed from the top of her thigh to her knee, over one shapely calf, and over to the other leg. Her breath raced and she shuddered as her fingers wound into Levi's hair and her nails scraped his scalp, giving him delicious chills that raced down his spine and settled in his sac.

"Levi . . ."

Lily's voice was a hoarse whisper. He loved the sound of his name on her lips. Thick with exhaustion and pleasure. Her fingers threaded through his hair as he continued to lay featherlight kisses against her thighs.

Tiny sighs filled the silence, the sweet melody of Lily's contentment feeding Levi's ego. He could lie here for hours, head cradled in her lap as she scraped her nails gently along his scalp. Chills danced along Levi's skin. He'd never felt so satisfied without having an orgasm. Knowing Lily's needs had been met was all the satiation he required.

Lily stirred and he looked up to find her studying him. "I hope you're not tired," she practically purred. "Because I'm just getting started."

Levi pushed himself up to sit. Lily leaned over him, her pert breasts brushing his arm as she reached for his belt. The button on his jeans came loose and she lowered his zipper tooth by agonizing tooth. She stood and maneuvered herself between his thighs before going down on her knees. Without a word, she gripped the waistband of his jeans and tugged. Levi lifted his ass from the cushion as Lily undressed him, pulling off his boots, socks, jeans, and underwear and at last stripping his shirt from his chest.

The tips of her nails dragged along the tops of his thighs and Levi's muscles went taut. He held his breath in anticipation as Lily's head dipped and her tongue swirled over the crown of his cock. Levi's back pressed into the couch as he blew out the breath he'd been holding. *Heaven.* The heat of her mouth was a welcomed balm as she sealed her lips over the swollen head and took him deeper. She adopted an easy rhythm, sliding along his shaft to the tip, where she grazed her teeth along the sensitive flesh before plunging downward again.

Lily's fingers wrapped around the base of his erection while her other hand reached down to stroke his sac. The layers of sensation drove Levi to the edge of his control. His breath came heavy and he let out a grunt of pleasure as Lily nipped the head of his cock.

Goddamn. He loved a little pain with his pleasure. "Just like that, baby. Don't stop."

His hips thrust up to meet the steady rhythm of her mouth. The fingers of his right hand wound gently in her hair, pulling and tugging as he urged her to increase the pace. She let out a low moan in response that vibrated down his shaft and settled in his balls, which grew tighter as she caressed them. He didn't know how much longer he could hold on, but he refused to finish until he was buried deep in the tight heat of her pussy.

"I'm close, Lily," Levi said. "But I've got to fuck you."

She responded with one last pass of the flat of her tongue along his shaft before working her way up his body. A trail of kisses that went over his torso to his chest, neck, and jaw until she'd settled herself, straddled, in his lap. They played a dangerous game as she teased his dick with the slick swollen folds of her labia. Sliding over his shaft with gentle thrusts of her hips without allowing penetration.

"Darlin'," Levi warned, "I'm barely holding on and you're tempting me to do something very reckless."

"You're tempting me too," she whispered against his ear.

Holy shit, he wanted to pull her down onto him, caution be damned. But he knew he'd hate himself for it once his brain was no longer clouded with passion. He could cool his jets for the thirty seconds it would take to protect them both.

"Hold on, Lily," he murmured against her throat. "I just need . . ."

She leaned away, her back arching, as she reached for his jeans. Levi used the opportunity, leaning in to take one pearled nipple into his mouth. Lily sucked in a breath as she lingered, allowing him to cradle her as her head dropped back. He paid the same attention to the other breast, suckling firmly before she came upright and handed over the wallet she'd fished from his jeans.

Levi took the package from the wallet and Lily plucked it from his grip, ripping it open and rolling the condom slowly over his erection. She positioned herself over him and gripped his shoulders as she lowered herself on top of him. Their mouths met as their bodies joined. Levi held Lily tight against him as they began to move together. With every sweep of her hips, his dick grew harder. Every brush of her nipples against his chest was a sweet torture he didn't want to end.

Unwilling to find release until she did again, Levi forced himself to wait. Lily's head rolled back onto her shoulders as she rode him, and he sucked her nipples until she once again moaned and sobbed her pleasure. Her pussy contracted around his shaft as she cried out and Levi's own orgasm overtook him as the powerful sensations ripped through him.

Lily collapsed against him. As he held her delicate frame in his arms, a sense of urgency rose up in him that he couldn't squash. He'd protect Lily at all costs from whatever or whoever meant to do her harm. He refused to let her go, no matter the consequences.

And damn it, things were about to get a hell of a lot more complicated. He could just feel it.

Chapter Fourteen

Lily never stayed up late on a school night, but here she was for the second night in a row. Blissfully exhausted, lucky to get even a few hours' sleep, and lying next to the most magnificent man she'd ever laid eyes on.

Levi had gotten creative in the second round of lovemaking, keeping true to his promise, and put the rest of the ice cream to good use, spreading it on her nipples and between her thighs before licking it off her. She'd returned the favor as well and they'd showered afterward, covering each other in luxurious suds before they'd succumbed to their lust for a third time, staying in the shower until the water had run cold.

A cool breeze blew in from the open window, stirring the curtains and bringing with it the scent of fresh lilacs. Lily had anticipated spending the evening alone and the night afraid. But with Levi here beside her, she felt safer than she had in years. Somehow, she knew that he would do anything to protect her. Strange that she'd feel so secure after knowing him for only a short time.

Lily didn't want to be protected, though. She didn't want to be a burden on anyone. She wanted to be able to protect herself. She wanted her life back.

"Levi, why did you bring a gun tonight?" The thought had gnawed at the back of her mind most of the night. Now she had nothing to distract her from it.

"I usually carry one with me." The warmth of his voice wound around her in the dark. "At least in the truck. Does it bother you?"

"No. Not really, anyway." Lily had grown up around firearms. "I mean, why did you have it on you when you came in the house, though?"

He pulled her a little tighter against him and she wondered at the almost desperation in the simple gesture. "I was worried when you didn't answer your phone. I know something's going on with you, baby, and it puts me on edge. You live all alone out here and the sheriff doesn't patrol regularly."

"But why?" Lily found herself unable to let it go. "Why were you worried?"

Levi's pregnant pause sent a jolt of anxious energy through her center. "You just never know," he said at last. "Bad things can happen in a single moment, Lily."

In the solemnity of his words, she knew a bad thing had happened to someone he loved. Levi spoke with the deep regret of someone who'd shown up a minute too late. Curiosity ate at Lily. She wanted to know everything, and afterward she wanted to help soothe his hurt and offer him the comfort and sense of security that he'd so easily—and unknowingly—offered to her.

"Thank you for looking out for me." She placed a kiss near his collarbone.

"I'll always look out for you, darlin'." Lily's heart soared, though she doubted it was a promise Levi could keep. Especially when he realized just how complicated and potentially dangerous her life was.

"Can you teach me to shoot a gun?" She might have been

raised around firearms, but she'd never actually shot one. It was time she took her own protection seriously. She couldn't always count on Shay or Sallie or even Levi or Jacob to be around. She didn't want anyone to ever be in danger because of her.

"If you want." Levi kissed the top of her head. "Maybe this weekend?"

Lily's stomach tightened. She hoped by this weekend there wouldn't be a reason for her to learn to shoot. "Sure. That sounds good."

"Don't think that means I'm going to stay away until then." Levi's hand wandered to Lily's breast and she let out a contented sigh. "You're going to have a hard time keeping me away from you after tonight."

Lily smiled into the darkness. She felt the exact same way. "You don't have to leave at all if you don't want to." A pang of selfish guilt tugged at her chest. If Levi stayed here with her, she wouldn't have to feel so alone and scared.

"Are you inviting me to stay with you?"

"Yes." Her voice sounded small and unsure in her ears.

She couldn't see him clearly in the darkness, but she knew he studied her. "For how long?"

"For as long as you want," she replied. Lily laughed and added, "Or until you get sick of me."

"Oh, darlin'." Levi gave her a tight squeeze. "I don't see how that could ever happen."

"Don't be so sure," Lily teased. "If I remember correctly, I've gotten on your nerves a time or two."

"And if I remember correctly," Levi countered, "I've done the same."

Lily nestled in closer. For the most part, their relationship had been physical. And while there was nothing wrong with that, now she found herself wanting more. To know more about Levi. His favorite color, foods, music. Was he a reader or more of a movie guy? All of the seemingly inconsequential things that were the building blocks for a relationship.

"Well, I guess we'll just have to see how it goes." Was it crazy to ask him to stay with her so soon? Did it reinforce her weakness, fear, and uncertainty? "I mean, you don't have to move your furniture in or anything, but . . ." Lily took a deep breath. "I just really want to get to know you."

"Well," Levi replied. "You're in luck, because I don't have any furniture." He reached for Lily's chin and tilted her head up to place a gentle kiss on her lips. "I really want to get to know you too."

Lily relaxed in the cradle of Levi's arms and let her eyes drift shut. For so long, she'd wanted intimacy, a relationship, to fall asleep next to someone every night and wake up next to that person every morning. They were moving quickly. No doubt about it. And it might complicate things with Levi working for Jacob if it didn't work out. But what if it did work out? What if this was the happiness Lily had always yearned for?

You won't be happy until Graham is back in prison.

Lily said a silent prayer that he'd be apprehended. Soon. Until then, she had to do her best to stay calm and keep it together. She wasn't ready to tell Levi about her past and how it haunted her still, and honestly, she didn't ever want to unless there was a reason to tell him. Lily didn't want her miserable past to screw up her chances at an amazing future.

"Sweet dreams, Lily," Levi said against the top of her head.

"You too."

She placed her palm over his chest and fell asleep to the gentle rhythm of his heart.

* * *

Levi tried like hell to sleep, but his mind was too damned active to settle down. His worry for Lily overrode his common sense. He knew that staying with her for any length of time was a bad decision. Already, he was too close to her. His judgment had become clouded. But he'd be damned if he left her side. In such a short space of time, she'd become important to him. Levi had spent most of his life pushing people away. He was good at building walls. High ones. But for Lily, he wanted to raze the defenses he'd spent years constructing.

There was no doubt he had feelings for her. But this was new and unfamiliar territory, and he had no idea what those feelings were.

She stirred beside him and let out an easy sigh. He could lie like this forever, listening to the sound of her breath and enjoying the weight of her body against his. She made him feel at peace and that was something Levi hadn't felt—ever—in his entire life. He settled down into the pillows, closed his eyes, and forced his mind to clear. Lily needed him at 100 percent, and he refused to be anything less for her. He could sort out his feelings for her later.

He just hoped that when all this was over she wouldn't hate him for the things he'd kept from her.

"Good morning." Lily smiled brightly as she placed a quick kiss on Levi's cheek. "There's coffee and blueberry scones in the kitchen."

Levi blinked several times to clean the sleep from his eyes. He stretched his arms high above him and arched his back as he let out a yawn. Lily was already showered and dressed, hair and makeup done.

"Good morning to you too." He grabbed her hand and placed a quick kiss on her palm. "How'd you sleep?"

Lily sighed contentedly. "Seriously, best night's sleep of my life."

Damn. Seeing her bright smile and the sparkle in her eyes made him want to wake up next to her every day.

Lily bounced up from the bed and went back into the bathroom to brush her teeth. "Did you sleep okay?"

"I slept great," Levi said with a grin. "But has anyone ever told you that you snore like a bear?"

Lily met his gaze through the mirror, the toothbrush held aloft. Her eyes went wide, and her mortified expression made him unable to keep a straight face.

"I'm kidding!" Levi said. "You're so quiet when you sleep, I considered holding a mirror up to your nose to make sure you were alive."

Lily rolled her eyes, but she gave him a wide grin. "Thank God I don't snore! If I'd kept you up all night, I would've walked out into the woods and died of embarrassment."

"Oh, come on," Levi scoffed. "Even if you'd snored like a chain saw, it would've been the best night's sleep of my life."

She held his gaze for a quiet moment, her sweet smile tightening his chest. She turned her attention to brushing her teeth and Levi wished they didn't have to start their day so soon and could stay in bed together for the next several hours.

They didn't have that luxury, though, so Levi got out of bed and went to the kitchen for coffee. "Do you mind if I turn on the TV and watch the news?" Levi called out toward the bedroom.

"Of course not!" Lily called back. "Feel free to do whatever you want!"

Levi poured himself a cup of coffee and headed into the living room. He didn't need to be at the ranch for another hour and a half. No point in crowding Lily in the bathroom. He turned on the television and found a news station. He had no interest in local news but instead kept to national outlets to see what—if anything—was being reported on the Susanville prison break.

A few minutes later, Lily joined him in the living room. "Anything good?" She tried to sound conversational, but Levi sensed the worry in her tone.

"Not a thing," he said, trying to keep his own voice conversational. Lily seemed relieved, but no news wasn't necessarily good news. He'd be briefed later, no doubt, but he was antsy as hell for information. "What do you have planned for this evening?"

Lily's brow furrowed. "I thought we'd spend the evening together. Unless you have something going on. Which is okay. I mean, you don't have to spend time with me."

They really did suck at communicating. Or at least they were still in that awkward phase of trying to find a comfort zone. Why did everything seem so much easier when there were no words spoken between them?

"I don't have anything going on. I want to spend the evening with you too. I just—hell, Lily—I'm not good at this. I want to cook dinner for you, get naked, and fuck you until we're too exhausted to keep our eyes open."

Blunt was the only way Levi knew how to get his point across. He wasn't romantic or particularly articulate. He was a hard-ass and even harder headed. He didn't stop until he got what he wanted, and he made no apologies for any of it. He liked Lily. A lot. Small talk wasn't his thing, but why did they have to pretend that they needed to experience that "getting to know you" phase? He already knew everything about her that he needed to know.

"Okay, then." Lily grinned as she changed course and

went into the kitchen. "Sounds like we've got a hell of a night ahead of us." She poured herself another cup of coffee and called out from behind the bar, "Better eat a good lunch, cowboy. You're going to need your strength!"

Hell. Yeah. That's what he liked to hear.

Levi had to remind himself of why he was in Deer Haven in the first place, though. As much as he was beginning to care for Lily, he had a job to do. A responsibility and oath to uphold. His obligations came first, no matter what. When the time was right, he'd tell Lily everything and lay it all out on the table. But until then, he had to keep a level head and not let emotions cloud his judgment.

"Okay, I gotta go." Lily unhooked a key from her fob and set it on the coffee table. "To the back door. I'll see you this evening."

Levi reached for her and she leaned in for a slow kiss before he eased her upright.

"Wow." Lily sucked in a quick breath. "It's tough for a girl to leave when she's getting goodbye kisses like that."

She flashed him a brilliant smile before grabbing her things and heading out the door.

Levi let his head fall back on the couch and stared up at the ceiling. The morning news anchor's voice became white noise in the back of his mind as he took a second to decompress. His ass was going to be in a sling. He'd fucked up this assignment big-time. Though he had always been the professional, always the by-the-book guy, all of his convictions had crumbled to dust the moment he'd laid eyes on Lily.

Timed to perfection, his phone rang from the bedroom. Levi let out a heavy sigh, aware of who the ringtone belonged to, and hustled to the other room to answer.

"Roberts."

"We've got a lead on Max Davis," Mitch McDonald, Levi's supervisor, said without preamble. "That doesn't mean he's with Brisbee, but I want you to check it out."

Son of a bitch. Levi had no intention of leaving Deer Haven. Especially if that meant leaving Lily vulnerable. The odds of Brisbee's former cellmate, Davis, traveling with him were slim to none and Mitch had to have known that. It had always been the U.S. Marshals Service's opinion that the three had parted ways after escaping the maximum-security facility. Their chances of being caught would be greater if they stuck together. And besides that, Brisbee was highly educated and would never lower himself to keeping company with what he would consider lowly criminals.

"What's the lead?" If he was given an order, Levi was expected to follow it. No questions asked. The only thing insubordination would get him was a one-way ticket back to Sacramento. He wouldn't do Lily a damn bit of good hundreds of miles away.

"Davis was allegedly spotted getting off a bus in Fairfield."

"Fairfield?" Levi's agitation grew. "That's almost three and a half hours away."

It would take him all day, maybe two, to drive down and follow the lead. If it panned out, he'd make an arrest and have to transport Davis to Sacramento. And then what? Processing, debriefing, paperwork. Days, maybe even a couple of weeks. And Lily would be here, unprotected.

"You're the closest deputy I've got to Fairfield right now. I don't want to lose him if it's legit."

Levi swore under his breath. Davis wasn't even his assignment. "Jimenez is assigned to Davis. Send him to Fairfield."

Mitch cleared his throat. Levi was about to get his ass handed to him, but he didn't care. He wasn't driving to Fairfield.

"There's no way Davis is there." He could at least try to plead his case before he was put on suspension. "The town is tiny. Like, what, a few thousand people tops? The last place you're going to go after escaping federal prison is a place where you can't blend in. Someone's trying to send us on a wild goose chase. If I had to guess, he's headed in the opposite direction, toward New Mexico."

"He's got a half sister who lives near Albuquerque," Mitch replied.

"Exactly." Levi trusted his instincts 100 percent and there was no way Davis was in Fairfield.

"It could be a misdirect. But . . ."

A stone of dread settled in Levi's gut. "I don't think it's Davis doing the misdirecting."

"Brisbee?" Mitch asked.

"Why not?" Goddammit, Levi would beat the asshole to a bloody pulp if his hunch was correct. "He's gone after victims before. He blames them for his being sent to prison. The guy's intelligent, but he's also angry and vengeful. Lily is the one who got away. Whether or not she testified against him, he knows she's the reason the other women came forward and she's damned sure the reason the janitor identified him when she was in the hospital. Maybe he's looking to finish what he started."

The idea that Brisbee could be on his way to Deer Haven filled Levi with a rage that left him shaking. He'd do whatever it took to keep Lily out of harm's way. Even if that meant putting her into protective custody. But she'd refused witness protection, and his hands were tied until the powers that be gave the green light. So far, they'd been operating on assumptions and behavioral patterns. Nothing was guaranteed.

"It makes sense, but I'm still not convinced," Mitch said. "Let me get in touch with the Freestone County Sheriff's

Department. Stay close to the phone. I'll call you back in an hour or so."

Mitch ended the call and Levi let out a slow breath that had nothing to do with relief. Things were about to get messy.

Chapter Fifteen

Lily could barely keep her mind on school. She might as well have been one of her students, watching the clock, anxious for the day to be over. Excitement warred with guilt, fraying her nerves and leaving her stomach raw and her limbs tense. She relaxed her jaw for what felt like the hundredth time that day.

"Miss Donovan?" Lily shook herself from her thoughts and looked up to find Lucy Bentley tapping her on the arm. "When I do that, my mom says I'm 'zoning out.'"

So, that wasn't embarrassing at all. Lily smiled. "I'm sorry, Lucy. I was definitely zoning out. What do you need?"

Lucy leaned in close. "Can I please go to the bathroom?"

"Of course, honey. Go ahead."

Lily rubbed her temples. Poor kid had probably been trying to get her attention for the past several minutes. She looked over the classroom; the rest of the students were still seated and silently reading. No hands were up, and no one else looked like they were about to have a bathroom emergency.

She'd really dropped the ball today. Both Sallie and Shay had checked in with her, and while she was glad she had people in her life who watched out for her, she was beginning to tire of it. All she wanted was a normal life. Hell, a day—or even a week—where she didn't have to look over her shoulder would be heaven. Even if Graham was arrested and taken back to prison, Lily didn't know if she'd ever feel safe.

Maybe she should have entered the witness protection program like the judge and the marshals had suggested. At the time it had seemed absurd. She'd been indignant, angry, and unreasonable. She was the victim, for shit's sake. It wasn't fair that her life should be altered for something that hadn't been her fault.

She was still angry.

Still unreasonable.

And it was still unfair.

Lily grabbed her phone from her desk drawer. She opened a new message and selected Levi's name from the contacts. Her fingers moved across the screen.

Hey.

She hit "send" and waited.

Not even fifteen seconds later, her phone vibrated. A sense of relief flooded her as she opened the message.

Hey. How's your day going, beautiful?

Lily smiled. Though he wasn't close, communicating with Levi made her feel immediately safer. It probably wasn't good that she'd become so dependent on him so quickly, but right now he was the only thing keeping her sane.

Pretty good, she typed. *What are you up to?*

Seconds later, his response popped up. *Running cows and thinking about you.*

A riot of butterflies took flight in Lily's stomach. *Thinking about you too. Can't wait for the day to be over.*

Levi replied: *Same. I'll be done at the ranch in about an hour. Headed straight to your place after.*

I'll see you soon, she replied, and put her phone back in her desk drawer.

"Okay, guys." Lily stood from her desk and walked to the whiteboard. "Let's put our library books away and get out our math books."

Knowing Levi would be at the house when she got home from work settled her nerves. It was the reassurance Lily needed to get through the rest of the day. She just hoped that forming such a strong attachment to him so soon wouldn't end up being one of the biggest mistakes of her life.

Lily walked to her car, glad the day was over. If Graham wasn't caught soon, she'd need to make some serious decisions in regard to her job, staying in Deer Haven, and how to explain to Levi why she was leaving. Moving from her childhood home and the only safe space she'd ever known didn't sit well with Lily, but neither did staying here if it meant potentially putting the people she loved in danger. She just wished she knew what the right thing was to do. There was only one person to go to for advice. No one else would understand.

She pulled up the contacts on her phone and dialed Sallie. She knew what it was like to hide from danger. To leave her life behind while constantly looking over her shoulder.

"Hey," Sallie answered after only one ring. Sallie was a ride-or-die friend. "Everything okay?"

"I'm good." Lily hated that everyone found it necessary to make sure she was okay all the time. "Just thinking a lot. Poor kids practically taught themselves today. My brain is way too occupied."

"Lily, you have every reason in the world to be out of sorts," Sallie said. "I honestly don't know how you're keeping it together as well as you have been. I've been checking the news all day for the past two days hoping to hear an update. He'll do something stupid and get caught. They always do."

Lily had hoped for the same thing. To see breaking news that escaped convict Graham Brisbee had been apprehended. It wasn't going to happen, though. Graham was too smart and the law enforcement agencies looking for him knew it too.

"I think maybe I should leave town." There was no sense in beating around the bush. Sallie had to know she'd considered it.

"I knew you'd say that," Sallie replied. "But believe me, it's not going to make anything better. It might actually made things worse."

"It worked out okay for you."

Sallie had come to Deer Haven because she'd been on the run from people who were searching for Jacob. At the time, Sallie hadn't known Jacob was living in the same town Sallie had come to hide in. She'd been bouncing around the country for years. Running. Never feeling safe. Fate—in the form of Sallie's stepfather and Stanley Dillerman, a man who'd owed her stepfather a favor—had brought Sallie back to Jacob. Jacob had protected her and killed the men who'd wanted to see them both dead.

"Yes," Sallie agreed. "But Lil, my situation was a little different than yours."

True, but at the same time, there were similarities.

"What if Graham finds out where I am and comes here?" Lily asked. "What if he tries to hurt you or Jacob or Shay? What if he comes looking for me and he finds Gran instead? What if Levi gets in his way and he hurts him too? I'd never be able to live with myself if anything happened to you guys."

"You have to trust us, then," Sallie said. "Let the people who care about you help to protect you. Let's talk to Jacob. You've been keeping this secret for long enough. He should know what's going on. You know he's got the connections to make sure Graham never gets close to you again."

Jacob was retired military and CIA. He certainly had connections and was deadly enough in his own right to scare off the baddest of the bad guys.

"I'm not ready," Lily replied. Jacob was certainly capable. Not to mention fiercely protective of his loved ones. But Lily didn't know if she could endure the shame of reliving what had happened or the guilt she'd feel when Jacob found out she'd kept it all from him. "I want him to know . . . just not yet."

"You can't leave town and not tell anyone," Sallie said. "I know firsthand how hurtful that that can be. I regretted every time I did it."

Sallie certainly knew what this would be like for Lily. And she heeded her friend's words. "You're right. I just don't know what to do."

"How about Shay and I come over for dinner tonight and we talk it out?"

"I can't. I promised Levi I'd have dinner with him tonight."

"Oh." Sallie's confused tone sent a jolt of nervous energy though Lily's center. "I didn't think he'd be back tonight."

"What do you mean?"

"Jacob said they were going to be a man short today because Levi needed the day off today to run over to Fairfield for something."

Lily's confusion grew. "That's strange. He texted me a couple of hours ago and said he was at the ranch running cattle."

A pregnant pause followed that did nothing to assuage her frayed nerves.

"I could be wrong," Sallie said at last. "Maybe I misunderstood Jacob."

"Strange." Lily tried not to let it bother her, but if Jacob had said Levi wouldn't be at work, how could Sallie have been wrong?

"Oh, I'm sure I just heard Jacob wrong. If not tonight, can we have lunch or dinner together tomorrow?" Sallie seemed to quickly divert the subject away from Levi. "You'll feel better if you talk about this with people who know what's going on. Together, we can come up with a solution."

"Okay." She had so much to worry about. She didn't want to think that Levi was keeping something from her, but she couldn't help but be a little suspicious. "I'll call you tomorrow."

"Sounds good. And Lily," Sallie said, "I'm sure I was mistaken about Levi. Hope you two have fun tonight."

"Thanks." Lily started her car. "Have a good night."

"You too!"

Lily ended the call and set the phone in the passenger seat. She'd had her fill of secrets over the past couple of years. She didn't want—or need—any more of them.

Levi tucked his phone in his back pocket. He hated lying to Lily, but now wasn't the time to come clean. He wasn't at the ranch running cattle. Instead, he was seated in the sheriff's office, waiting to brief him. Levi knew damn good and well that after this keeping his real reason for coming to Deer Haven a secret would be next to impossible. Jacob was tight with local law enforcement. Levi wanted to make sure he talked to Jacob as well before anyone else got to him first. And he'd be lucky if he didn't walk away from that conversation with a black eye or worse.

Damn, he'd really managed to fuck this assignment up.

"Marshal." Dwight Davidson walked into his office and took a seat at his desk. He fixed Levi with an apprising stare as he rested his elbows on the desk. "I just got off the phone with your supervisor in Sacramento. Gotta say, doesn't sit well with me to know that the U.S. Marshals are sending their guys into my jurisdiction without letting me know first. I know I'm just a small-town cop, but things always run smoother when we work together, if you know what I mean."

"I understand completely, Sheriff, and I apologize. But I'm here now."

It was protocol to let the local authorities know when the USMS was in their jurisdiction, but Levi, as well as Mitch and the chief deputy, had decided that the best way not to alert Brisbee to their presence was to make sure that absolutely no one knew he was in Deer Haven. Secrets were impossible to keep in small towns and Levi had wanted Brisbee to feel safe if he'd managed to track down Lily and pay her a visit. But that had been before he'd gotten to know—and care for—Lily.

His focus when he'd come here was apprehending a fugitive. Now nothing mattered more than protecting Lily and keeping her safe.

"Mitch McDonald seems to think that Graham Brisbee might be headed this way. Said you'd fill me in on why that might be."

"That's true, Sheriff. I'm pretty damned certain he's headed this way."

Davidson fixed Levi with a serious stare. "I'm listening."

Levi drew a deep breath into his lungs and held it before letting it all out in a gust. *Damn it.* Talking to Sheriff Davidson about the Brisbee case felt like a betrayal to Lily. He'd studied her case file before coming to Deer Haven. He knew she'd chosen to keep her identity a secret during the trial and afterward. She'd declined witness protection and fought so hard to maintain not only her anonymity but also her autonomy. He couldn't remain impartial any longer, though. Hell, he hadn't been impartial since the moment he'd laid eyes on her. She might eventually hate him for this, but he had to do whatever it took to protect her.

"Brisbee's last victim is a resident of Deer Haven. We have reason to believe he's looking for retribution."

"I followed the trial," Davidson replied. "He's a real sick son of a bitch. That girl was lucky to get away from him with her life."

That was the truth. Brisbee had been a favorite professor of a lot of students. But that's how he operated. He targeted young women. Gained their trust. Acted as a friend and mentor. And raped seven and managed to murder one unfortunate young woman before he'd been caught. Lily would have been number two in what had been an escalation of his violence, but she'd fought tooth and nail and called for help. In fact, Lily was the reason Brisbee had been arrested at all. His other victims had refused to testify against him. Lily had been brave enough to tell her story, giving the others the courage to come forward and tell theirs, and Levi had no doubt Brisbee wanted nothing more than to make Lily pay for it.

"She was named as 'Jane Doe,'" Sheriff Davidson continued. "Are you going to disclose her name?"

Levi didn't want to. But damn it, Lily's safety was more important than her privacy. "Lily Donovan."

Davidson's eyes went wide, and he sat back in his chair. "Son of a bitch," he muttered under his breath. "Do you have any idea who her family is?" he asked, his tone almost panicked.

"I do," Levi said.

"Does Jacob know?"

Levi shook his head. "Not yet. But I plan to talk to him soon."

"Soon?" If it was possible, Davidson's eyes went wider.

"You're going to have a hell of a lot more on your hands than an escaped fugitive, son, once he finds out."

And Levi knew it. Jacob was ex-military, former CIA, and a man whose reputation preceded him. He was infamously protective of his family and had been known to go to . . . extreme measures when his loved ones were in danger. Lucky for Levi, he wasn't some young pup new to the job. He knew what he was up against.

"I can handle Jacob," he said. "But until I have a chance to talk to him, I'd appreciate it if you could keep this under wraps."

Davidson snorted. "I'll do my best, son, but like I said, this is a small town, and even the best-kept secrets don't stay secret for long. Shit's going to hit the fan when Jacob finds out what's going on. Deer Haven is overflowing with men just like Jacob and every single one of them has his back."

Levi knew that as well. Besides the men at the ranch, the Culpeppers were just a few of those who had Jacob's back, and every one of the brothers was a force to be reckoned with. He was happy to know Lily had so many capable men in her corner, but the last thing Levi needed was a bunch of ex-military hotheads trying to supersede his authority. This was his assignment and he was in charge. The sooner everyone involved realized it, the better.

"It's going to be a delicate situation to navigate," Levi agreed. "But the USMS is good at what we do as well. I've hunted my fair share of fugitives," he said. "And if Brisbee is anywhere in this county—or this state—I'm going to get him." He owed that much to Lily. And damn it, he'd hunt Brisbee to the ends of the earth if that's what it took.

"And you can be assured that the entire Sheriff's Department will assist you in any way you need us to," Davidson said.

"Thank you." Shit was about to get sticky and Levi could use all the help he could get. He reached out a hand and Davidson took it in a firm handshake. Levi stood and retrieved a card from his wallet. He presented it to the sheriff, who took it from him. "I'll be in touch."

"I'll make sure to have our deputies patrolling the area by the ranch and Lily's house in the meantime," Davidson said.

"I appreciate that." Levi had gotten lucky today by convincing Mitch not to send him to Fairfield. But he might not be that fortunate again. The more people looking out for Lily, the better.

Levi checked the time as he left the sheriff's office. He guessed he had about a half hour before Lily would be home from work. There were still things he needed to do—including talking to Jacob—but he didn't have time for that today. He'd told Lily he'd be at her place when she got home. Jacob could wait. Lily was his priority.

For the first time in his career—hell, his life—Levi was putting his personal life before his duty, and he prayed it was worth the gamble.

Chapter Sixteen

Lily pulled up to her house, her earlier elation replaced with a sense of foreboding. She couldn't shake the worry that ate at her and the doubt that plagued her after talking to Sallie this afternoon.

Levi's truck was parked in the driveway. He'd kept his word and was waiting for her. If he'd gone to Fairfield for the day, there was no way he'd have beaten her home. The tightness in Lily's chest loosened as she let out a slow breath of relief. Was it sane to feel such a sense of safety with a man who might not have been entirely forthright with her?

Was she blowing all of this out of proportion? Sallie hadn't seemed particularly troubled by it. In fact, Sallie had been totally dismissive of it. Maybe Lily was simply looking for holes to poke in Levi's so far perfect package. Too good to be true. Self-sabotage was something Lily was good at. Perhaps she was simply cherry-picking excuses to make herself believe that Levi might end up being Mr. Wrong. Wasn't he allowed a little secrecy? God knew Lily had her own secrets.

She got out of the car and headed up the front steps. The aroma of barbeque wafted from the back of the house. He'd made good on his offer to cook dinner and Lily couldn't help but smile. No man had ever made her dinner before. It was the sort of thing that only happened in rom-coms. Their relationship—if that's what this was—was still new.

"Something smells delicious!" Lily put her worries to the back of her mind as she walked in the house. It felt so good to come home to someone. Did it matter if Levi had driven to Fairfield today or not? She'd been so worried about what Levi might or might not have been forthright about today. He didn't owe her any explanations. She wasn't his keeper, or his wife, or even his girlfriend for that matter. He was here now and that's what was important. "I'm starving."

Levi greeted her with a wide smile that took her breath away. He wore her gingham apron as he basted a rack of ribs with barbeque sauce.

"How was school?"

"Good. I'm not sure who was antsier for the day to be over, the kids or me."

Levi's eyes sparked with mischief. "Why's that?"

Lily swore she'd never seen anything sexier than Levi in her frilly apron. He wore it with confidence, and why shouldn't he? She averted her gaze, heat rising to her cheeks. "Because I wanted to see you."

Levi rounded the counter to where she stood. He took her in his arms and put his mouth to hers in a quick but passionate kiss. When he pulled away, Lily reached out to steady herself on the countertop. Good grief, that man made her literally weak in the knees. He returned to cooking and gave her a wide, sensual smile.

"I've been antsy to see you too."

Lily took off her jacket and hung it, with her purse, on the hook by the front door. She kicked off her shoes and went back to join Levi in the kitchen. "Can I help with anything?"

"No." Levi nudged her away with his wide shoulder. "You worked all day and should be relaxing."

"You worked too." The worry she'd tried to ignore reared its ugly head. She didn't want to catch him in a lie, but she couldn't help her curiosity. "Harder than me, I bet. I should be cooking you dinner, not the other way around."

"Harder than you?" Levi's brow scrunched up adorably as a corner of his mouth quirked into a crooked grin. "You spent the past eight hours wrangling thirty little kids."

"Cows are harder to handle than kids." She pressed on, despite the voice in the back of her head that urged her to stop.

"Cows are easy," Levi replied. He opened the refrigerator and produced a bowl of homemade potato salad. "They get out of line, you tie them up. Can't exactly do that with kids."

Lily laughed. "No. I think my principal and a few parents might take issue with that. How did it go today? You guys should be pretty much done with the calves, right?"

Levi transferred the ribs from the pan to a cutting board and began to slice them. Lily waited for his response, half holding her breath as she fought to keep a façade of nonchalance.

"Just about." Lily let out a breath. He was so good at giving noncommittal answers. "But you know how it is; there's always something to do on a ranch."

She wanted to relax. To force her brain to stop overthinking. It would take a bottle of wine to get that job accomplished and she wasn't exactly interested in having a hangover in the morning. If she outright asked him about Fairfield, she risked upsetting him or, worse, ratting out Sallie and Jacob. If she held her tongue, she might just drive herself crazy worrying about it.

Lily already had more than enough to worry about.

"I talked to Sallie today," she began. "She mentioned that she thought you'd gone up to Fairfield for the day."

Levi's attention shifted from the ribs to Lily. He studied

her for a quiet moment, as though trying to climb inside her head and get a good long look at what was going on up there. A stiff, closed-lipped smile belied his relaxed posture. "I was going to drive up there, but my plans got canceled."

"Not because of me, I hope?" Something about his response seemed off, but Lily couldn't put her finger on it.

"Well, sort of because of you." His gaze went dark and sultry as his intense attention heated her blood. "A drive to Fairfield and back takes up most of the day. I didn't want to waste a single second of it not being with you."

"Oh, come on." Lily tried to keep her tone light. But damn it, she was tired of being messed with, and if Levi was just another player looking to screw her over she'd rather find out now rather than later. "You're laying it on pretty thick, aren't you?"

Levi put a couple of ribs on a plate along with a large scoop of potato salad and a biscuit that he placed on the bar in front of Lily. He pulled a glass from the cupboard and got a bottle of wine out of the fridge. As if he already knew the place by heart, Levi opened another drawer and produced the corkscrew. How long had he been here today and exactly *how* acquainted was he with the layout of Lily's house? She didn't have anything to hide, but it definitely made her wonder just how comfortable Levi had made himself. He poured her a glass of wine and she took a generous sip—and then another—before digging into the potato salad.

"Maybe I am," Levi agreed as he dished himself some food. He didn't bother to sit beside her but ate standing at the kitchen counter. "I don't know. I don't have any experience in this area."

Lily nearly choked on her wine. "No experience in what area?"

Levi shrugged. "This. Dating."

There was no possible way a man who looked like Levi

Roberts didn't have any experience with women. Lily imagined that women threw themselves at him quite regularly. The shy, unsuspecting hottie routine wasn't going to fly with her. He certainly didn't perform in bed like a man who had no experience with "this."

She fixed him with a stern eye. "You expect me to believe that?"

"You can believe what you want," he replied.

Lord, but he frustrated her. It was that cocky, who-gives-a-shit attitude that turned her on as much as it made her want to give him a solid kick to the shin.

"You're hardly virginal," Lily quipped. She took a bite from one of the ribs and nearly swooned at the delicious blend of flavors. *Damn it.* Was there anything Levi wasn't good at?

"I never said I was," Levi agreed.

Not even close. She thought about that thing he did with his tongue. . . . "Okay." She forced herself out of the memory to keep herself from spontaneously combusting. "So, what did you mean then?"

Levi hiked an unconcerned shoulder. How could he possibly be so low-key all the damn time? "I've never really been in a relationship before."

Lily hiked a skeptical brow. "No girlfriends?" Forget the ribs, she needed popcorn for this show.

"Depends on what you mean by 'girlfriend.'"

Lily nearly threw a rib at him. "You know exactly what I mean by 'girlfriend.'"

Levi focused his attention on his biscuit, slathering it with butter. Lily swore he was dragging this out on purpose to drive her crazy. He ate with gusto, as if he'd do anything to avoid the current conversation. Well, too bad. Lily was tired of feeling like she had no control in her life. For once, she was going to take charge.

She waited him out. Refusing to eat or do anything until he answered her. When his eyes finally met hers, they possessed a sadness that sent a pang through the center of Lily's chest. What could possibly hollow out his usually easygoing expression?

Levi focused his attention on the ribs. Unfortunately, he'd have to answer Lily no matter how full he managed to keep his mouth. Her expectant gaze drilled into him, waiting for a response. He should have known that she would have found out about Fairfield. It was damn tough to keep a secret in a small town. Even tougher when family was involved. He'd tried to be as honest as possible without blowing his cover. Unfortunately, it wasn't honest enough, and he swallowed down the bitter gall of guilt.

With every passing day, he worried more that Lily would hate him once she learned the truth.

"It's going to sound bad no matter how I answer," Levi finally said. He didn't want to give Lily the wrong impression, but there really wasn't any way to sugarcoat it for her and she deserved some measure of honesty from him. "I've just never had more than a third or fourth date."

Lily's brows raised and her mouth quirked into a smirk. "So you're a hit it and quit it type of guy." She took a good, long sip from her glass. "Typical cowboy, I guess."

Yep, it definitely sounded bad. The worst part was that she wasn't exactly wrong. "I don't know how typical I am of anything," Levi said. "But I've never met anyone that I wanted to be with for more than a couple of nights. Is that wrong?" He took a pull from his bottle of beer, needing a little liquid courage himself. "I'd think it's worse to stay with someone you're not connecting with and just dragging out the inevitable."

"How do you know if you're not connecting?" Lily asked. "You've gotta give it more than a day or two."

Ouch. Lily went straight for the jugular. "It doesn't take me a day or two. I usually know pretty immediately."

"Is that so?" Lily picked at her potato salad with her fork. "I mean, what's your impression of me so far? We've been together for a few nights. This might be the longest relationship of your entire life."

She wanted him to cringe. Maybe even to feel bad for his many one- or two-night stands. But Levi wouldn't do that. He made no apologies for the way he lived his life. "My impression of you so far?" If she was trying to bait him, she'd be disappointed. He was determined to avoid a fight. "You're the sexiest woman I've ever laid eyes on. Stubborn, feisty, and a pain in the ass when you want to be. Every night I go to bed knowing I'm going to want another day with you."

Damn it, that was the truth too. The realization was like a fist to the chest.

"You're full of shit." Lily gave a sad shake of her head. "How do I know that's not just some ridiculous pickup line?"

Levi sighed. He forgot to add "infuriating" to his list. "Sorry, but I don't need pickup lines, darlin'."

Lily snorted. "I suppose you don't."

"What was your first impression of me?" Levi wanted the heat off himself for a second. "I mean, I can probably guess."

"I thought you were an arrogant ass," Lily said without hesitation.

Well, he'd asked for it, hadn't he? "I am that," he agreed.

"You're also persistent," she added. "And a pretty good guy despite being an ass. I wouldn't mind a few more days with you either since we're laying it out on the table."

"Aren't we the romantic pair?" Levi had never been one

for emotional confessions and cheesy sentiment. But he had to admit it made him feel damn good to know that Lily wanted more.

"Yeah, we're something all right," Lily said. "The past few days have been fun. But we don't know each other well. If this is going to ever turn into something more, we're both going to have to work on letting down our defenses."

It was the most emotionally real thing Lily had said to him since they'd met. They both had their secrets, though, and a lot stood between their chances at this—whatever it was—becoming anything substantial.

"You're right." Levi wasn't about to pretend that he didn't have a giant wall up. "I guess until then, we'll just agree to keep it strictly physical?"

Lily laughed. He absolutely loved that sound. "Seems like a good plan. We get along best when our clothes are off."

Witty, tough, beautiful, thoughtful, and just as jaded as he was . . . He might have only been with her for a few days, but Levi *knew* Lily. And he was beginning to realize that he didn't want to be without her. Ever. Was he falling for her? And if so, did it even matter? Once she found out the truth about him, he might lose her. If that happened, he knew he'd do whatever it took to win her back.

"Is that an invite to be naked?" The thought of Lily without her clothes was enough to curtail his overly introspective thoughts. "Because I can clean up the dishes later."

"No way." Lily shook her head, but her eyes sparked with a mischievous light. "I'm not done eating and I know you've got dessert in the fridge."

"You're right." Levi grabbed the tongs and put a couple more ribs on Lily's plate. "But full disclosure, I didn't make dessert. I bought it at the Sunrise Bakery."

"Oh, I know," Lily said. "I recognized the yellow bag on the counter. Good choice. They're the best."

Levi looked over his shoulder at the discarded paper bag and grinned. He liked that he could make her happy. And once dessert and the dishes were done, he planned on making her *very* happy.

"Eat up," he said as he scooped up a forkful of potato salad. "You're going to be burning off all of those calories soon."

She responded with a sexy wink that stirred his cock to attention.

"It's a good thing the counter is covered with dishes." Levi remained conversational, but he planned to talk Lily right into an orgasm if he could. "Because all I can think about is lifting you up onto the counter and making a meal of *you*."

Lily paused midbite.

He'd get her wet and ready for him. If he had it his way, she'd be too wound up for dessert. *To hell with dinner.* He wanted her. Right now.

"That cheesecake might be good, but I'd rather have your sweetness on my tongue right now." Levi leaned in close and let his gaze drop between Lily's thighs. "You smell so good, darlin', you have no idea."

Lily's lips parted on a breath. She knew exactly what he meant, and her reaction was all the encouragement he needed. "I could get drunk on you," he continued. "Your taste, smell, the feel of you. I want to glut myself on that beautiful body of yours."

Levi brushed Lily's full bottom lip with the pad of his thumb. He wouldn't kiss her. Not yet. He wanted to build up the anticipation until she couldn't wait for him to take her. Her lids drooped and she leaned toward him.

"I want those glorious nipples hard for me. I want you dripping wet and ready for me. I'm going to make you come hard and often, Lily. I want you screaming my name by the end of the night."

Her breaths came in quick little bursts. Levi held her gaze, refused to let her attention wander. Lily was right. They were damn good together when their clothes were off. He let his hand wander to her legs, brushing against the juncture between her thighs.

"When I'm done with you, baby, you'll never think of another man ever again."

And damn it, he meant it.

Chapter Seventeen

If Levi said one more sexually charged word to her, Lily was going to spontaneously combust. Heat swamped her. The sound of her own pulse rushed in her ears and her clit throbbed between her legs. Her mind raced with the images Levi had painted with his dirty talk and all she wanted was for him to follow through with every single filthy promise he'd made her.

When I'm done with you, baby, you'll never think of another man ever again.

Hell, she hadn't realized there was any other man on the face of the entire earth since she'd met Levi. He'd already ruined her for any other lover. And the more she got to know him, the more she began to think that no one would ever compare. She just hoped he wouldn't run when she finally decided to fill him in on the trouble that followed her.

Levi's gaze didn't leave hers. He took both of their plates and silverware and put them in the sink along with her wineglass. He meticulously cleared the countertop, letting Lily know without a single word that she was about to be laid out on the surface just like he'd described to her.

He rounded the counter and Lily spun in her chair, mimicking his movement until they were face-to-face. His eyes burned bright with passion as he wrapped his large hands around her waist and lifted her onto the countertop. Lily rested her hands on his shoulders as he guided her hips up, unbuttoned her pants, and dragged them off her body. Slowly, he guided one leg, and then the other, to the stools on either side of her, opening her legs fully to him.

She braced her arms behind her as Levi lowered himself. He buried his face against the silk fabric that separated him from her intimate flesh. Her stomach clenched as he inhaled deeply, holding her scent in his lungs.

"Goddamn, you smell good, baby."

The deep timbre of his voice vibrated against her and Lily shivered. The heat of his breath caressed her, a tease that she could barely endure. His teeth grazed her clit through the fabric and Lily moaned. It wouldn't take much for her to come. He had to know that, and he'd no doubt make her wait for it.

He kissed from her inner thigh to one hip before gripping the hem of her shirt. Lily sat up and lifted her arms as he took off her shirt but left her bra right where it was. As he moved the center barstool aside, he placed a soft, teasing kiss on her lips. She leaned into him, trying to deepen the kiss, but he pulled away, brushing his thumbs lightly over her nipples as he moved his mouth to one shoulder.

Though Levi was sure to keep their contact to a minimum, what parts of him did touch Lily left an impact. She pushed herself up again, reached out to touch him, and he seized her wrist firmly in his grip, guiding her hand back to the countertop.

"No touching," he scolded. "Sit still. Understand."

Lily couldn't find her voice. She simply nodded her acquiescence.

"Good girl."

He took his time with her. Careful to touch every inch of her skin. He started at one foot. Smoothed his work-rough palm over a shapely calf, up and around her thigh. Without missing a beat, his palm found her hip and caressed her torso. Lily shivered as he continued his path, moving up to the swell of one breast, his fingers dancing over her collarbone, and then from shoulder to fingertip, back to her shoulder, and across her back. The intensity of sensation scattered her thoughts. The only thing she could do was *feel*. Her nerve endings fired from his callused touch and oh, did she love the rasp of his skin against hers. From her back, he worked his way to her opposite shoulder and down the other side of Lily's body, letting his fingertips once again dance over her skin until goose bumps rose after his passage.

A soft sigh escaped Lily's lips. Levi kissed her, once, and abandoned her mouth for her throat, the skin behind her ears, her jawline. His hands and lips danced over her until Lily quivered from his touch. She wanted—needed—more, but he held back. Did he want her to beg? Because Lily would gladly do that and more. If he continued with his slow assault on her senses, she might just explode from frustration.

"Levi." Lily sucked in a deep breath as he brushed a thumb over her nipple. Her pussy clenched each time he touched her, desperate for the same lavish attention. "I can't take any more. Kiss me. Touch me." She swallowed, unable to play demure for another second. "I need you to fuck me."

"I'll fuck you in good time," Levi growled close to Lily's ear. "But only after you come for me."

Lily let out a low moan at the seductive promise in Levi's tone. He didn't move to take off her bra or panties and Lily's frustration mounted. If he wanted an orgasm out of her, she'd be happy to oblige, but she'd get there a hell of a lot faster if he got her naked. She moved to unhook her bra and he stayed her hands.

"No," he ordered, his tone deepening. "Leave it on."

Levi leaned in and placed a leisurely kiss on Lily's mouth. His tongue danced at the seam of her lips, urging her to open for him. Their tongues met as he deepened the kiss and Lily nearly sighed her relief. Her mouth slanted against his. She nipped at his bottom lip, sucked it, and he did the same. His palm found the back of her neck as he tilted her head back, their breaths becoming one as he continued the onslaught.

His other hand moved against her and Lily let out a tight whimper as his fingertips brushed her clit through the fabric of her underwear. The swollen bud pressed against the silk as though straining toward Levi's touch. The barrier between their skin frustrated her as much as it titillated her. No man had ever touched her the way Levi did. He knew exactly what to do to get the reaction he wanted.

He drove her mad with want.

With only the pad of his thumb, Levi brought her closer to the edge. Slow passes that sent jolts of sensation through Lily's body and flooded her with heat.

"You're soaking wet, baby," Levi murmured against her mouth. "Do you have any idea how hot you're making me right now? How badly I want to hear your sweet moans when you come for me?"

He kissed her again as his hand abandoned the back of her neck and moved to her breast. Through the lace that covered the swell he teased her nipple to a stiff, aching peak, alternating with a firmer, tighter grip on the hard tip. Lily's panting breaths became hitched, desperate moans as he brought her closer to release. Her thighs quaked and her stomach muscles clenched. She kept her palms planted firmly on the kitchen counter, her feet anchored on the barstools, knees wide. Her head rolled back on her shoulders and Levi's mouth moved to her exposed throat. His pace quickened as he teased her clit and nipples, and Lily gasped as her world turned in on itself, becoming small as a pinpoint before exploding outward.

Waves of sensation crested from her core and spread through her body. Lily's moans became impassioned cries as the wild crescendo waned before bursting over her once again. Her body quaked, her muscles tensed. She wondered if the onslaught would ever end as wave after wave of sensation crashed over her. Adrenaline coursed through her veins as the storm that raged within her passed and her body began to calm. Levi continued to kiss and pet her, easing her from the intensity of sensation until her limbs felt liquid and her breathing slowed.

"Levi." His name was nothing more than a whisper. How was it possible to feel such mind-shattering pleasure and still want more? "I want you inside of me. Please."

"You're so damn beautiful, darlin'," Levi said as he continued to kiss along her throat. "The way you feel, the sounds you make. I can't get enough."

Lily knew exactly how he felt. She couldn't get enough of him either. With every passing second, she became even more enamored with him. With every kiss, every touch, he became an addiction she couldn't escape. Did it matter that their relationship was mostly physical? They had plenty of time to get to know each other. Levi gave her so many things she hadn't had in so long. Companionship, comfort, pleasure, security. And already, she knew she wanted more.

Damn, Lily painted a pretty picture. Legs spread, silk panties damp from passion, and her tight little nipples straining against the lace of her bra. It was torture for him to see her this way. He was more than ready to strip her completely bare and fuck her until his legs could no longer bear his weight.

Levi wrapped his arms around Lily and hauled her against

him. She wrapped her arms around his neck and their mouths met in a ravenous kiss as he made his way to the bedroom, their bodies bouncing off the walls in the hallway as they went. Lily laughed. A low, sensuous ripple that turned Levi's cock to steel and drew his balls tight. He'd been dying to bury himself to the hilt in her wet heat since the second he'd pulled her pants off. It had taken all the self-control in his reserves to not simply take her.

Once in the bedroom, he deposited her on top of the down comforter. He reached for her panties and tore them from her thighs, reached behind her, and unhooked her bra, stripping it away from her as well. Levi stepped away from the bed and took in the glorious sight of Lily's naked body. He toed off his socks and stripped off his shirt and jeans, anxious to have what he had denied himself all evening.

"Top drawer," Lily said.

Levi crawled up the length of Lily's body, sliding his shaft along her silky skin as he reached for the drawer. The sensation of skin on skin sent a ripple of heat down his spine. He grabbed a condom and rolled it on. Lily's back arched as he moved over her and sucked a delicate nipple into his mouth, eliciting a sweet gasp from her lips. He'd never get enough of those sounds.

"I'm like a wound-up kid with you, Lily," Levi said with a laugh. "So damned anxious to have you, I can barely handle myself."

Lily's eyes became hooded and her lips curled into a sweet smile. "I like that I can have that effect on you." Her voice was a warm purr that fired every nerve in his body. "I don't want to give you a reason to ever think about another woman again."

He loved her confidence. The way she owned her sexuality and inherent strength and beauty. "Darlin', I haven't thought of another woman since the moment I laid eyes on you."

Lily smiled brightly and her eyes sparkled with an emotion that hollowed him out and then filled him to bursting. No woman could ever compare to her.

Levi braced an arm on the bed beside her, and the other he wrapped around her shapely thigh. He guided her leg up, opening her to him, and drove home in a single thrust. Sweet hell, she felt good. They fit together as though their bodies were made for each other.

He moved slowly at first, holding back as he pulled out to the crown and dove deep once again. Lily's mouth moved in a silent *yes* as she reached for his shoulders, nails digging in as she tried to pull him deeper still.

"Careful, baby," he warned. "I'm holding on to my control by a thread."

"Don't hold back." Lily's breath was warm in his ear. "I want all of you."

Damn, she drove him wild.

Levi did as she told him. He lost himself to the moment, the sensation that coursed through him. His teeth gnashed as he went hard and deep, his shaft pressing against Lily's clit with every thrust. She met his rhythm, her hips rolling with his. Her scent swam in his head; the satin flesh of her pussy stroked him, squeezed him. He fucked her with abandon, every muscle in his body rigid. Lily's tight breaths once again turned to desperate moans and he went harder. Deeper.

"Come for me, baby," he growled. "Do it. Now."

Lily broke apart with a keening cry. Her core contracted around him, and Levi let out a shout as she milked him. He continued to thrust as the orgasm shook him. His arm trembled under the strain of his weight and he didn't stop until his body no longer obeyed his commands. Levi collapsed on top of Lily and they lay in a tangle of limbs, panting breaths. Their unintelligible words filled the dark space between them.

"You're amazing." Levi pushed himself away, worried he'd crush her beneath his weight.

"Don't." Lily pulled him back. "Don't leave. I like it."

"I don't want to hurt you."

Lily laughed. "I'm tougher than you think. And your weight doesn't hurt at all. It's . . . comforting," she said after a moment. "Your body on mine. It makes me feel safe."

He wanted her to always feel safe with him. "Nothing will ever happen to you as long as we're together," Levi promised. "Anyone who ever tries to harm you is going to find himself in a world of hurt." It was the most honest oath he could give her and he hoped she'd understand—to some extent—exactly what he meant.

Lily's breath hitched. She wrapped her arms around him and held him tight. "Thank you," she said on a breath. "I—" Lily stopped short.

"What?"

"Just, thank you."

A few quiet moments passed, and Levi rolled to his side, bringing Lily with him. He missed the heat of her body, the connection that kept them joined. But as he held her in his arms, a different kind of comfort washed over him. A contentment he'd never felt before. As though everything was as it should be. She felt like home.

"I have a tendency to put up some pretty high walls." Pushing the words past his lips took a concentrated effort. Levi didn't like opening up to anyone, but because of what he'd had to keep from Lily, he knew he owed her some measure of truth. "I try my damndest to push people away. Which is why I've never had anything more than a one- or two-night stand here and there. It's easier to distance myself than to risk losing someone. You can't get hurt if you don't let it happen, you know?"

"I understand." Lily's hand found his chest and she drew little circles with her fingertips. "It's hard to let someone in."

"I don't have a lot of people in my life." He couldn't hold back the rueful laugh that came on the heels of the admission. "I don't have anyone in my life."

"Why?" Lily came up on an elbow. He could barely make out her features in the dark, but he knew she studied him. "What happened to you, Levi?"

His throat grew tight. Goddammit, he didn't know if he had the stones to talk about it. To finally, after so long, let down his guard.

"I joined the Army right out of high school. It was something I'd wanted for most of my life. My parents weren't sold on the idea, but it's what I wanted. I excelled. Joined the Army Rangers. It consumed so much of my life. There's a lot of secrecy when you're a part of an elite government agency." He didn't know how much of Jacob's life Lily knew about, but he assumed she had at least enough knowledge to relate. "Times when I was overseas and couldn't check in at home. I was young, a hell of a lot cockier than I am now, and thought I had the world by the balls."

"There's nothing wrong with that," Lily said softly. "I'm sure your parents are proud of you."

Levi's jaw flexed. He'd rather walk barefoot over glass shards than have this conversation, but he owed it to her. "I wouldn't know." His throat became thick with emotion. "They were killed in a car accident while I was on assignment."

"Levi." Lily's hand came to rest over his heart. "I'm so sorry."

He took several slow breaths as he fought to suppress the sadness that welled up inside him. "There was a high-speed chase involving an escaped fugitive. The guy lost control of the car and hit them head-on. They were in the wrong place at the wrong time, I guess."

"There's nothing I can say that would be enough." Lily's own voice quavered on the words.

"You don't have to say anything." Levi held her close against him. The heat of her body comforted him. "It was years ago. But I didn't have any other family. Both of my parents were only children. There was just my baby sister and me. If we have any other family, I'm unaware of it. My sister, Erin, was a teenager. She stayed with friends and I returned to my unit. I was alone after that. Erin and I meet a few times a year, but we're not really close."

Lily pushed herself up. She leaned over him and placed a gentle kiss on his lips that conveyed so much tenderness, Levi felt the impact like a fist to the chest. No one had ever evoked these sorts of emotions from him. He didn't know how to handle it.

"She's your sister," Lily murmured. She teased her fingers through his hair and a chill raced down Levi's spine. "You may not live close, may not see each other often, but she's in your heart."

"That's true." Levi had certainly felt a sense of family with the Rangers and he'd felt it with the marshals service as well. Erin was his sister, though, and like Lily said, he might not see her often, but he knew he'd kill or die for her. And right now, in the quiet dark, their bodies entwined, he felt it with Lily.

And that scared the shit out of him.

Chapter Eighteen

Lily's heart ached for Levi. The isolation he must've felt had to have been difficult. She could relate to a certain extent. She'd isolated herself from friends and loved ones after leaving school without an explanation. Even a little over a year later, Lily separated herself. She'd put up walls of her own and Levi was slowly making her realize that it might be okay to bring them down.

"My regiment was like family, though." Levi's rich voice cut a swath through the quiet. "You have to be able to trust the members of your team with your life. They were my brothers for eight years."

"Why did you leave the military?" Despite having to be up early the next morning, Lily didn't want to sleep. She wanted to stay up all night and learn everything about him.

"I felt as though I'd served my country and my purpose. It was time to move on."

The warmth of his voice stirred something in Lily's chest. Her heart felt as though it would burst from emotion. There was a depth to Levi she'd never known existed. And why would she? She'd never given him a chance to show her any other side of himself.

"Do you feel like you made the right decision?"

"I do," he answered without hesitation.

She couldn't imagine what the transition had been like for him, going from being a member of an elite military organization to picking up odd jobs at ranches here and there. But his being in Deer Haven made so much more sense now that she knew a little more about him. Jacob had been in the military as well and had worked for an elite government agency. He'd left that behind—well, mostly behind—for the life of a cattle rancher. Jacob tended to surround himself with men like him. Smart, resourceful, dedicated, and in some instances deadly. It was obvious why she'd always felt so safe with Levi. He'd been trained to protect. And she had no doubt that Levi could be equally deadly.

"I, um . . ." Lily didn't know if she could be as honest with Levi as he'd been with her. Her wounds were still so fresh and her fear still ruled so much of her life. But she wanted to let her guard down with him. Even if all she could offer him were half-truths. "I'm pretty good at keeping people at arm's length too. I had a bad experience when I was at college and I had a hard time dealing with the trauma. I left school and came home. Finished my classes online and made arrangements to do my student teaching in Deer Haven. I didn't open up to anyone about it for a long time. I don't trust easily."

The breath she'd taken lodged somewhere between Lily's sternum and lungs. She'd hit Levi with a lot of pretty vague information quickly. She braced herself, ready for the questions, not sure if she'd be able to answer them or not.

"Were you hurt?" Levi's voice went low, tentative as though he shouldn't ask but wanted to know just the same.

"Yes. But physical wounds can fade, you know? It's the emotional and mental damages that take the longest to heal." The words came as a hoarse whisper. "And it changed me. I've always been a smart-ass and too tough for my own good. But I was always a good sport about it. I could laugh at myself. Now . . ." Lily fought the tears that threatened. "I don't know. I'm just harder now. More defensive. A little jaded, I guess."

"You have every right to be." Levi's strong arms encircled her, held her secure. She never wanted this feeling of comfort and security to end. "Something obviously terrible happened to you, Lily. Something you didn't deserve."

Guilt nearly choked her. "How do you know I didn't deserve it?"

Levi cupped her cheek in his palm as though he saw her perfectly in the dark. "*No one* deserves to be hurt. I don't care what you think you did to invite what happened to you. I know without a doubt that you did nothing wrong."

"Thank you." Though he didn't have all of the facts, she valued the reassurance. "I needed to hear that."

"As long as I'm in your life, no one will ever hurt you again." Levi's voice bore a deadly edge to it that sent a cold chill over Lily's skin. "I promise you that."

"And as long as I'm in your life," Lily said, "you'll always have a family."

A solemn silence settled over them both. The weight of their words, their promises as sacred as vows, settled over Lily. In the space of an hour, their relationship had changed. They'd turned a corner and there was no going back. Through Levi, Lily felt as if she might have finally found a path to healing from everything that had happened to her. She only hoped that nothing would happen to destroy the new life she was on the verge of building.

As long as I'm in your life, no one will ever hurt you again.

She could so easily fall in love with a man like Levi. But if she couldn't find the courage to be completely honest with him, she worried she might lose the chance to find out.

* * *

Hands wrapped tightly around Lily's neck and squeezed. Her face throbbed from where his fist had connected with her cheek and her eye was nearly swollen shut, distorting her vision in the already dark room. Her airway became constricted and she fought for the tiniest thread of breath. She struggled against the body that held her down, kicked and scratched even as her world became darker at the edges and her mind slowed. She chided her own stupidity in the midst of dying, wishing she could go back and change the events that led up to this. No amount of wishing would make that happen, however, and she had no choice but to resist, or let him choke the last breath of air from her lungs.

Lily refused to die.

She twisted and managed to free her arms that had been pinned at her sides by the weight of his body. Remembering the self-defense move Jacob had taught her, Lily brought her arms between his and twisted outward, forcing him to release his grip on her throat. Air filled her lungs in deep, rasping gulps as she used his imbalance to her advantage and tipped his body from hers as she wriggled free. His fist swung out, catching Lily in the ribs. Pain exploded through her torso, but the adrenaline rush pushed her forward. A bright swath of light cut into the room from the open door. If she could just make it to the light. If she could just close the door behind her, she might buy herself enough time to run. If she could just get enough air in her aching lungs, she could call for help—

A desperate scream tore from Lily's throat as she sat upright in bed. A hand reached out to steady her and she flailed, arms and legs kicking and swinging at the unknown threat.

"Lily!"

The memory clung to her mind, sending her into a spiral of panic. Her heart beat a wild rhythm in her chest and her breaths raced as she fought to fill her lungs with sufficient air. The familiar surroundings of her own bedroom became foreign, as confusion won out over calm. She had to get out of here! Had to get help. But her arms and legs were so heavy, she had no idea if she had the energy to run.

Glaring light filled the room and Lily shielded her eyes against the sudden brightness. A man's face came into view, his brow furrowed as he held his arms aloft, palms out as though trying to calm a wild animal. He kept one knee on the mattress, the other leg planted firmly on the floor, half standing as he gave her ample space.

"Lily. You were having a nightmare. You're home. You're safe. Everything is okay."

She fought to form a coherent thought. The past held her in its grip and, though familiar, the voice speaking to her didn't spark any recognition. Her hazy vision fought to reconcile dream with reality and she reached up to lay her fingers gingerly on her swollen face only to realize she was unmarred.

"Lily, listen to me, darlin'." Her breathing began to slow. Her pulse no longer rushed in her ears and her vision cleared with her mind. "You're okay. You're safe." He reached out to her but stopped short and pulled back. "Take a deep breath, baby. Let yourself wake up."

Slowly, Lily came back to awareness. The details of her bedroom, the light above her, and Levi, resting tentatively on the edge of the bed, so much concern etched into his handsome face that it brought tears to Lily's eyes. Her hands went to her mouth, her embarrassment at what she'd just put him through flashing hot in her cheeks.

"I'm sorry, Levi. I . . ." She took a shuddering breath as tears spilled over her eyes. "I'm so sorry."

"God, no." Levi reached out, and when she took his hand in hers he sat on the bed and pulled her tight against his chest. "Don't you dare apologize. Do you understand me? Never apologize. You went through hell and sometimes the demons follow us to the other side. But it's going to be okay." Levi laid a palm on the top of her head and let his hand caress the length of her hair. "You're going to be okay."

Silent tears pooled in Lily's eyes and fell like soft rain. The patience and understanding he'd just shown her was so much more than she could have expected or even thought she deserved. But they'd both experienced traumas in their life and maybe Levi understood what she was going through better than she'd thought. How did she ever get so lucky for him to find his way into her life?

Quiet sobs wracked Lily's body as Levi held her and rocked her in his embrace. "Get it all out," he crooned next to her ear. "Feel it all and then put it away."

Levi was no therapist, but he knew a little bit about the pain Lily felt. The fear that plagued her and the ghosts of her past that wouldn't loosen their grip on her. Wherever he was, Graham Brisbee had better pray that one of the other marshals got to him before Levi did. Because he'd be hard-pressed not to beat the shit out of the bastard before he managed to put the cuffs on him.

He'd make sure that son of a bitch never saw the light of day again. Lily deserved that much.

Minutes passed as they sat in the silence of Lily's bedroom. Levi made sure not to make any sudden adjustments or jostle her unnecessarily. He did what he could to contribute to an atmosphere of calm as her silent cries turned to sniffles and then, finally, ceased. Levi had never felt so helpless. In the field, he had an objective. A target. A goal and a plan of attack to attain it. He had backup and resources. The tools necessary to get the job done.

If he couldn't help Lily in even some small way, what the hell good was he?

Lily's silky soft lips met his shoulder. She kissed across his chest, over his collarbone, to his opposite shoulder as she came up on her knees and straddled him. The wet heat of her pussy brushed against his cock and Levi sucked in a breath. He held himself completely still, worried to do anything that might trigger her.

"Will you touch me, Levi?" Lily whispered close to his ear before she took the lobe into her mouth and sucked. "I want to feel your hands on me."

He let his hands wander up her naked back. Lily let out a contented sigh as she continued to kiss his neck, behind his ears, and along his shoulders. Her hips began to undulate in a slow rhythm, deliberate as she brushed the softest part of her flesh against the steel of his erection.

"You're playing with fire, darlin'." Levi sucked in a breath as she pressed downward, dipping the head of his cock into her heat. "Give me a second to—"

"No." Lily continued to tease him as she kissed and nipped at his skin. "I want you like this."

Levi's jaw clenched. She tested the limit of his control with each roll of her hips. "Are you sure, Lily?" He pulled away to force her to look into his eyes. She'd been through hell tonight and her emotions were still raw.

"I'm sure." She put her lips to his and kissed him deeply at the same moment she settled over his cock.

Levi groaned at the intense stab of pleasure. His arms held Lily tight as she rode him, her fingers gripping his shoulders. Nearly every inch of their bodies touched. The heat they generated caused beads of sweat to form on their skin. Lily's mouth slanted over Levi's. She kissed him as though she was starved for him, desperate and wanting more.

"You feel so good," Lily murmured against his mouth. "I need this. I need you."

He needed her too. "Lily." The word slipped from his lips like a prayer. "My Lily."

His. Levi's heart stuttered in his chest. He wanted Lily to be his. In the short time they'd been together, she'd become important to him. Special. The thought of losing her filled him with fear. He knew without a doubt that he'd never be able to let her go. He'd reached the point of no return. He was lost to her and he'd accept the consequences for his action, whatever they may be.

Levi's rhythm matched hers as their bodies met and parted again and again. Lily's back arched as her breaths quickened. Her pussy squeezed him, stroking the length of his cock until Levi's balls drew up tight and the pressure built to a near-unbearable level. Rational thought gave way to passion and sensation. Nothing mattered but this moment. The soft caress of Lily's skin, her nails as they grazed his back, and her soft cries that grew louder with each roll of her hips.

"I'm close." Lily nipped at his earlobe once again and the gentle shock of pain only spurred him on. "So close."

A cry escaped Lily's lips as she came, and Levi let go of his meager control at the same moment. They rode the waves of their passion as one, bodies, mouths, and breaths joined in synchronicity.

Lily relaxed against Levi's chest, draping her arms over his shoulders. Her quick breaths brushed his neck and her fingertips drew a lazy pattern up and down his spine. Levi held her. His own heart continued to race despite coming down from the high of loving Lily. A knot of uncertainty tied itself in his gut and he fought to shut down the worry that assuaged him.

Damn it, what did you do?

Levi chided himself as the path of Lily's fingers over his back began to slow and finally stilled. Her breathing became steady and deep and her body went limp in Levi's arms.

She'd exhausted herself both emotionally and physically and he was glad that she'd been able to find the easy rest she'd needed so badly.

Carefully, he eased her onto the bed. Levi reached for the light switch and the room once again plunged into darkness as he lay down beside her and tucked his body protectively against hers. Lily reached for him in her sleep, took his hand in hers, and guided it around her body until his palm cradled her breast. She let out a soft sigh as her head sank deeper into the downy surface of the pillow and she stilled.

Levi wished that sleep would find him as easily. He'd been reckless and it didn't matter that Lily had been the one to suggest it. She'd been through hell tonight and her emotions had been volatile. He should have been the responsible one and insisted that he use protection. He'd never not used a condom with a partner before. He'd always been so careful. Shame welled up hot and thick in his chest, not only that his actions were disrespectful toward Lily but also that he'd wanted to be reckless with her.

Levi wanted Lily to be the last woman—the *only* woman—he was ever with again.

For the first time in his life, he began to envision a future with someone. Hell, his heart nearly soared at the thought that Lily could be pregnant with his child. The thought of having a family of his own . . . It was more than he'd ever dared to hope for. For so long Levi had resigned himself to being alone for the rest of his life with nothing more than random hookups to fill his lonely nights. Now he envisioned a different future. One with companionship and laughter, with children and love.

Love.

Levi's breath stalled in his chest. Was it possible that he'd fallen in love with Lily without even realizing it? Had she wormed her way into his heart with her fiery personality, her fierce beauty, and the deep hurt that had made her put her guard up and helped to shape the woman that she was?

He'd never been in love. Wouldn't know what it felt like if it walked up to him and kicked him right in the face. But he knew that Lily made his day brighter. That the sound of her laughter was music to his ears. He knew that a day without her in it was incomplete, and he also knew that if anyone ever dared to hurt her again he'd hunt the bastard to the ends of the earth and make him pay.

If that wasn't love, Levi didn't know what was.

As Lily slept beside him, Levi knew the only way they could have a future together was if he was honest with her. Every day that he continued to keep things from her would only hurt them. He had a duty, not only to the marshals service but also to Lily, to find and arrest Graham Brisbee. She would never find peace until the son of a bitch was behind bars for the rest of his life. A plan began to form as he held her next to him. He didn't want to waste another day. It was time to come clean. With Lily, Jacob, everyone. Before they found out on their own and hated him for it.

He prayed, as he placed a quiet kiss on the top of Lily's head, that it wasn't too late.

Chapter Nineteen

Five days turned into two weeks. Lily had worried that Levi might tire of her. That he'd become weary of playing house and go back to the ranch. Instead, the days bled into one blissful moment after another. Lily never suggested he leave, and likewise, Levi never asked if she wanted him to. A change of clothes grew to a duffel bag of clothes and then a couple of drawers, space in the closet, and his deodorant, razor, and other toiletries next to Lily's in the bathroom.

Were they crazy to be moving so quickly? Honestly, Lily didn't care.

Their relationship evolved daily. From a one-night stand to deep, meaningful conversations and random chats. They talked about everything and nothing. They went to dinner together, spent the weekends together, and enjoyed lazy days at home watching movies, sitting on the couch. Fourteen short days might as well have been fourteen months. She and Levi simply clicked. Lily felt as though she'd finally found the life she'd always wanted.

And yet at times she sensed that Levi was still holding back.

"Lily! Are you even listening to me?"

She snapped back to reality and forced her attention back on Shay, who'd been talking for the past five minutes. She was tired of going over the same points, over and over, without really forming some plan of attack. It wasn't that Lily didn't appreciate Shay. But the past two weeks hadn't been all butterflies and rainbows. Graham was still on the run and had yet to be apprehended. There had been no news updates and, as far as Lily knew, no leads on his whereabouts. And Shay was just as tired as Lily of the waiting and not knowing and worrying and she wanted Lily to do something she wasn't quite ready to do.

"He could be anywhere," Shay pointed out for what felt like the hundredth time today. They'd decided to meet at Rizzo's, a cute little Italian place with plenty of secluded booths for them to have a private conversation. Right now, Lily was more interested in her fettucine than Shay's arguments. "Go to Sacramento; tell the marshal that called you that you want to go into the witness protection program and wait this out until that asshole is arrested and back in prison where he belongs."

Lily had decided a long time ago that she wasn't going to let what had happened to her dictate her life. So far, she had no reason to believe that Graham was anywhere near Deer Haven, let alone anywhere in the United States, and she wasn't willing to give up her freedom—or Levi—based on hunches and conjecture.

"No."

Shay snorted derisively, and Lily amended, "Not yet. If I run and hide, he wins."

"You're wrong." Shay raised her empty wineglass in the direction of the waitress. It was definitely going to be a bottle sort of lunch. "If you live, he loses. You got away with your life the first time. What if he's not willing to let that happen again?"

It sounded dramatic, but Lily knew that Shay had a point. Another student—a senior, and one of Graham's research assistants—had been killed on campus a week before Lily had been attacked. Because of Lily, the renowned psychology professor had been caught before he could hurt anyone else. Graham had been arrested and the police and FBI asserted that he'd graduated from serial rapist to potential serial killer. The thought terrified her. She'd managed to get away with her life, but not before her former professor had beaten and nearly raped her. Even over a year since the trial, it felt like a dream. Someone else's life events that she'd watched unfold like a TV show.

Very few people knew what had happened. Lily's parents, of course. Sallie and Shay, the law enforcement officers, and the district attorney. She'd fought hard for her anonymity, arguing that life at the university would be unbearable if her identity had been made public. In the end, it hadn't mattered. Staying at school had proven to be more than she could shoulder and she'd come home. She'd kept her secret, though, not wanting anyone to see her as a victim. And she wanted to keep it that way.

"We don't know anything," Lily argued. With each passing day she wanted to believe less that she was in danger and needed to take the necessary precautions. "The media doesn't even know anything and I'm sure that the marshals' office would tell me if they thought he was anywhere near Deer Haven." Things were going so well with Levi. If she gave in to Shay's urgings, it could ruin everything they'd begun to build together. "If I was a murderer on the run, I'd be getting myself out of the country as soon as possible, not wasting my time chasing someone who doesn't matter anymore."

"That's the thing, Lily," Shay said. The waitress approached their table and she leaned toward her. "It's been a day, honey. I'm gonna need the bottle." She set her empty glass down and turned her attention back to Lily. "You do matter. Psychos like that don't just brush it off and move on. It's been eating at him for over a year. He's got to have someone to blame for why he is where he is. And since he's too damned arrogant to blame himself, he's going to lay it on you."

It made sense. Graham was insufferably full of himself. He'd often compared his intelligence to that of men whose genius far surpassed his, but Lily had always seen it as a reflection of low self-esteem. He'd wanted to be a world-renowned academic but had been too self-involved to be anything other than a local sensation. Although, at the time, Lily had fallen victim to his charm. His dedication to the study of the human psyche. His good looks and supposed interest in his students and their educations. Now she realized it had all been an act. He'd used his students as experiments in manipulation and exploitation. He'd played sick games with countless women and a few men. He'd escalated from toying with students, to sleeping with them, to physically abusing them, and then, finally, murder.

"I'm not his only victim." God, she hated that word. It made her feel so weak. "Other women have come forward and admitted to being abused by him."

"That was before," Shay said.

"Before what?"

Shay leveled her gaze on Lily. "Before he'd graduated from a vile piece of shit to a fucking monster."

A finger of fear stroked down Lily's spine. She'd be stupid not to be terrified, but that wasn't the point. It was about losing her freedom. It wasn't fair for her to become a virtual prisoner while her attacker roamed free.

"You put an end to what he'd started, Lily." She knew that Shay was right, but that didn't make the pill of truth any easier to swallow. "Please, for once, just play it safe and hide out. Just for a little while."

"What if it isn't a 'little while,' Shay?" Lily's temper began to crest. The waitress returned with the bottle of wine and she snatched it before her sister could get her hands on it and poured herself a generous glass. "What if they never catch him and I have to spend the rest of my life hiding? I'll have to change my name!" Her heart beat faster as her anxiety crested. "I'll never get to talk to my parents again. I won't get to see you or Jacob and Sallie or anyone else I love again." Emotion rose in her throat and she washed it down with a gulp of wine. "I'll never see Levi again."

"Please tell me you're not basing this decision on a guy you've only known for a couple of weeks." Shay's words were delivered with all the care of someone being passed a live grenade. "Your life is worth more than something that might not even be a thing in a month or two."

Lily knew that her relationship with Levi seemed trite to Shay. And that it was too soon to think it would ever turn into anything substantial. It wasn't like they were getting married or even anywhere near an engagement or something serious. But what if she walked away now and gave up her one chance at real love? Maybe Levi wasn't the one. But what if he *was*?

"It's not only about Levi." That was the truth. "I don't want to lose anyone that I love. Including you," she said with a sarcastic edge that made Shay crinkle her nose. "I'll go crazy if I have to cut everyone out of my life. I know I make it seem like I'm a bad bitch who doesn't need anyone, but the loneliness and separation will kill me. I won't be able to handle it."

Shay's expression softened. "I know, Lily. This isn't an easy decision to make. And do you think I want to live without you in my life either? I'd fucking hate it! But I'd rather know you were alive and never talk to you again than have you die and know that you would have been okay if you'd just let yourself be protected."

"Levi can protect me." She knew how it sounded. It's not like she'd ever asked him to, but he'd promised her that he'd always keep her safe and she believed him.

"But what if Levi can't?" Shay said. She added, quietly, "What if you tell him everything, and he won't?"

"He wouldn't do that," Lily replied. "You don't know him like I do, Shay."

"Lil, you don't know him at all."

Lily sipped from her glass. "I know enough."

The conversation quieted and Lily pretended to be interested in her lunch. The pasta, usually delicious, might as well have been cardboard. Shay had made some good points, not that Lily wanted her to know it. She had to consider Levi in all of this as well, and not simply from the standpoint of her own selfish wants. He had no idea how complicated her life was right now. It wasn't fair to keep it from him. And she wouldn't blame him if he decided it was more than he wanted to deal with. Likewise, Lily couldn't bear to think of something bad happening to Levi because she'd been too foolish to leave her protection to professional law enforcement.

"I'll think about it," she said at last.

"Thank you," Shay said with a smile. "Don't think I ever want to get rid of you. There's no one else on the planet I'd rather ruffle feathers with."

"Back at ya," Lily said.

Shay was right. Lily knew it. She just wasn't ready to admit it.

The past two weeks had passed in a blur of unaccustomed happiness. Levi couldn't remember ever feeling so damned content and he had Lily to thank for it. Though he'd planned on coming clean and telling Lily everything, the fact that Brisbee had seemed to virtually disappear from the face of the earth made him reconsider. He still had his responsibilities to consider and his commitment to the USMS and the fugitive recovery team. Levi had managed to make a mess of his life and managed to further complicate it with each passing day, but he'd be damned if he wasn't happier than he'd been in a long time.

Levi bounced a leg as he sat in the debriefing. He didn't want to waste another minute in Sacramento. He was antsy as hell to get home to Lily, and though Sheriff Davidson was a good man, had kept his word to keep Levi's purpose in Deer Haven under wraps, and was a competent cop, Levi didn't trust anyone but himself to keep the woman he loved safe.

And he did love Lily. Though he hadn't said the words out loud yet, he'd known it the night he'd told her about his parents' deaths. Since that night together, he'd practically moved in with her. And he wasn't planning on leaving unless Lily told him to.

They'd caught a break from an anonymous tip. A credible lead had placed Derrick Bloom, another escapee, not far from Durango and the fugitive recovery task force in Colorado was closing in on him. It might be the break they needed to locate Brisbee, because so far the bastard was a ghost. Levi wouldn't stop hunting him until he was either in custody or dead.

At this point, it didn't matter which.

"What about Max Davis?" Chief Deputy Seth Miller asked.

"Tip lines have several leads," Mitch McDonald, Levi's supervisor, replied. "You know how it goes, though. It takes a while to weed through what's credible and what's just fucking crazy."

"He was Brisbee's cellmate," Seth continued. "And we're working on the supposition that he and Davis planned this together. I have no doubt Brisbee was the mastermind so to speak, and knowing his pattern, he likely used Davis for whatever he could offer to the success of the escape and whatever Brisbee had planned afterward. That's what we need to figure out if we want to get our hands on Brisbee. Knowing what made Davis valuable to him is what's going to get us our first break in this manhunt."

That was the mystery. Brisbee was a smart son of a bitch. He didn't do anything without good reason. Max Davis was a thug who'd landed himself in prison because he'd been too stupid to be a successful drug dealer. Brisbee had had a solid year to get to know his cellmate, however. In that time, it made sense that he would've learned something about the other man that he could use to his advantage. He never would have included him in his plans otherwise.

It drove Levi crazy that he'd yet to put the pieces of that particular puzzle together.

"What about family connections?" Seth asked. More times than not, fugitives ran to family members, girlfriends, or friends for protection. They stayed close to what was familiar and that's why most fugitives were apprehended soon after escape. "Ex-girlfriends? Old roommates? Buddies from his trafficking days?"

"So far, nothing," Mitch replied. "We followed a couple of leads. His parents basically disowned him after his first arrest at twenty-five. No ex-girlfriends recent enough for him to think they might be willing to help him out. As for his street connections," he sighed, "that's a dead end too. Most of his former associates are either dead or in jail."

Levi dragged his fingers through his hair. His frustration mounted as they continued to hit one dead end after another. "Brisbee's a psychologist." They needed to talk everything through, brainstorm every angle, until something viable presented itself. "He had plenty of time over the past year to dig around in Davis's head. There has to be information that we're missing. It's probably a detail we've overlooked more than once. Something seemingly inconsequential."

"What's the one thing Brisbee wants that would keep him from heading straight to the Mexico border?" Seth asked.

"Revenge," Levi said, already knowing the answer. "Retribution."

"Exactly," Seth said. "I still believe Brisbee is too arrogant to simply run."

An icy chill danced over Levi's skin. He hadn't wanted to believe it, but there was a reason he'd been sent to Deer Haven undercover and everyone on his team had been betting on it. So far, there'd been no trace of Brisbee anywhere close to Deer Haven. "Could it be that Brisbee has somehow found a connection to Lily through Davis?" If so, he needed to get to the bottom of it, ASAP.

"That's where we need to focus our attention," Seth said. "We'll need to look at Davis's file again. Interview the guards, prison officials, and anyone else who knows anything about him. See if there's anything that might lead Brisbee to Lily Donovan through him. It has to be ruled out, regardless. If we don't find anything, we switch up tactics and, Levi, you'll have to follow the evidence."

Levi nodded. His emotions were all over the place. Though he knew he needed to keep his head in the game, be a good investigator, and do the work, there was a part of him that was reluctant to leave Deer Haven for any reason, even if it meant following the bread crumbs to Brisbee. He didn't trust anyone other than himself to protect Lily. She was the one thing he couldn't afford to lose.

The meeting continued, swinging focus from Brisbee to Albuquerque and Davis's possible connections there. Levi tried to pay attention, but his mind wandered. He agreed when he needed to, scribbled a few sparse notes, and kept his eyes focused dutifully on the chief deputy director. But Levi couldn't stop the worry that ate away at him. He couldn't tear his thoughts away from Lily.

"Roberts, can I have a word with you in private?" Seth asked as the meeting concluded and the other deputy marshals filed out of the conference room.

Levi sucked in a deep breath and let it all out in a single gust. He kept his ass parked right in his seat and waited for the chief deputy director to drop the hammer.

"Is everything okay?" Of course it wasn't. He wouldn't still be sitting there otherwise.

Seth took a seat beside Levi and adopted a casual posture. Looked like they were going to have the "just between guys" chat as opposed to a formal reprimand. As though it mattered how the words were delivered. Levi knew he was in deep shit.

"I was talking to Mitch this morning and he has some concerns. This job isn't for the faint of heart," Seth began. "It falls on us to hunt down some pretty scary sons of bitches and protect people whose lives will never be the same because of what they saw or what happened to them. A lot of guys sign up for the adrenaline rush. They focus on the job, the chase, and nothing else. But not you. You signed up because you care about protecting people and making the world a safer place."

Levi nodded. He didn't need to be told about his character or why he did the things he did. "I wouldn't be on the fugitive recovery task force if you didn't think I was good at my job," Levi replied. "So why don't you just tell me what this is about."

"You always take the job personally." Seth propped his elbow on the chair back. He shifted to his right and focused his gaze on Levi. "Every time you go out in the field, everyone in this office knows you're doing it to make sure no one has to be victimized ever again by whoever you're hunting. And it's damned admirable. But you're too close this time, and all it's going to do is land you in a world of hurt."

Levi settled back into his chair. Was it that obvious that this time was unlike any of the others?

"You barely passed your psych evaluation when you entered the program," Seth continued. Levi cringed. He hadn't been dragged this hard since basic training. "People who've lost loved ones like you did have a hard time separating themselves when they go out into the field. Every fugitive you take down is the guy who killed your parents. And I've kept a close eye on you to make sure you toe that line between professionalism and vendetta. But I can't protect you if you let your feelings for this girl get in the way of doing your job."

In other words, if Levi didn't do what he was told when he was told to do it, he was toast. Insubordination wouldn't be tolerated. Proceed by the book or start looking for a new job. Levi sat for a few quiet moments and digested everything Seth had said. If he argued now, it would only expedite what the chief deputy director didn't want to happen.

"You're one of the best deputy marshals the service has right now," Seth said. "It would be a damn shame to lose you, and I know that's not what you want either. You've gotta trust in the process, stick to your training, and remember there's a reason we're the best there is. I don't know what's going on with you and Miss Donovan and I don't want to have to know. Just do your job."

"Understood, sir," Levi replied. There was nothing else to say. No other option. He just hoped he could do as Seth asked . . . and trust.

Chapter Twenty

Hey. I'm feeling a little cooped up. Meet me at the Broken Horn this evening.

Levi looked down at the text message and a stone of dread settled in his gut. He reluctantly sent off a text to Lily agreeing to meet her there as he pulled out from the parking garage and put the pedal to the metal to get back to Deer Haven sooner rather than later. Maybe Seth had been right and his feelings for Lily were beginning to cloud his judgment. Because the thought of allowing her to be out in public—so exposed—made him break out into a cold sweat. If he had it his way, he'd have her locked safely in a fortress somewhere until he had Brisbee in custody and securely back in prison where he couldn't harm Lily, or anyone else, ever again.

She'd never forgive him if he pulled something like that, though. Lily's autonomy was important to her. Levi had to do what he could to make sure her life was as normal as possible, while still doing his job. And damn if that didn't seem a hell of a lot harder than it sounded.

A half hour later, Levi pulled up to the Broken Horn. The microbrewery and sports pub was a favorite hangout for locals as well as the cowboys who occasionally blew through town to run cows or pick up rodeo stock. He hadn't been there since the night he'd first tried to win Lily over, only to be shot down. He noticed her car across the street and he took the lanyard with his badge from around his neck and tucked it, along with his sidearm, in the glove box. He was tired of the deceit and sickened that he had to keep this part of his life a secret from her. He needed to lay everything out on the table and let the cards fall where they may instead of continuing to drag out the inevitable. If Lily loved him like he loved her, surely she'd understand.

Did she love him?

Levi pushed that worry to the soles of his feet as he locked the pickup and made his way into the sports bar. Several big-screen televisions lined the walls of the bar and outward. The large space was sectioned off into the bar, a dining area, and another with pool tables. Lily waited in a booth and raised her hand to get his attention, even though he'd zeroed in on her the second he'd walked through the door. Levi's eyes gravitated to wherever she was. He returned her bright smile, despite the rolling waves in his stomach, and made his way to the table.

"How was your day?" She almost seemed too chipper. Levi was on edge. Tired from a long-ass day and his nerves raw from his talk with Seth.

"Good," he said. "Long." He slid into the booth next to her and placed a gentle kiss on her lips. "How about yours?"

"Same," she said with a laugh. "I wish I had the endless drive of a second grader. They're little Energizer Bunnies."

Their waitress brought over a water for Levi and another glass of wine for Lily. "Can I get you something to drink, hon?"

"I'll take a sweet tea."

"Coming right up."

"How long have you been here?" Levi tried not to pry, but

he worried about Lily being anywhere public until they had Brisbee's location locked down.

Lily shrugged. "I don't know. A half hour or so."

"Next time, we'll meet at the house and come together."

Lily's brow furrowed and her lips formed into a petulant pucker. "I'm perfectly comfortable waiting by myself in a restaurant, Levi."

"I'm sure you are." Irrational as it was, his temper rose. "I'm not comfortable with it."

Lily's frown transformed into an absolute scowl. "Excuse me?"

Levi raked his fingers through his hair. Their weeks of bliss would come to a screeching halt if he didn't shut his mouth. He couldn't exercise control over Lily simply because he had no control over the current situation with locating Brisbee.

"I'm sorry, darlin'." He reached over and gave her thigh a gentle squeeze. "Bad day, you know? I'm an asshole."

"Yeah," Lily said without humor. "You are. But . . . we've both had long days. Wanna just start over?"

"Yeah." Levi squeezed Lily's thigh again. "I do."

"Hi!" Lily began brightly. "How was your day?"

Levi leaned in and kissed her. It was a slow, purposeful kiss to let her know exactly how he felt about her. Lily reached for the back of his head and her fingernails scraped his neck. Levi's dick jumped to attention behind his fly. If she didn't watch out, he'd take her right here on the table and not give a damn who watched.

It took an actual act of will to break the kiss. He pulled away first and Lily's dreamy eyes opened slowly. "I had a long day," he said as he reached for her hand and brought her fingers to his lips. "But it's much better now. How was your day?"

"Same." Her expression brightened. "Much better now."

Once again, Levi pushed his worry and the preoccupation with work to the back of his mind. Dinner was spent in amazing company and good conversation. Lily's presence was a balm on his soul. She had quickly become his comfort, his home base, a part of his life he didn't think he could live without. Attachments were dangerous, and an attachment to someone he was technically staking out was taboo. He could lose his job over this and he couldn't even be bothered to care. He was lost to her. In a few short weeks, Lily had managed to capture his heart.

"Can we go shooting tomorrow?"

She'd asked him before to take her out, but in the blur of their quickly budding relationship Levi had forgotten about it. He suspected the topic would continue to come up until he followed through. It was a good idea for her to know how to protect herself, but damn it, he never wanted her to be in the position to have to.

"Absolutely." Tomorrow was Saturday. It was the perfect opportunity to teach her how to handle a gun while simultaneously keeping her close. "We can go to the shooting range."

"I was thinking we could do it out at the ranch. I know a spot that'll work good."

Even better. "That sounds good. How about we go after breakfast in the morning?"

"Perfect."

Lily's smile brightened, but a shadow crossed her gaze. She was afraid and Levi so desperately wanted to assure her that he'd make sure Brisbee would be in custody and back in prison soon.

"Shooting tomorrow and now"—Lily grinned—"I'm going to kick your butt at pool."

"Want to make it interesting?" Levi asked.

"Name your price."

Forget pool. Levi wanted to get Lily home, strip her naked, and throw her in bed. "Winner gets five bucks *and* loser cooks breakfast in the morning."

Lily's wicked grin was enough to turn his dick to stone. "You're on."

They found an empty spot at the back of the bar. Lily put some quarters into the slot at the side of the table and released the balls. "I'll rack; you break."

He loved her feisty, assertive nature. Lily bent over the table, her skirt hiking up her thighs, dangerously close to being indecent, and arranged the balls in the rack, her pert little ass in the air. If this was a seduction tactic, Levi approved. She gingerly removed the plastic triangle from around the balls and slid it back into its slot. She walked over to the wall and carefully selected a cue.

"This one feels lucky." She stroked her hand along the length of the wood and Levi swallowed a groan. If he made it through the next half hour without losing his composure, it would be a miracle. The innuendo, coupled with that sexy body of hers, could tempt a saint down from heaven.

"Five bucks and breakfast," Levi said. "You ready?"

"Please," Lily scoffed. "It's in the bag."

Levi leaned over the table and calculated his shot. He hit the cue ball head-on and the balls broke with a resounding crack. Lily smirked as they scattered, but nothing managed to make its way to a pocket.

"Looks like the table's open. I can already taste the French toast."

She leaned over the table, giving Levi another glimpse of her perfect ass. She lined up her shot and effortlessly dropped the four in the corner pocket. He'd never seen anything so damn hot in his entire life. Lily readjusted and banked the two. Her satisfied grin became smug as she rounded the table, brushing seductively against his groin as she passed.

"Excuse me."

If Lily didn't stop, they wouldn't make it to the end of the game to determine a winner. He was already too wound up to focus on what he was doing. And she was definitely using it to her advantage.

Was it wrong to be enjoying herself amid so much turmoil in her life? For the first time in a long time, Lily felt free. As though her past wasn't a heavy stone around her neck that had become too cumbersome to carry. Levi made her feel safe, and even though he hadn't been happy about her being in the bar alone, she knew he'd never let anything bad happen to her.

The alpha-male protectiveness had thrown her a bit off guard. In fact, Levi had seemed particularly on edge when he'd shown up tonight. They'd both admitted to having long days at work, and she wondered what could have possibly happened on the ranch today to have him so tightly wound.

No matter what had happened, she was determined to make sure his night was far better than his day had been.

Lily hadn't played the flirty seductress in a while, but she was holding her own. As she brushed her backside against the fly of Levi's jeans and the hard length of him hidden there, a thrill raced through her center. Knowing she could affect him that way gave her a sense of power and she was letting it go to her head.

With a careful eye, Lily chose her next shot. She lined up the stick to the cue ball and gently tapped. The seven ball dropped lazily into the pocket and a surge of smug confidence fueled her already raging fire. "Want to make our wager a little more interesting?"

She turned to find Levi watching her. The fire that sparked hot in his expression made Lily's limbs tingle and her core pulse with need. He gave her a swoon-worthy lopsided grin and rested the bottom of the cue against the toe of his boot. "Why not? I'm thinking I'll have biscuits and gravy for my victory breakfast."

"Keep dreaming, cowboy." Lily walked around the table and assessed her next shot. "Let's say winner now gets breakfast and a full-body massage? Oh, and bragging rights, of course."

"Of course." Levi chuckled.

It was a risky shot but would be totally worth it if she made it. Lily hiked a hip onto the ledge of the table and leaned over the felt. All she had to do was cut the six to the far-right corner pocket.

The hairs rose on the back of Lily's neck and her arms. The sensation of being watched—and not by Levi—overwhelmed her. She pulled back and the stick connected with the ball, hitting it straight in the middle. The shot went wild, sending the six in the opposite direction.

"Shit." Lily hopped off the table, the sense of unease refusing to release its grip on her. She looked around the crowded bar area, searching for the source of whatever had tripped her instinct.

"You okay?" Levi studied her, his brow furrowed.

"Yeah." Lily hoped the lie was convincing. In the short time they'd been together, Levi had learned to read her moods. A double-edged sword right now. She didn't want to alarm him just because she'd managed to spook herself. "I should have had that shot, though." She forced a laugh. "Lucky you."

Levi studied her for a beat. He took a quick glance around, as though assessing their surroundings, before he focused on the table and his shot.

Lily watched him slide the cue between his thumb and finger, but her brain refused to process any of it. He paused to reevaluate and moved from one end of the table to the next, his gaze wary, as he seemed to keep his attention more on their surroundings than the game. Lily tried to maintain a façade of calm, but something wasn't right.

"Nice," she remarked as Levi made his first two shots. And a third. "Very nice." Lily forced a smile and wiggled her fingers at her sides to keep from tensing up. "It's not enough to earn you biscuits and gravy, though."

"Oh, you don't even know," Levi teased. "I'm just getting started."

He managed to make his next two shots as well, showcasing a skill that Lily couldn't help but admire. With every passing day he became more perfect for her. And as that happened, she knew it would soon be impossible to let him go.

Levi rose to the challenge of Lily's competitive nature. He brought his A game, and it turned her *on*. He missed his next shot, and she rocked back on her heels, practically bouncing with excitement. Lily loved to win and beating a sexy as sin cowboy only made the victory that much sweeter. She was going to win that breakfast and massage. No way was she going to lose.

She bent over the table just as Nate Jackson, one of Jacob's former ranch hands, walked by. He paused and turned back with a smirk. "If that isn't the perfect target, I don't know what is."

She liked Nate well enough, though Jacob hadn't been able to tolerate his brawler mentality. Lily straightened, a grin tugging at her lips. But when her eyes met Levi's, the grin dissolved in an instant. Apparently, her cowboy didn't think the remark had been quite as funny as Lily had.

"Um, Nate, this is Levi." Lily tipped the pool cue in his direction. "Levi, Nate used to work for Jacob."

Lily looked from one man to the other, uncertain of how to proceed without making an already awkward situation worse.

"Nice to meet you, Levi," Nate replied. "Watch out for her." He jerked his chin in Lily's direction. "She's a ringer."

"I have no idea what you're talking about." Lily made sure to infuse her tone with innocence. "But speaking of asses, Nate, I heard yours got handed to you the other night right outside on that sidewalk."

Levi rounded the table. He came up behind Lily, standing so close to her that his wide, muscular chest brushed her back.

Nate snorted. He pushed his hat up a little higher on his head to give Lily a clearer view of a once-blackened eye that had healed to a sickly yellow. "Rancor Culpepper popped me a good one," he said. "But he didn't hand me anything."

Levi pressed tighter against Lily's back. His body went rigid and she let out a nervous laugh. He wrapped his arm possessively around Lily's torso and remained intimidatingly silent behind her as he sized the other man up.

"It's my own fault, though," Nate continued. "I was bored and decided to push his buttons." He looked from Levi to Lily and gave her a wry grin before addressing Levi. "You'll have your hands full with this one."

Levi stepped to the side as though to move forward and Lily shadowed him, placing her body between his and Nate's. She knew he was teasing her and having a little fun, but apparently Levi hadn't gotten the memo.

"I'm a handful?" Lily poked her finger toward his chest. "I'm not the one riling up Rancor Culpepper just because I'm bored. You've definitely got me beat in that department."

Nate's brow quirked with amusement. He glanced again in Levi's direction and Lily was suddenly worried that Nate might just be bored enough to pick another fight in the Broken Horn. Levi didn't seem a damn bit pleased either. His suddenly growly, rigid posturing was about to get on her last nerve. It shouldn't matter if Nate wanted to give her a hard time. Lily was a grown-ass woman. She had plenty of male friends in Deer Haven, not to mention a couple of ex-boyfriends. It's not like she'd been a virgin when she'd met Levi, and likewise, they'd already been over his dating history. Why the jealousy all of a sudden? His aggressive, caveman attitude tonight was throwing her for a loop.

"Who's winning?" Nate turned his attention to the pool table, as though sensing the tension, which embarrassed Lily even more.

"I am."

She and Levi responded at the same time. Lily laughed and gave Levi a playful elbow to the ribs that she hoped would help lighten his mood.

"Guess that's still to be determined," Lily replied. "But I'm pretty sure I've got it in the bag."

"I don't doubt it," Nate said. He gave Lily a playful grin. "You two have a good night. See you around, Levi."

As he walked away, Lily let out the breath she hadn't realized she'd been holding. Levi had certainly shown a new side of his personality tonight. Good grief, she'd seen agitated bulls that were less protective.

Levi turned his attention back to the table. "It's still your turn."

Lily fought to keep from rolling her eyes at his suddenly abrupt tone. If it was going to get under his skin every time a guy talked to her, living in Deer Haven wasn't going to be any fun for him at all. Lily had grown up around the ranch. She'd tagged along with Jacob and his friends and made lifelong friendships with a lot of them. Levi was going to have to get used to a little teasing here and there. And if he didn't like it? Well, too damn bad.

She'd needed tonight to keep her mind off of all of her troubles and the recent turn of events had her mood quickly plummeting. She scratched her next shot and sighed with frustration as Levi retrieved the cue ball. He lined up and slammed the stick into the ball, sending the ten ball with enough force to bounce off the back of the pocket before falling down into the hole. His next two shots found their homes with equal force, and before Lily realized it he'd managed to clear the table, leaving nothing but her remaining solids.

"I win." There was no joy in his victory, though. Levi scowled across the bar in Nate's direction. "Let's go."

So much for having a good night. As Lily returned her cue to the rack on the wall, she couldn't help but wish they'd just stayed home.

Chapter Twenty-One

Levi knew his behavior was childish, but he couldn't stop himself from acting like an ass. He'd never felt an ounce of jealousy in his entire life until tonight. Watching that smug son of a bitch checking out Lily's ass before walking up to the pool table had sent his blood to boiling.

Lily had seemed to think that Nate was a good enough guy. From what he could tell, a little rough around the edges and—as evidenced by his healing eye—a bit of a brawler. Levi shouldn't have cared about him one way or another. But the second he'd started flirting with Lily, his brain had gone into possessive caveman mode.

Lily was his, damn it. And he wanted every single man in Deer Haven to know it.

He watched as Lily huffed out a frustrated breath and went over to the wall to put up her cue. Levi followed, unable to shake his sullen attitude, and hung his stick next to hers. She didn't look at him, barely acknowledged his existence as she grabbed her purse from their bar table and marched toward the door. He followed behind her, no less angry but smart enough to know when not to press his luck.

Lily went straight to her car and without a word got in and pulled out into traffic. Levi raked his hands through his hair as he headed for his truck. He'd managed to fuck up a perfectly good evening and he knew the rest of the night wasn't going to get any better. He hustled to catch up with Lily, starting the engine and getting out into traffic behind her. His cell rang and he reached for the phone, swiping his finger across the screen and putting it on speaker before placing it on the dashboard in front of him.

"Roberts," he answered.

"I put a call in to the warden at California Correctional," Seth Miller said without preamble. "I'll send you the details for the in-person meeting when we have them. Make certain you're available."

He would have preferred to make his own arrangements for follow-up interviews at the prison, but considering their timeline, he wasn't surprised the chief deputy director had already made the call. If Levi had any chance of getting his hands on Brisbee, he needed to do the legwork. Even if that meant leaving Lily in Deer Haven, virtually unprotected.

"Sounds good." He knew Seth wouldn't expect any other response. "I'll be there, sir."

Seth let out a chuff of breath. "Leave early. I don't want to hear any excuses about traffic or anything else. I'm not in the mood for wasting any more time. I want these bastards—and especially Brisbee—in custody before any of them makes it to the Mexico border. An international manhunt requires too damn much red tape. Understand?"

"Completely." Levi had no choice but to be 100 percent compliant after their talk this afternoon.

"I'll expect an update tomorrow when you're done."

"Of course."

"One more thing." Seth's pregnant pause made Levi's gut clench. "I'm arranging for witness protection for Miss Donovan in the event we hit another dead end. She's not going to like it, but if we don't get our hands on Brisbee soon, she's got no other choice."

"I understand." Levi's heart sank. He couldn't manage more than the words his superior demanded to hear at this point.

"I'll look forward to hearing from you tomorrow. Have a good night, Levi."

"You too, sir."

The call ended and Levi stared ahead at the back end of Lily's 4Runner as she turned down the lane toward her house. With a white-knuckle grip, he spun the wheel behind her. His already shitty mood had become downright foul. If the chief deputy director made the decision to put Lily into witness protection, there would be little either of them could do about it. He needed to come clean with Lily, soon. Otherwise, he ran the risk that when she did find out the truth about him the USMS would hide her away somewhere and he'd never get the chance to explain himself or apologize.

Lily pulled up to the house, got out of the car, and walked straight into the house. He pulled up beside her car and killed the engine. His hands remained firmly planted on the steering wheel as he stared straight ahead. He'd never felt so damned helpless in his entire life. He'd lost control of the situation a long time ago, and his impartiality had flown out the window the moment after his very first conversation with Lily.

What a clusterfuck.

He gave her a few moments to decompress before going into the house. The sliding glass patio doors were open and a spring breeze stirred the sheer curtains and brought with it the sweet scent of blooming lilacs. Levi set his keys on the entryway table and headed for the patio. Lily sat in a chair, her legs tucked beneath her, staring out at the western horizon.

The sunset had nothing on her fierce beauty. The golden

glow played off the highlights in Lily's hair, casting an ethereal halo around her. Her expression was no longer angry but contemplative as she hugged her arms around her body as though trying to keep herself whole. Her skin tone warmed with a rosy hue as the sun sank lower on the horizon. Levi had never seen anything on this earth closer to perfection than she was at this very moment, bathed in the setting sun.

"I'm an asshole," Levi said after a moment.

"Yeah," Lily said without turning to look at him. "You are. But I think we've already established that."

Ouch. She could lay him low with the simplest of words. He deserved it, though.

"I'm also a jealous son of a bitch."

"I noticed that." She still refused to look at him. "Not a good look on you."

At least she didn't hold back.

"I'm sorry."

"You should be."

"Lily." Levi paced the length of the porch, feeling very much like a caged animal. "You've got to understand. I'm in uncharted territory here and I—" Damn it, why did he always find himself so tongue-tied with her?

"What?" Lily still refused to look at him.

"The thought of another man looking at you or thinking about you in the way that I do makes me want to beat the shit out of him."

Well, that oughta do it. Levi looked up to the heavens, hoping for some sort of divine intervention, or maybe for a large hole to open up in the earth and swallow him whole. Either would be okay at this point. Lily had just told him she didn't appreciate his jealousy and he responded by going all in with it.

Lily's head turned and she studied him from the corner of her eye. "How do you think of me?" she asked.

"Every time I look at you, all I can think about is how badly I want to get you home, get you naked, and get you on top of me."

Lily turned fully to face him. Her skeptical expression tore at his heart. Did she have no idea how damned beautiful she was? How sexy and desirable? Everywhere they went, men looked at her with open admiration. It took every ounce of control Levi had to keep his mouth shut.

"On top of you?" A smile flirted with the corner of Lily's mouth.

"On top, beneath, in front of . . ." Levi stepped closer to where she sat. "Do you want me to go into detail about all of the ways I want to fuck you?"

"I see." She turned more fully toward him, her earlier anger no longer present in her expression. Instead, Lily's gaze heated and her full lips parted slightly. "How about on the back porch?"

A few simple words were all it took to turn Levi's cock to stone. Any common sense he might have had vanished under the onslaught of Lily's seductive suggestion. He thought of her nipples pebbling in the chilled evening air and swallowed a groan. Not a goddamn thing on this earth would ever tame his desire for her.

"Absolutely." The word came out a little hoarse and rougher than Levi had intended. He could barely form a coherent thought, let alone speak. All he knew for certain was that he had to have Lily.

Right now.

When she'd made the suggestion, she'd never expected Levi to take her up on it. But he'd gotten her so hot and bothered with his gruff voice and sexy talk, she hadn't been able to help herself.

She pushed up from her chair and walked toward Levi. She

kicked off one sandal, and the other, before resting against the porch railing. "If that's the case," she purred, "right here seems as good a place as any."

Levi's heavy boots made the only sounds as he slowly approached her. Lily's heart thundered with anticipation as a riot of butterflies took flight in her stomach. She hoped that feeling never went away. The thrill was intoxicating.

He didn't stop until the walls of his muscular chest touched hers. Lily's nipples tingled from the contact, hardening in an instant. He bent his head to hers, his mouth coming to rest at the shell of her ear. Hot breath met the chill of her skin. "There's something you need to know right now. You're mine, Lily. I don't share, and I won't like it when another man looks at you like Nate looked at you tonight."

Her fingers gripped the porch railing as he nipped at her ear, sending a renewed cascade of chills over her skin. A thrill zinged through Lily's core. Though she'd professed her disappointment in his jealous attitude, his possessive words sparked her desire. There was something decidedly seductive about the way he laid claim to her, and Lily wanted that. She wanted to belong to Levi and no one else.

His hands found her ass as he lifted her up and positioned her on the railing. Lily held on, her breath stalled in her chest as he reached beneath her skirt and moved her underwear aside. His fingers slid across the swollen wet flesh at her core and she sucked in a sharp breath as he dipped briefly inside her.

"This is mine," he murmured before circling her clit. The backs of his fingers stroked along her inner thigh. "This is mine." His hand ventured under her blouse and cupped one breast. "This is mine. Do you understand me, Lily?"

Words refused to form. Lily nodded as her thoughts spun out of control. She was lost to the sensation, lost to Levi's commanding words and the wicked vibration of his voice as he claimed ownership of her body. It was easy to agree. To give herself to him. She never wanted to be touched by another man. She was his. And likewise, he was hers.

He pulled away to look at her. The sun had retreated into the western horizon, leaving nothing more than a dull, gray light. His features sharpened in the shadows, though his gaze burned with an intensity that rivaled the harsh light of day. He reached for the buttons of her blouse and one by one unfastened them, his eyes never leaving hers. A gentle tug pulled one cup of her bra away, and then the other. The cool night air met Lily's breasts and her nipples hardened to pearls as goose bumps dotted her skin.

"You're so beautiful," Levi said. "I don't even think you realize how damned desirable you are."

The pad of his thumb brushed against her nipple and Lily shivered. He kept one hand around her, supporting her on the narrow railing, while he cupped her breast with the other. He teased one nipple and then the other until Lily practically ached with need. The walls of her core contracted, as desperate for attention as the rest of her body. Levi bent down and closed his mouth over one breast and Lily let out a soft moan.

For what felt like forever, he licked, sucked, and nibbled the sensitive flesh. Pleasure coiled and twined within her, and her breaths quickened with every deliberate flick of his tongue. She could come like this. With his mouth at her breasts and her legs wrapped around him. When he pulled away, Lily whimpered. She wanted to beg him not to stop. To continue to tease her until she couldn't take any more of the intense sensation.

The sounds of spring surrounded them. Frogs sang for them. The breeze stirred the trees. Insects buzzed and rustled in the bushes and grass. Lily's senses were awash with nature, her body as exposed as her soul in this moment, her heart close to bursting with love and fulfillment.

She was in love with Levi Roberts, and the realization took her breath away.

Levi reached for his jeans. He loosened his belt and freed the button. A quiet whoosh of the zipper followed, and he reached for the length of his erection, freeing it from his underwear. He guided the swollen head to Lily's opening, brushing against her for a moment.

"You're so damned wet, baby," he said with a groan. "You feel so good."

He drove home and Lily moaned. He filled her completely, perfectly, as though they were made to fit each other this way. She gripped the railing tighter as he pulled out and thrust again, eliciting a gasp from the stab of pleasure. Her heels dug into his ass, urging him deep as he found the perfect rhythm.

"Say you're mine, Lily." His gruff command brooked no argument. "Say it."

"I'm yours, Levi," she said through pants of breath.

"Again."

His thrusts became harder, more desperate as his pace intensified.

"I'm yours." Lily's body felt as though it would collapse on itself. Coiling, drawing inward as her muscles tensed. "Always."

"Come for me, baby." He pushed the words through gritted teeth. He reached for her nipple, rolling it between his thumb and forefinger. "Now."

Lily's universe broke apart in an instant. Waves of sensation pulsed from her core outward, a never-ending tide of pleasure that rushed to the top of her head and tips of her toes. She cried out, wondering how much more she could take. Levi was relentless, refusing to let up as he demanded more.

His body went rigid against hers and he put his forehead to hers as a low groan escaped from between his lips. His wild thrusts stuttered and finally stilled as he came to rest inside her.

The sound of their mingled breaths drowned out everything around them. Evening gave way to night and still they didn't move. Lily abandoned her grip on the railing as her arms wrapped around Levi. She held him to her, refusing to let the heat and comfort of his body go. Tears welled in her eyes and she bit them back. How could she possibly go to the marshals and ask to be placed in protective custody when it would mean leaving her heart behind? She'd rather be dead than live without Levi. She knew now with certainty that she could never let him go.

"You're shivering," Levi said close to her ear. "We should go inside."

Lily nodded, too afraid that the thickness of her throat would betray her emotions if she spoke. She missed the heat, the feel of him, as he pulled away. He hiked up his jeans and scooped Lily into his arms, holding her against his chest as he carried her across the porch to the patio door.

"I can walk, you know."

"I know."

She sensed the smile in his voice as she let her head rest on his shoulder. "I weigh a ton."

"You weigh about as much as a sack of feathers."

Lily snorted as he stepped over the threshold into the house. "I don't, but thanks for saying it."

He continued through the kitchen and dining room, down the hall, and into Lily's bedroom. He set her down on the bed and kicked off his boots as Lily slipped out of her clothes and climbed beneath the covers.

Levi went into the bathroom and Lily turned her eyes from the bright light that flicked on. She'd never known such contentment. The world could crash down around her and as long as she had Levi by her side it wouldn't matter a bit.

The room went dark again, and he climbed into bed beside her. He pulled her close, molding his chest to her back, and she nestled against him as exhaustion began to overtake her.

"Do you need anything, darlin'?" He kissed the back of her head. "You thirsty? Hungry?"

Lily smiled. "I'm okay," she said sleepily. "Do you need anything?"

He gave her a tight squeeze. "Nope. Just a good night's sleep next to you."

The dangers in her life seemed to fade into the background of her mind as sleep overtook her. With Levi's arms around her, nothing could harm her. Lily didn't require another thing to make her happy. She had everything she needed right here.

Chapter Twenty-Two

Lily woke more refreshed and excited to face the day than she had been in years. A beautiful May sun rose higher in the sky and it didn't even bother her that she had to pay up on the bet she'd lost to Levi the night before. He'd kicked her ass fair and square. He'd get breakfast in bed today . . . and a full-body massage tonight.

Her cheeks heated as she relived last night's escapades on the porch. Levi made her brazen. Drove her to the point that the rest of the world melted around them and all was left was the two of them. This morning marked three weeks since they'd ridden the field together at the ranch. Last night had been a turning point for her. Levi's passionate declaration that she was his made her believe that maybe his feelings for her had moved beyond something casual. Lily had begun to hope that perhaps they could have a life together.

A sheet pan of freshly baked biscuits sat on the counter. She split one and put the two halves on a plate before scooping a large ladle full of sausage gravy over them. The savory aroma filled the air and Lily smiled. Every weekend could be like this. Lazy mornings with breakfast in bed and an entire day together ahead of them.

They only had one obstacle to overcome and everything could be perfect.

Lily placed the plate on a tray along with a cup of coffee and a glass of orange juice. She balanced the tray in her hands, careful not to slosh anything as she carried Levi's victory breakfast down the hall. It appeared he'd been up for a while, already showered with a towel wrapped around his narrow waist. Lily's gaze dropped. A simple tug would reveal the glorious length of his manhood and breakfast would be cold by the time they were done.

"A bet's a bet," Lily said as she placed the tray on the bed. "Biscuits and gravy."

"I'm starving."

Levi's heated gaze let Lily know that breakfast wasn't the only thing he was hungry for. Her cheeks heated at the innuendo, but she forced her libido to take the back seat if only for a few minutes. She had an agenda for today and was bound and determined to stick to it.

"I don't doubt it. You worked up quite the appetite last night." Just because she was being a good girl didn't mean she couldn't flirt.

Levi sat down on the bed and swung his legs up onto the mattress. He patted the space next to him and Lily picked up the tray and sat beside him.

"I'd say we both deserve a little breakfast, don't you?" He grabbed the fork and cut off a chunk of gravy-drowned biscuit. Instead of trying it for himself, he brought the fork to Lily's mouth. "Ladies first."

Lily grinned and took the first bite.

"Enjoy your victory breakfast," Lily teased as she hopped off the bed and headed for the bathroom. "It's going to be your last."

Levi's laughter followed her as he dug into the biscuits and gravy. "What are you doing?"

"Jumping in the shower."

Levi leaned forward on the bed, craning his neck to get a look as Lily shucked her pajama bottoms and T-shirt.

"Damn it," he said. "I knew I should have waited to shower."

Lily grinned. She loved his playfulness. She turned on the water and slipped behind the shower curtain. "Next time!" she called to Levi.

"Absolutely, darlin'."

Absolutely was right.

Their lazy Saturday morning had Lily completely relaxed when they pulled up to the ranch. Jacob, Sallie, and Gran had driven to Sacramento for the day, so they had the place to themselves. Because she wasn't interested in spooking the horses and cattle with a bunch of gunshots, she led Levi to the large garage at the south end of the property.

"Let's take the ATVs," she suggested. "It'll be a nice ride."

"Sounds good," Levi said as he loaded a couple of handguns and ammo into a cargo box. "No racing, though."

"What?" Lily said with mock innocence. "Do you actually think I'm that competitive?"

Levi chuckled. "Yes."

Lily shrugged. "Okay, you've got a point. No racing." She reached out her hand and hooked her pinky with Levi's. "Promise. But . . . you have to follow me since I know where we're going."

"Somehow, this feels like a loophole to the whole not-racing thing," Levi said as he climbed onto his machine.

"Of course it is!" Lily replied. She swung a leg over the seat of her ATV and started the engine. "And I don't feel a bit bad about it."

Lily pulled out of the garage and led the way past the

southern end of the property to a dirt trail where two tire tracks had been cut into the grass from continuous wear. The grass was green and lush here, not yet dry from the heat or eaten down by the herd, and wildflowers had begun to pop up from the last rainstorm to roll in.

The sound of the engines drowned everything out, a lovely white noise that left Lily alone with her thoughts. The sweet smell of spring filled her nostrils, the wind blew her hair back from her face, and the sun shone down on her shoulders. She couldn't have asked for a more perfect day.

Levi followed close behind on the trail and Lily waved her arm to urge him beside her. She shouted over the engines, "As much as I like being in the lead, I don't want you to literally eat my dust!"

He offered her a grin that did wicked things to Lily's body. He could affect her with nothing more than a look. But aside from their physical relationship—which couldn't be better—Lily valued Levi's companionship. He had quickly become her best friend. There wasn't anyone she'd rather spend the day with.

A thirty-minute ride found them in one of Lily's favorite spots on the ranch. The terrain wasn't as flat here, and pecan, oak, and mesquite trees dotted the landscape. She pulled up to a grouping of mature red oak and killed the engine. Not far from there, a stream cut into the land, filtering down into the lower fields where the water was used for irrigation.

"It's beautiful here," Levi remarked as he climbed down from his machine. "Like a different world."

"Isn't it?" Lily turned to him and smiled. She'd wanted him to love this place as much as she did, and his reaction was exactly what she'd hoped for. "I used to play here all the time when I was a kid. I'd get in so much trouble."

"Why's that?"

"We were only allowed to go as far as Gran's voice could

carry," Lily said. "If we couldn't hear her calling for us, we were in for it later."

"I can imagine," Levi said. "That's one woman I wouldn't dare cross."

"Oh, she's the queen bee, all right," Lily replied. "The best grandma any kid could ask for."

"I'm sure she was."

Levi's sad smile had Lily backtracking. "I'm sorry. That was insensitive of me. I—"

"You're okay, darlin'," he said. "I'm glad you had her growing up."

Her heart ached for him. Lily's family was so important to her, she couldn't imagine growing up without Shay, her parents, or her grandparents, aunts, uncles, cousins. . . . "I'm glad too. She taught me a lot about strength and fortitude."

"I'm glad for that too."

Their eyes met, and in Levi's honeyed depths Lily saw so much earnest emotion that she had to look away. It seemed impossible that in such a short time she'd fallen so deeply in love with him. There would never be another man for her.

"You ready for your lesson?" Levi opened the cargo container of his machine and retrieved the two guns, a stack of paper targets, and the ammo. He looked around and assessed their surroundings. "Not sure where to hang the targets, though. I don't want to poke any holes in these trees."

Lily knew exactly where the targets could go. With a flourish of her arm, she invited him to follow her and led the way to a section of fence that had fallen into disrepair years ago. She pointed to a tall, sturdy corner post that was still standing. "Will this work?"

Levi walked over and held one of the targets up to judge the width. "This will definitely work."

He secured one of the targets and walked back to the

ATVs. Lily followed and watched as he removed a clip from one gun and opened the cylinder of the other.

"Okay, here we go," Levi said as he jumped right in and began the lesson. "The Ruger is a nine-millimeter. The clip holds fifteen rounds and the casings will eject from the clip with each shot. The Smith and Wesson is a .38 Special, and the cylinder holds six rounds. The casings stay in the cylinder. You have to remove them when you reload."

Lily watched carefully as he pointed out both the clip and the cylinder. "Which one is better?"

"Either one is good," Levi replied. "The clip can easily be replaced in the Ruger, which means if you empty a clip, you can eject it and insert another one quickly. The cylinder is going to be slower. But for self-defense, I think the S and W is going to be the best for you. It's smaller, and if you learn how to shoot it well and with intention one shot is all you're going to need."

Lily hoped she'd never be in a situation where she could test that theory out, but until Graham was found she wanted to know she could at least try to defend herself if she had to.

"I'm going to let you shoot both guns today," Levi continued. Lily marveled at his all-business tone. As though he'd been through this drill before. "The nine-millimeter packs a punch. The S and W is going to be a little gentler. But I want you to get a feel for both of them."

Lily nodded. "Okay. I've shot a twelve-gauge shotgun before. When I was a kid. It definitely had a kick."

"This won't be like shooting a shotgun," Levi explained. "But we'll practice until you feel confident. We have a couple of boxes of ammo and I'm in no hurry."

"That's good," Lily said with a laugh. "Because it might take me all day to get the hang of it."

"No way," he said. "My girl can do anything."

My girl. Lily loved being his. And his confidence in her gave her a renewed sense of strength. She could do anything.

Levi tried to keep it light, but deep down he was all business. This wasn't something to be taken lightly, and he wanted Lily to leave this place today confident that if she had to she could aim the gun at another human being and pull the trigger. It was something he'd been trained to do, first in the Army, and then with the marshals service. He knew it wasn't an easy thing to do, even in a situation where it was your life or the other guy's.

"Before we load the weapons, I want you to get a feel for them." He closed the cylinder on the Smith & Wesson and handed it to her. "Just hold it. Let your fingers wrap around the grip, but not too tightly. Get used to the weight of it."

He held the pistol, barrel toward him, and handed it to her. Lily took the grip in her palm and turned the barrel away from him—her common sense putting her ahead in the lesson—and studied it. She held it out in front of her and looked down the sight. Rotated her wrist, tilting it to one side and then the other.

"It's heavy," she said, turning to look at him. "But not as bad as I thought it would be."

"You can handle both of these, no problem," Levi said. "I just think that one will be easier for you to shoot."

She turned and set the revolver on the back end of the ATV next to the 9mm. Levi picked it up and handed it to her.

"This one will be heavier with the clip in place," he explained. "The grip is a little wider too."

"Yeah." Lily studied it in much the same way as the revolver. "My hand doesn't fit it quite as well. And even without the clip, it's heavier than the other one."

"Yep." Levi waited while she acquainted herself with the

gun. "It's got stopping power but is going to be tougher for you to aim if you have to act quickly."

"How do you know so much about all of this?"

Levi cleared his throat. He tipped back the brim of his hat to get a good look at her. Lily studied him, a single brow arched with curiosity. Damn, he loved her inquisitive nature and inability to accept something at face value. Lily wasn't happy until she knew something inside and out. Including him.

"The Rangers," he answered simply. "I'm a trained marksman."

Lily looked to the sky. "Of course." She let out a humorous snort. "I don't know why I asked."

"I'm glad you did." Levi never wanted her to apologize for something like that. "You can ask me anything."

Lily gave him a wry grin. "How good a shot are you?"

Levi held out his hand. Lily passed him the 9mm and he grabbed the clip from the back of the ATV and slid it into place. He dug in the bag and produced two pairs of earmuffs. He handed Lily a pair and put a pair on himself. When her ears were properly protected, Levi brought up the weapon, sighted it to the target, and gently squeezed the trigger.

Lily gripped the cups of the earmuffs tightly against her head with the report of the gun. Levi lowered the weapon, fighting the urge to appreciate his shot while at the same time staying humble. But damn, he hadn't missed a beat.

"Wow!" Lily shouted over the ear protection. "That was amazing!"

Levi fought back a grin. He hiked a casual shoulder. "It's okay."

"Are you kidding?" She removed the earmuffs and he followed suit. "It was better than okay. You hit the center of the target."

"If you practice enough," Levi said, "you'll be able to do it too."

"I doubt that," Lily scoffed. "But I'm ready to give it a try."

"That's my girl."

Lily's gaze warmed as a bright smile lit her face. The midday sun had nothing on her brilliance and Levi was struck by her beauty. She had his heart. If anything ever happened to her, he'd never recover from the loss.

"Can I try that one?" Lily pointed to the Ruger in his hand.

"Absolutely."

It was going to kick, but Levi wanted her to experience the power behind the weapon. The revolver would be easier for her to handle, but he didn't want her to be afraid to shoot the 9mm. He hoped that in time he could help her to become confident to use a wide array of firearms and be accurate as well.

"Can you help me?"

As though he'd turn her loose without any instruction. Levi waved her over and she came to stand beside him. He pointed her toward the target and put the Ruger in her hand.

"Don't put your finger on the trigger until you're ready to shoot," he said close to her ear. "This is the safety." He flipped it on and then off. "This is how you disengage it. There's going to be recoil, but as long as you keep a firm grip, it's not going to kick much. Stand with your legs hip width—a little more if you feel more comfortable—and bring your arms up."

Lily did as he asked, taking care to position her body. She brought the gun up and aimed it at the target. Her heady perfume wafted to Levi's nostrils and he took a moment to breathe in the sweet scent.

"Don't hold your breath." Levi needed the reminder as much as Lily. "Breathe through the shot. Slow and steady. Sight it just high of where you want to hit. The bullet is a little heavy and will fall a bit after you shoot. When you're ready, move your finger to the trigger. Don't squeeze it. Just increase the pressure. Hold the grip tight," he reminded her. "Don't lock your arms, but keep them strong."

Lily let out a quiet laugh. "That's a lot of information to take in all at once."

"You've got this," he said. "We'll stay here all day if that's what it takes."

"It might."

Levi placed a kiss on her temple. "Nah. You're going to be a natural. I can feel it."

"Okay," Lily said on a breath. "Here goes."

"Hang on." Levi chuckled as he brought the earmuffs from around Lily's neck and placed them over her ears. He put his on as well and gave her a tap to the backside. "Okay, darlin'. Now."

Levi took a step back and to the left. Lily stood still as she looked down the barrel of the Ruger. Her finger slid over the trigger. She took a few breaths.

Pop!

The report of the gun rang out. Her arms kicked up, but Lily was able to control the recoil—much better than he'd expected for her first time. She engaged the safety, the barrel of the gun pointing down, and turned to face Levi.

"You okay?" Levi removed his ear protection. His brow furrowed as she appeared a little shaky.

"I'm okay." Lily reached up and removed her earmuffs. "Not gonna lie, I hope I never have to use this thing in a real-life situation. That's a lot of power to try and control. How did I do?" She shielded her eyes against the sun. "I didn't look."

Levi looked past her to the target. *Damn. Not bad at all for a first-timer.* "You did amazing," he said. "But I hope you never have to use it in real life too."

"Whew." Lily blew out a relieved breath. "Now that that's out of the way, let's try the revolver."

Levi couldn't be prouder of her. His brave Lily.

As she placed the Ruger on the ATV and reached for the revolver, he made a silent promise that he would always be there to protect her, so she would never again have to know the fear of having to protect herself.

Chapter Twenty-Three

The sharp chime of Levi's phone woke him. He pushed up on an elbow and looked over Lily's shoulder to find her still fast asleep beside him. The glow from the screen illuminated the bedroom and he reached for the nightstand, unlocking the cell to check the text message.

Davis is in custody. Meet tomorrow in Susanville for questioning. Plane is still scheduled for pickup.

Levi fired back a quick 10–4 and put his phone back on the nightstand. Looked like he had a long day ahead of him, and he needed a few more hours' sleep before he headed to the prison in Susanville. This could be the break they needed in locating Brisbee and getting his ass back to prison where he belonged. He reached over and smoothed a hand over Lily's hair while she slept.

"I love you, Lily," he whispered. "I'm going to do my best to make sure this is over soon."

Levi parked his truck and walked to the black SUV waiting for him a few parking spaces away. The back passenger side door opened as he approached, and Levi climbed inside to find Mitch McDonald sitting behind the driver. This was a high-profile case and at the top of his department's priority list. The rest of the fugitive recovery team was in Albuquerque, so it looked like today's interrogation was going to be a two-man show.

"He was apprehended just about to cross the border at Juárez," Mitch said, all business. "Air marshals flew him in last night and he was transported to Susanville. He's in isolation. I didn't want him to have the opportunity to talk to anyone and get a message to Brisbee or Bloom. The press doesn't know he's been taken into custody and it's going to stay that way for the time being. It's a pretty good assumption they're watching media outlets."

Levi rolled his shoulders to try to release some of the tension that had settled there. The less Brisbee knew, the better.

"I put a call in to Dwight Davidson to give him a heads-up and I'm going to send a couple of deputy marshals to Deer Haven and the surrounding towns, in case our theory about Brisbee is correct. As of right now, and because of Lily Donovan's request for autonomy and anonymity, Miller wants it kept quiet, but he's ready to put her into witness protection if need be, depending on what Davis tells us—or doesn't tell us—today."

"What makes you think he'll say anything at all?" Levi was glad there would be deputy marshals looking out for Brisbee in Deer Haven, but he didn't trust anyone other than himself to protect Lily. He couldn't get back to town soon enough. "Brisbee has to have threatened both of his accomplices to buy their silence in the event either one of them was caught."

"I don't doubt it," Mitch agreed. "We're prepared to offer Davis a very sweet deal in order to buy his cooperation."

Levi scoffed. "What makes you think Brisbee hasn't already bought his unconditional loyalty?"

Mitch hiked a shoulder. "If he wants to rot in prison, that's his choice."

Levi's jaw clenched. He hated hypotheticals. He'd beat the truth out of the bastard if that's what it took. He wasn't leaving that prison today until he knew *everything* Davis knew.

With the mini briefing concluded, Levi retrieved his lanyard with his badge from his pocket and looped it around his neck. He checked his cell for any messages from Lily—nothing—and set the ringer to silent before exiting the SUV with Mitch. As they walked to the prison's entrance, nervous energy pooled in his gut and he stretched his neck from side to side. He had years of experience in interrogation and negotiation. He knew the tactics. But he'd never been about to step into a room with a fugitive whose information might determine the safety of someone he loved.

Seth had been right to call him out on his attachment to Lily. Levi could no longer be objective and he knew it. All he had to do was hold it together long enough to get through their interview with Davis without succumbing to the urge to beat the bastard to a bloody pulp. He took a deep, cleansing breath and let it out slowly.

Keeping his cool would be easier said than done.

"I want to get right to the point with him," Mitch said as he reached for the door handle. "I'm not dicking around. We'll present our offer, give him a chance to play ball, and if he won't, he'll go back to solitary. I'm not wasting time."

"Perfect." Levi couldn't agree more. The last thing he needed was to waste a day—or more—in Susanville when where he needed to be was back home with Lily. "Let's see what he knows."

Once inside the prison, Levi and Seth presented their badges and IDs. They were required to hand over their sidearms and cell phones, which was protocol, and Levi reluctantly handed his phone over to the prison guard, who placed it in a plastic bin just outside of the metal detector.

His nerves ratcheted another notch and he rolled his shoulders. He'd only been awake for a few hours, and already it had been one hell of a day.

"You okay?" Mitch gave him a sidelong glance as they followed a guard to the interview room where Davis would be. "I need you to be one hundred percent today."

"I'm good." It was only sort of an exaggeration. He simply needed to put his worry on the back burner and he'd be fine. "Long night."

"I know Seth already laid into you," Mitch replied. "And you probably don't need to hear it from me too, but you're not going to be any good to anyone if your head isn't in the game."

Levi wasn't surprised that Mitch had been made aware of his conversation with the chief deputy director. God, it was a wonder he was still on the job as badly as he'd managed to fuck this up. Mitch was right, though. Levi owed it to Lily to be at the top of his game. Emotions aside, he needed to focus on the task at hand and doing the job he was here to do. Instead of obsessing over his worry for Lily, he needed to focus on his training and the objective: locate and arrest Graham Brisbee.

The interview room they were led into was empty. Gave them the upper hand for Davis to see two U.S. Marshals waiting for him when he walked in. Levi took a seat while Mitch spoke briefly with the guard. He grabbed a chair and they waited in silence until the guard returned and approached the door a few minutes later.

"You sure you're good?" Mitch asked again.

"Five by five."

The door swung open and Max Davis was escorted into the room. His eyes widened slightly and his step faltered before the guard urged him forward to the empty chair opposite the table from Levi and Mitch. His handcuffs were secured to a length of chain attached to the table and his ankles were left bound. Aside from a black eye and a scrape to the forehead, David didn't look as bad as Levi had expected.

Too bad.

"This is Deputy U.S. Marshal Levi Roberts, and I'm Assistant Chief Deputy Director Mitch McDonald. Let's go ahead and just cut the shit right now and lay it all out on the table. We know that Brisbee put you up to the prison break. We also know he used you to get out of here. You had information he found valuable; otherwise, you'd likely be dead right now. So, here's the deal: You tell us what we want to know today, and there might be a possibility you'll see the light of day again before you're ninety. If you decide to make this difficult for yourself, we can make sure the only view you have for the rest of your life is four concrete walls. Understand?"

A moment of silence passed as Davis sized them up. He'd been sentenced to ten to fifteen for drug trafficking and assault with a deadly weapon. Not the hardest criminal Levi had dealt with, but just wily enough to know how to work the system—and other criminals—in order to come out on top.

"You wouldn't be talking to me right now if you had Brisbee in custody," Davis stated with a smirk. "What about Derrick Bloom? What makes you think Brisbee didn't use him for his escape and I just tagged along?"

Levi rolled his eyes. Did he really think they were that stupid? "You were Brisbee's cellmate. According to prison records, Bloom had little to no contact with Brisbee. While you, on the other hand, worked the kitchen with him four days a week. That's how you got out of here, right?" Levi leaned forward in his seat, braced his elbows on the table as he studied Davis. "You hitched a ride on a food service truck on delivery day."

As though to mock Levi's uptight posture, Davis took the opposite stance and leaned as far back as his shackled wrists would allow. The defiant show did nothing more than piss Levi off and he coached himself to keep his temper in check and stick to Mitch's plan.

"You're not getting out of here," Levi stated. "And we're going to catch Brisbee. The question is, do you want to be left in general population with him when he gets back here, or do you want to know what we can do to protect you from him?"

The cocky smile melted from Davis's face as realization sank in. He sat up straighter in his chair and looked from Levi to Mitch.

"I'm listening."

Monday morning, Lily sat in Sallie's office at Dillerman's, thumbing through a *Better Homes and Gardens* magazine while she finished up a phone call. They were meeting Shay and a few other friends for lunch, but Sallie had to run by the office for a few minutes first to clear up a delivery issue with one of their suppliers. Levi had traveled to Sacramento for the day—he was meeting one of his old Army buddies—and though she appreciated a girls' day, she couldn't wait to be home again, snuggled up on the couch with him.

". . . I appreciate your help. I'll let you know if we run into any more problems. Thanks." Sallie ended the call and let out a slow sigh before shutting down her computer. "I swear, ranchers never rest. This is a twenty-four-seven job."

Lily laughed. "No rest for the wicked."

"Are you ladies talking about me again?" Justice Culpepper leaned into Sallie's office doorway, a smug grin on his handsome face. "Sallie, you're a married woman," he chided. "But Lily, you can talk about me as much as you want."

Sallie looked over at Lily and rolled her eyes. Justice's overabundance of confidence never let him miss an opportunity to put his notorious flirting skills to good use. He should have known better than to pull that crap on Lily, though. She'd rather swallow glass than flirt with Justice.

"Oh, I talk about you all the time," Lily remarked. "Just yesterday I was telling Sallie that no one pulls off the Hells Angels wannabe look better than you."

Justice smiled, but the expression didn't reach his eyes. The Culpepper brothers were raw, rowdy, and tantalizing. But lord would they ever be a handful for the women stalwart enough to take them on. Especially Justice. If he simply learned a little humility, it would do him wonders in the dating department.

"If I didn't know any better," Justice said, "I'd think you pride yourself on being a pain in the ass, Lily."

"I absolutely pride myself on it." Lily showcased her pride with a wide, Cheshire cat grin. "Especially when it's in regard to you."

Justice pretended not to hear her as he turned to Sallie. "Hey, what's Jacob up to today? I stopped by the ranch a while ago and he wasn't there."

"You know," Sallie mused, "it's not my day to look after him, Justice. He didn't say what he was doing today. Want me to give him a message?"

"No thanks, Sallie. I want to talk to him in person."

His gaze wandered to Lily and lingered there. She nearly squirmed under the intense scrutiny. If he didn't watch it, she was liable to throw Sallie's stapler at him.

"Okay," Sallie said, perplexed. "If you can't get him on his phone, I'm sure he's around the ranch somewhere."

"Probably right," Justice agreed. "Ran into Sheriff Davidson last night." His gaze remained locked on Lily. "Had a pretty interesting conversation that I'm pretty sure Jacob would be interested in."

"Huh." Lily was tired of being looked at like she was about to sprout a third eye at any second. "I'm sure he'll be positively thrilled to hear your gossip. I swear, you're all as bad as a bunch of old hens, cackling."

The humor faded from his face, followed by a dark intensity that made Lily's nerves crank even tighter. "What's Levi up to today? I heard you two have been spending a lot of time together."

Lily's hackles rose. It was no one's—especially Justice Culpepper's—business who she spent time with. She swore he gossiped more than Gran, and that was saying something. First Jacob and now Levi? What was he getting at?

"I don't really think that's any of your business," Lily quipped.

"Maybe not," Justice said with a shrug. "But it should be yours, don't you think?" He made a show of tipping his hat in Lily's direction. "Ladies," he said in parting as he pushed himself from the doorjamb and left.

Lily and Sallie exchanged curious glances.

"What in the hell was that all about?" Sallie's perplexed expression echoed Lily's feelings completely. "I mean, Justice is always a little . . . you know . . ."

"Nosy, cocky, bossy, and generally annoying?" Lily shook her head ruefully. "I have no idea what motivates him. And he thinks I'm a pain in the ass."

"Yeah." Lily laughed. "But seriously, that was just weird."

"I guess I'll find out what it's all about when I get home tonight. How much do you wanna bet Justice is headed back out to the ranch to hunt Jacob down right now? He'd better watch out, though. If he cops an attitude with Gran, she'll toss him out on his ass."

Lily nodded solemnly. "No one messes with her family."

A sense of unease settled like a stone in Lily's stomach. Was Justice trying to tell her that Levi was hiding something from her? Sallie had been sure Levi had taken the day off to go to Fairfield a couple of weeks ago, and when she'd asked him about it he'd brushed it off, saying he'd been at the ranch all day. And now Levi was in Sacramento—or at least that's where he said he was going, only to have someone drop in on her and cast doubt on him yet again.

"What do you think he meant?" The more she thought about it, the more Lily couldn't let it go. "Do you think he wanted to talk to Jacob about Levi?"

Sallie shrugged. "Your guess is as good as mine. I think Justice just likes to stir the pot. Likely he's just upset that he has a little competition. He doesn't like it when he's not the center of attention and lusted after by every woman in Deer Haven."

Sallie had a point. Not that Lily would ever revisit that again. "It's still weird, though."

As she sat down at the restaurant with Lily and Shay, Sallie said, "Let Jacob deal with Justice."

"Sounds good." Lily could use a little levity. She had so much on her mind, all she wanted was a day where she didn't have to overthink anything. "The less I have to think about Justice at all, the better."

But she couldn't erase from her mind the encounter with the smug rancher no matter how hard she tried.

Lily had never been the sort of clingy type to check up on a boyfriend when he wasn't around. But she stared at the home screen of her phone now, wondering if she should do just that. She opened a new message, her fingers hovering over the keyboard as she tried to think of an excuse to text Levi and check in with him. But what if Justice had been pushing her buttons? Purposely trying to plant a seed of doubt in Lily's mind. She wouldn't put it past him, but it seemed as though Levi had been taking a fair amount of time off of work the past week. The last thing she needed was something else to overthink. She wished Justice had just kept his big mouth shut.

"Hey? You okay?" Shay leaned in toward Lily and spoke close to her ear. "You're sort of disconnected today."

Her mind was a million miles away. "Would you say Justice is malicious or just an asshole?"

Shay's brow furrowed. "Is this a loaded question?"

"Sort of."

"Definitely an asshole," Shay replied. "But I don't think he's malicious. Why? What did the son of bitch do this time?"

"Nothing." It was bad enough that Sallie had been there to hear the doubt Justice had cast on Levi. She didn't want Shay to know as well. "He just likes pushing my buttons."

"We've known that for a while now." Shay reached for her glass and took a pull from the straw. "But nothing's going to change that."

True. And maybe that's all his visit to Sallie's office had been. Another attempt to get under Lily's skin.

"You give any more thought to our conversation the other day?" Shay angled her body toward Lily's to block out the rest of the women at the table and give them a little privacy.

"Yeah." Lily let out a slow breath. It would be hypocritical to be upset at Levi for potentially hiding something from her when she had been anything but forthright with him. If she wanted a future with him—and she did—it was time to come clean. "I'm going to talk to Levi tonight. I can't make this decision on my own."

"I've got your back no matter what," Shay said. "You know that, right?"

"I do. Thanks."

Lily just hoped that she could be brave enough to tell Levi the truth. Because it might end up costing her everything.

Chapter Twenty-Four

Lily sat on the couch, her legs resting on Levi's lap. She'd lost her nerve to sit down and talk to him about her past, and the possible present threat to her life, the moment she'd walked through the door. Something was eating at Levi as well. He wasn't in a bad mood per se, but he'd been quieter than usual and the silence between them was more disconcerting than any conversation they may or may not have had.

His thumbs kneaded the bottom of one foot as they watched some obstacle course show. Lily had lost interest somewhere around contestant number three and flipped on her tablet to browse social media in order to distract her mind from the worry that ate away at her. Tiny rivulets of pleasure ran from the soles of her feet to the top of her head, making her feel more liquid than anything solid. Forget social media. Levi was the best distraction on the planet.

A contented sigh slipped from between Lily's lips as she peeked up from the screen to admire Levi's strong profile, the sharp cut of his jaw, and the dark lashes that nearly brushed his eyebrows. His attention was focused on the television, but she couldn't take her eyes from him. He was perfect. How did she ever get so lucky to find someone so perfect for her?

Or was all of this too good to be true?

This was all she'd ever wanted. Peace, love, security. To feel content with another person, to draw from an endless well of passion. To laugh and experience the freedom that only comes from being with someone who understands you, truly loves you, and wants you to thrive. Lily had known control. She'd known abuse and manipulation. Levi had shown her that it was possible to overcome the traumas in her life—or, at the very least, learn to live with them—by allowing herself to be vulnerable, to bare her heart and soul, and to trust someone to treat her the way she deserved to be treated.

Levi would never lie to her or deceive her. If Justice thought he had something to hide, that was his problem. He'd wanted to rile Lily and pique her curiosity, but honestly, she didn't care. Whatever had gotten Justice's shorts in a knot today, she was certain it had nothing specifically to do with Levi.

"That feels so good." Lily set her tablet on the end table and sank deeper into the couch cushions. She patted the space beside her. "If you put your legs up here, I'll rub your feet too."

"As much as I appreciate the offer, I'm going to pass." Levi applied pressure to the insole of Lily's foot and she nearly groaned with pleasure. "My feet are so ticklish, you wouldn't make it past getting my socks off."

She loved that she learned something new about him almost every day. "Seriously?" She flashed a mischievous grin.

"Don't even think about it," Levi warned.

"Where else are you ticklish?"

"Rule number one: Never volunteer information that exposes a weakness."

Levi traced the tip of his finger along the bottom of Lily's foot, over her toes, to the top of her foot and her ankle. She shivered as he made his way along her shin, to her knee, and then slowly circled under her leg and back down. A tiny spasm shook the muscle as she stifled a giggle.

"You're not playing fair," she pointed out.

"Who said anything about playing fair?"

Lily reached for Levi's foot, but he was too fast. He sat upright and grabbed Lily around the waist. She let out a squeal as he rolled her from the couch onto the carpet, careful to cradle the fall so he took the impact. He pinned her to the floor and Lily sucked in a breath through her laughter. She exhaled in a loud snort that caused Levi to laugh as well, and he let go of her, rolling to his back as he guffawed at the ceiling.

"God, I love you."

Lily stopped laughing and turned to look at Levi, his laughter still shaking his chest. She turned and crawled over him, her mood no longer playful. A quick swing of her leg had her straddling his thighs. Levi's laughter died as well and the look in his eyes sparked with heat.

She reached for his belt and tugged it free of the buckle. The button of his jeans popped open beneath her fingertips, followed by the quiet tick of his zipper as she lowered it tooth by tooth. She curled her fingers around his underwear, the backs of her fingers skimming the V where his hips met his torso. Levi sucked in a breath and Lily let her hands venture beneath his shirt to trace the topography of washboard muscle that lined his stomach.

"I love the way your hands feel on me."

Lily's emotions heightened her desire for him. His words twined around her heart like unyielding vines, securing her permanently to him. She pushed up his shirt higher on his chest and placed a kiss between his pecs. Along his torso, and lower to where the delicate trail of hair formed a line from his belly button to below the waistband of his underwear.

She eased his pants down over his hips. Levi thrust upward, lifting Lily as well, and she teetered for a moment before grounding her toes on the carpet and sliding the denim over the tight globes of his ass.

The hard length of his erection sprang free and Lily bent to place a wanton kiss on the top of the swollen head. Levi's thighs tensed beneath her, twin steel beams that held her weight with no effort. She braced her hands on either side of his hips and she pushed herself lower, over his shins, as she laid her body against his and placed the flat of her tongue at the base of his cock and licked the length of his shaft.

"Sweet mercy, Lily." Levi's hips bucked as he drew in a sharp breath. "You sure know how to torture a man."

She gripped the thick base of his erection, which her fingers could barely enclose, and held him tight as she sealed her mouth over the crown. She sucked deeply before sliding downward, taking as much of him as she could. A low groan was all the encouragement she needed to repeat the motion, pulling up to the head and sucking it gently before sliding back down.

He was almost too big, but oh how she loved it. She teased him for a while. Let her mouth linger on his cock with slow, easy strokes, languorous licks, and deep sucks that made his body rigid and his breathing labored.

"Just like that," Levi rasped. "Take it all, baby."

His heated words encouraged her wanton behavior. She made a meal of him, devouring every inch of him as she found a rhythm that Levi matched with the thrust of his hips. God, she loved the feel of him sliding against her lips, filling her mouth. Lily couldn't get enough, couldn't take him deep enough to satisfy her want of him. His fingers wound through her hair, gripping but not demanding as he held her where he wanted her. A moan vibrated in Lily's throat and Levi shuddered. His muscles grew tense and his thrusts became more desperate.

"Baby, if you don't stop, I'm going to come."

She wanted him to. Wanted to taste him and have him at her mercy in the midst of his pleasure. She wanted to be in control. To decide when it was enough. And she knew she wouldn't be satisfied until he was.

Lily squeezed the base of his cock in her hand as she kept up the unrelenting glide of her mouth over his shaft. She came up high on her knees, brushing the sides of her breasts along his inner thighs as she brought him closer to the edge. Levi's head fell back against the couch cushion. He groaned and tightened his grip on her hair, sending a heated, wet rush through Lily's core.

"Lily."

Her name was a low, sensual growl as his pleasure overtook him. His cock pulsed against her lips as a rush of warmth coated the back of her tongue. Lily took ownership of the moment, reveling in the pleasure she'd given him and taken for herself. It was an aphrodisiac like no other. Her clit throbbed and her nipples ached. She'd never known such ecstasy. Such sweet, delicious torture.

Levi's thrusts became shallow as his body relaxed. He released his grip on Lily's hair, caressing the length of it as she continued to lick, kiss, and suck.

"Lily . . . ," Levi said on a deep sigh. "My Lily."

Her heart soared as emotion welled in her chest. She pulled away to look at him. So many words—the truths she'd kept from him—formed on her tongue, but fear kept her from saying them aloud. Lily was afraid to love. Afraid to trust. Afraid of the uncertainty, the fragility, of her life and the knowledge that it might crumble around her at any minute. She was afraid of Levi and everything he made her feel and dare to hope for.

And mostly, she was afraid of what she might have to do to protect herself and the possibility of having to leave her life as she knew it—including Levi—behind.

"Let me love you, Lily." Levi's voice was still rough with passion. Her eyes met his and she wondered if he realized the double meaning in his words. "Let me make you feel as good as you make me feel. Let me take care of you."

That's all she wanted, and it went so much deeper than something simply physical. Lily wanted real and honest and she'd finally found that with Levi. She just had to be brave enough to trust him with the truth.

The vulnerability reflected in the depths of Lily's hazel eyes nearly gutted Levi. There was so much she didn't know. So much he needed to tell her. What had started out as a cut-and-dried undercover assignment had turned into an emotional roller coaster that was bound to get Levi fired.

And honestly, he didn't have a single shit to give. If he had to do it all again, he wouldn't change a thing. He'd risk it all to have her. His reputation, his career, everything he'd worked so hard for. He'd give it all up in an instant to make her his forever. Levi was in love with Lily Donovan. Nothing else in this world mattered to him but her.

He'd put it off long enough. They'd talk. Tomorrow. He'd lay it all out, tell her everything, and pray that she'd forgive him for his duplicity. But for tonight, he'd love her, hold her, and cherish her in the way that she deserved.

Levi reached out for Lily's hand and pulled her to her feet. He undressed her, first stripping her shirt from her torso and up her arms and then unhooking her bra and slowly urging the straps from her shoulders to reveal the glorious swell of her breasts. He eased down her pajama bottoms and underwear, steadying her as she stepped out of them.

Every inch of her was perfection. He sat before her in worship, in awe of her beauty. Levi's palms swept over her satin skin with purpose, laying claim to her. He held her waist between his hands before gliding upward, cupping the weight of her breasts as his thumbs brushed the erect nipples that seemed to strain for his touch. His fingertips rotated inward, over her chest, and outward again as he smoothed his hands over her shoulders, down her arms to her fingertips, back to her hips and down the outsides of her thighs, to the roundness of her calves, up the backs of her legs, to hold her perfect ass in his grip as he bent to place a kiss on the softness of her belly.

She let out a slow, contented sigh and the sound slipped over his skin like a caress. Simply touching Lily was electric. He was hard as stone, ready for her again.

He pulled her to him, settling her knees on either side of him so she straddled him. She lowered her body, to glide over him, but he stopped her. "Not yet."

Levi reached between her thighs and swept his fingertips through the slick folds of her pussy. Lily sucked in a breath as a tremor shook her. She was so wet for him, practically dripping, her thighs coated with the evidence of her arousal. He wanted her shaking with need before he took her.

He bent to one breast and sucked her nipple into his mouth while his fingertip found the hard knot of nerves at her core. Lily's hands went to his shoulders, her nails biting into the skin. Levi moved in slow circles while he suckled her, nibbled at her nipple, and brought her to the edge of her control.

It didn't take long before her thighs trembled and her mewling sobs of pleasure echoed in his ears. Levi didn't waste a moment to pull her down on top of him, driving home in a single stroke.

He'd never get enough of her. The moment her tight heat enveloped him Levi was ready to go off again. She cried out and her inner walls squeezed him, the contractions milking him dry. They came together, instantly, almost violently, and when it was over they collapsed against each other, breathing through the remnants of their pleasure until Levi wasn't sure where his body ended and Lily's began.

"I love you, Lily." Levi buried his face in her hair as he spoke. "So much. I fell in love with you the moment I saw you leaning over that fence. I love your fire and your wit and your determination. I love your mind and your body and everything that makes you, you. I've built a wall around myself that I refused to take down for anyone or anything. I don't let people get close, but I let you, and that scares the shit out of me. I don't know how to be in a relationship; I have no fucking clue what I'm doing. But I want to try. For you."

Quiet moments passed and Levi's gut bottomed out. Had he said too much too soon?

Lily's arms wound tight around him. She kissed his shoulder. His neck. Below his ear. One hand reached up, her fingers grazing the back of his neck before winding in his hair to tease the strands. She took a deep breath, pressing the generous swell of her breasts against his chest. When she breathed out, a shudder passed through her, into him.

"Levi." The word was little more than a whisper. "I love you too."

He held her tight and kissed her temple.

"I don't know what I'm doing either." Lily's throat constricted with emotion and fought to keep her tears at bay. "I—" Words lodged between her chest and lips, her fear preventing her from speaking. So she started with what was easy. "There's so much I love about you. And sometimes I wonder how it's possible to fall so deeply in love in such a short time. I haven't even learned everything about you, but

I know that I'll love each new thing. I love your confidence and your strength. Your humor and mind. Your dedication and work ethic. I even love your jealous streak and the fact that you can frustrate me just as easily as you can make me laugh. I love that there's depth to you and that I haven't even hit the bottom of it yet. I love the way I feel when I'm with you. Like nothing in the world could ever hurt me."

He held her tighter and buried his face in her hair. "I'll always protect you, darlin'."

"It's been hard for me." Lily's chest tightened. "Sallie knows. And Shay. But sometimes I don't think they even realize." She rambled, unable to articulate the damage that had been done to her. She prayed that Levi might understand. "I was so stupid. So trusting and just . . . naïve. I thought he was brilliant and edgy and sophisticated. I thought he was pushing me, teaching me. But it was all a lie. He manipulated me. Used me." Lily bit back a sob. "And when he was done playing his games and had messed me up emotionally, he—"

"Shhh." Levi stroked her hair as he held her tight. "It's okay, Lily. You don't have to say any more."

"Anxiety. Panic attacks. Nightmares. It makes me feel weak and pathetic. It's not fair for you to have to deal with that. I've been pretty good lately about keeping it bottled up, but I wouldn't blame you for not wanting to live with someone who's so screwed up."

Levi pulled away. A deep crease marred his handsome brow as he studied her. His gaze burned, and his jaw squared. He reached up to swipe the tears from her cheeks. "You are a victim, Lily, and there's no shame in that. Someone you trusted took advantage of you and hurt you. You don't have to feel any blame for it either. You went through hell and you deserve to feel however the hell you want about it. I've seen what trauma does to a person. I know stalwart soldiers who've grappled with PTSD. And not a goddamn one of them is weak or pathetic. There is no expiration date on healing or how you get to find peace. And I would *never* abandon you because of it. I'm in love with you, Lily Donovan. And there isn't anything on this earth that's going to come between us. I'm not going anywhere."

"You're stuck with me too. I hope you know that."

"Good." Levi kissed her gently. "Now that that's settled. Let me take you to bed."

Tomorrow. She'd tell him the rest tomorrow. But for tonight, all she wanted was to lie in bed next to him and feel his strong arms around her.

Suddenly, Lily's future didn't seem quite as uncertain or frightening. As long as she had Levi, she had everything she'd ever need.

Chapter Twenty-Five

Lily woke up refreshed, despite having slept less than a few hours the night before. What a roller-coaster ride of emotions. She'd gone from passion, to sorrow, to fear, and right back around to passion. They'd solidified their relationship last night. Spoken words of love and devotion that anchored them to each other. Nothing and yet everything had changed last night. And there was no turning back from it.

The hot water sluiced down Lily's body. Levi had left early for the ranch. According to Levi, the crew had a long day ahead of them and Jacob wanted everyone ready to go before the sun was up. He'd kissed Lily goodbye and told her that they needed to talk tonight. A tiny shiver of trepidation raced through Lily's veins. They definitely needed to talk. She wondered what he could possibly want to talk about. It couldn't possibly be as bad as what she wanted to discuss with him.

After everything they'd said to each other last night, Lily hoped he wouldn't be too upset with her. He'd told her he loved her and promised to protect her. The connection between them had deepened last night. He'd opened himself up to her and she'd done the same. They'd revealed the darkness that cast shadows on their lives to each other and found comfort in it. With his touch, Levi had banished the demons that plagued her and distracted her from her own traumatic memories. She'd put her trust and faith in Levi last night. And in the depth of her soul, she knew that trust hadn't been misplaced.

But it definitely took them into new territory as far as their relationship went. Levi had readily admitted that he wasn't a "relationship" guy. He'd been open and honest with her, but at the same time Lily didn't think he was the kind of person to take his—and his partner's—safety lightly. What would his reaction be when Lily revealed to him just how much danger she might be in?

After being afraid for so long, Lily was ready to move forward with her life. She wanted a future with Levi. She wanted him to be a part of her life. And not temporarily. She wanted him forever, and the only way to make sure that could happen was to be 100 percent honest with him.

She realized that they would have some obstacles to overcome. Just because she was ready to live her life didn't mean that she was instantly healed from the trauma she'd experienced. In fact, she'd never be completely healed. It would remain with her for the rest of her life. But she hoped that Levi would be by her side while she grew and reshaped her reality because of it.

She'd almost told him everything last night but stopped short of diving into the criminal investigation, trial, and Graham's subsequent escape from prison. Talking about it required her to relive every horrible detail. But Levi deserved to know what had happened to her and what was still happening to her until Graham was finally apprehended and put back behind bars where he belonged. Lily only hoped that her considerable baggage wasn't enough to scare Levi away.

Lily had fallen in love with the cocky cowboy. She didn't want to imagine her life without him.

* * *

For the rest of the morning, Lily felt lighter and more carefree than she had in a long time, despite the danger that still presented itself and the worries that came on its heels. She smiled for the sake of smiling and hummed a familiar song as she finished putting on her makeup and doing her hair. She thought about what they'd have for dinner tonight and what they might do later. The prospect of coming home at the end of the day no longer filled Lily with dread. Rather, she couldn't wait to get to school and start her day, because she knew Levi would be here to greet her with a bright, sardonic smile when she got home.

An hour later, Lily pulled up to the parking lot at Deer Haven Elementary School. Her phone rang as she killed the engine, and she reached in the passenger seat for it, grinning as she hoped it might be Levi calling.

"Hello?" She'd been too excited to even check the caller ID.

"Lily," a menacing voice growled into the receiver. "You sound happy. Why is that?"

Her blood turned to ice in her veins and Lily began to tremble. She'd never forget that smooth, velvety tone. Or the personification of evil that it now represented. Her mind raced with fear and too many questions to process. First and foremost, how had he gotten her phone number and did he know where she was?

"How in the hell did you get my number? For your sake, I hope you're calling from somewhere in Mexico." Lily forced herself to speak with bravery she didn't feel. "Because if you're not, it's only a matter of time before you're arrested, or worse."

"You know I'm incredibly resourceful." Graham's dark laughter reached out through the receiver, and Lily's stomach nearly heaved with revulsion. "And what could you possibly wish on me that's worse than prison?"

"A slow and torturous death." Lily didn't hold back. If he knew how terrified she was, she'd be giving him exactly what he wanted.

"You never were one to mince words." Even after losing his job, his reputation, his freedom, and being exposed for the monster he truly was, Graham couldn't help but be arrogant.

"You disgust me," Lily continued. "And don't think I won't go to the police and let them know you've called me."

"I'm counting on it," Graham replied.

He was absolutely insane. Only a lunatic would want to alert the police to his presence when he was trying to elude them. "What do you want?" Lily demanded through the panic that threatened to overtake her. "I know you like the sound of your own voice, but I've got things to do."

"Diversion is a funny thing," he practically purred. "You were a good one for me for a while. Certainly a challenge. So strong willed and confident. You weren't starry-eyed like those other, weak-minded girls. Harder to break."

"You were a shitty psychology professor," Lily deadpanned. "Don't give yourself too much credit."

"That's what I enjoy about you," Graham said with a rueful laugh. "Never one to needlessly bolster a man's ego. In fact, you managed to bruise mine quite significantly. And I'm going to make you pay for it. Tell the police that."

"You're a disgusting piece of shit," Lily spat into the receiver. "And they're going to find you."

"We'll see," Graham crooned. "We'll see."

The call ended and Lily dropped the phone into her lap as though it burned her. She took several shuddering breaths and gripped the steering wheel to keep her hands from shaking. How? She'd never told him where her hometown was. And she'd used her parents' address at their second home in Sacramento when she'd registered for school. Even during the trial, her identity had been kept a secret from the press. Her perceived anonymity had been the only reason she'd refused witness protection. It had all been an illusion of security. He'd known all along. Everything about her. It was the only explanation.

Inside the building, a classroom full of kids waited for her to guide them. Lily refused to let them down.

It took every ounce of courage in her stores to leave her car and walk into the building. But Lily was tired of being scared, and damn it, she wasn't going to run away. Graham had intended to rattle her. To make her look over her shoulder. He was a psychologist. The human psyche was his wheelhouse. He was toying with her.

Bastard.

"Good morning, Lily!" Stacey Ambrose, the school secretary, greeted Lily cheerfully from her office window.

"Good morning." Lily tried to sound just as chipper.

"Someone called for you this morning." She handed a slip of paper with a name and phone number scrawled on it. "I apologize if I got his name wrong. I could have sworn he said it was Grant. Anyway, he said to give him a call at that number regarding a case study you were involved in a couple of years ago."

Case study. So that's how he saw it? Lily wanted to scream. Lily looked down at the number written on the paper, certain it was fake. More games. More scare tactics. "Thanks, Stacey. Oh, while I'm thinking about it, I'll need a substitute for the next week. My folks need some help at their place in Sacramento. Do you think that might be possible?"

"Absolutely," Stacey replied. "I'll make some calls this morning and get someone lined up."

"Thanks so much," Lily replied, way calmer than she felt. "Have a good day."

"You too!"

Lily walked down the hallway, her temper and anxiety rising to a near-unbearable level. It would be a miracle if she made it through the day without losing it completely, but she had to. Looked like she might be spending some time in witness protection after all.

With any luck, they'd let her see Levi one last time before the marshals hid her away somewhere. So much for the life she'd wanted to build. Lily entered her classroom and sat down at her desk to prepare lesson plans for the rest of the week. Graham Brisbee was the devil. And she prayed someone would find him before he managed to get to her first.

Levi waited in Jacob's office, prepared for anything. He'd been ready to talk to him about who he really was and why he was in Deer Haven, but between his trips to Sacramento and Susanville, Jacob had beaten him to the punch. He'd gotten a text from him early in the morning to request that he meet him at the ranch ASAP. Levi had reluctantly made his excuse to Lily, telling her that they had an early morning and Jacob wanted everyone at work before the sun rose. And he supposed that was sort of true. Jacob had ordered his ass out there at daybreak. Things were likely about to get ugly.

Jacob stalked into the office and slammed the door behind him. Levi flinched but kept his spine ramrod straight. The other man rounded his desk to face Levi, his brows drawn down over his eyes and a scowl pulling at his lips.

"Do you want to tell me what the hell a deputy U.S. Marshal is doing on my ranch pretending to be a retired Army Ranger?"

Yeah, Jacob was pissed. Levi took a deep breath. "You're a Company man. You should know better than to get bent out of shape over undercover work."

Jacob's palm slapped down on his desk. "Not when it involves my family. What in the hell is going on?"

"I guess you've been talking to the sheriff." Small towns. So much for keeping things on the down low until he could take care of business.

"Not yet," Jacob spat. "But you can bet your ass I'll be talking to him later. If Justice hadn't decided to stop by the ranch yesterday, I'd still be in the dark."

Justice Culpepper. Great. Levi forced his jaw to unclench. He was going to pop that cocky SOB right in the nose for getting involved. "It's not my place to tell you why I'm here and I'm under no obligation to," he began.

"Bullshit," Jacob spat. "You *will* tell me. Now."

"I didn't lie to you, Jacob. Just omitted some things."

Jacob snorted. "Don't use that bullshit on me. I wrote the playbook."

"I'm not bullshitting you. You have connections; use them."

Jacob looked him up and down with contempt. "Don't think I'm not doing that right now."

Of course he was. Levi expected nothing less. "Levi Roberts, U.S. Army Rangers, retired. And deputy U.S. Marshal, fugitive recovery task force, active."

Jacob's nostrils flared. His jaw flexed, and though he seemed to calm, he was obviously still pissed. "What fugitive?"

Jacob was about to get a hell of lot angrier, or he might just come to his senses and listen. Either way, Levi braced himself for Jacob's reaction and replied, "Graham Brisbee."

"Graham Brisbee," Jacob repeated slowly. It took him a moment to place the name before an expression of recognition lit his face. "What in the hell does my family have to do with that asshole?"

Jacob was a smart man. Levi suspected he was already putting the pieces together. He gave Jacob a minute, hoping he'd come to the conclusion without Levi having to betray Lily's confidence. It was a loophole for sure, but one he'd willingly take.

"Lily," Jacob said under his breath. "Goddammit!"

Levi averted his gaze. His protective instinct reared its ugly head and he resisted the urge to tell Jacob to stay out of it and mind his own business. He didn't want Lily to have to endure any more hurt or humiliation because of what had happened. She'd kept it private for a reason, and Levi didn't want to be an accessory to her family finding out the truth if she didn't want them to.

Fast as a flash, Jacob lunged across his desk and grabbed Levi by the collar of his shirt. He jerked Levi to him until they were nearly face-to-face. The snarl became a deadly growl as Jacob gave Levi a brain-rattling shake. "You've been seeing her. Does she know who you are? Have you been using her for information or as bait?"

Damn, this looked bad. There was no way to put a positive spin on what was going on and Levi wasn't sure that at this point he wanted to. What was done was done and he was man enough to own up to it and accept whatever Jacob wanted to throw at him.

"She refused protection after the trial," Levi explained. "And she was notified when Brisbee escaped and refused protection then as well. There was always the possibility that Brisbee would want revenge and would go looking for her. We made the call. But Lily is *not* bait," Levi stressed. "I would never put her in danger. I'm here to make sure that nothing happens to her."

Jacob snorted. "How in the hell did she manage to keep this a secret?" Jacob said more to himself than Levi.

Jacob shook his head as he released his grip on Levi's shirt. He let out a slow breath as he settled himself in his chair, and Levi followed suit, taking a seat.

"You know Lily," Levi said. She's tough and just as stubborn. "She's not willing to do anything that's going to erase her control over her life. WITSEC has been off the table since day one."

"That definitely sounds like Lily," Jacob mused. "She'd never leave her life behind to enter into witness protection."

"Exactly. I care about Lily, Jacob. I'm not going to let anything happen to her. You have my word." He took a breath, wondering how much of his feelings for her he should admit to Jacob. "I love her."

Jacob's brow quirked as he studied Levi. "That's a surefire way to lose your job."

And Levi knew it. Ranching might be in his future permanently if he found himself released from duty once this operation was wrapped up. "Some things are worth the risk," Levi replied.

"Yes, they are." Jacob steepled his fingers in front of him as he leveled his gaze on Levi. "The trial was one of the most publicized criminal court cases in the past two years. At least statewide. I understand why she wanted to remain anonymous, but she should have told me. I could have done something. Helped her."

Levi understood Jacob's hurt and confusion. "I'm sure she had her reasons for not sharing with you what had happened. But those are her reasons, and it's not my place to tell her story."

"Do you have any leads on Brisbee?" Levi was thankful that Jacob wanted to change the course of the conversation and get right down to business.

Levi knew he could trust Jacob. "The media doesn't know yet, but one of his accomplices was taken into custody two nights ago."

"That explains the time you've been taking off," Jacob remarked ruefully.

"We interviewed him yesterday. There's a deal on the table and he's got until tonight to decide if he's going to flip on Brisbee or not. I think he'll do it. The assistant chief deputy is staying in Susanville and I'll know more as soon as he knows. I'd like nothing more for the bastard to be halfway to South America by now, but my instinct says Brisbee's not going anyway until he takes care of some unfinished business."

"Lily."

Levi looked Jacob square in the eye and gave a nod of his head. "She helped put him away. He's going to want retribution."

"Damn it, Lily," Jacob said under his breath. "Why couldn't you trust me to take care of you?"

"I don't think this is a trust issue, Jacob," Levi said. "I think it's a pride issue and I also think—"

"She was embarrassed," Jacob finished.

Levi didn't disagree.

"This isn't something to be embarrassed about," Jacob went on, already in problem-solving mode. "That piece of shit manipulated countless women. Used his knowledge and position of power to play his sick, twisted games with them. He"—Jacob stopped short, his voice hitching with emotion—"killed one of them. Lily could have been that woman."

"But she's a Donovan," Levi said. "And whether you realize it or not, she's a fighter and a survivor because of you and your family."

"She's like a sister to me." Jacob turned in his chair and stared out the window. The sun rose over the eastern horizon, painting the sky in shades of gold and red. "What can I do to help? Whatever resources we have are yours."

Levi appreciated the help. He doubted the USMS would share his opinion. Sometimes it wasn't a good idea to have too many big egos working on a single problem. But as former

CIA, Jacob could bring a lot to the table. And he surrounded himself with equally talented—not to mention connected—people.

"I appreciate that," Levi said. "But ultimately this isn't my show. I answer to the chief deputy director in Sacramento."

"What he doesn't know won't hurt him," Jacob offered.

True. As long as it meant Lily would be safe, Levi would take any resulting punishment he might receive for allowing Jacob to assist him.

"Full disclosure?" Levi asked.

"Whatever is said between us stays between us," Jacob assured him. "And if anyone asks, this conversation never happened."

"Works for me," Levi replied.

Jacob rested his elbows on the desk. "All that matters is making sure Brisbee goes back to prison for the rest of his life."

Levi nodded. "That's my plan."

"Good," Jacob replied. "Let's get to work."

One confession down, one to go. Levi sure as hell hoped that Lily would be as understanding as her cousin. One thing was certain, though: Her wrath scared him a hell of a lot more than Jacob's.

Levi's meeting with Jacob had gone slightly better than he'd anticipated. At least it hadn't come to blows. But he was feeling less than relieved. Now that Jacob knew the truth, he needed to come clean with Lily. He just hoped she'd understand why he'd done what he'd done. He loved her and he'd do anything to protect her.

He jumped in the truck and pulled out from the ranch. Lily would be just about done with school for the day and he wanted to talk to her before anyone else got the chance to. Jacob had already begun to pool his resources, phoning in favors and mobilizing the men he had on the ranch in preparation for joining the manhunt for Graham Brisbee. So far, the bastard had managed to elude some of the most reputable manhunters in the country. With any luck, they'd be able to flush Brisbee out of hiding and set a trap for him. Already, Levi and Jacob had a plan in place.

All they'd need to execute it was Lily's cooperation.

Chapter Twenty-Six

Lily could no longer pretend as though her life wasn't in danger. By calling not only her cell but also the school this morning, Graham had made it 100 percent clear that he knew where she was. And that he was coming for her. She'd lost control of the situation a long time ago. Hell, since she was being honest with herself, it was time to realize that she'd never had control at all. She needed help and she wasn't willing to put her loved ones in danger because of her own stubbornness.

She needed to leave Deer Haven. For a little while.

Or maybe forever.

Stacey had managed to line up a substitute for the next week. Lily was thankful there was only a month of school left before summer break. It would make replacing her for the rest of the term easier. Tears stung at her eyes and she willed them to cease as she looked over the classroom of young faces intently focused on their social studies worksheets. She'd miss them. Miss saying goodbye to them and wishing them a good summer. She'd miss welcoming a new group in the fall and getting to know them.

She'd miss her life.

As soon as three o'clock hit, Lily planned on calling Seth

Miller at the U.S. Marshals' office in Sacramento. Maybe they could trace where Graham's phone call had originated. Either way, she planned on asking for the help he'd offered her weeks ago. It was time to put her safety into capable hands.

But first, she needed to talk to Levi.

The thought of saying goodbye to him broke her heart. She didn't want to leave him. Didn't want to give up what they'd built together over the course of their passionate, albeit short relationship. God, she hoped he'd understand and wouldn't hate her for keeping this secret from him.

The next three hours passed in a blur. Time worked against Lily, thrusting her closer to the moment she dreaded. Acid churned in the pit of her stomach and her limbs practically quaked with unspent adrenaline. The bell rang to signal the end of the school day and Lily's chest tightened as she said goodbye to her students, knowing this was likely the last time she'd see them.

Back at her desk, she continued to outline her lesson plans past the week she'd scheduled to take off. The more prepared she could be for a substitute, the better.

"Lily. We need to talk."

Her head jerked up from her work at the gruff male voice. Justice Culpepper strode into the classroom, closing the door behind him. The sound of his heavy boots echoed with a dull thud on the floor as he approached Lily's desk. As if Lily's day couldn't get any worse. What in the hell was he doing here?

"I can't think of a single thing you and I have to talk about, Justice." Her temper rose by the second as Lily fumed over his audacity. "Why don't you take yourself out of my classroom and piss off."

"I'll gladly piss off if that's what you want, but I'm not

going anywhere yet. After you hear what I have to say, you might change your mind about kicking me out of here."

She couldn't think of a single thing he could say to convince her not to have him escorted off school property. She didn't have time for his bullshit games. "I'm busy, Justice. Go bug someone else."

"Levi isn't who you think he is."

Levi again? Lily's blood boiled. Her life was in a state of turmoil and Justice had the nerve to bring this childish alpha-male, bruised-ego bullshit to her attention yet again?

"Get out. Now."

"I told you, I'm not going anywhere until you hear me out. He's been using you, Lily. And because of it, you're in a shitload of danger."

Danger? Lily snorted. Justice had no clue. "I don't have time for this."

"No," he agreed. His gaze burned into hers. "You don't."

Lily's stomach did a backflip at the intensity of his eyes, the stern set of his jaw. She knew that expression, and Justice wasn't messing around. Anxious energy crept up her spine, spreading out through her limbs. Lily's mind spun as she tried to hold on to a coherent thought. She wasn't sure how much more she could take before she suffered a complete nervous breakdown.

"What are you talking about?" Lily needed to get out of here. She had a lot of bases to cover and not a lot of time to get it all done. "Just spit it the hell out."

"Levi is a deputy U.S. Marshal," Justice said. "He's in Deer Haven hoping to find and arrest an escaped convict. And he's using you at bait."

It took a few seconds for what Justice said to register in Lily's mind. Shame heated her cheeks as she averted her gaze and looked out the window, trying to collect her thoughts.

She refused to believe what Justice was saying. "Why would he do that?"

"You know why, Lily." Justice's voice dropped to a murmur. "And I'm not going to add to your stress by saying it out loud."

Oh God. Lily's stomach heaved and she forced herself to stay calm. It wouldn't do any good to play dumb. Justice would see right through it. This explained his strange behavior at Dillerman's the other day. He'd been so hot to talk to Jacob. Which meant her cousin now knew everything as well. So much for anonymity. Justice had managed to blow her secret wide open. And why? To satisfy his own damn ego and knock Levi down a peg?

Lily's world spun further out of control. Levi had lied to her. Was all of this—their relationship, his proclamation of love—just a ruse to get him closer to finding Graham? Her breath began to race, and Lily forcefully pushed her chair from her desk. If she didn't calm down, she was going to pass out.

"You asshole," Lily said between breaths. "Does it make you proud to know you got one up on me? Do you feel good about your smug-ass self for coming here to tattle on Levi?"

Justice's jaw squared. Apparently, he'd expected a different reaction from Lily. Well, too damn bad. She'd deal with Levi when she got home. Right now, Justice was as good a target for her wrath as anyone.

"You are a stubborn pain in the ass, Lily Donovan. Do you know that?"

Lily's eyes went wide. "I'm a pain in the ass?" She stood from her chair, her anger overriding her anxiety. She marched right up to Justice and poked her finger into his chest. "You have some nerve, Justice. Am I supposed to be grateful? Do you want me to thank you for coming in here and not only humiliating me, but destroying my entire world?"

"He lied to you, Lily!" Justice's nostrils flared with his agitation. "What part of that don't you get?"

"I've been lied to before," Lily reminded him. "This is nothing new."

Justice had the good sense to look chagrined. He took a step back and drew in a deep breath. "Lily, I'm not trying to hurt you," he implored. "I want to help you."

"Oh yeah?" she scoffed. "How? By telling my family all about my sordid past?" It wasn't that Lily believed Jacob, or anyone else, would think less of her because of what had happened. It was simply that she didn't want to burden anyone with her baggage. Sallie had managed to wrangle the truth out of her shortly after Lily had moved home. And Lily had never kept anything from Shay. But it was her experience to share and neither Justice—nor anyone else—had the right to talk about it without Lily's permission.

"Jacob loves you," Justice said. "He can protect you."

"That's not what I want." How could he be so blind to her nature? He knew her well enough to realize that she'd never place that sort of responsibility on Jacob's shoulders. She'd had a plan, and in a matter of minutes Justice had managed to throw a monkey wrench into it. "I'm not putting anyone I care about in danger."

"Quit being so damned stubborn, Lily." Justice blew out another frustrated breath that gave Lily a small measure of satisfaction. "Do you think we're all a bunch of inexperienced hicks?"

"Of course not." Lily knew just how capable Jacob, Justice, and most everyone they associated with were. "But that still doesn't mean I'm willing to risk anyone else's safety in order to secure mine."

"What about Levi?"

Lily stared at Justice, unable to say a damn thing. She didn't want to address Levi's betrayal. The pain of it was simply too much, and simply none of Justice's business.

"What about me, Justice?"

Lily flinched as Levi's imposing frame filled the doorway of her classroom. Things were about to get messy.

It took every ounce of self-control Levi had not to haul off and lay his fist into Justice Culpepper's face. He hadn't heard anything that had been said between him and Lily, but from the look on her face, it wasn't good. Levi didn't have time for this shit; he had enough on his plate without having to deal with the fallout of whatever had just transpired between the two. He planned on sending Justice on his way. Right now. He and Lily needed to talk.

"Just making sure Lily knows the truth about you."

Son of a bitch. Levi should have known that if Jacob had been made privy to his real reason for being in Deer Haven, others would have known too. Small towns. Impossible to keep anything secret.

"And what's that?" Levi maintained his calm, refusing to be ruffled by the other man.

"I thought she should know why you were really here, *Deputy Marshal*," Justice stressed. "So she could decide on her own if she wanted to put her life in danger so you could use her as bait."

That son of a bitch. Levi's teeth clenched to the point that he felt the enamel grind. "You don't know a goddamn thing." He looked over at Lily and the doubt etched into her beautiful face. The damage had already been done. "What you should have done was minded your own fucking business."

"You'd like that, wouldn't you?" Justice puffed up, his confidence bolstered. "So you could keep on using her."

This was a complication Levi didn't need. He'd already been worried about what Lily's reaction to the truth would be. Justice, in his arrogant foolishness, had managed to make things a thousand times worse.

"You really shouldn't talk about things you know nothing about." Levi's ire rose with each passing second. "It just makes you look stupid."

Justice's shoulders squared as he took a menacing step forward. Levi didn't want to fight in the middle of Lily's classroom, but he'd lay the bastard out right here and now if he didn't back off.

"Is it true?" Lily's soft voice cut through the outrage coursing through Levi's veins.

There was no way to put a positive spin on it at this point. Levi had no choice but to own up to it. "Yes," he said. "But—"

Lily held up a hand to silence him.

"I am such an idiot." Her voice hitched with emotion and it cut through Levi like a knife. "I should have known this was too good to be true."

"Lily," Justice said. "Let me take you out to the ranch."

"Shut the hell up," Levi quipped. "Don't you think you've done enough damage?"

Lily shook her head. "I never should have let my guard down with you."

"Don't say that." Damn it, Levi wished that Justice would get the hell out of there so he and Lily could talk. "Lily, you have the wrong impression about all of this."

"Do I?" Her voice rose with anger. "What do I have wrong, Levi? That you're a deputy marshal? That you already had all the background you needed about me and let me spill my guts to you like you didn't know any of it? Or that you're here trying to get your hands on Graham? Which part of that do I have wrong?"

"I would never put you in danger, Lily." Levi took a step toward her and she took an answering step back. "I love you."

Lily let out a rueful laugh. "I seriously can't take any more lies."

Justice moved toward Lily as well and she pointed an accusing finger his way. "I don't want to have anything to do with you either. Take your sorry ass back to your ranch and stay out of my business." She went to her desk, yanked open one of the drawers, and pulled out her purse. "If you'll both excuse me," she said as she pushed her way between them, "I've got some phone calls to make."

The door slammed shut in her wake, leaving Levi alone with Justice.

He turned on Justice, his anger cresting to a near-uncontrollable level. "Are you always this fucking stupid, or did you reserve it all for right now?"

"You're a piece of work, Roberts, you know that?" Justice wasn't any taller than Levi, but he had a good fifteen pounds of extra muscle on him. That didn't mean Levi couldn't kick his ass, though. "I'm not the one keeping secrets or dangling Lily in front of some sick bastard, hoping to get his attention."

At least now Levi knew how Jacob had found out why he was really in Deer Haven. Problem was, Justice was filling in the blanks and making dangerous assumptions about things he didn't know dick about.

"What you did today," Levi said, dropping his voice to a menacing growl, "was put Lily in more danger than she was already in. And if anything happens to her because of this, I'm going to beat your ass to a bloody pulp."

He knew his anger was slightly displaced, but Levi didn't care. He was pissed off and Justice was the perfect target for him to take his frustrations out on. Justice didn't seem the least bit concerned with the threat, but he didn't know Levi.

He'd be wise to do as Lily told him and take his sorry ass home.

"Is that what you're doing?" Justice asked. "Protecting Lily? Because if that's the case, I think you're doing a piss-poor job of it."

Levi bit back a sharp retort. He was wasting time arguing with Justice. He needed to talk to Lily and straighten this out. This had nothing to do with Justice, no matter how badly he wanted to insert himself—unwanted—into the situation.

"If you want to make yourself actually useful," Levi said as he headed for the door, "then go talk to Jacob. If not, mind your own damn business, and stay out of mine."

Without another word, Levi jerked open the door and shut it behind him.

He took off at a run down the hallway, hoping he could catch Lily before she left. He'd run out of time and couldn't afford to waste another second. At the end of the long hallway, Levi burst through the double doors, toward the staff parking lot. Lily's 4Runner was still parked in its spot, not far from where Levi had parked his truck. He let out a sigh of relief as he continued to run, desperate to catch her before she sped off.

"Lily, wait!"

Levi got to the car just as she pushed the ignition button. He pulled the door open, reached across Lily, and killed the engine. Her look of indignation should have frozen him right in his tracks. She was pissed and he was playing with fire.

"You can't just drive off without letting me give you an explanation."

Lily looked him up and down. "I don't have to let you do a damned thing, *Marshal*." She did nothing to hide the sneer in her voice. "I know everything I need to know."

"No," Levi said. "You don't. You can't take what that asshole told you at face value."

"Really?" Lily arched a curious brow. "That asshole seemed pretty damned convincing to me. But sure, go ahead and tell me, what did he get wrong?"

Levi didn't have much time to get the truth out. He'd planned this so much differently. "You refused protection. We knew there was a possibility that Brisbee might come looking for you. I was undercover. Not to use to you draw him out of hiding, but to protect you in case he does show up." Levi took a breath. "Lily, I wasn't supposed to get close to you, but I couldn't help myself. I couldn't stay away. I fell in love with you. If you don't believe anything else that I've said, you have to at least trust in that. I. Love. You."

She studied him for a quiet moment. "Whether or not you've been trying to draw him out of hiding, that's what happened," Lily said. She reached for the ignition button and once again started the engine. "He knows where I am, Levi, and he's coming for me, just like you thought. I have to get out of here."

"What do you mean he knows where you are?" Fear and frustration fueled the adrenaline that rushed through Levi's veins. "What happened?"

"You're all so high-handed, aren't you?" Lily asked. "Justice decided to stick his nose in my business even though he knows he's the last person on the planet I want involved in my private life. I told Seth Miller I didn't want protection and he sent you anyway. And now here you are, demanding that I divulge information to you like you have some sort of right to it."

Damn it, she was right. The more Lily asked to be left alone, the more everyone tried to control her. She was entitled to every ounce of rage she felt and then some. But damn it, this wasn't something she could do on her own and she needed to realize that. "Lily, you can kick my ass, and anyone else's that you want. Later. Right now, I need to get you out of here and somewhere secure."

"You don't need to do anything," Lily spat, "but leave me the hell alone."

She jerked the door closed, shutting Levi out as she started the car and put it in gear. The tires squealed as she pulled out of the parking lot and sped away from the school. Levi cursed under his breath as he hustled for his truck, hell-bent on catching up to her.

Keeping Lily safe might just be the death of him yet.

Chapter Twenty-Seven

Tears blurred Lily's eyes as she sped out of the parking lot. She'd called the marshals' office from the parking lot before Levi had chased her down but had only managed to get Seth Miller's voice mail. Justice's unwelcome revelation had sent a spear of betrayal through Lily's heart and she wasn't sure if she'd ever recover from the damage.

Levi wanted her to believe that he loved her. How could she possibly trust him now that she knew the truth? Lily had been less than forthright with Levi about her past, but it was hardly the same thing. She'd agonized for weeks over it. Worried about what he would think of her, how he would treat her, and whether or not he'd want to be with her, knowing what had happened to her and the sort of danger she might be in because of it.

What a joke.

All this time, he'd known everything. A sob lodged itself in Lily's throat and she swallowed it down. She'd never felt such crippling humiliation. Not even Graham had managed to make her feel so absolutely pathetic. God, she wished the highway would open up and swallow her, car and all, and put an end to her misery.

Lily had nowhere to turn. She had no idea what her next move should be.

She wished she'd had the presence of mind to give Justice Culpepper a fist to the gut before she'd left her classroom. Small towns don't keep secrets, and someone had obviously known about Levi being here and let the cat out of the bag. Who? Jacob? Lily couldn't imagine that being the case. Her cousin would have gone to her first if he'd known the U.S. Marshals Service had a deputy in Deer Haven to look after her. Though she had to assume if Justice knew the situation, Jacob also knew. Which was why he'd been looking for Jacob yesterday. Lily felt so far removed from all of this alpha-male bullshit. Justice and Levi seemed more interested in posturing for each other than worrying about her.

They sure knew how to make a girl feel loved.

Lily's phone rang and she looked at the caller ID, hoping to see Seth Miller's number pop up. Instead, she swiped her finger across the screen to answer Sallie's call.

"Hey."

"I hate to tell you this," Sallie said. "But the cat's out of the bag. And there's something else. . . ."

She didn't have to ask Sallie to elaborate. "I know. Justice just stopped by the school."

"Justice?" Sallie said, perplexed. "What in the hell did he have to say?"

"Oh, nothing much. Just thought I needed to know that Levi was an undercover U.S. Marshal in town to use me as bait to lure Graham out of hiding."

"That's what he said?" At least Lily wasn't the only one outraged. "Lil, that's not exactly true."

"Yeah, well, it's not exactly untrue," Lily said.

"What are you going to do?"

Lily turned onto the road toward her house, slowing on

the dirt road. She noticed a pickup following behind her and let out a slow sigh. And Levi thought she was stubborn?

"I don't know." Lily had never felt so directionless. "Was Jacob upset with you? For not telling him."

"Of course not," Sallie replied. "He cares about you, Lily. He wants to make sure you're safe."

Seemed to be a running theme: Keep Lily Donovan Safe. She hated it. She was no one important, and she didn't expect anyone to sacrifice their own safety for hers. It was time to put Deer Haven behind her. No matter what anyone else tried to convince her of.

"Sallie . . ." If Lily could trust anyone, it was her. "Graham knows where I am."

"What do you mean?" Sallie's concern reached out through the receiver. "How do you know that?"

"He called me. This morning. And he called the school and left a message for me with the secretary. He knows where I am and he's coming to get me. Hell, he might even already be here. I can't stay. I can't put any of you in danger. I've called the U.S. Marshals' office in Sacramento, but the chief deputy hasn't called me back yet. If I don't hear from him, I'm going to leave town anyway."

"Oh my God, Lily." Sallie let out a gust of breath. "Don't you dare worry about us! And don't you dare run off without a plan in place. Take my word for it, you don't want to do that."

Lily wasn't about to disregard Sallie's advice. She'd lived through something similar and was speaking from experience.

"Where are you now?"

"Almost to my house," Lily said.

"Pack a bag and come to the ranch," Sallie replied. "We'll form a solid plan and mobilize from there."

It seemed like the best starting point. "What about Gran?"

"Please," Sallie said with a laugh. "She's tougher than anyone on the ranch, including Jacob."

That was the truth. "Okay." Maybe in between the time it took to pack and get to the ranch, she'd get a phone call from Seth Miller or someone at his office. Of course, wasn't Levi a part of Seth Miller's office? It didn't matter. Lily didn't want to have anything to do with him.

"What about Levi?" Sallie seemed to read Lily's mind.

"What about him?"

"I can only imagine how hurt and angry you are right now, but maybe he could help?"

"No." Lily didn't want his help. He'd lied to her. Used her. He could take his ass back to wherever he'd come from and stay there.

"Are you sure? Because he might—"

"No," Lily cut her off. "I don't want anything to do with him."

"Fair enough," Sallie said. "Where are you now?"

"About to pull into my driveway."

"Okay. Call me as soon as you get your things packed. If I don't hear from you in twenty minutes, I'm calling the sheriff and sending Jacob over."

Sallie didn't mess around and Lily was so grateful to have someone like that in her life. "Deal. I'll call you in twenty minutes."

"It's going to be okay, Lily."

"I hope so," Lily replied. "Bye."

She pulled into her driveway and killed the engine. If Levi wanted to fight, he'd have to do it while she packed, because Lily had exactly twenty minutes to get out of here and she wasn't going to let anything—not even Levi—stand in her way.

She jumped out of the car and headed for the front door. Cold dread settled like a stone in Lily's stomach as she noticed the bouquet of calla lilies leaning against the porch railing. Her breath stalled in her chest and her limbs began to quake. That son of a bitch had been to her home. For all she knew, he could still be there.

Enraged, Lily kicked the bouquet, sending the delicate flowers scattering across the front porch and into the driveway. She reached for the door handle and barged into her house with little care for her own safety. If Graham had the balls to be waiting for her, then she'd give him the fight of his life before he tried to finish what he'd started. Otherwise, she was going to pack her shit and go to the ranch. Lily was tired of being afraid and of living her life on someone else's terms. *Fuck it.*

She pushed open the door and went inside. The house was empty. Of course, Graham wouldn't be there. That's not how he operated. He'd want to play his little mind games with her first, push her to her emotional and psychological limits, so he could study her reactions to it later. He'd build the tension, cat-and-mouse bullshit, to drive Lily to the edge.

Well, that wasn't going to happen.

She was through playing Graham Brisbee's games.

As she stalked through the house to her bedroom, the sounds of tires crunching on the gravel outside interrupted the quiet. *Great.* Looked like round two with Levi was about to begin. He could bring it. Lily had reached her capacity for bullshit today and she wasn't putting up with any more.

He—and everyone else who'd ever messed with her—could kiss her ass.

Levi pulled into Lily's driveway, his phone pressed to his ear. He listened again to the message Mitch had left him thirty minutes ago, wishing he had time to call the assistant chief deputy back. Shit was hitting the fan in a major way.

His cover had been blown, and apparently, Graham Brisbee had found his way to Deer Haven despite the USMS's intel telling them otherwise. Another diversion tactic. Seth had flown to Arizona to meet with the team to follow the lead there, leaving Mitch in charge of the team in California. They'd pulled the deputies who had been sent to keep a lookout in Deer Haven and redirected them, giving Brisbee exactly what he wanted.

"Son of a bitch!" Levi's fist came down hard on the steering wheel. He'd wring Justice Culpepper's fool neck if he managed to do irreparable damage to his relationship with Lily.

You have no one to blame but yourself, you stupid ass. Levi's common sense wouldn't allow him to put the responsibility for what had happened on anyone but himself. He'd fucked up. He'd violated the rules. He'd fallen in love with someone he was supposed to be surveilling. He'd made a mess of everything and it was on him to fix it.

He just prayed that once Lily calmed down she'd hear him out. Otherwise, Levi feared he might lose her forever. His heart would never survive if that happened.

Levi got out of the truck and headed for the porch. Pale white lilies were scattered on the driveway and the porch, sending up a red flag. He reached for the holster at his side, freeing the snap that secured the grip of his Glock and slid it free.

"Lily?" Levi walked through the front door, his senses alert, ready for anything. She didn't reply and his heart raced in his chest. "Lily?" A little louder this time.

"The last pushy bastard who thought he could tell me what to do nearly got a skillet to the head," Lily said from the bedroom. "You want to try your luck, Levi?"

He couldn't help but smile. Damn, he loved her fire. But

this wasn't the time for amusement. She was pissed off and he needed to do damage control. "What's up with the flowers in the driveway?" He didn't go into the bedroom but continued his sweep of the house.

"Lilies," she said simply. "Meant to rattle me."

"Brisbee?" That son of bitch had been there? Levi gnashed his teeth as a renewed rush of anger surged through him.

"Yeah." Lily snorted. "He's such an asshole."

Her cavalier attitude was enough to send Levi over the edge. He finished his quick sweep of the house and headed for the bedroom. He needed to get her out of here. Now.

"What are you doing?" Levi marched into the bedroom to find Lily folding clothes. She set a sweater on the bed and reached for a pair of jeans. "Lily, we need to get the hell out of here."

"You can do what you want," Lily stated. "You're a big boy. I'm packing a bag and then I'm going to the ranch."

"The hell you are." Levi hadn't meant to sound so commanding, but whether Lily liked it or not, he needed to take control of the situation. "We're driving to Sacramento and you're going into protective custody."

Lily rounded on him, fire burning bright in her gaze. "You do not get to tell me what to do!"

"Yes," Levi argued. "I do. Especially when your life is in danger."

"Would you listen to yourself?" Lily exclaimed. She continued to fold her clothes and angrily stuff them into a duffel bag. "Why in the hell would I do a damned thing you told me to after what you did?"

"I want to protect you, Lily!"

"You lied to me!" she shouted. She no longer folded her clothes but gathered them into balls and shoved them in the bag. "The entire foundation of our relationship is fake!"

Levi ran his fingers through his hair and let out a frustrated breath. "You have every right to be angry with me. I deserve it. I withheld information, yes."

"You *lied*," Lily corrected.

"I had my instructions."

"Were part of your instructions to get me into bed?"

Levi cringed. Lord, he'd fucked this up. "No. My instructions were to get close but not too close. To keep an eye on you."

"And keep an even closer eye out for Graham," she deadpanned.

"I'm part of the fugitive recovery team, Lily." How could he possibly make her understand? "It's my job to keep an eye out for him. That doesn't make him a priority over you, though. You will always be my number one priority."

"Why's that?" Lily did nothing to hide the disdain in her tone. "You up for a big promotion or something?"

"No." Levi took a step forward despite Lily's warning glance. "Because I love you."

Lily stuffed a pair of boots into the bag and headed for the bathroom. "Yeah? Then why did you lie to me?"

"I've wanted to tell you," Levi said. "I've tried. I'd planned on telling you last night but put it off because I was worried."

"Worried I'd send your sorry ass packing?"

Levi turned toward the bathroom. "Yes. And the thought of losing you scares the shit out of me."

Lily paused whatever it was she was doing, but the silence didn't last long. Levi's appeal didn't garner any sympathy and she continued to pack. "You should have thought of that before you decided to trick me."

"I wasn't trying to trick you, Lily." The sadness that permeated his voice nearly broke his heart. "I wanted to protect you."

"Do you know what he did to me?" Lily appeared in

the doorway, framed by the bathroom light. Shadows hollowed her eyes and sharpened the angles of her face. "Of course you do, I mean, to some extent. But I don't think you understand." She crossed the bedroom and set a toiletry bag next to the duffel. "He lied to me. He charmed me, complimented me, challenged me, educated me, seduced me, used me, amused himself with me, and then"—her voice hitched—"when he was bored of me, he tried to rape and kill me. Knowing even some minor portion of that, how could you possibly think I'd be okay with being deceived and played with again?"

Her words laid him low. "I was selfish." The admission burned on his tongue. "I didn't think about that at all. I wanted you and I didn't consider the consequences. I hurt you and I'm sorry. I deserve your anger and everything that comes with it. But, please, Lily. Let me protect you now. Let me do my job."

She looked away and swiped at her cheek. God, he was a bastard. He didn't know if he'd ever be able to earn her forgiveness, but he'd do whatever it took.

"Who told Justice?" Lily's bitter tone reached out, sharp as a knife. Levi didn't know their history, but it must have gotten under her skin that he'd found out what had happened to her at school.

"Sheriff Davidson, if I had to guess," Levi said. He owed her as much honesty as he could provide. "I met with him a couple of weeks ago and asked him to keep our presence here under wraps for the time being."

"Small towns," Lily said ruefully. "Can't keep a secret if you try."

"I never intended to keep it a secret," Levi said. "I wanted to tell you. Every day. I've risked everything for you, Lily and if I had to do it again, I wouldn't change a thing."

"You've risked everything? Well, isn't that magnanimous

of you. Do you think because you jeopardized your job that I somehow owe you something?"

"Absolutely not. I made that decision, and no matter how things play out with us, I won't regret it."

Her dubious expression didn't give him much hope. Levi wasn't easily fazed. He'd spend the rest of his life apologizing if that's what it took. They could deal with their relationship issues later, though. Right now, Levi needed to do his job.

"I want to talk to someone else at the U.S. Marshals' office," Lily said finally. "I'm sorry, but I simply can't take your word for it on anything right now."

Every blow she dealt knocked him down another peg and made him realize just how badly he'd screwed this up with her. He couldn't fault her for not trusting him. At this point, he was unreliable.

"The chief deputy, Seth Miller, is in Arizona now chasing a lead on Brisbee. My supervisor left me a message this afternoon letting me know that resources were being redirected to follow the Arizona lead."

Lily let out a chuff of laughter. "Graham sure likes throwing his big brain around. He's probably getting off on sending you guys all over the country to look for him."

"More importantly, Lily, he's distracting us to allow him the opportunity to get closer to you."

Lily's expression became serious. "I know that."

"Then can we please get out of here?"

"I'm going to the ranch."

Damn, she was stubborn. But Levi could use it to his advantage. Now that he knew Brisbee was in Deer Haven, he needed to talk to Jacob and Sheriff Davidson and, most important, Mitch.

"All right," he said at last. "We'll take my truck."

Lily shook her head. She grabbed her bags and stalked past Levi. "You can drive your truck. I'm taking mine."

He'd let her have her anger. She was entitled to it. For the first time in his life, Levi had brought down his walls and let someone in. And he wasn't about to let Lily's wrath undo that. He refused to give her up.

Chapter Twenty-Eight

Lily called Sallie to let her know she was on her way with three minutes to spare. Levi's truck followed close behind her on the highway and Lily did her best to keep her eyes off the rearview mirror and focused on the road in front of her. She had more to worry about than her love life right now. That didn't mean she wasn't still pissed off as hell at Levi. Lily didn't know if she'd ever be able to forgive him for his deception. But for now, she knew she wouldn't be able to get rid of him, so she'd have to do her best to tolerate him.

She parked near the house. Sallie waited for her at the end of the walkway and opened the gate for her. Lily didn't bother to look behind her as Levi's truck pulled into the driveway. She didn't give him the satisfaction of acknowledging him. This was Jacob's house. If her cousin wanted him gone, he could boot him off the property.

"You okay?" Sallie looked past Lily to the driveway as they walked toward the house.

"I'm fine." Lily couldn't offer anything but a standard response. "I need to talk to Jacob, though, and Shay too." She wanted Jacob to know how close Graham was. It didn't sit well with Lily to put her family in danger and she was hoping he could help hide her out somewhere until someone from the U.S. Marshals' office—who wasn't Levi—called her back. It was time to admit that she wasn't in control of the situation and turn the reins over to someone more qualified.

"I called Shay," Sallie said as she opened the door. "She wanted to come over, but I told her it might be a good idea for her to stay home for now."

"That's a good idea," Lily said. She deposited her bags on the kitchen table and plopped down on a stool at the bar. "I'm not even sure how long I'll be here."

Sallie's brow furrowed. "Why's that?"

Jacob walked into the kitchen. He walked straight to Lily and without saying a word wrapped his arms around her in a tight hug. Tears threatened, but Lily kept them at bay, determined to remain strong no matter what. Crying wasn't going to accomplish anything.

"He was at my house," Lily said quietly. Jacob pulled away and studied her.

"What?" Sallie walked to the bar. "Who was at your house?"

"Graham."

"Goddammit!" The expletive shot angrily from Jacob's mouth.

"Oh my God." Sallie put a staying hand on Jacob's shoulder as though to calm him. "How do you know?"

"He left a bouquet of lilies on my front porch," Lily said. "He's just trying to scare me."

"That's a threat," Sallie replied.

"Damn right it is," Jacob agreed. "And when I get my hands on the bastard, he's going to pay for it."

"That's the thing," Lily said. "I don't want any of you to be in danger because of me."

"If you think I'm going to let this go without doing everything in my power to make sure you're safe, Lily, you don't know me very well."

Lily wasn't the only stubborn member of the Donovan clan. Jacob was like a dog with a bone. When he set his mind to something, he was unstoppable. And while they were on the subject of stubborn . . . she glanced toward the kitchen door, half expecting Levi to walk through at any minute. Maybe he was sitting out in his truck, brooding.

"What can we do?" Sallie asked Jacob. "We need some sort of plan."

Jacob nodded. "Levi and I are already on it."

Lily snapped to attention. "Is that so?"

"Lily, don't get upset." Jacob knew she was pissed. *Good.* "You have to understand the position Levi is in. Undercover operations are tricky. Especially when—"

"Don't you dare defend him," Lily said. "He lied. He intentionally deceived me. It was shitty of him to get me to—" Lily stopped short of saying "fall in love with him." "He shouldn't have pretended to be someone he wasn't."

Jacob averted his gaze. When he brought it up, his eyes met Sallie's and they shared a moment of silent communication. *Oh lord.* The realization made Lily wish she could swallow her tongue to keep herself from saying another insensitive thing. She'd really put her foot in her mouth this time.

"I'm sorry," she said. "I didn't mean it that way."

"Yes, you did," Jacob replied. "And it's okay. I understand. It caused a fair amount of trouble for Sallie and me as well, so I absolutely know where you're coming from."

Jacob had been undercover in Europe when he'd met Sallie. He'd told her his name was Jake Rossiter and they'd ended up spending the night together. When Jacob had lost his memory during a failed murder attempt by a terrorist group, Sallie had come home thinking the man she'd fallen in love with had ghosted her. Only after she'd moved to Deer Haven did she realize that Jacob wasn't the man he'd said he was and that he'd lost all memory of their time together.

Jacob had lied to Sallie about who he was when they'd met, and she'd forgiven him. Was Lily being too hard on Levi for doing the same?

Sallie remained silent. She pulled out a barstool next to Lily and sat down. What were the odds that they'd both fall in love with men who practiced deception in order to make sure innocent people were kept safe? Lily knew Levi was a good man. She'd never question that. But she was hurt and what she needed was time to process everything before she could break it all down and actually analyze how she felt.

"Let's just forget I opened my stupid mouth," Lily said. "What do you have planned? Because I honestly have no idea what to do."

"Don't get upset, but I actually got the idea from Justice."

"He's on my shit list too," Lily groused.

"When isn't he?" Jacob countered.

"Good point."

"Anyway, I made a couple of calls and I have an old military associate who looks a lot like you. Close enough that it might trick someone from a distance."

"Bait," Lily said. "You're going to use her to draw Graham out."

"Essentially, yes."

Lily was certain that Jacob's "military associate" could likely decapitate a man with her bare hands if she wanted to. That didn't mean Lily was interested in anyone risking their life for her. "I don't know. . . . I don't want anyone to get hurt."

"Believe me, Lily. The only one who needs to worry about getting hurt is the son of a bitch who's stalking you."

Lily appreciated that Jacob hadn't said his name. It made it easier somehow to talk about it without feeling ashamed. "Levi thinks this is a good idea?" She didn't want to admit it, but his opinion mattered. Where was he? She hated that she couldn't get him out of her head.

"He thinks it's a viable option," Jacob said. "Though we're wondering how to execute it when we don't have any way to actually make contact with the bastard. We could plant her in your house. Now that we know he's been to your place, he might come back."

"Or maybe we could just call him," Lily said.

"You think?" Sallie asked.

Jacob's brow furrowed with curiosity.

"He called me this morning," Lily explained to him. "The number wasn't blocked."

"Do you think he'd be stupid enough to call from a number that could be traced?"

Lily looked over at Sallie and shrugged. "I don't think Graham is stupid. But he might be arrogant enough."

"For sure," Jacob agreed. "It's worth a shot, anyway. No doubt it's a burner phone, but he might be hanging on to it in the hope that Lily will call him. Arrogance is sometimes a criminal's greatest weakness. Their egos get the better of them." Jacob reached for a pad and pen on the counter and set it front of Lily. "Can you give me the number?"

Lily retrieved her phone from her pocket and searched her recent calls. She scrawled the number on a sheet of paper and tore it from the pad before handing it to Jacob. "Here. I don't know if it matters or not, but he called the school too this morning. He left a message for me with the secretary."

"Do you know around what time that would have been?"

Lily shrugged. "I'm not sure. It was before I got to school, so sometime between seven and seven-thirty."

Jacob nodded. "Thanks." He folded the paper and slid it

into his pocket. "I've got some things to take care of. You two sit tight for a while. No leaving the house. Understand?"

Sallie gave Lily's arm a reassuring squeeze. "I understand. Where's Gran?"

"She's going to go to bingo with a friend of hers, and is staying the night in town with her," Sallie said. "One less thing to worry about, you know?"

"Good." Lily let out a slow breath. Sallie was right; the less they had to worry about, the better. She just wished that one of her worries wasn't Levi and what he was currently doing.

Levi paced the confines of Jacob's office. Not the one in the main house, but something closer to a mini command center he'd set up in the bunkhouse, proving you could take a man out of the CIA, but you couldn't take the CIA out of the man. Jacob was damned prepared, and Levi was thankful for it. He'd likely get his ass in a sling for going over his supervisor's head and joining forces with ex-CIA, but he figured if he was going to fuck up, he might as well go all in.

The sound of a vehicle pulling into the driveway got Levi's attention. He kept his right hand positioned on the grip of his Glock as he eased toward the doorway. The crunch of footsteps on the gravel signaled multiple bodies converging and he waited, breath stalled in his chest, as the door swung wide.

Levi froze as he came face-to-face with Justice Culpepper. He moved his hand from his sidearm so he wouldn't be tempted to draw it on the man whose face he wanted to smash. Jacob stood directly behind him and sidestepped Justice to put himself between them.

"I'm not going to have to worry about you two, am I?"

"Depends," Levi said, "on whether or not he plans on staying."

"I'm staying." Justice folded his arms across his wide chest and gave Levi a shit-eating grin that he wanted to smack right off his face.

Levi stepped up to Justice. "You're a real piece of work, you know that?"

"Both of you knock it the hell off," Jacob interrupted. "I don't give a shit if you beat the tar out of each other after Graham Brisbee is behind bars, but for right now, you're going to play nice and at least pretend to get along."

Levi snorted. Though he'd like nothing better than to take it outside, Lily was what mattered right now and he could put his anger and annoyance on the back burner. For now.

"I'm golden." Justice really was a smug SOB. "I've got nothing to worry about."

"You think so, huh?"

"That's enough," Jacob barked. "I don't want to waste any more time. Let's get to work. Lily said Brisbee left something at her house this afternoon, so he knows where she lives. We have to assume that if he knows that, he knows her familial connections and who her friends are. Have you heard anything from your assistant chief?"

"No." Levi was frustrated as fuck that he hadn't been able to get Mitch on the phone. "My chief is in Phoenix, and as far as I know, the assistant chief is in Sacramento now. He left me a message this afternoon that they were pulling resources in Deer Haven and redirecting to Arizona due to a credible lead there. He had a follow-up interview with Max Davis today. He agreed to sign a deal and agreed to talk."

"What do you think he said?"

"Initially, we were hoping we could connect Davis to Deer Haven. We thought maybe he somehow knew Lily and provided information to Brisbee about where she lived. I haven't heard anything from the assistant chief yet, but

I'm assuming Davis told them something that pointed them toward Arizona instead."

"Davis." Justice thought for a moment. "There are plenty of Davises in the area. One of them might be related. But there are a lot of Davises everywhere, if you know what I mean."

True, it was a common name and Brisbee's cellmate being from Deer Haven would be quite a coincidence. Grasping at straws in hopes of making a connection.

"Your superiors don't know he's here?" Jacob asked.

"No." Levi combed his fingers through his hair. "I haven't been able to get ahold of anyone since this morning. Not that it would matter. No one has technically seen him, so there's no actual proof that he's in Deer Haven."

"The flowers?"

"Anyone could have left those," Levi replied. "He could have called from anywhere and had the flowers delivered."

"Lily believes he's here," Jacob said.

"And I agree with her," Levi said. His gut feelings were never wrong, and Levi's gut told him Brisbee was close. "I've always suspected he'd come here."

"Well, let's do a little investigative work of our own." Jacob produced a piece of paper from his pocket and handed it to Justice. "Can you trace this number? Also, Lily said he called the school this morning. Sometime between seven and seven-thirty."

"I'm on it." Justice turned and headed for the computer at the far end of the room. He fished his cell from his pocket and dialed, talking quietly to whoever was on the other end, more than likely one of his brothers.

"What about your decoy?" Levi asked.

"She's on her way from Langley," Jacob said. "Flying into Sacramento tonight. She'll be here first thing in the morning."

If Levi could keep Lily safe for the next twelve hours, he hoped he could hand her over into Mitch's care and set a trap for Brisbee. "In the meantime?"

"We try to figure out a way to flush him out," Jacob suggested. "I'm assuming he's using a burner, but maybe he's arrogant enough to hold on to it in the hopes that Lily reaches out to him."

"He's arrogant, all right," Levi agreed. "I don't know that he would think Lily would reach out to him, though. He has to know she'd go to the police. My bet's on the Davis connection."

"If Davis is a local," Jacob began, "there's a chance he'd know everything about Lily."

"Including where her family members live," Levi said.

"Shit," Jacob hissed.

"Exactly." They had to assume that nowhere was safe.

"We need to get Lily out of town," Jacob said.

"We need to get anyone that Lily *cares about* out of town," Levi stressed. "Brisbee isn't above using someone she cares about to get to her."

Jacob cursed under his breath. "You've got a point."

"That's potentially a lot of family." Levi didn't know exactly how many of Lily's family members lived in Deer Haven, but they needed to cover all the bases.

"Me, Sallie, Gran," Jacob began. "Tara. There are a few third and fourth cousins as well. Shay . . ."

Shay. "Fuck." The word burst from between Levi's lips. He'd been so worried about Lily he hadn't stopped to consider the person most important to her: her sister.

"You have anything on that phone number?" Levi called to Justice.

"It's a burner for sure," he said, not bothering to look up from the screen. "Trying to get a ping on it now."

Levi unlocked his phone and selected Mitch McDonald

from the contacts. The call went straight to voice mail and he swore under his breath as he waited for the announcement to conclude. "It's Levi. Call me ASAP. Brisbee is in Deer Haven." He ended the call and turned to Jacob. "We need to get Shay out here immediately. Can you call her?"

Without a word, Jacob made the call. The stretch of silence that followed caused a knot of nervous energy to tie up Levi's stomach. He waited. Jacob's gaze met his, the other man's brow furrowed with concern.

"Shit." Jacob brought the phone down. "Voice mail."

"I got a ping." Levi and Jacob turned their attention to Justice. "It's near the intersection of Briar Street and Johnson Creek Road."

Jacob's eyes went wide. "That's near Shay's house."

"Lily!" Sallie's voice carried to the bunkhouse and all three men froze. "Lily, wait!"

The sound of tires against gravel drowned out Sallie's voice. Levi burst from the bunkhouse at a sprint in time to see Lily's 4Runner racing down the dirt road. Sallie ran toward the bunkhouse and straight to Jacob. Her panicked expression turned Levi's blood to ice as he tried to keep his mind from spinning.

"I don't know where she's going," Sallie said, nearly out of breath. "She got a phone call. I think it was Graham Brisbee. I-I don't know what's going on, Jacob; she didn't say a word, just ran out of the house to her car."

Levi looked at Jacob.

"Go! I'll be right behind you with backup!"

He sprinted for his truck, rage and fear fueling every single step. He yanked open the door and launched himself inside the cab, turning the key and throwing the truck into gear as he pressed the gas pedal to the floor. The back end of the pickup fishtailed on the loose gravel as he sped after Lily. He had no idea where Lily was headed, but his best guess was

Shay's house, and he had no idea where she lived. He had to keep up; he couldn't risk losing her. Lily maneuvered the 4Runner through traffic recklessly, speeding down the highway as she passed cars and swerving nearly into the ditch to avoid a collision. Levi cursed as he tried to keep up, his half-ton pickup too bulky for some of Lily's tight squeezes. She put two cars between them before traffic would no longer allow for Levi to keep up. His phone chimed from the dash and he checked the message, relieved to find that Jacob had been one step ahead and texted him Shay's address, making the same assumption as Levi. He opened the location in navigation and only half listened to the electronic voice that gave him pleasant directions as he tried to get around the slow-moving vehicles and closer to Lily.

If anything happened to her, he'd never forgive himself.

Chapter Twenty-Nine

Lily's heart threatened to beat right out of her chest. The sound of her sister's enraged shout on the other end of the receiver had been enough to spur her into action, giving Graham exactly what he wanted. The highway blurred in Lily's tear-filled vision and she swiped at her face, forcing herself to try to remain calm.

She wouldn't be any good to Shay if she let herself fall to pieces.

From her rearview mirror, Lily checked for Levi's truck. He'd fallen behind in traffic, which was exactly what she'd intended to happen. Her cell rang and she sent the call to voice mail. It rang again and she declined the call once again. It started up for a third time and Lily simply ignored it. She wasn't going to answer and let Levi try to talk her out of going to Shay. Graham had made it abundantly clear that he wouldn't hesitate to hurt her sister if Lily brought anyone with her. She wasn't exactly an expert at ditching someone who was tailing her—and considering Levi's experience, she figured he was pretty damned good at pursuit—but she'd do her damnedest to shake him.

Traffic slowed on her left, giving Lily the opportunity to leapfrog ahead on the highway once again. She stomped the pedal to the floor and passed several cars, lengthening the distance between her and Levi. She checked her phone for the address Graham had given her and veered off onto a side road no longer maintained by the county. It was overgrown with foliage, masking Lily's presence as she left the highway behind.

She was officially on her own.

How in the hell did Graham know the area so well? Had he been in Deer Haven for weeks? Not that it mattered. He was here now, and he had her sister. Lily said a silent prayer that Shay was all right as she drove as quickly as she could on the rut-worn road. It dead-ended at an old schoolhouse that had been a part of a historic registry at one point. Few people knew about the little chunk of property except for a few locals and some of the staff at the school. It belonged to the elementary school secretary, Stacey Ambrose. Her parents had purchased the seven-acre plot and had planned to renovate the school into a vacation rental. The building had flooded three years in a row, squashing those plans, but they'd held on to the property. Lily had brought her class here on a field trip a few months ago. They did an ecosystem lesson at the stream and a history lesson at the school site.

Had Graham learned about the property somehow? And who had he hurt in order to get his information?

Lily's stomach heaved at the thought.

Remains of afternoon sunlight filtered through the trees and Lily flipped down the visor to shield her eyes. In a few short minutes, the sun would set, casting a gray shroud over the landscape, making visibility almost impossible. Leave it to Graham to set the stage, creating an eerie backdrop to further taunt Lily's already racing mind. Her anxiety crested, threatening to overtake her, but she had to keep it together. She could do this. She had to. For Shay.

The dirt road wound over a little knoll to a bridge that

spanned a shallow creek. The trees were thick here, blocking out the highway altogether. Three more agonizing miles passed before the little school came into sight. A pickup—Shay's—was parked next to the building, but Lily saw no trace of either Graham or Shay. She swore if anything had happened to her sister, she'd use her last ounce of strength to do as much damage to Graham Brisbee as possible.

Lily slowed the 4Runner to a stop and cut the engine. She reached for her phone and turned it off like Graham had instructed, before taking a few deep breaths, kicking her feet back toward the seat as she stretched her back. Her heel knocked something under the seat and Lily felt beneath her, the holstered .38 right where Levi had left it after her shooting lesson. Lily grabbed the revolver and tucked it into her waistband at her back like she'd seen Levi do once. Adrenaline coursed through her veins, causing her limbs to quake. She'd be lucky if she could hit the broad side of a barn at this point, but all she had to do was immobilize Graham long enough for her and Shay to get out of there.

She could do this. She had to do this. Lily mustered every ounce of bravery she could as she got out of the car and pulled on her jacket to better hide the revolver. She lifted her chin high and steeled herself for what was to come. Shay deserved nothing less.

"I'm here!" Lily called out, forcing her voice to sound strong. "Where in the hell is my sister?"

The door to the schoolhouse swung wide. Graham Brisbee stepped into the doorway, looking every bit as handsome and larger-than-life as she remembered him. But just a year in prison had hardened him, lending a dangerous edge to his appearance and darkening his gaze to make it appear even more menacing.

Lily's hatred for the man standing before her far outweighed her fear. He'd stolen her peace of mind and her confidence. He'd been the cause of countless sleepless nights and anxious days. If she could manage to get close enough, she could reach for the revolver and pull the trigger. She could bury a bullet in his chest. But she had to make sure Shay was okay first. Once her sister was safe, Lily would act. He might take her down with him, but that was a risk she was willing to take as long as the world was rid of him.

"You're not really in the position to be so demanding, Lily," Graham said with a bone-chilling calm.

"You kidnapped my sister. I have every right to be demanding." He wanted her to play his game, but she wasn't the easily impressionable girl she'd been when they'd first met.

"I didn't kidnap anyone." Graham postured himself in the doorway as though he were standing at the podium, about to lecture a class. "She came on her own."

"What did you say to her to coerce her?"

He hiked an unconcerned shoulder. "The same thing I told you. That if she didn't come with me, I would kill her sister."

Asshole. A scream of pure rage built in Lily's chest and she swallowed it down. He thought he was so brilliant, but what she'd come to realize was that he was nothing more than a coward and a bully.

"Where is she?"

"She's fine, Lily," Graham assured her. "She's not who I want."

A shiver danced down Lily's spine. She knew that feeding Graham's ego, keeping him engaged, would buy her some time. Maybe if she managed to stall long enough, she could put herself in the position to pull the revolver from her waistband and pull the trigger.

"How did you find out about this place? This is a pretty obscure location for someone who hadn't been in town long."

"I thought an old schoolhouse would be a nice backdrop for a reunion with my favorite student who is now a teacher herself. How are you enjoying shaping young minds, Lily?"

Graham was so good at turning the microscope away from himself. "I'm not discussing that with you." Her students were none of his damn business. "How did you find this place?"

Graham grinned. Lily couldn't believe there was ever a time when she found the expression charming.

"It's a small world, isn't it?" He mused. "I'd never put much thought into that six degrees of separation theory until I was forced to spend so much time with another human being in a confined space."

He wasn't going to tell her anything, and frankly, Lily didn't care. Her only priority was Shay.

"Where is my sister, Graham?"

He let out a long-suffering sigh. "I suppose we aren't going to get anywhere until we address that, are we? Come in." He made a wide sweeping gesture with his hand. "You can see her for yourself."

Lily forced one foot in front of the other. The weight of the revolver at the small of her back was her only comfort as she climbed the rickety stairs to the doorway. The last bits of gray light were fading from the sky, giving way to darkness. Soon, Lily wouldn't be able to see anything. All the more reason to hurry up and get Shay out of there. If she was forced to be trapped in the dark with Graham again, Lily was certain she wouldn't survive.

"Son of a bitch!"

Levi's third call went to voice mail. Lily was blatantly ignoring him and his lack of control was about to send his temper over the edge. He punched his palm against the steering wheel as he lost sight of her car. Damn her, she'd managed to shake him in the string of evening traffic congesting the highway. He swerved into the left lane, punching the gas as he rounded a couple of slower-moving cars. Levi hit the brakes, cursing under his breath as he waited for another opportunity to get farther ahead. The string of vehicles thinned in the opposite lane, and he gained another three car lengths, but still no sign of Lily. She'd disappeared into thin air, adding to Levi's fear-fueled frustration. Fear for Lily's safety, and frustration at her stubborn impetuousness.

He continued to scan the traffic ahead of him as he followed the directions of the navigation app and turned off the highway toward the town proper. Levi wound through town, past businesses, and into a more residential area. He turned down the lane toward Shay's house, his heart pounding in his chest. No lights on in the house, no cars parked in the driveway, and no trace of Lily.

The pickup came to a stop and Levi left the engine running as he got out to take a look around. He drew the Glock, holding it at the ready. He tuned out the surrounding sounds of traffic and his own footsteps as he slowly approached the house. The hairs on the back of Levi's neck stood on end as his suspicion grew. Up the steps to the front door. He knocked. Nothing. He walked the perimeter of the house, looking into the windows to find the house empty. As he rounded the east side corner, Levi's toe kicked at something and he looked down to find a discarded cell phone.

"Motherfucker!"

Another goddamned misdirect. Levi holstered his gun and fished his cell from his pocket as he rushed back to the truck. Jacob answered on the first ring.

"I'm almost there. Three minutes out."

"They're not here," Levi forced the words through clenched teeth. "It's another distraction."

"What about Lily?"

"I lost her on the highway." Levi hated to admit that she'd

managed to shake him. "She was never coming to Shay's house."

"Goddamn it." Jacob ended the call without another word.

Levi dug through his glove box and found a tissue. He went back to the side of the house and carefully wrapped the phone to preserve any fingerprints. By the time he got back to the truck, Jacob had pulled into the driveway. He slammed the door of his pickup closed as he stalked toward Levi.

"I did a perimeter check," Levi said. "The doors are locked and the lights are off. From what I can tell, no one's in the house."

"I have a key."

Levi followed Jacob back to the house. As much as he knew they needed to check inside and do the investigative work, his worry for Lily overrode his common sense. He wanted to get the hell out of there and find her. Problem was, as long as she refused—or was unable—to answer his calls, he'd have to do the legwork in order to track her down.

He swore when all of this was said and done he'd never let Lily out of his sight again.

Jacob released his sidearm from the holster as he opened the front door. This was some real renegade shit they were pulling. If Levi hadn't lost his job yet, pursuing a fugitive with a civilian—albeit ex-CIA—was bound to get it done. Levi covered Jacob as they swept the house, only to confirm Levi's assumption that the house was unoccupied, and Lily had never intended coming here. They closed up the house and went back to the truck to regroup, leaving Levi even more frustrated.

"Brisbee knew she'd be followed," Jacob said. "The bastard did his homework."

That he did. Levi was convinced that Max Davis was the link between Deer Haven and Brisbee. His inability to get ahold of Mitch was as maddening as Lily ignoring his calls. And now he was out of time.

"I don't suppose Justice was able to dig anything up that might connect Max Davis with the town?"

"I've got resources," Jacob said. "But they're not unlimited. I'm retired, Levi. I don't exactly have security clearance and access to databases like I used to."

He knew that, but damn he wished they had something.

Levi's cell buzzed and he answered in an instant, hopeful for what could be a huge break. "Roberts."

Mitch's service was sketchy, and Levi had trouble making him out through the garbled speech.

"You're breaking up. Say again."

"Got—message. Dav—"

Damn cell phones. "Mitch, I didn't get that."

"Davis was found dead in his cell this afternoon. He—moved from solitary. We—inside job. I'll be back in Sacramento tonight. I'll—Deer—Lily Donovan with you until I—"

The line went dead. Levi immediately selected Lily from his contacts and hit "send," but the call went directly to voice mail. Either she'd turned it off or the battery had gone dead. Levi damned near threw his phone across the street. So far, nothing had gone his way, and they were running out of time.

"What's wrong?"

Levi turned toward Jacob and blew out a gust of breath. "Cell service was shit. I couldn't make it all out. Davis was found dead in his cell this afternoon. I think he was moved from solitary, which means someone at the prison was likely paid off to make sure Davis could be taken care of. Whatever information he was going to provide us, it's gone now. The assistant chief is on his way back to Sacramento, but I have no idea what the plan is from there."

"So it's up to us," Jacob said.

"It is." And with limited resources, it was going to be tough.

"Justice called Rancor out to the ranch. He's a lot better with the cyber stuff."

"We need a ping on Lily's phone, if we can get one," Levi said. "But I think she might have turned it off."

"If that's the case, we focus on Davis," Jacob paced as he talked. "I'll turn this goddamned town upside down to find her if I have to."

Thank God Lily had Jacob in her corner.

Jacob got on the phone and turned on the speaker function as Justice answered. "What's the update?"

"Dead end," Jacob said. "The cell was planted to get us out here and away from wherever Lily had been told to go."

"She shook the marshal, huh?"

Levi swore he was going to knock Justice on his ass before all this was over.

"You know Lily," Jacob said.

"Don't feel bad, Levi," Justice said. "She's shaken the best of us."

He wasn't interested in the backstory to Justice's comment. "We need to find a connection between Max Davis and Deer Haven, more specifically, to Lily."

"I can only do so much." Levi assumed the voice speaking now belonged to Rancor.

"Well, do more," Justice complained.

"Did you get ahold of Tara?" Jacob asked.

"Yeah. She's at the ranch now with Sallie. We're ready to go to get everyone out of town as soon as you give the green light."

"Okay, good."

Levi saw the indecision in Jacob's eyes, and he understood it all too well. He didn't want to separate himself from the people he loved, and the decision was tearing him up. Even as close as Sacramento might as well be a world away. Levi didn't want this. He didn't want to see an entire family up-rooted because of one lousy son of a bitch. He'd help Levi turn the town over to find Brisbee so none of that had to hap-pen.

"Hang on!" Rancor called from the background. "I think I might have something."

Thank God. Levi sent up a silent prayer as he let out a sigh of hopeful relief. Lily had given herself over to a psychologi-cal sadist to save her sister, and if Levi didn't get to her, fast, he was going to lose the woman he loved forever.

Chapter Thirty

A shiver raced down Lily's spine as she walked past Graham into the schoolhouse. Shay sat on the floor, her back against the wall, looking as absolutely fearless as Lily expected her to. Everyone thought Lily was the tough one, but it was Shay who'd been forged from steel.

"You okay?" Lily knew better than to make a big deal. Shay knew how she felt.

"Perfect," Shay replied. "I've always wanted to check this place out at night. And I get the added bonus of doing it with a legit psychopath. Totes creepy."

She sounded stalwart, but Lily picked up on the quaver in her sister's voice. "Wanna go home?"

"Yeah. I need a beer," Shay said as she pushed herself from the wall and edged closer to Lily. "Scratch that; I need a case of beer."

"Your sister is a lot like you, Lily." Graham spoke from behind her and the sound of his voice sent a lick of terror up her spine. "Full of bravado to mask so many insecurities."

"Why don't you go fuck yourself? Ted Bundy wannabe."

Shay's mouth was her only defense mechanism, and usually Lily was on board. But not now. Shay didn't know how sadistic Graham could be when his switch was flipped. Lily wanted a few more years on this planet. She wasn't ready to check out yet.

"Let her go, Graham." Lily hoped he'd listen to reason. "You don't want to add a kidnapping charge to your sentence."

"Concerned for me, Lily?" He didn't wait for a response. "I haven't kidnapped anyone. Your sister is free to leave whenever she wants."

Shay snorted. "I'm not going anywhere without you, Lil."

Graham shrugged. "Sibling bonds are some of the strongest."

The son of a bitch knew Shay wasn't going to leave.

Lily made sure to keep her back turned away from Graham. Her timing needed to be perfect because she'd likely only have one opportunity for escape. He hadn't shown a weapon so far, but Lily would be a fool to believe he wasn't armed. She had herself and Shay to worry about and they needed a clear path to the doorway. All she had to do was keep Graham's attention focused on himself. His own ego would likely provide the distraction they needed.

"Please save your psychobabble for someone who cares, Graham." Lily might have wanted to placate him, but she wasn't about to bow down to him.

"You should have majored in psychology, Lily," Graham mused. Could he not see how utterly ridiculous it was to have an intellectual conversation amid his prison break and subsequent kidnapping of her sister? Not to mention the fact that he'd tried to kill her. "You're wasting your mind on snot-nosed rug rats."

"You're seriously stuck-up for someone who's done time, you know that?"

The smile melted from his face, causing a cold stone of fear to congeal in Lily's stomach. "Would you like to discuss the circumstances that led to my imprisonment?"

He spoke of his prison sentence as though he were some sort of martyr being unjustly persecuted. Of course, that's probably how he'd seen it. He didn't view the women he'd victimized—including her—as human beings. They were props to him. Toys to play with. Items to be carelessly damaged and thrown away. He'd killed an eighteen-year-old woman on campus and shown no remorse for it. Lily needed to remember exactly who she was standing here talking to. She needed to remind herself of what he'd done to her—the damage he'd inflicted—and take heed.

"Seems to me, you have no one to blame for your imprisonment but your own fucked-up self."

"Shay," Lily warned. She'd encouraged her sister's mouthiness, but it was time to settle down and play it safe.

"No, Lily." Graham's voice seethed with poison. "Let her speak her mind. Exactly what did I do to earn a place among common criminals?"

Shay's eyes went wide. "Are you fucking kidding me? Rape, exploitation, assault, attempted murder, oh, and the actual murder they pinned on you."

Lily needed to calm her sister down. Graham already knew his list of nefarious deeds. The only thing Shay accomplished by repeating them was to stroke his sick ego.

"Is it exploitation," Graham wondered, "when those young women volunteered for the treatment they received?"

Shay lurched forward, and Lily grabbed her arm. Graham's hand twitched by his side, and Lily caught a glimpse of dark metal in the gray evening light.

"Graham." Lily spoke with as much calm as she could muster. "Let Shay leave." No matter what he'd said to the contrary, Lily knew he'd never intended to allow her sister to walk out of there. He had too much to lose. "She hasn't done anything to you. Please."

"Lil, I told you—"

"No, Shay." Lily cut her off. She wasn't going to go through all of this so that her sister could die alongside her. She needed to get her out of there so she'd at least stand a fighting chance. "Don't argue with me."

"You have no bargaining power here, Lily," Graham said simply.

Lily was about to do something goddamn rash. The last dregs of light would soon be gone and they'd be engulfed in darkness. She had one opportunity and she had to take it.

"Shay," Lily instructed in her most polished teacher voice, "run."

Lily pulled the .38 from her waistband and fired off a wild shot. It wasn't meant to do anything other than scare Graham to buy some time for Lily to aim and fire a proper shot, but she hadn't prepared herself for the recoil and the revolver flew from her grip, flying behind her somewhere. Shay didn't hesitate and sprinted through the doorway. Lily followed close behind, leaping over the stairs after her. Lily hit the ground flat on her chest, knocking the air from her lungs.

Shay was already at the car. The keys were in the ignition and Lily's cell was on the passenger seat. Shay was her best chance at getting help and she swore, if her sister turned back for her, she'd kick her ass. Lily fought to draw a breath as her vision darkened at the periphery. The sound of a gunshot exploded overhead and Lily watched as Shay dropped to the ground near the back of the vehicle.

A mournful scream lodged in Lily's throat. Had the bullet hit her sister? Lily swore as her world went dark that if she was going down, she was taking Graham Brisbee with her.

Pain radiated from Lily's face as her cheek slid against gravel. She twisted to one side, fighting against the hands that held her ankles, dragging her backward. The pressure released from her chest, allowing her lungs to fill with air. Lily gasped, desperate to replenish the oxygen to her body as she became more fully aware of her surroundings and what was happening to her.

Graham continued to drag her back to the schoolhouse, apparently unconcerned for her handling. Lily's face burned where the dirt and rocks scraped the side of her face and her ankles ached from the firm grip that held them. With each breath that filled her lungs, Lily became more aware, more in control of her mind and body. She thought of Shay, lying in the dirt next to her car, and she swallowed down a sob, forbidding herself from thinking of her sister until she could secure her own freedom. She'd be no use to Shay if she was dead.

Lily fought against Graham's hold, twisting and rolling until he was forced to release her. She scrambled forward, her knees nearly touching her chest as she tried to propel herself upright, but not before Graham wound his fingers in her hair, jerking her backward with enough force that she couldn't believe he hadn't yanked it out by the roots.

"I'm not letting you go, Lily," Graham said with the same calm he'd exhibited the night he'd attacked her in his classroom. "You have to pay for what you did to me. Every action has a consequence."

What she did to him? "Fuck you!" Lily spat. She was done trying to play his games. There was no reasoning with a psychopath. "The U.S. Marshals already know you're here, Graham. And when they find you, you'll be right back in prison and this time you'll be on death row. You're not going to win."

He pulled her up the stairs, and Lily kicked at the risers to give her leverage so he wouldn't free any more strands of hair from her head. Blood trickled from a cut at her temple, coating her face in sticky warmth.

"It's not about winning, Lily."

Flashbacks of Graham's abuse assaulted Lily's mind. She'd been alone in his classroom, finishing up a research project she'd been assisting with after hours when the lights went out. A shadow approached her, illuminated only by the faint glow of lights on the campus below. She hadn't known it was Graham until they were face-to-face. Lily's relief had turned immediately to fear as his fist swung out and made contact with her jaw. She'd blacked out for a moment, and when she came to, Graham was on top of her, one hand wrapped tightly around her throat, while the other forced her legs apart beneath her skirt.

Lily was relieving the worst nightmare of her past. But this time, she didn't think she was going to survive the encounter.

"Okay, so I didn't find a Max Davis, but I searched public records and found a Maxwell Davis on a divorce petition filed by a Stacey Ambrose Davis six years ago. She requested to revert to her maiden name and that's literally the only record of anything close to Max Davis in the entire county."

Levi had gone over Davis's prison records and his legal name had been listed as simply "Max." That didn't mean he couldn't have gone by Maxwell or used it as an alias.

"What was the reason for the divorce?"

"Fraud," Rancor said through the speaker. "Stacey Ambrose filed the petition."

That sounded more like the Davis Levi knew. "It's a starting point. Can you find anything on Stacey Ambrose?"

"This'll be a lot easier," Rancor replied. The sound of keys clicking in the background filled the silence. "A Google search should be sufficient—hang on—" The clicking of keys drilled into Levi's brain. "I found Stacey Ambrose on the staff directory for the Deer Haven Elementary School."

"Shit," Jacob spat. "She works at Lily's school?"

"Secretary," Rancor said. More clicking. "I can't find anything in the county jail's repository, so no arrests. No criminal history at all as far as I can tell without hacking into law enforcement databases."

Levi was less interested in her criminal history than possible locations Lily might have gone to. If Max had been familiar with Deer Haven, he could have given Brisbee all the information he needed. "Can you do a search of the county's tax assessment records for property Ambrose might have owned or still owns? Also, someone should probably reach out to her. I don't necessarily think she's involved, but we need to cover all of our bases."

"On it!" The voice must have belonged to Pride Culpepper. The brothers rarely weren't together, and frankly, they seemed to work better as a team. Levi was grateful for all the help he could get. Nothing mattered more than finding Lily and making sure she and Shay were safe.

"There's a seven-acre parcel belonging to a Clare and Ed Ambrose off the highway," Rancor continued. "Twenty-Three Red Oak Road. It was assessed for acreage and a structure, nonresidential, last year, but I'm not seeing anything else under that name. I'm not even sure where Red Oak Road is, and I've lived here my entire life."

Jacob remained silent, though his expression was contemplative. "Nonresidential structure, off the highway?"

"According to the county records," Rancor said.

"Google the address," Levi suggested. "Maybe we can get a visual."

The sound of the keyboard started up again. "Thank you, Google Earth. It's definitely off the beaten path. Looks abandoned. Maybe a barn or something?" He continued to type. "The address was listed on a historic registry about ten years ago."

"It's a school," Jacob said. "I know where it is now."

"Let's go. You drive."

Levi hustled to Jacob's truck and jumped into the passenger seat. Jacob was right behind him, giving instructions to Rancor to keep digging and call if he found anything out in case this lead didn't pan out. As Jacob threw the pickup into reverse and backed quickly out of Shay's driveway, Levi entered the address of the school into his navigation app. The app was more of a backup, however. He was relying on Jacob to get them there.

He couldn't afford another dead end.

The sun had gone down ten minutes ago, making visibility less than ideal. Despite his weeks in Deer Haven, he was still unfamiliar with a large portion of the area, and he was grateful to have Jacob working alongside him. The highway blurred as Levi focused on the white lines to the right, looking for any break, any indication of a side street, or even Lily's 4Runner maybe parked alongside the road. The headlights proved less than useful in the gray dusk, making it necessary to adhere to the speed limit in order to keep an eye out for any kind of signage to mark Red Oak Road.

"Goddamn, I hate driving this time of night. Visibility is for shit," Jacob groused. "It's along here somewhere. I'm just not sure where."

"In point-five miles, turn left," the serene electronic voice on Levi's phone announced.

There was nothing up ahead, just a bunch of trees and bushes. Levi's frustration mounted. He forced his jaw to relax lest he bite right through his lip. He drummed his fingers on his knee as he searched the road ahead. The navigation system had to be wrong. There was no trace of—

"Turn left."

Jacob obeyed the navigation app's command, jerking the wheel sharply to the left. The pickup hit a rut in the road, damned near jarring Levi right out of his seat. He gripped his phone in his left hand and the oh-shit handle with his right. This was a road? It was barely passable.

"Hang on."

Jacob didn't bother to slow down, despite the rough terrain. The pickup could handle it, but Levi wasn't sure he'd survive the ride. Trees and shrubs grew thick on either side of what he could only consider a wagon trail, blocking out any natural light that might remain. At least the headlights illuminated the landscape better now. Levi could make out a bridge up ahead that, frankly, didn't look sturdy enough to support a bicycle, let alone a half-ton truck. Jacob slowed and carefully passed over the bridge. Goddamn, tonight's drive presented a good case for never leaving the city again. Country roads fucking sucked.

"You see that?" Jacob pointed ahead at the reflective light that played off what appeared to be a taillight.

Hope blossomed in Levi's chest. It could be Lily's car. But they weren't close enough yet to be sure.

"Stop." If Lily was there with Brisbee, the last thing he wanted was to alert the bastard to their presence.

"Got it," Jacob said. He stopped the truck without question, obviously understanding Levi's reasoning before he even had to say it. Intuitive partners were invaluable, and Jacob had quickly proven himself to Levi.

The headlights went dark and Jacob killed the engine. Levi tucked his cell into his pocket, checked the clip of his Glock using the dome light. Jacob did the same with his sidearm and they exited the truck, easing the doors closed so as not to make a sound.

It would be a miracle if he didn't fall and break his damn ankle before he made it to the school. As Levi negotiated the rough, rut-worn road, he kept his gaze focused on the path ahead of him, his senses alert for the slightest sound or movement. Jacob walked beside him on the opposite side of the road, giving ample space between them in case they found themselves in a hostile situation. The car came closer into view and the dark outline of a body on the ground beside the rear driver's side tire caught Levi's attention. His heart leapt into his throat as he rushed to the car and dropped to a knee, rolling over the body that lay there, still.

Shay.

Levi put his ear to her mouth to listen for any breath sound. It was there, but she was unconscious. Jacob knelt beside him, and even in the absence of light Levi knew the expression that marred Jacob's face was that of pure rage.

"Go find Lily," he said, low. "I'll take care of Shay."

"Get some backup out here," Levi said. "We're going to need it."

"Ten-four."

The sound of an enraged scream cut through the quiet and sent a lick of fear down Levi's spine. He'd know that indignant fury anywhere, and Lily was pissed. What came on its heels was a muffled sound of fear and pain and it spiked an anger so intense that it nearly blinded Levi's vision. He picked up his pace as he stayed low, desperate to get to the woman he loved before she endured any more pain.

As Levi hustled up the stairs toward the looming façade of the school, he swore that if anything had happened to Lily, Graham Brisbee would pay for it, tenfold.

Chapter Thirty-One

Graham's only interest was in finishing what he'd started. Lily wasn't going to survive this time and her only regret was that she'd be leaving this world while Levi believed that she'd turned her back on him.

Time slowed, almost dreamlike, as Lily fought her attacker for the second time. He could have ended her life with a gunshot, but instead, Graham chose to drag it out. Her suffering was his entertainment.

Graham crushed her with his weight as he pressed his body on top of hers. Lily gagged, sickened by the stench of sweat and filth that clung to him. He was even more of an animal now. Hardened by prison and his need for revenge. One hand squeezed Lily's wrist, holding her right arm in place, cutting off the circulation until her fingers tingled and finally went completely numb. She wriggled her left arm free from where he'd pinned it with his chest and reached for his face, digging her nails into the flesh as she scraped downward. Graham let out a growl of pain and he released her long enough to flip her onto her stomach.

Lily's enraged scream echoed through the empty building. She kicked, flailed, and fought to get to her knees, but Graham overpowered her. His palm slammed into the back of her head, forcing her face to the floor, sending a renewed shock of pain from the scrapes that already marred her cheek.

"Is this how you want it?" Graham seethed next to her ear.

A shiver of revulsion traveled the length of Lily's body. If she was going to die tonight, she was going to make sure she fought till the bitter end.

"You're a fucking coward!" Lily forced the words past her swollen lip, half pressed against the aging floorboards. "Lowlife piece of shit!"

Graham took a handful of her hair and yanked her head backward, and Lily arched with the motion as best she could to protect her spine. "I'm going to squeeze the life out of you. By agonizing, slow degrees. When the sun finally rises, I'm going to enjoy extinguishing the light from your eyes. Until then, I'm going to have you every way imaginable, Lily. By the time I'm through with you, you'll beg me to take your life."

Lily's panic crested with Graham's sadistic promise. He shoved her head back to the floor, slamming it against the boards with enough force to rattle Lily's senses. Stars floated in her vision and a hazy cloud muddled her thoughts. Her body went limp and she tried to shake her head enough to keep herself conscious, but Graham held her immobile. She was going to pass out and that scared her more than anything. What would he do to her while she was unaware? Somehow that was far worse than being lucid for this torture. Lily fought with every ounce of willpower she had to stay awake, to keep her mind sharp.

Graham thrust his knee between her legs, forcing them wide. Tears stung at Lily's eyes, spilling over onto her cheeks and adding to the sting of her injuries. She was so tired of fighting. Tired of fear. Tired of the anxiety that hadn't left her in over a year. Maybe it was better to let go. To accept her fate and pray that Levi would find Graham and make him pay for what he'd done to her.

I love you, Levi. Lily forced herself to focus on that thought alone. If anything, this tragedy had led her to the love of her life. She just wished they'd had more time together.

Footsteps pounded against the stairs. Graham paused, pushing himself from Lily's body as he turned toward the open doorway. Lily used the opportunity to push herself to her knees, but before she could scramble out of the way, Graham caught her around the ankle and put his knee down hard on her back.

In the low light, Lily could barely make out the imposing form that filled the doorway. But she didn't have to see his face to recognize Levi. Elation soared in her chest, followed closely by fear-fueled dread. She already may have lost her sister tonight. She couldn't bear it if she lost Levi too.

He lurched forward just as Graham swept his right arm toward Lily's head. The cold barrel of a gun rested against her temple and Levi stilled in an instant.

"I don't know who you are," Graham all but purred. "But I'd advise against coming any closer unless you want this lovely young woman to lose her life."

It floored Lily how Graham could continue to be so calm and civilized. As though he were chatting with colleagues at a university function. She didn't dare move. Her lungs ached from the effort it took to draw even a shallow breath with his weight on her back. His knee dug into her back and a sharp cramp sent jolts of pain through Lily's body.

"You okay, darlin'?" Levi disregarded Graham entirely, though he stayed put.

The sound of his voice sent a renewed rush of tears to Lily's eyes and she spoke through the emotion that thickened her throat. "I'm hanging in there." It was barely true, but she wanted him to have some sort of reassurance.

"Hang on for a little bit longer for me." The rich, smooth tenor of his words was a balm to Lily's soul. "This'll be over soon."

"I think I'll determine when this is over." Graham's annoyance at being ignored became quickly apparent. He loved being the center of attention. "Let's not forget who's in charge here."

"A team of U.S. Marshals and FBI is about to converge on this location, Brisbee." Levi's tone because authoritative, matching Graham's. "Make it easy on yourself and toss the gun to me. We can do this peacefully. There's nowhere for you to go."

"What if I don't believe you?" Graham asked.

"Whether or not you believe me isn't any of my concern," Levi said. "I've got a job to do, and you can trust I'm going to do it."

"Follow-through and completion are so important," Graham acknowledged. "Admirable qualities. And so I'm sure you'll understand that I must also follow through. I'd appreciate it if you discarded your weapon. It's beginning to make me nervous."

"That's not going to happen."

"I'll pull the trigger," Graham warned. "It won't be as fulfilling, but I'll do it if that's what it takes to get my point across."

A moment of silence followed, marking Levi's indecision. Graham pressed the barrel harder against Lily's temple and the gash there, until she cried out from the pain. He wanted Levi to see her suffer. And to make sure that Levi knew, without a doubt, that neither of them was getting out of there alive.

Levi raised his hands in supplication, holding his gun aloft. He tossed it gently toward Graham just as a bright light shone through the broken front window. Graham reared backward, taking the bulk of his weight from Lily's back. He lifted the gun from her temple and she used his imbalance to her benefit, bucking him backward as she propelled herself semi-upright.

Lily dove for Levi's gun. Her brain had switched over to autopilot the moment Graham had leaned backward. Adrenaline pumped through Lily's bloodstream, banishing the pain that had nearly crippled her. She pushed herself to stand and turned toward her former mentor, the gun raised in her shaky hands.

"Lily," Levi said gently. "Give me the gun, baby."

"No." The rational part of her brain knew Levi was there to help. That he was the capable one and she needed to do what he'd told her. The irrational side of her, the side that had been beaten twice and subjected to endless nightmares and fear, continued to point the gun at the source of all of her trauma as her rage built to a nearly uncontrollable level.

"How does it feel, Lily?" Graham asked. "To hold someone's life in your hands?"

All she had to do was pull the trigger and she'd be rid of him forever.

"It's powerful, isn't it? A high unlike any other. It's the closest thing to omnipotence you'll ever experience. But are you strong enough to give yourself over to it?"

"Shut up!" Lily cried at the top of her lungs. She was so sick of the sound of his voice.

Levi's footfalls became louder as he approached her. Lily began to shake, and the gun nearly rattled in her hands. She placed her finger gently on the trigger just as Levi had shown her to.

"Careful, Lily," Levi said. "You don't want to do this. It's okay. You're safe. He's not going to hurt you again."

"That's what they told me last time." Her own voice

sounded foreign in her ears. Hollow, and emotionless. "And here we are. If I don't kill him, he's going to kill me."

Lily would never know peace until Graham Brisbee was gone from the world. And if she had to do the world a favor by taking care of it herself, then so be it.

Levi knew that Lily wasn't thinking clearly. His own rage had been so overpowering that it had taken everything in him to think past his anger and need for revenge in order to protect Lily and uphold the law in the way he'd sworn to do.

Brisbee was a lowlife piece of shit who didn't deserve to live. But Lily would never be able to live with herself if she took his life and Levi didn't want her to add to her distress by letting her do something she'd never be able to take back.

"I'm not going to let that happen, love." Levi spoke gently. "I promised you I'd protect you and I meant it. I'm sorry it took me so long to get here. It's over, Lily. Give me the gun. I promise you, he won't ever see the light of day again."

"I hate him," Lily said more to herself than to Levi. "I hate you!" she screamed this time, all of her anger directed at the man standing casually before her. A sob lodged itself in her throat and Levi's heart broke for her. If he could take all of her suffering away, he'd do it in an instant. But he wouldn't be able to do a damned thing if she wouldn't listen to reason and let him help her.

The bright headlights of the vehicles they heard approaching flooded the single room with light. Lily's face was streaked with blood, her lip was swollen and cut, and she had a nasty cut on the side of her forehead. Levi's jaw clenched until it began to ache. It was a good thing backup had arrived, because if left alone with that piece of shit Levi would have gladly given up his badge in order to beat the living hell out of him.

"Lily," Levi tried again to soothe her, "Jacob is here. The police are here. Let's let them do their job."

"Shay." Lily's shoulders shook as she began to cry in earnest. "He killed her."

"She's alive, Lily." Levi didn't know her status, but she'd been breathing when he turned her care over to Jacob. "I swear, baby. She's alive."

Lily cried harder and it was more of relief than pain. "Are you sure?"

"As sure as I can be." Levi would never lie to her or deceive her again. "She was breathing when I found her. Jacob took over with her so I could go to you."

"I don't feel omnipotent at all," Lily said to Graham as she began to lower the weapon. "You're wrong."

Brisbee used the opportunity to rush her. Levi wrapped an arm around Lily's waist and jerked her out of his path. The gun landed on the floor as Levi was knocked off-balance by Brisbee's impact and he lost his grip on her, sending her sprawling several feet from the doorway.

"Lily, get the hell out of here!"

He didn't have time to check on her as Levi dove for the discarded gun at the same moment Brisbee did. They fell to the floor, and the Glock slid just out of reach. Brisbee connected a right hook, but without any momentum behind it, the blow had little impact. He reached for the Glock yet again, only to have Brisbee kick it out of the way. His other foot came down on Levi's hand, giving him the advantage as he reached for the gun.

Levi scrambled to his knees and swept at Brisbee's ankles with his left hand, knocking his feet out from under him. He landed on his back with a resounding thud but didn't lose control of the weapon that he swung toward Levi and fired.

Pop! With the report of the Glock, searing heat shot through Levi's left arm. It went limp at his side, nearly useless, as the blinding pain overtook him. It was a flesh wound, nothing major hit, but it still hurt like hell. Levi's legs crumpled beneath him and he went to his knees as he hissed in a sharp breath, reaching for his injured arm. Brisbee brought the gun up again and used Levi's momentary incapacitation to his advantage and fired off three more quick shots.

Levi ducked and rolled as the voices shouting from outside were suddenly drowned out by the sound of a helicopter overhead. Wood splintered with each shot, but nothing hit its mark.

The blue and red strobe of police lights cast their colorful shadows on the walls as armed law enforcement stormed the school. Something hard poked at Levi's side and he reached down to find a discarded .38 Special identical to the one he'd given Lily.

His smart, beautiful Lily. She'd come prepared.

"Don't move!"

"Hands in the air!"

"Drop your weapon!"

Brisbee held the gun aloft, pointing it toward the bodies that converged. Panic etched his face and Levi felt a smug sense of satisfaction that the bastard might know some of the fear he'd caused so many.

"It's over, Brisbee," Levi told him once He kept his voice level through the pain screaming through his arm and the blood that flowed freely, soaking the sleeve of his shirt. He wanted to be the one who made this arrest. He'd made a promise to Lily and he'd be damned if he didn't keep it. "Put the gun down."

"I can't do that." No longer smug, Brisbee's defeat came through in his words.

A half-dozen armed law enforcement officials stood face-to-face with the escaped convict. There was no chance he was going to escape again. He had two choices, go back to prison and serve his time, or die. Graham Brisbee wasn't going to go back to prison.

Brisbee opened fire.

Levi brought up the .38 and pulled the trigger. Six shots exploded, adding to the surrounding chaos. Brisbee dropped to the floor. His body remained still, but the officers inside the school remained on guard, their weapons pointed at him. Wet warmth coated Levi's sleeve and now his jeans, where a second bullet had grazed his thigh.

The pain barely registered thanks to the adrenaline high. He stood and approached Brisbee slowly, before kicking the gun away from where he'd dropped it. "Clear!" he called out to the officers on scene, who mobilized in an instant, securing the building and giving the ambulance the all clear to proceed to the scene.

Levi turned toward the doorway in a daze as his brain played catch-up. He stared without recognition at the man who entered the building and strode toward him with purpose.

"Levi!"

His ears rang and the garbled speech came to his ears as though he was underwater. Levi gave his head a solid shake as he tried to dislodge the fog that clouded his mind. He knew the man speaking to him.

"Levi, we need to get you out to the ambulance."

"Mitch?"

The assistant chief deputy reached out and placed a steadying hand on Levi's shoulder. He couldn't shake the disorientation as his body did its best to keep from going into shock.

"You've lost some blood. We need to get you checked out and taken to the hospital. We'll get this buttoned up here. You did good, son."

Mitch's words barely registered. Levi once again fought

to shake the cobwebs that clung to his mind. Lily. He needed to find Lily and make sure she was okay.

Levi pushed past Mitch. The assistant chief deputy followed close behind and tried to steady him, but Levi shook him off. "Lily!" he shouted over the din of activity as deputy marshals and local sheriff's deputies swarmed the area. "Lily!"

He'd rather bleed out on the dirt than live another second without her. He needed to see her, touch her, assure himself of her safety, before he would even consider attending to his own injuries. He fought and pushed his way past the bodies that crowded the area, frantic as he searched for her.

"Lily!"

"Levi!

"Levi!"

Someone called out his name, but he ignored it. He needed Lily. Nothing else mattered.

"Roberts! Stop!"

The barked command snapped him back to reality.

"Sir," Levi acknowledged his superior with the respect due to him. He took a deep breath, steadied himself, and put his concern for Lily on a brief hold. "Before I get checked out, I need to see—I need to know—Lily and Shay Donovan are okay. They were injured. I need to talk to Jacob Donovan." He might have come to his senses, but Levi was still having a hard time articulating himself. He'd definitely lost some blood. He felt like he could sleep for a month.

"They're okay," Mitch said. "Lily and Shay have already been transported to the hospital." He snorted. "Lily didn't go without a fight. She fought us tooth and nail. Refused to go anywhere without you. I finally got her in the car, but she swore she'd have my badge if anything happened to you."

His Lily. So full of fire. "Get me to the ambulance." He'd

jump on board willingly if it meant getting to the hospital quickly.

Levi staggered and stumbled to the ground. The adrenaline rush had worn off and his injuries had begun to take their toll. In the back of his mind, he heard Mitch shout for assistance. He wanted to reassure him that he wasn't going to die yet, but he was just so goddamn tired. Levi's eyes drifted shut as the not-so-soft gravel driveway slammed against his face.

There was never a dull moment with Lily, and Levi could use a little rest.

Chapter Thirty-Two

The first thing Levi noticed when he woke up was that he wasn't wearing any pants. He lay in a hospital bed, groggy as fuck and annoyed by the rubber IV tubing that might as well have been a shackle. The last thing he remembered was passing out just outside of the old school, on his way to the ambulance. As he came more fully awake, he took in his surroundings: the small flat-screen mounted to the wall, the rolling cart to his left, the sink at the opposite end of the room, and the empty chair to his right. It should have been occupied by someone he loved. Someone who loved him and might be concerned for him.

Lily should have been in that chair.

His head came to rest on the pillow and Levi closed his eyes. His arm and leg ached, but he'd been hurt worse. To be honest, if he hadn't lost so much blood, he wouldn't even be in this bed right now. Where was she? In another room? Maybe next door? Or perhaps she'd been discharged and didn't want to see him. Levi's gut twisted. If that was the case, he'd find her as soon as he got out of this place and beg her to forgive him. Whatever it took to win her back. Without Lily, his life would be incomplete.

The door whispered open and Levi brought his head up from the pillow. Lily walked into the room with a paper cup in each hand. Levi's heart nearly burst in his damn chest at the sight of her. He tried to push himself up to sit, and Lily gave him a disapproving frown as she rushed to the bed and placed the cups on the side table.

"Don't you dare sit up," she ordered. "Let me adjust the bed."

"I'm fine." His brow furrowed as he looked her over. She should be the one in bed, not him. "Why aren't you resting? Are you okay? What did the doctor say? Is Shay all right?"

She tried to smile, but her lip was still swollen and instead it ended up as a wince. Levi cursed Graham Brisbee. The bastard had gotten off easy and should have been made to pay for his crimes. The only comfort Levi took in what had happened last night was the knowledge that he could never harm Lily—or anyone else—ever again.

"I'm going to live." Lily was joking, but Levi sensed the sadness behind the words. "I'm a little scratched up, but it'll heal."

"Shay?"

"She has a mild concussion. Banged her head pretty good on a rock. She had to get a couple of stitches, but she got a date out of the deal, so overall, she's pretty happy."

"A date, huh?"

"Yeah." Lily laughed. "The ER nurse. According to Shay, he might be the perfect man. Doesn't own a single pair of boots, only wears baseball caps, and can't ride a horse to save his life."

Levi wasn't sure why those particular things made the guy such a catch, but he suspected he'd hear all about it soon enough.

"Jacob was here earlier." Lily reached beside Levi and found the switch to raise the bed. She brought the mattress up to a sitting position before taking a seat beside him. "He said he'd come back this afternoon."

"I'm hoping to be out of here by this afternoon," Levi remarked.

"We'll see what the doctor says," Lily shot back. "You're not going anywhere until they give you a clean bill of health."

"I'm fine." Levi hated being fawned over. "I've been stitched up before." Levi didn't want to upset Lily, but he needed to fill in some blanks for his own peace of mind. "Who took your statement?"

"Mitch McDonald. He's your boss?"

"Yeah." Levi was glad it had been Mitch who'd talked to Lily. "He's a good guy. I would have rather been with you when you talked to him, though. How did it go?"

"Pretty standard." Lily let out a rueful laugh. "Sort of sucks that talking to the cops is pretty much old hat at this point, huh?"

"I'm sorry you had to go through that again, Lily." It broke Levi's heart that she'd had to endure Brisbee's abuse for a second time. "If I could go back and change it for you, I would."

Lily looked out the window for a moment, her expression pensive. So much had happened in such a short period of time. Levi wished he knew where to start. There was so much to say.

"I'm sorry I took off like that," Lily began. She continued to look out the window and not at Levi. "It was reckless and dangerous and I could have—" Her voice cracked with emotion and she took a breath. "He told me not to tell anyone or— I couldn't let him hurt Shay."

"Lily, look at me."

She reluctantly met his gaze.

"You did what you had to do. There's no point in looking back. What's done is done. You're safe now and he can't ever hurt you again."

"You're right," Lily said, barely a murmur.

"I'm the one who needs to apologize." Levi had thought about what he would say to Lily if she'd give him a second chance. And now that he had her attention, he found himself searching for the right words. "I lied to you. There's no excuse for it and I'm sorry. I made decisions about your life that I had no right to make. That's not how you treat someone you love. And I love you, Lily, with all of my heart. I was wrong. And if you'll forgive me, I'll spend the rest of my life making it up to you."

"Thank you for saying that." Lily placed a gentle hand on Levi's uninjured arm. "But you never would have been in that position if I hadn't been so damned stubborn. I should have listened to the people who knew better than me. I should have agreed to witness protection. I should have trusted instead of closing myself off to everyone. I was so hurt and angry when Justice told me about you, I didn't stop to really think about the situation or the position you were in."

"I love that you're stubborn," Levi said. "And no matter what happens, I want you to know that for me, it was worth it."

Lily's brow furrowed. "What's going to happen?"

Levi reached up and gently brushed his thumb against her temple where the flesh was raised and bruised. Lily had no idea how strong and resilient she was. Levi was in awe of her. He admired her. She was one of a kind, and she was his.

"I don't know." He brought his hand to hers and gave her a reassuring squeeze. "I toed the code of conduct line by pursuing you. I might be able to find a loophole to talk my way out of it. If I can't"—Levi shrugged—"I'll just find another job."

"You pursued me, huh?"

Levi grinned. "Oh, absolutely."

"I'm glad you did." Lily bent over Levi and put her forehead to his. "I've been in love with you since the first day I saw you."

"No, you haven't," Levi teased. "You thought I was an obnoxious pain in the ass."

"I still think you're an obnoxious pain in the ass." Lily tried to smile again and winced. "But you're my obnoxious pain in the ass."

"And you're mine," Levi said.

A mischievous gleam shone in Lily's bright hazel eyes. "You wanna get out of here?"

"More than anything," Levi said with a groan.

"Let me see what I can do. Where do you want to go?"

He grinned. "Your place."

"We're a little beat up; it might be a while before we do anything friskier than sit in front of the TV."

"That sounds amazing," Levi said. "Throw in a bowl of ice cream and I'll be good to go."

"Deal."

A knock came at the door, and Mitch McDonald walked into the room. Lily eased off the bed to stand beside Levi and he fought the urge to pull her back to him. He stayed calm and gave his supervisor a friendly smile, but inside, Levi's nerves churned like an angry sea. He'd worked so hard to get where he was in the USMS, and he'd give it all up again for the opportunity to be with Lily. But he loved his job, and the good that he did, and it might all be coming to an end today.

"Levi, glad to see you're up and okay," Mitch remarked, all business. "You up to talking?"

Yep. His ass was in a sling. "Of course, sir."

Lily reached over and gave Levi's hand a reassuring squeeze. "I'm going to go see about that ice cream." Levi's eyes didn't leave her until she went through the door and turned down the hall.

Time to face the music.

Shay waited for Lily in the lounge. She thumbed through a magazine while intermittently checking her phone. A gauze bandage covered the stiches on the left side of her forehead and there was some bruising, but other than that, she looked okay on the outside. They'd yet to talk about what damage, if any, Shay had sustained emotionally and mentally. Lily wasn't going to push her. Shay would open up when she was ready.

"How's Marshal Hottie?"

Lily could always count on Shay for levity. "He's okay. I'm sure they'll let him go this afternoon. He's talking to his supervisor now."

Shay cringed. "That probably won't be any fun."

Lily couldn't imagine it would be. "Nope."

When she'd given her statement to the assistant chief deputy, he'd asked her point-blank about the nature of her relationship with Levi and how it came about. Lily hadn't lied. She'd simply stated that their relationship developed over time and very naturally. That Levi's presence at the ranch where she spent most of her time had put them together in a situation where their mutual interest in each other had found an opportunity to grow. She also pointed out that had the assistant chief deputy not sent Levi there to surreptitiously keep an eye on her, they never would have gotten the opportunity to know each other. She hoped the gentle dig at the sneaky way Mitch had planted Levi in Deer Haven would someone lessen the blow when, and if, Levi was reprimanded for their relationship.

Lily took a seat next to her sister. "The hospital's social

worker gave me the names and numbers of a couple of counselors."

"You gonna go this time?" Shay asked.

"Yeah." Lily was done trying to shoulder everything on her own. "It'll be good for me."

"I think so too."

They sat in silence for a while, Lily leaning against her sister's side as they looked through the issue of *Vogue* together. Shay broke the ice and made a comment about the functionality of one of the model's feather bikinis. Lily giggled and swatted at her sister.

"Don't make me laugh. It hurts to smile."

"It's always hurt you to smile," Shay teased. "What's new?"

"I love you," Lily said. "You know that?"

"Back at ya, Sis," Shay said. "There's no one I'd rather get into trouble with."

Lily put her arms around Shay and hugged her tight. "Same."

"Okay, that's enough of that." Shay batted her away. "I've reached my limit for sappiness for one day."

"I'm going to go talk to someone at the nurses' station and see if they're going to discharge Levi."

"Good idea," Shay said. "I'm ready to get the hell out of here."

"That makes two of us." Lily was ready to go home and get some much-needed rest.

"You have beer at your house?" Shay asked.

"Of course." When had Shay not known Lily to have a fully stocked fridge?

"Good. Because I need one. Or three."

"We deserve it," Lily said as she headed for the doorway.

"Hell yeah, we do."

* * *

Levi insisted on opening Lily's door for her. She waited in the passenger seat as he rounded the truck, first reaching for the back door, to let Shay out. They'd all left the hospital together and Shay was planning to stay at Lily's for a few days. They'd all been through hell and she couldn't think of a better way to decompress than with the people who'd suffered together with her. Lily handed Shay her keys and she walked ahead to the house, giving Lily and Levi a few private moments. It felt so good to be home with the man she loved. Lily couldn't think of a more perfect way to end the day.

"When do you have to be back in Sacramento?"

"Mitch gave me a couple weeks off. He said I've earned it." Levi held out his hand. Lily took it as he helped her down from the truck. "I'm not out of the woods yet and I'm sure I'll be reprimanded for more than a few things, but my record speaks for itself and I think that it's enough to keep me employed for a little while, at least."

Lily couldn't imagine Levi in any other role than protector. The job suited him well and the U.S. Marshals Service would be crazy to get rid of him.

"Two weeks at home." Lily had extended her substitute till the end of the month. She wasn't going to be ready to go back to school for a little while and she wanted to get some counseling sessions under her belt first. "What are we going to do?"

"I can think of a few things," Levi said as he leaned down to place a kiss on the top of Lily's head. "And none of them require us to be wearing clothes."

"You have no idea how badly I want to kiss you right now." Lily leaned her body into his, rubbing her breasts seductively against him.

Levi replied with a low, sensual growl. "Same. But my lips

are perfectly okay and there's about five feet of you that I can kiss until your lip is feeling better."

A shiver of pleasure danced over Lily's skin. "Oh yeah? I have to say, that sounds pretty damn good."

She tucked herself against Levi's body as they walked to the house, careful to avoid the injury to his arm. It was the worst of the two gunshot wounds and was going to take the longest to heal. Lily had promised to help him shower, though, and he'd promised to take her up on the offer.

"Are you okay with Shay staying here for a while?" Lily didn't think Levi minded, but it was important to her that he knew his opinion mattered. This was his house now as well, and she wanted him to be comfortable.

"Of course." They climbed the stairs together and Levi paused on the front porch as he turned Lily to face him. "She's family. I have a feeling you two will be sick of me before our two weeks are up, though."

"I don't know about Shay," Lily said, "but I could never get sick of you."

"Are you sure?" Levi teased. "I can be a real pain in the ass."

"Me too." Lily reached around his waist and squeezed. "That's why we're perfect for each other.

They were too. Lily had never felt surer of anything in her entire life. Levi Roberts had been made for her and no one, nothing, would ever come between them again.

"It's funny that you think you're getting rid of me in two weeks when you go back to work," Lily remarked as she opened the front door. "Because you're stuck with me forever."

Levi grinned. God, how she loved that wicked expression and the gleam in his honeyed eyes. A rush of heat spread from Lily's core outward. She'd told him it would be a while before they'd be getting frisky, but she doubted she'd be able to wait a couple of hours to have him, let alone a couple of days.

"And you're never getting rid of me," Levi said.

"What about work?" It was too soon to worry about it, but Lily couldn't help but wonder if they'd stay in Deer Haven or she'd have to move to Sacramento.

"What about it?" Levi asked. "I can commute. I like it here."

"You know how small towns are, though," Lily warned. "Nothing is ever private."

"I'm an open book," Levi said. "Besides, someone's got to stay here to keep Shay in line."

"I heard that!" Shay called from the kitchen. "Are you two done making kissy-faces at each other? I'm starving."

It was going to be an interesting few days. But one thing was certain: They wouldn't be bored.

"I'll call in a pizza!" Lily called back. "Sallie said she'd run errands for us if we needed her to."

"Woo-hoo!" Shay pulled open the refrigerator and rifled through the contents. "Tell her to bring more beer. And ice cream. Oh, and some Oreos. What do you guys want for breakfast tomorrow? We could do omelets or French toast. We should rent some movies too. . . ."

Shay's voice faded into the background as Lily turned to Levi and gave him a gentle, albeit stiff, smile. Her life couldn't be more perfect. She had everything she needed right here.